She wasn't about to let him get away...

Before Lani could get her bearings, her assailant punched her and pushed her back off the side of the boat. She splashed into the water, plunging beneath the surface as the boat sped out into open water.

Feeling defeated, she turned and swam back toward the beach. Noah rushed out into the water up to his knees. She gasped for air.

"You all right?" He wrapped his arm around her and helped her to the beach.

The suspect had gotten away.

She stared out where the flashing light of the assailant's boat merged with other flashing lights.

If a training exercise could go so far off the rails, what would happen when she worked the field?

USA TODAY Bestselling Author

Sharon Dunn

and

New York Times Bestselling Author

Shirlee McCoy

On His Watch

Previously published as *Courage Under Fire* and *Sworn to Protect*

LOVE INSPIRED
INSPIRATIONAL ROMANCE

Special thanks and acknowledgment are given to
Sharon Dunn and Shirlee McCoy for their contributions
to the True Blue K-9 Unit miniseries.

LOVE INSPIRED®

INSPIRATIONAL ROMANCE

ISBN-13: 978-1-335-20965-8

Recycling programs
for this product may
not exist in your area.

On His Watch

For questions and comments about the quality of this book,
please contact us at CustomerService@Harlequin.com.

Love Inspired
22 Adelaide St. West, 40th Floor
Toronto, Ontario M5H 4E3, Canada
www.Harlequin.com

Printed in U.S.A.

CONTENTS

Ever since she found the Nancy Drew books with the pink covers in her country school library, **Sharon Dunn** has loved mystery and suspense. Most of her books take place in Montana, where she lives with three nearly grown children and a hyper border collie. She lost her beloved husband of twenty-seven years to cancer in 2014. When she isn't writing, she loves to hike surrounded by God's beauty.

Books by Sharon Dunn

Love Inspired Suspense

Cold Case Justice
Mistaken Target
Fatal Vendetta
Big Sky Showdown
Hidden Away
In Too Deep
Wilderness Secrets
Mountain Captive
Undercover Threat
Alaskan Christmas Target

True Blue K-9 Unit: Brooklyn

Scene of the Crime

True Blue K-9 Unit

Courage Under Fire

Visit the Author Profile page at Harlequin.com for more titles.

COURAGE UNDER FIRE

Sharon Dunn

Be of good courage, and he shall strengthen your heart, all ye that hope in the Lord.
—*Psalm* 31:24

For the dog who saved my life and is
my writing companion, Bart the hyper border collie.

ONE

Rookie K-9 officer Lani Branson took in a deep breath as she pedaled her bike along the trail in the Jamaica Bay Wildlife Refuge. She could hear birds chattering. Water rushed and receded from the shore just over the dunes. The high-rises of New York City, made hazy from the dusky twilight, were visible across the expanse of water.

She sped up even more.

Tonight was important. This training exercise was an opportunity to prove herself to the other K-9 officers who waited back at the visitors' center with the tracking dogs for her to give the go-ahead. Playing the part of a child lost in the refuge so the dogs could practice tracking her was probably a less than desirable duty for the senior officers. As a new recruit to the NYC K-9 Command Unit, she understood the pecking order. If she did a good job tonight, she'd be given more responsibility.

Though she was in solid shape, her leg muscles strained as she willed herself to pedal even faster. The trail ended. She pushed her bike into a hiding place in the brush and headed toward the tall grass that surrounded the shore. A flock of birds took to the air.

Their squawking and flapping of wings filled the gray sky. Her heart beat a little faster. God's creation never ceased to amaze her.

She stuttered in her step, squinting to make out details in the early evening light. She wondered what had alarmed the birds. Though people might be around the surrounding area, the rangers had secured this part of the refuge for the training exercise. That didn't mean someone curious about what the NYPD was up to hadn't snuck into the area. Could be anything or nothing at all, sometimes birds just decided to fly away.

She ran through the tall grass that bordered the salt marsh and then toward the open area of the dunes. She needed to get far enough away for it to be a challenge for the dogs to find her.

As a sense of unease invaded her awareness, she stopped. She had felt on edge for the last few days. A car had tailed her through traffic just this morning and more than once she'd felt the press of a gaze on her only to turn and see no one.

Reaching up to her shoulder, Lani pressed the button on the radio. "I'm in place."

The smooth tenor voice of her supervisor, Chief Noah Jameson, came over the line. "Good, you made it out there in record time."

As she hurried steadily toward the tall brush, Lani had an extra bounce in her step. Since her training as a K-9 officer had begun, that was the first compliment Noah had given her. Noah had been appointed the interim chief of the NYC K-9 Command Unit after the untimely death of his brother Jordan—the former chief. A permanent replacement was yet to be named.

Noah's voice floated over the radio. "Remember, move like a five-year-old would."

"Ten-four." In fact, Noah always seemed to be quite tight-lipped whenever she was around. He had a great deal on his mind. Jordan had been murdered months ago and the investigation had stalled. All the same, Noah seemed to be extra quiet around her. She took his silence to be disapproval. Maybe like some of the other officers, he didn't think she was up to the job.

Lani was a natural athlete with a background as a self-defense instructor and a dancer. She'd graduated from the academy with flying colors and she had an older brother, Reed, who was also with the unit. It was her former profession as an actress that probably made them wonder if she would make the cut. All officers earned a nickname sooner or later. Hers was less than flattering. They called her Cover Girl. Never mind that she'd never worked as a model. She was stuck with the name…for now. Lani gritted her teeth. The rest of the team just didn't know what she was made of.

She entered a grove of trees. The dry autumn leaves crackled as the breeze rushed over them. It could be up to an hour before the dogs found her. The refuge was thousands of acres. The places a child could get lost were infinite. She passed a wooden box on a stake. A barn owl peeked out of the round hole in the box. Jamaica Bay was home to hundreds of species of birds. This time of year, the raptors showed up.

Lani was New York City born and bred. One of her favorite memories was of her grandfather taking her to see the eagles.

Knowing that a child would not move in a logical way, she headed back toward the shore and ran along the beach for a while before zigzagging back into the brush. Her heart pounded in her chest. Though she still had her radio, her instructions were not to communicate with the rest of the team.

Up ahead she spotted an object shining in the setting sun. She jogged toward it. A bicycle, not hers, was propped against a tree.

A knot of tension formed at the back of her neck as she turned a half circle, taking in the area around her. It was possible someone had left the bike behind. Vagrants could have wandered into the area.

She studied the bike a little closer. State-of-the-art and in good condition. Not the kind of bike someone just dumped.

Still puzzled by her find, Lani hurried deeper into the trees and then sat down on the ground. A five-year-old would stop and rest, she reasoned, maybe even fall asleep. She stared at the sky.

The noisy chatter of the gulls and other birds feeding hummed in the background. Wind rustled the leaves, some of them already golden and red, others still green, creating a sort of song.

She listened, thinking she might hear the baying of the dogs as they picked up her scent and tracked her. No. It was too soon for that. Though it would have been a welcome sound.

A branch cracked. Her breath caught in her throat. To the best of her knowledge, there were no large animals on the refuge, only squirrels, rodents and raccoons. Fear caused her heartbeat to drum in her ears. She touched the radio on her shoulder.

More noise landed on her ears. Whatever was in the thick brush that surrounded her was on the move.

She took her hand off the radio, shaking her head. It would not go over big for her to push the panic button over some nocturnal creature looking for its dinner.

Lani rose to her feet and headed toward the tall grass where she would lie down as though she'd fallen asleep. The dogs and their handlers needed to read the signs she left behind. Her feet pounded the hard-packed ground as she turned back to the shore. The cacophony of the birds feeding by the water's edge grew louder.

Out of the corner of her eye, she caught movement, a bright color. Human? The rest of the team couldn't have found her that fast.

"NYPD." She hadn't worn her gun for this exercise. Her eyes scanned all around her, searching for movement and color. "You need to show yourself."

Seconds ticked by. Her heart pounded.

Someone else was out here.

Again, it was possible that a junkie or vagrant had found a way to avoid detection and was making the refuge his or her home.

The birds quieted as the sun slipped lower in the sky. All she heard was the sound of her own heartbeat. Her hand moved to the radio. She needed to at least inform Noah that someone else was lurking in the bushes. She clicked the radio on and turned her head to speak into it.

A hand slapped hers and yanked the radio off her shoulder. Automatically, she reacted with an elbow punch to her assailant's stomach.

Her attacker groaned in pain but did not relent in his attack. He restrained her by locking her neck in the crook of his elbow while he pulled her arm behind her and pushed it up at a painful angle with his other hand.

The fear that invaded every cell of her body was

overridden by her years of training in self-defense. She kicked him hard in the shin. His grip didn't loosen at all. The man was strong and had a high tolerance for pain.

He held on tight, dragging her toward the tall grass and the water. Her arm burned from pain as he bent it behind her back and pushed it upward.

She planted her feet.

Her resistance seemed to fuel his anger. He squeezed her neck tighter.

She struggled for air. She kicked him several times even as dots formed in her field of vision. He jerked back and up with his crooked arm. She landed one more intense blow to his leg.

His grip loosened enough for her to twist free. She ran only a few steps before he grabbed her shirt and dragged her back toward him. She spun around landing a chop to his neck designed to cause pain by pinching nerves. The move disabled her attacker long enough for her to get a head start.

The ground was softer this close to the shore. The water of the bay shimmered in her peripheral vision as she sprinted. She needed to get back up to the trail to find her bike before he could grab her again.

The landscape darkened and shadows covered the trees and bushes as the last light of the sun faded. His footsteps pounded behind her. She willed herself to go faster. Air filled her lungs and her breathing intensified. She veered off, hoping to head back up toward the trail and her bike.

She attacker remained close at her heels. Just as she arrived at her bike, he grabbed her. She whirled around, getting in several solid blows. He grabbed her by the shoulders and spun her around.

The attacker wrapped his arms around her, coming at her from behind. He seemed to want to restrain her rather than fight back. His arms suctioned around her like an anaconda. His mouth was very close to her ear.

"There now," he said.

His warm breath and sickly sweet words sent a new wave of fear through her. When she tried to twist free, he tightened his grip on her waist.

Then she heard a most welcome sound, the dogs baying and barking. Still some distance away but clearly headed toward her.

The man let go of her and stepped back. He wore a hat and she could not see his face in the dim light. Clearly frightened by the approaching dogs, he turned to go. She wasn't about to let him get away. She leaped through the air, seeking to knock him to the ground. The attacker did not fall, which left her hanging on to his back.

"NYPD," she shouted.

He shook her off, ran a few paces and then bent over.

She caught up with him. He swung around. In the darkness, she had not seen him pick up the rock he now had in his hand. It hit the side of her head. Her knees buckled.

The ground drew ever closer as dots filled her field of vision.

Her attacker loomed above her. "Next time."

She heard his retreating footsteps as her world went black.

Noah Jameson's heartbeat ticked up a notch as he let his Rottweiler, Scotty, pick up the scent of Officer Lani Branson. Three dogs on their long leads sniffed, barked and circled back to spots before taking off on the trail. Officer Finn Gallagher's K-9 partner, a yellow Lab trained in search and rescue, took the lead. Reed Branson, Lani's brother, followed with bloodhound Jessie, a tracking K-9.

The dogs' enthusiasm was infectious. This kind of excitement made him feel alive. This was what he loved about police work, the action. Being out in the field nourished him even if it was just a training exercise. It beat sitting behind a desk putting out administrative fires and keeping the upper brass happy.

Until his murder last spring, Noah's older brother Jordan had been the chief of the NYC K-9 Command Unit. Though there had been some jockeying for the job, Noah had been the one appointed to fill his brother's shoes, temporarily at least. He missed working the street with Scotty, chasing down leads and suspects. More than anything, he missed his older brother. That the NYPD, himself included, had been unable to track down Jordan's killer only made the wound more raw and the grief harder to bear.

Scotty kept his nose to the ground as they worked their way along the path. Scotty was trained in emergency services which meant he could do a little of everything. The other dogs kept pace with Scotty.

So far the trail had been easy enough to follow, but they hadn't found Lani's bicycle yet. Once she got off the bike, she'd been instructed to move in the same erratic pattern a five-year-old might take. Though he had his concerns about Lani's ability to be a K-9 officer, she had a good attitude about being the guinea pig.

A tightening in his chest indicated his doubts were getting the better of him. Once she was in place, Lani was to have no communication with him or anyone on the team. He thought he'd heard the radio turn on and then off suddenly. It was probably nothing. Lani was in great physical condition and had done well at the academy, it was just that her chattiness made her come across as lacking confidence. Anytime he had interacted with her, Lani tended to talk a mile a minute.

The sky darkened as they headed up the trail. Noah and the other officers jogged to keep up with the dogs. They worked their way on the path running for at least twenty minutes. The dogs stopped and split off the trail, each of them alerting and then sniffing in a circle. This must be where Lani had left the trail.

Noah followed Scotty through the tangled brush.

"Come on, boy, you can find her."

Scotty raised his head, sniffed the air and then put his nose back on the ground. He picked up the scent again. They headed off the trail into the tall grass. Scotty lifted his head and sat on his back haunches. That was his hard alert. Noah stared into the brush. Metal shone in the waning light.

He'd found the bicycle.

Noah spoke into his radio. "Scotty's picked up the trail."

The two other dogs bayed and fell in behind Scotty. The dogs took them across the dunes back into the trees and down to the shore. Though he could still hear the barking, the dogs spread out as they moved through the trees.

Reed's panic-filled voice came across the line. "We got a problem. You better come see this."

Noah could see Reed and Jessie through the tangle of brush. Judging from the high-pitched baying, Jessie was excited. No sign of Lani. He shortened the lead on Scotty and hurried through the trees.

"What is it?"

Reed held up a police radio. Lani's. Reed's voice filled with concern. "She wouldn't tear it off herself. Something's gone wrong."

There was only a small chance the radio had gotten hung up on something as she ran. Noah's thoughts raced as he took in the scene around him. Both dogs indicated a high level of excitement. The grass was smashed down. Some sort of struggle had taken place.

"The dogs will find her. If someone else is out here too, we'll find him as well."

Noah radioed the other handler, Finn, to see if his Lab picked up on any new scent.

As they followed the dogs through the brush, Noah pushed away any negative thoughts. If he'd learned anything from his K-9 partner, it was to stay focused.

Reed and Jessie headed in a different direction, maybe toward whomever else was out here.

Scotty worked methodically. Jessie sniffed a different area, more toward the shore, trying to find the trail. A new level of panic invaded Noah's awareness as Scotty worked his way through the brush and then sat down, head held high.

Noah saw Lani's blond hair visible in the moonlight. Her motionless body twisted at an odd angle set off alarm bells as he hurried toward her.

He drew close and kneeled beside her. Scotty emitted a whine and then leaned to lick Lani's face. Still, she did not move.

"I'm worried too," said Noah. As he gazed at her motionless body, the grief over the loss of his brother hit him like a semitruck. Another officer wasn't going to die, not on his watch. His fingers touched Lani's neck. Her pulse pushed back on his fingertips. He breathed a sigh of relief. She was still alive. There was a bruise on the side of her head. Her hair had worked loose of the tight bun she kept it in when on duty. Signs that she'd been in a fight.

While Noah radioed for medical help, Reed rushed toward them through the tangle of brush.

He let out a groan as he knelt beside his sister.

Lani's eyes fluttered open, and she lifted her head and shoulders. On impulse, he gathered her into his arms.

"She's alive," said Noah. His voice filled with elation. "We need to call for backup. Get some more searchers to the refuge. Someone attacked Lani and we need to find him before he escapes."

TWO

Lani stared into Noah's calm face. He'd wrapped his arm around her back holding her up as he kneeled and faced her.

In the waning light, she could just make out the tiniest of smiles. "Hey. Good to see you coming around." His voice held a note of joy. Normally very stoic, it was the first time she had seen any emotion at all from Noah.

"Hey, sis." Reed's voice drew her attention as he kneeled off to the side. Jessie lay down beside him. The bloodhound's big floppy ears touched the ground.

Scotty leaned in and licked her face.

The Rottweiler's affectionate response stirred her into full consciousness. "Whoa, what a greeting." She sat up rubbing Scotty's barrel chest and nuzzling her face against his.

Both Reed and Noah laughed at Scotty.

Petting the dog behind the ears, Lani pulled away from Noah. Silence fell between the three of them. Her breath caught as the memory of the attack invaded her thoughts, breaking the moment of levity.

Reed spoke up. "You all right?"

"My head hurts," she said. It was easier to think about her physical pain. She touched the sore spot where the rock had hit her.

Noah cleared his throat. "What happened?" He pulled back and squared his shoulders, returning to his old professional self. So much for the small sign that Noah Jameson was human.

Heat rose up in her cheeks. Now she would have to explain why the training exercise had gone sideways. She still didn't know who the man was or why he had come after her. She hadn't even gotten a good look at him. She leaned forward to get to her feet but sat back down. Pain shot through the side of her head. "Ouch." Scotty edged in close to her, emitting a whine that suggested deep concern.

Reed leaned a little closer as well. "Take it easy."

Noah repeated his question. "What happened? There was someone else out here. Who was he?"

The memory of that man talking into her ear, of not being able to subdue him, hit her full force. "Yes, I was attacked." Her voice faltered, but she took in a breath and regained her composure. The last thing she wanted was for Noah to think she couldn't handle herself.

Scotty licked her cheek. Reed put a hand on her shoulder.

Noah rose to his feet. "I thought that might be the case. We've got reinforcements coming in to search the area."

"Did you see the guy?" Reed rose to his feet.

"No, it was dark. We struggled." She glanced nervously at Noah. His expression gave nothing away. "I can give a full statement as to what happened. The guy was in good shape. I found a bike that might be his."

She gave them a summary of the attack but then kept talking. Lani bit her lip. She was rambling because Noah's silence made her nervous. "We should try to locate that. It might be his means of escape. Certainly, it might have fingerprints or other evidence." Why was she talking like it was going out of style?

"We'll start searching before the others get here. Time is precious." Noah had already signaled Scotty to stand beside him.

"I'll help with the search. I can at least lead you to where I saw the bicycle." She moved to get to her feet.

"You've had physical trauma. Maybe you should stay put," said Reed.

Reed had shown considerable restraint. She could tell from his expression he was worried. He knew when they were out in the field, she wanted to be treated like a fellow officer not the little sister.

"I'll be fine." She stood up. Already she could feel the bruising and strained muscles from the fight she'd been in, but she wasn't about to let Noah know that. "I can show where I found the bike, maybe the dogs can pick up a scent."

Noah nodded. He pulled his flashlight off his belt and handed it to her. "If you are fine with that. Lead the way."

Lani took the flashlight. Was that approval she heard in his voice? In all other settings, she was a confident person. She had a black belt and good instincts. Why did she always second-guess herself around Noah?

With Reed, Noah and the dogs following, Lani made her way back to where she remembered seeing the bicycle. She saw the tree where the bike had been propped.

Of course, it was gone. The man must have taken off on it.

"Right here. It was right here." She shone the light all around.

The dogs circled giving a soft alert to some sort of smell.

She saw the most likely path the bike could have gone on. The dogs picked up the scent and headed in that direction. The sky had become black with the city skyline glittering in the distance. Always a beautiful sight. She loved the city at night.

The brush grew denser as they got closer to the shore. She saw a flash of light up ahead. The dogs barked and bayed excitedly. That had to be her attacker.

Lani ran, following the light as it winked in and out of view and then disappeared close to the shore. The light must be on the attacker's bicycle.

She ran faster despite the terrain becoming more treacherous and the pain from her injuries. With Reed and Noah right behind her, she made her way down the steep incline. The faint silhouette of a boat was visible in the moonlight. She heard a motor roar to life. The man had loaded his bike into the boat and was preparing to take off.

She wasn't about to let him get away.

The boat had just eased away from the shore when she jumped into the water. In the distance, she could see the flashing lights of other boats.

This boat wouldn't be able to get up speed until it was in open water out of the bay and the tangle of peninsulas and islands that made up the refuge.

Her arms cut through the surging waves. Her head bobbed above the surface. She was within feet of the boat. She willed herself to move faster. Her hand reached for the edge of the boat. She held on.

She could see the back of the man as he steered. The bike occupied two of the backseats. She pulled herself up. Water cascaded off her body. The noise was enough to alert her assailant. He shifted the boat into Neutral and whirled around.

Before she could get her bearings, he had punched her and pushed her back off the side of the boat. She splashed into the water, plunging beneath the surface like a weighted rag doll. She bobbed back up just in time to see the boat speeding out into open water.

She could hear the dogs on the shore going ballistic.

Feeling defeated, she turned and swam back toward the beach. Noah rushed out into the water up to his knees. She gasped for air.

"You all right?" He wrapped his arm around her and helped her to the beach.

The suspect had gotten away. Noah eased her down to the beach where Scotty waited to give her moral support and doggie kisses. The cold water had masked the pain of her attack. Now she could feel where there was probably going to be some soreness and bruising.

She stared out where the flashing light of the assailant's boat merged with other flashing lights. Not many boats out at this hour. "Maybe the coast guard can catch up with him." She didn't hold out much hope for that happening.

Noah spoke on his radio, giving a description of the boat and the direction it was headed.

Noah sat down beside her. "That was something else, jumping in the water like that."

That Noah was impressed with her was only a small

victory. The suspect had gotten away. She was exhausted, beat and wondering if she had made the right choice following in her brother's footsteps.

Her only consolation was that Scotty seemed to pick up on her despair. The Rottweiler rested his chin on her leg and made a sympathetic noise. Now she remembered why she wanted to be a K-9 cop. She rested a hand on Scotty's head. Someday she would be assigned her own K-9 partner.

Tonight though, she felt defeated. If a training exercise could go so far off the rails, what would happen when she worked the field?

Noah sat beside Lani, catching his breath. "Maybe they'll nab him when he comes to shore."

The other dogs and officers were farther inland.

"Maybe." Lani's voice sounded weak. She stroked behind Scotty's ears.

Noah's Rottweiler usually didn't warm up to people so fast, but the dog seemed to like Lani from the moment she'd become a part of the K-9 unit. His brother Jordan had always said that dogs were a good judge of character. If he closed his eyes, he could almost hear his brother's voice. He rubbed his chest though the pain he felt was emotional, that deep chasm inside that would never be filled. His younger brothers Zach and Carter were probably the only two people who understood about the hole Jordan's death had left for all of them. His parents were going through a whole different kind of grief.

"I appreciate your tenacity in going after the suspect," he said. Noah remembered that only a month before, Lani had stopped an intruder in her and Reed's house by shooting him. Though she had handled herself well, she had been put on administrative leave to help with her emotional recovery, which had stalled her training. Remembering that and seeing firsthand how she had done tonight made Noah think that maybe he had underestimated Lani.

Lani wrapped her arms around her body. "He got away though."

Noah took off his jacket and wrapped it around her shoulders. His pants were wet up to the knees, but he wasn't cold. "If medical hasn't shown up yet at the visitors' center, let's get you checked out in the ER."

She drew the coat around her. "I'm fine. I just need to change into some dry clothes and get some rest."

"You took quite a blow to the head." Though Lani seemed like a strong woman, he was concerned about the psychological fallout from having been attacked tonight in addition to her physical well-being. Sometimes there was an accumulative effect from dealing with violence and then an officer just cracked up.

"I know about the possibility of a concussion. Reed gets off duty in a bit, he can keep an eye on me through the night. As soon as that suspect is picked up, I want to be called. I don't care what the hour is."

"Sure, Lani." Always at the back of his mind, the fear of something bad happening to another of the K-9 officers plagued him. He felt a strong responsibility to the team. "At least ride home with me in my patrol car."

He rose to his feet and held out his hand to help her up. Her fingers felt silky soft in his calloused bear paws. They stood for a moment facing each other. The rhythm of water rushing the shore and the gulls feeding in the distance seemed to be the only sounds.

"Fine, I'll ride back with you, but I will report for duty for my regular shift tomorrow. Don't treat me with kid gloves." Lani turned and headed up the sandy shore toward the tall grass. "I can handle myself just fine. I've had first aid training as part of being a martial arts instructor..."

Lani continued to talk as they moved through the grass.

He wasn't sure if her talking was a sign of confidence or insecurity. His estimation of her had gone up a notch. It took guts to jump in the water after a suspect, especially one that had just attacked her.

Noah's radio glitched and Reed's voice came across the line. "I got Lani's bike loaded up in my patrol car."

"Ten-four. She's riding home with me, but you need to keep an eye on her through the night."

"She's not going into the ER?" Reed's voice filled with concern.

Lani grabbed the radio. Standing on her tiptoes, she spoke into it. "Reed, quit being a big brother. When we're working, treat me like you would any other officer."

"Copy that, sis."

"Do you call all the other officers, sis?"

Noah chuckled at the banter between the siblings. His brothers razzed each other and him on and off the job.

"Yes, Officer Branson." Reed's voice held a note of amusement.

Lani addressed Noah. "We'll swing by the ER, but I'm sure I'm fine," Lani said.

They hiked back up to the trail and out to the visitors' center. Several patrol cars were parked there. More had arrived once the alert about the suspect had gone out.

"Any news on the boat?" Lani stepped toward one of the other officers, who shook his head.

Noah loaded Scotty in the back of his Tahoe SUV. Lani got into the passenger seat. They pulled out of the visitors' center. Noah veered toward Cross Bay Boulevard, Lani doing most of the talking sharing about the kids' class she taught at the martial arts center.

They stopped in the ER where a doctor examined Lani and gave her the okay to go back to work after a day off, but cautioned her to watch for any pain or loss of focus for the next couple of days. They got back into the Tahoe and headed home. Lani continued to talk about working with dogs at the training center.

As they drove through Queens at night, her voice trailed off. She touched her hand to her shoulder.

He'd gotten so used to the sound of her voice, the silence felt awkward. He glanced over at her. "Everything okay, Lani?"

"My radio. He yanked it off of me. I don't have a radio anymore." Her voice, normally very animated, had become monotone.

Noah had been braced for the emotional shock to set in. "We'll issue you a new one when you come on shift after your day of rest. Lani?"

He was only a few blocks from her house in Rego Park. Lani and Reed lived on a quiet street. At this hour, there was no one outside. He spoke again to get her attention. "Lani?"

"I'm all right." She stared straight ahead.

He knew she wasn't. "It's pretty normal to feel off-kilter after what you've been through." She hadn't been an officer very long and already she'd seen a degree of violence. "It wouldn't hurt to make an appointment with the police psychologist. I know it was required you meet with one after you shot that guy who came into your house. It wouldn't hurt to make another appointment."

She lifted her chin slightly. "I just need a good night's sleep and run in the park in the morning. That's my therapy."

He had a feeling the bravado she showed was because she didn't want to appear incapable in front of the chief. Sometimes he didn't like his title. It put a barrier between him and his fellow officers.

After circling the block, he found a parking space not too far from her house. He appreciated how tough she was acting. He'd been a cop long enough to know that denial didn't make the trauma go away. "At least let me stay with you until Reed gets off shift."

She lowered her head and pushed open the car door. "Okay, but only if Scotty can come in too."

Scotty let out a low-level woof of approval.

Both of them laughed.

"Scotty seems to like the idea," said Lani.

He had to hand it to his square-jawed partner. He could be very entertaining. Noah walked Lani to the house which had a stone facade and pillars. The flower beds were covered in straw. Though he could picture them in full bloom. Lani struck him as a plant kind of person. Who was he kidding? Lani was a people person and a dog person—warm and connecting, vivacious about all aspects of life. That's why it bothered him to see her so quiet.

With Scotty heeling beside him, they went up the steps and onto the porch. Lani unlocked the door.

Noah stared up at the second story. "This whole place is yours?"

"No, we have an upstairs tenant." She pushed the door open.

Once inside, Lani invited Noah to sit on the couch while Scotty sniffed his new surroundings. She excused herself to change out of her wet clothes.

Family photos, many of Reed and Lani doing sports together, adorned the wall in the living room. There was a picture of them attending a Yankees game with an older couple. Judging from the resemblance, the older couple must be Reed and Lani's parents. His eyes rested on a picture of a teenage Lani in a leotard with her arms around two other dancers. A more recent one showed Lani on stage in a Western costume with other actors.

Noah understood why Lani was referred to as Cover Girl by the rest of the team. Her vitality and positive attitude came across in the photos and she was beautiful enough to be a model.

Several photos featured Reed working with his K-9 partner, Jessie.

Lani entered the room dressed in an oversize orange sweatshirt and jeans. "Do you want some cocoa or something?" Her blue eyes did not have their usual sparkle. He detected the weariness in her voice. It was important that she not be alone after having gone through such an ordeal.

"Sure, that sounds good," he said. "Let me help you."

While Lani filled the kettle and put it on the stove, Noah rooted through cupboards for mugs.

Lani pulled a basket filled with tea bags and hot chocolate packets from a cupboard. "Pick whatever you like."

The toll of the attack was evident in her movement

and on her face. He placed a hand on her shoulder. "Why don't you go sit down and I'll bring you the drink?"

She nodded and stepped back into the living room. Again, he knew something was up because she didn't argue with him.

He opened the packets of cocoa and sprinkled them into the mugs. The kettle whistled. He poured the water into the cups. He carried the steaming mugs into the living room where he found Lani standing, not sitting, staring at the wall of photographs. Scotty had finished sniffing his surroundings and now sat at attention. His ears perked up when Noah entered the room.

She pointed to a bare space on the wall. "Do you know what goes there?"

Noah shook his head.

"A picture of me with my dog when I'm assigned one." Her face shone with a sort of inner glow.

The bare space was next to a photo of Reed with his Jessie. The bloodhound's saggy-skinned expression seemed to contradict the dog's tenacious personality.

He knew from Lani's file that she was twenty-nine, old for a rookie. His estimation of her abilities had changed, but he still had his doubts. Her background was not the normal career route for a cop. "That will happen soon enough." It had been months since Lani had been accepted to the K-9 unit and a suitable dog had still not become available. She'd tried out several. The dogs were either not compatible with her or they washed out of the program. Jordan's death and Noah getting used to being chief had slowed everything down as well.

"Tonight didn't go like I expected." She stared at the floor.

He stepped toward her, touching her chin so she

lifted her eyes. "But you handled the unexpected. That's what a good cop does."

A little light came into her blue eyes. That spark of energy that he liked about her returned.

"Thanks," she said.

She let out a heavy breath and sat down on the couch. Noah sat down beside her sipping his beverage. Scotty lay down so his butt rested against Noah's feet and his head rested close to Lani's feet.

Noah pointed toward the photos. "So you did a lot of plays?" It was important to keep her mind off the attack.

"Mostly off Broadway, and I did a couple commercials and even some stunt work," she said.

"I know I've lived here my whole life, but I think I made it to the theater twice in my life and one time it was with my school."

Lani laughed, "I know. There are people born and raised here who have never been to the Statue of Liberty."

He reached down to pat Scotty's head. "My family goes to the Mets games quite a bit."

"Sounds like fun." Lani took a sip of her cocoa.

They talked awhile longer. When the door opened and Reed stepped in with Jessie, Noah glanced at the clock. An hour had passed without him realizing he'd been so caught up in his conversation with Lani.

Jessie loped over to Lani, who leaned so the dog could give her a sloppy kiss.

"Long night?"

"Something like that. Had a couple other calls after we got stuff wrapped up at the refuge." Reed took his coat off and hung it up on a coatrack. "Sorry I'm late. I stopped in to talk with Abigail for a little bit."

Abigail was Reed's fiancée and an outreach coordinator for troubled teens.

"Can I talk to you for just a moment?" Noah gestured for Reed to enter the kitchen.

"What's up?"

"Keep an eye on her through the night. Not just to make sure she doesn't lose consciousness. Wake her up a couple of times. The ER doc said to look for dilated pupils. I'm more worried about her emotional health. Maybe she's just acting tough in front of me. I don't know."

Reed nodded. "We got this handled. I know my sister."

"She'll push to come into work tomorrow, but she needs to take the day off," said Noah.

Reed nodded. "Will do."

When they returned to the living room, Lani had fallen asleep on the couch. Jessie curled against her belly. The bloodhound was so huge she hung halfway off the couch. Lani's blond hair, loose from the tight bun, framed her face and fell across her neck.

Scotty lay at Lani's feet. He stared up at Noah while his tail thudded on the floor.

Noah commanded Scotty to come and he fell in line. "I'll see myself out." He glanced once again at the sleeping Lani. She looked at peace. "Take care of her. Maybe you can talk her into making a counseling appointment."

"You can't talk my sister into anything once she's made up her mind."

"So true." Noah stepped to the door, swung it open and headed up the block toward his SUV with the dog padding softly on the sidewalk beside him. He looked back. The curtains were drawn in the living room. Still, he could picture Reed placing a blanket over his sleeping sister. She was in good hands.

As he loaded Scotty into the patrol car, he felt that tightening in his chest.

He only hoped that what had happened to Lani tonight was an isolated incident. He didn't want another cop harmed...or worse.

THREE

Lani clicked the leash onto the collar of the six-month-old yellow Lab and headed out of the training center to walk the pup. She was glad to be back to work after a required day off. Oscar was one of eight puppies born to Stella, a yellow Lab, who had been a gift to the unit from the Czech Republic. The dogs had all been put into foster homes. Oscar had been brought back to the training center to assess if he would be good K-9 material and maybe assigned to Lani. She tried not to get too hopeful about Oscar. Other dogs she'd trained with had initially seemed like a good fit. She pushed aside the frustration she felt over not getting her own K-9 partner after so many months.

As she stepped out into the early morning to walk the dog, the sun bathed her skin. She turned the corner.

The idea of taking the dogs out was not only for exercise but getting them used to staying focused with a million distractions around them. This street usually had fewer people and less traffic than Ninety-Fourth Street where the K-9 offices and training center were.

All the same, the streets already bustled with activity, visual and auditory. Oscar heeled with his head up, taking in the buzz of the city. Pedestrians brushed past them on the sidewalks. Car horns blared as traffic rolled by. In the distance, she detected the intense rhythm of a jackhammer.

This was her city. Walking the dogs was part of her routine while on duty. Still, a fearful hesitation made her a little less confident in her step. The boat her attacker had escaped in was never found. She'd gone for a run on her day off which usually cleared her head, but not this time. Her sleep had been fitful.

Oscar's tail wagged when a group of children walked past him. She gave the leash a slight jerk to let him know that as much as he wanted to, he couldn't interact with the children.

"We're on duty," she said.

The crowd thinned as they approached an abandoned building that used to be a multistoried department store. She could feel the soreness from the attack. She increased her pace. Oscar's little legs kept up with hers. If she slowed, he responded. The dog was sharp. She loved all the K-9 recruits, but she liked how quickly Oscar picked up on her cues. They seemed to be dialed into each other, a quality that was essential in working with a partner, K-9 or human.

She'd requested that he be brought out of foster care to see if he'd be good K-9 material. Not all dogs had the temperament to be K-9s. In her first encounter with Oscar, when he was just weaned at eight weeks, he had sat back on his haunches and looked up at her, tilting his head to one side as if to say, *At your service, ma'am.*

Oscar seemed to have alerted on something across the street. She followed the line of his gaze. Noah Jameson stood beside a coffee cart waiting for his morning cup. He offered Lani a small wave before he turned back toward headquarters. He must be busy today if he was getting his coffee from a street cart. Most of the officers went to Griffin's diner for coffee. Scotty wasn't with him. He must be back at Noah's office.

"He's all right, isn't he, Oscar?" Noah had always struck her as being emotionally closed down. She had seen a more caring side to him after the training exercise fell apart. Maybe he was human after all.

A scraping sound above her caused her to tilt her head. A large square object came right toward her at a rapid speed, filling her field of vision. She jumped to one side, falling against the brick exterior of the building. The few people on the sidewalk scattered as well. In her panic, Lani had let go of Oscar's leash.

An air-conditioning unit shattered on the concrete. Some of the pieces still vibrated from the impact.

An older man rushed toward her. "Are you all right?"

Dazed and in shock, Lani got to her feet with the man's help. She brushed the dust off her uniform.

"What a bizarre accident." An older woman approached Lani. She tilted her head. "It must have been loose or something." The woman patted Lani's shoulder. "Are you all right, dear? That was quite the scare."

Lani's heart raced a mile a minute. She glanced around. Where was Oscar? "Did you see where my dog went?"

Both the old man and woman shook their heads. People had begun to move past her on the street, stepping around the pieces of the shattered air-conditioning unit. She stared through the forest of feet, not seeing the puppy as fear gripped her heart all over again. The poor thing had probably gotten frightened and run off.

A yelp came from inside the building. She pressed her face against the dusty window. She could just make out Oscar's face by a pile of scrap wood. The poor dog had been so afraid he'd run for shelter.

"Hang on, Oscar. I'm coming to get you."

She tried one of the double doors that were the main entrance to the building. Locked.

Oscar had gotten in somehow. She saw then a hole in the display window. Not big enough for her to slip through. She walked around to the side of the building and found a door that looked like it had been jimmied. Someone desperate for a place to sleep on a cold fall night had probably done that. Knowing that she might surprise someone, she pulled her gun.

She rushed in. She heard Oscar's whimper before she saw him in the dark corner. Broken display counters and pieces of mannequins still remained in the dust and debris.

A sense of relief flooded through her as she ran over to the puppy. She holstered her weapon and gathered him in her arms. "It's all right, buddy. That was scary for me too." The pup licked her face.

Thudding sounds came from the floor above her. Footsteps. Her heart beat a little faster. Maybe the air conditioner had had a little help by being pushed. Maybe the lock was jimmied by someone up to no good, not just looking for a place to sleep.

"Tell you what, buddy. You've had enough excitement for one day." She wrapped his leash around a door knob. She still hadn't been issued a new radio. Protocol would be to call for backup. That wasn't possible right now. She'd neglected to get another cell phone after hers was damaged by the water last night.

Chances were she was dealing with a vagrant, nothing more. He or she could have leaned against the air-conditioning unit…or the destruction might have been on purpose. Or just someone so high or drunk, they didn't know what they were doing.

Oscar yipped as if to offer encouragement. More footsteps sounded above her. She pulled her weapon and headed up the wide staircase in the center of the floor. The second floor was an open area with broken glass and display counters largely dismantled and probably used for firewood. Mattresses and dusty clothing scattered throughout the floor indicated the homeless had taken up residence at one time. Maybe they were still here. None of the big front display windows on this floor contained air conditioners.

She scanned the open floor area one quadrant at a time. There were places someone could hide, behind the piles of busted furniture and boxes and the display counters. She detected no movement. She held her own breath and listened, sensing that someone was watching her. Her mouth went dry. "NYPD. Please show yourself."

Turning quickly and aiming her weapon, she thought she saw someone in her peripheral vision. She let out a breath. Just a mannequin. She shook her head and dryly laughed.

There were smaller rooms on the south side of the building that might have been offices or storage spaces. Some had doors, some did not. With her heart drumming in her ears, she made her way toward the rooms.

Her own footsteps seemed to echo on the floorboards. The first room had no door, she peered inside seeing only empty shelving. She lifted her weapon and made her way to the second room. She held her gun in one hand while she opened the door with the other.

A hand went over her mouth and jerked her back. The attacker had come up from behind. "I got you." He pinched the nerves on her wrist. "Drop the gun."

Pain shot up her arm, but she held on to the gun. She angled her body side to side trying to escape his iron hold on her. In the struggle, she dropped her gun. She broke free, whirled around and slammed him hard in the stomach. The man, who was wearing a blue baseball cap, bent over. She scrambled to get her weapon.

The man recovered quickly and took off running just as she picked up her gun. Footsteps pounded behind her. Not another one. She whirled around aiming her weapon just in time to see Noah coming up the stairs.

On reflex, Noah pointed his gun at her. "Whoa."

Unable to form the question, she shook her head as if to ask what he was doing.

"I saw movement on the third-floor window where that thing fell out. I was just getting ready to walk around the corner to headquarters, but there was a construction accident that blocked the sidewalk, so it took me a minute to run back over here."

But he was here. That's what mattered.

She pointed. "He went toward the stairwell leading up."

They both raced across the floor. The culprit must have been trying to get out via the first floor when Lani had interrupted him on the second floor. Noah took the lead as they headed up the stairs.

The third floor consisted of a hallway and a series of rooms that were probably offices and storage. There was no obvious exit.

Lani pointed, signaling that they could work their way from either end toward the middle, clearing each room. She moved into the first room, cleared it and stepped back into the hallway just in time to see Noah disappear into a room on the opposite end of the hallway.

She stepped into the second room, which featured a large window that looked out on the street. A knocked-over file cabinet and pieces of a desk that must have been quite beautiful in its time cluttered the floor. This could have been the CEO's or store manager's office. There was no evidence a transient lived here, though she did see the hole that likely contained the air-conditioning unit that now lay in pieces on the street.

She shuddered. What was in the mind of someone who would push something out a window knowing there were people down below who could be hurt?

She heard the thunder of footsteps. Heart racing, weapon drawn, Lani stepped back out into the hallway just in time to see Noah sprinting toward the far end of the building.

Noah looked over his shoulder. "He's headed up to the roof."

Noah disappeared around a corner. Lani followed after him, praying they would catch their suspect.

Moments before, Noah had stepped out on a fire escape and spotted the suspect climbing out on a different fire escape and taking a ladder up toward the roof. He had raced back inside to see if there was an easier way to get to the roof. That's when he'd seen Lani and told her the suspect was headed up to the roof.

He hurried out to the landing where the suspect had

gone. The fire escape, which looked like it was hanging by maybe one bolt, was clearly not a safe route down. He peered up just in time to see the suspect's feet disappear over the top of the building.

Noah holstered his weapon and leaped up the uneven brick facade that the suspect had used as a sort of climbing wall. His muscles strained as he pulled himself up. He glanced down only for a moment to see the throngs of people and metal of cars glinting in the early morning sun. He found another foothold as his hands wrapped around the protruding brick above him.

Lani came out on the balcony. She groaned. "Are you kidding me."

Noah looked down at her. "Join the fun." He scaled the rest of the wall and pulled himself up to the flat roof. The suspect raced from one corner of the roof to another. He was trapped.

Noah pushed himself to his feet. He pulled his weapon just in time to see the man leap to the adjoining building. As chief, Noah was not out in the field enough to warrant having a radio. There was no time to make a call on his cell. He had to rely on Lani for backup. The suspect did not appear to be armed or he would have pulled a weapon by now.

He raced across the roof. There was about a five-foot chasm between the two buildings. Without hesitation, Noah pushed off. He stretched his right leg out in front, watching the edge of the building looming toward him. He landed with a thud. His knees buckled screaming with pain from the impact. The suspect had reached the edge of the second building. He hesitated, glanced back at Noah and then disappeared over the side. The guy must have found a safer fire escape.

Noah's heart pounded against his rib cage as his leg muscles strained. He sprinted toward where the suspect had gone. He peered down and saw only the top of his blue baseball cap. The guy had already made it to the top floor down the fire escape ladder. Noah swung down onto the ladder. He'd gone down only four rungs when Lani's voice reached him. She'd made up the distance between them pretty easily. "I'm going to look for a faster way down. See if we can cut him off."

He glanced up to see her head and shoulders as she looked down. Her bright expression and blue-eyed gaze met his. "Go find it."

She disappeared.

The suspect had only a short way to go down the ladder before he reached the street. Noah climbed faster narrowing the distance between them. When the suspect was halfway down the last part of the ladder, he jumped the remainder of the distance.

Lani emerged from the side of the building just as the man ran toward a crowded street market. She must have found an elevator in the building. Noah climbed two more rungs and then jumped, landing on his feet. He whirled around.

He could see Lani's blond head. She was in uniform but had lost her hat somewhere. The tight little bun on top of her head was easy enough to track in a crowd. He didn't see the suspect anywhere, but Lani ran like she still had sight of him.

He hurried past booths selling handbags and scarves. The aromatic scent of street vendor food swirled in the air, the mingling scent of salt, a heady sweetness and other spices. Noah kept his eyes on Lani. He didn't see the suspect anywhere. Still running, Lani merged with a throng of people. She towered above them. She stopped, glancing side to side.

He surveyed the area. Then he saw a blue baseball hat on the ground beside a food cart that sold gyros. The guy had ditched the hat knowing it would be an easy way to track him.

Lani turned back to face Noah, shaking her head before pushing deeper into the crowd. She wasn't one to give up easily even though he had a feeling the suspect had managed to give them the slip.

Taking slow steps, he ambled past the vendors, scanning the crowd one more time while he caught his breath. He didn't see the suspect anywhere. He retraced his steps, searching for the baseball hat thinking it might have DNA on it, but it had either been picked up or kicked out of view. He worked his way back to the edge of the street market, asking several of the vendors if they had seen the man in a blue baseball cap or seen a man take the cap off and throw it on the ground. All of them shook their heads.

When he glanced over his shoulder, Lani was headed toward him. As she drew closer, he knew that wrinkled forehead indicated her frustration.

She stood beside him and crossed her arms. "I guess that is that. I don't know what gets into people thinking it's okay to endanger public safety by pushing an air-conditioning unit out a window."

Concern niggled at the edges of Noah's brain. Lani had been attacked twice in forty-eight hours. "You don't think maybe that guy was aiming specifically for you?"

Her face went pale and she didn't answer right away. "He was probably just someone with mental illness issues or a drug problem. Don't you think? Besides, how would someone know that I would be walking by that building at that time?"

"You keep the same routine every day, don't you?"

"Well I…why would someone want to hurt me?"

"Do you think it might be the same man from last night?"

Her face blanched. "I didn't get a good look either time." She turned away from him. "I left Oscar back in that building by himself." She took off at a jog.

Lani clearly did not want to believe that the attacks were personal or connected. And he suspected she knew something she didn't want to share. Noah followed her back to the open side door of the building. They stepped from the brightness of day into the dim gloom of the abandoned building. Even the big display windows were so covered in dust not much light got in.

Oscar wagged his tail and yipped when he saw Lani. After untying him, she gathered the pup into her arms. "There's my little guy."

"Little guy?" Noah kneeled beside her, so he could pet Oscar's head and velvety ears. "Don't go all mushy on him. We're trying to turn him into a tough police dog." The dog licked Noah's face, melting his heart. So much for being tough.

"Oscar did all right. He did freak when that unit nearly fell on us, but he didn't seem too bent out of shape for having been left here." She let the dog kiss her face. "Next time you'll be a part of the action, won't you?"

Noah was concerned that Lani wasn't being realistic about the attacks. But grilling her wouldn't do any good. Right now, she was in denial. If he started slinging questions at her, she might become defensive.

He needed to get information out of her without making her feel pressured. "What do you say that after we get the crime scene people over here, I grab Scotty and we get Oscar used to working around people and staying focused?"

She put Oscar down on the floor and stood up. "That would be good for Oscar and for me. But do you have the time for that?"

The last thing he wanted to do anyway was sit in that office on this beautiful fall day. "I'll make the time." Maybe the attacks were random. He needed to make sure one of his officers was not in danger. That someone would not come after Lani a third time.

FOUR

Lani and Noah waited for the forensics team to show up at the abandoned building before heading back to headquarters. Lani loaded Oscar into the backseat of Noah's patrol car where Scotty already waited. Scotty remained at attention while Oscar jumped and nipped excitedly.

She laughed and shook her head. "Talk about the senior officer putting up with the rookie's misplaced enthusiasm." She ruffled the top of Oscar's head. Scotty let out a groan of protest. She reached across the seat past Oscar and stroked the Rottweiler's ear. "I love you too."

Scotty remained in position but licked his chops and leaned into her touch.

Lani climbed into the passenger seat. Noah already sat behind the wheel.

"The park is always a nice place to do training. Teach the dogs to deal with the distraction," he said.

She buckled herself in. "Yeah, sure." Her throat constricted. Noah was up to something. He wasn't in the habit of dropping his desk duties to hang out with her or any other rookie. Any of the other officers could have trained with her today. He'd wanted to know if she thought her attacker from the refuge and the one they'd chased in the abandoned building had been the same guy. The question made her chest feel tight.

While it was true, she hadn't got a good look at the attacker either time, there were similarities. Same height and build. But it was the assailant's unusual strength both times that made her wonder if they were dealing with the same man. Though she was a black belt and more agile than her attacker, he was an equal match for her due to his level of fitness. He'd spoken to her both times. She couldn't say for sure if the voice was the same. Why would anyone want to harm her though? That was what didn't make sense.

Noah pulled out onto the street and into traffic just as a call came over the radio.

"Missing child at the GallopNYC stables, Forest Hills."

"That's right up Scotty's alley." Noah picked up the radio. "This is unit twelve. Depending on traffic, I can be over there shortly with a K-9." Noah glanced over at Lani. "So much for a training exercise. This is the real thing."

Lani's heart beat a little faster. Though she was concerned about the missing child, the prospect of working a real case was exciting. She said a prayer of gratitude that she wouldn't have to deal with Noah's questions right away.

Maybe it was just the bliss of ignorance that she could be in denial a little longer. If the attacks were personal, would they let her continue in her K-9 training? She'd worked hard to get to this point. She didn't want to lose all that or even have it be delayed.

Noah wove through traffic with a high level of skill by slipping into the pockets between moving cars and avoiding construction by taking side streets.

Noah checked his rearview mirror. "What's with this guy?"

Lani craned her neck at the line of cars behind them. "I don't see anything."

"That black sedan two cars back has been doggin' us since we left the station."

Her muscles tensed at the sight of the car.

Sensing her unease, Oscar leaped up and licked Lani's hand where she rested it on the back of the seat. She gave him a hand signal indicating he needed to sit. Oscar complied but shifted his weight from foot to foot as he sat back in the seat. He stretched his chin out indicating that he wanted affection from Lani.

Lani shook her head and waved her finger at the pup.

"He's a little unfocused to be good K-9 material," Noah said.

"He's still young. The initial testing showed he had a strong defense drive." She glanced one more time at the dark sedan. Encroaching fear made it hard to get a deep breath.

Noah hit his turn signal and slipped around a corner. After he'd driven several blocks, he checked the rearview mirror. She didn't need to look over her shoulder at the traffic behind them. Noah's expression, the tight lips and narrowed eyes, told her the sedan had turned as well.

The fenced dirt arena for the therapeutic horse stable came into view with the stables behind it. City apartment buildings and homes surrounded the little oasis for horses. She had volunteered here as a teenager. "I know the layout of this place."

A cluster of maybe ten people with two uniformed police officers stood on the edge of the arena. A rider— a young girl—with three adults, one on each side and one by the horse's head, trotted alongside the horse skirting the edge of the fence on the other side of the arena.

Noah pulled onto the grass beside the other patrol car where there was no fence. "I'm glad you know the lay-out. Let's go get the details from the uniforms." He got out, opened the back door and gave Scotty the command to hit the ground. Noah hooked the Rottweiler into his leash and headed toward the crowd. Lani glanced at the forlorn-looking Oscar. "You gotta stay in the car, buddy. Be good. We're both being tested." She shut the door just as the pup's tail thumped on the seat.

One of the officers noticed Noah and Lani. He broke away from the crowd. Lani recognized him from the academy. He'd graduated the same time she had.

She stepped forward. "Officer Langston."

Scotty sat at attention at Noah's feet.

Officer Langston was short and maybe twenty pounds overweight. His physical stature was deceiving. He'd played football in high school and was strong and quick on his feet. He smiled. "Officer Branson, good to see you." He tipped his hat toward Noah. "Chief Jameson. Just want you to know all the street patrol units have kept their ears to the ground for any news about your brother's killer."

A shadow seemed to fall across Noah's face at the mention of his brother's name. "Thank you, Officer." The change in mood was momentary. Lani wondered if she was the only one tuned into it. "Time is of the essence in finding this kid. What is the story here?"

"More tracking dogs and search-and-rescue dogs are on the way." Officer Langston held up a child's red coat. "Brendan is five, he's autistic and deaf. He comes here for lessons. The usual thing. His mom was distracted for just a second. She turned back around and her son was gone. They searched the grounds for twenty minutes before calling us."

Lani didn't have to have Brendan's mom pointed out to her. It was clear the woman who gripped her purse to her chest with glazed eyes and an expression that looked like it was chiseled from stone was the distraught mom. They didn't need to make her more upset by peppering her with questions she had probably already answered. Officer Langston would give them all they needed to know.

Lani said a quick prayer for the mother and son.

"The mom says the son might think he's in trouble, so he'll hide," Officer Langston said.

And if the child was deaf, he wouldn't hear people calling for him.

Noah grabbed the coat and let Scotty sniff it. "Let's head up there and see what he can find."

"Two more dogs are on their way. I'm just glad you were able to get here so fast."

They made their way across the grounds toward the stables. Lani stared out into the streets that surrounded the little oasis of peace. Her throat tightened with fear. A five-year-old could wander out into the street pretty quickly.

"We've got a unit circling the block and officers on foot as well." Officer Langston explained before break-

ing away and heading back to where the cluster of concerned people huddled together.

Eager to work, Scotty lurched forward, causing the
long leash to go taut. They headed into the stables where
the boy had last been seen. A teenager stabbed hay with
a pitchfork and tossed it into a stall.

Scotty sniffed the ground. And hurried through the
building.

Lani lagged behind.

"You're here to find the kid?" said the teenager.

"Yes," she planted her feet. "Did you see anything?"

"No, I was in another building. All I know is that kid
loves animals. I can't help but think he was chasing after
a barn cat or became fascinated by a squirrel outside."

But where was he now? She didn't even want to think
about what could have happened to Brendan if he had
wandered off the grounds.

Noah exited the stables and headed toward another
building with Scotty sniffing the ground.

An idea flashed through Lani's brain. She called to
Noah that she would return quickly. She headed down
the hill toward the patrol car. She swung open the back
door and put a leash on Oscar. He ruffled his ears while
he licked her face. "Time for some on-the-job training.
Let's use your cuteness to draw out a little boy."

Oscar leaped down to the ground. They headed back
toward the stables. Her theory could be totally off base.
Something sinister could have happened to Brendan.
He could be miles from here by now. If he'd wandered
out into the street, someone in a car could have picked
him up.

She shuddered at the thought. Brendan was the age

of some of the kids in one of the martial arts classes
she taught.

Oh God, let there be a happy ending to all this.

She hurried across the arena just as another patrol
car with another search dog pulled up. She waved at
the officer as he unloaded his dog. She caught up with
Noah and Scotty inside a different barn that was filled
with hay.

"Scotty loses the scent inside here." The barn appeared to be used mostly for storage of farm-type equipment, hay and other bags of feed.

"You think he's still on the grounds somewhere?"
she asked.

"Yeah, but there are a thousand places where he
could be. What if he's fallen and hurt himself." Noah's
jaw tensed. "I hate when bad things happen to kids."

"Let's pray this isn't one of those cases."

Noah pointed at Oscar who tugged on his leash.

"The teenager feeding the horses said that Brendan
loves animals. If he's hiding because he thinks he's in
trouble, maybe a puppy will be enough to lure him out."

Scotty gave a soft alert to a smell by the door. They
hurried outside and back around the grounds before returning to the storage barn. The barking and baying of
the other search dog reached her ears. That dog wasn't
headed in this direction. Either the other dog or Scotty
had picked up on a false scent.

Scotty circled again, nose to the ground. Oscar
nipped at the twirling dust in the sunbeams. Maybe
the pup was too big of a goofball to be K-9 material.
She suppressed a smile at the puppy's antics.

Lani studied the barn, which had a loft on one end

where bales of hay and bags of feed were stored. Scotty kept coming back to this barn for a reason.

"I checked up there. I didn't see anything," Noah said.

She handed Noah Oscar's leash. "Hand him up to me when I get up there." Even though the responding officer had said a search had been done, there were a thousand cubbyholes a kid could hide. And Brendan wouldn't be able to hear people calling for him.

"I'm going to search that loft." She climbed up the ladder. The platform was so stuffed with supplies she had to maneuver over the tops of the bags of feed to get to the corner. Lani sat down on a hay bale.

"Anything?" Noah's voice came from below along with Oscar's yipping and barking.

Lani sat very still as her eyes scanned every inch of the dark space. Gradually, her eyes adjusted to the light. Again, she studied the shadows until her gaze landed about a foot from the far corner of the loft where what looked like tarps were tossed in a pile. Beneath the tarps she was able to discern the tips of a child's fingers. Though she could not see a face or eyes she sensed that she was being watched.

Lani spoke. "Noah, can you get Oscar up here? And then run and get Brendan's mom. I found him."

"Sure."

Shuffling sounds came from down below while Lani remained very still. To move toward the child might terrify him even more. She listened to her own heartbeat drumming in her ears. Oscar's yipping grew louder. She turned to see Noah's head as he placed the puppy on a pile of feed bags.

Oscar made his way across the treacherous landscape while Noah remained at the top of the ladder. Oscar wagged his tail as he drew closer to Lani. She gathered the pup in her arms before setting him down, and Noah left to fetch the anxious mother. Judging from the position of the fingers, Brendan was lying on his belly peeking out from beneath the tarp.

Oscar sniffed around, stepped over a pile of hoes and rakes and headed toward the tarps.

The puppy sat down then looked over at Lani. Lani gave him the hand signal to lie down. Oscar complied.

The seconds ticked by.

Slowly, little fingers came out from underneath the tarp and touched Oscar's belly. Dragging his belly, Oscar moved closer toward the tarps and stuck his head in.

A giggle came out from beneath the tarp.

Tension left Lani's body like a hundred birds taking flight. Though Oscar had broken the ice, she doubted that Brendan would trust her, a stranger. And she didn't know sign language. Hopefully, Noah would be back with Brendan's mom soon.

Oscar came back out from beneath the tarp. The tarp lifted. She saw fear in the boy's expression and the round brown eyes. The boy remained very still as he pushed himself into a sitting position.

Lani hoped her hand signal communicated that she wasn't going to hurt him. She held a palm out toward him, indicating he could stay where he was.

Oscar licked Brendan's hand. The boy's fear seemed to melt as he gathered the pup in his arms and let it kiss his face.

Within minutes, Brendan's mother arrived to coax

him out of the loft, hold him and reassure him that he was not in trouble.

While a crowd had gathered outside the storage barn, mother and son were left alone. Lani and Noah headed outside toward the patrol car with the two dogs in tow. Scotty heeled beside Noah while Oscar galloped ahead, heeled for a moment and then got distracted by a bug.

Lani gave Noah a friendly punch in the shoulder. "See, even goofballs like Oscar can be helpful."

"I'm just glad this all ended on a positive note."

They arrived at the SUV. "I think the four of us make a pretty good team. Scotty knew that boy was in that barn. Oscar drew him out."

"And you knew enough to do a deeper search. And how to deal with the kid." Noah's hand brushed over her cheek. "Good job."

Her skin felt hot from his touch, though it was a gesture that he had done probably without thinking. Noah took a step back. The look of embarrassment on his face told her that he knew he'd stepped over a line.

She shook herself free of the heat of the moment.

Once her heart stopped fluttering from Noah's touch, she focused her thoughts on her work. A sense of satisfaction filled Lani as she loaded Oscar into the back of the patrol car. They did make a good team. She swung open the door on the passenger side and stared out at the busy street. Her mood took a nosedive as tension threaded anew through her body.

The dark sedan that had been following them earlier eased by on the street.

FIVE

As they drove back to headquarters, Noah knew Lani was upset. Not because her expression gave anything away, but because she was quiet. Lani had two speeds, fast and faster. If she was being silent, it meant something was wrong. He could understand her fear in seeing the sedan after the two attacks.

Noah turned on his signal and slipped into traffic. "We did good work back there." He'd already said as much at the stables but wanted to reiterate it. He checked the rearview mirror. No sign of the sedan.

She stared down at her fingers which were laced together. "Thank you." Her voice remained monotone.

He drove for several blocks struggling to figure out what to say to her that might alleviate her fear. Dealing with a woman's emotions had never been his strong suit. He'd grown up with brothers and his dating history was far from stellar. Most women told him he was too quiet and didn't give anything to the relationship or they didn't want to date a cop. Zach and Carter had both met wonderful women in the last few months. He was starting to feel like the odd man out.

He cut a look at Lani and shook his head. Why was

he thinking about dating at a time like this? He was Lani's direct supervisor, so that wouldn't even be an option.

Lani turned to stare out the window. "So what if this guy is stalking me." She shot him a quick glance. "I'm not quitting the force. I can handle this."

"No one says you have to quit, Lani." She might need to be put on desk duty though. He turned and headed toward Jackson Heights where headquarters was. He slowed down. "Look, it's past lunchtime. We can take a break, grab a bite at Griffin's. Maybe we can figure out who might be targeting you."

She massaged her temple. "Guess you already figured out it was the same guy from the refuge and the abandoned building."

"That's what you were thinking, right?"

"I didn't get a good look at the guy either time." Her voice faltered. "But the way he fought me…he didn't have any training, but he was really strong."

Without thinking, Noah reached over and patted Lani's shoulder. He pulled away after the second pat. What was it with this compulsion he had to offer her a comforting touch? When he'd brushed her cheek back at the horse stables, he'd felt a spark between them. A spark he would have to throw cold water on. He was her supervisor. Their relationship had to remain professional.

Lani stared out the windshield and let out a heavy sigh. "My stomach is growling. I could use a bite to eat."

Noah circled the block several times before a parking space opened up. With the dogs in tow they walked the few blocks to Griffin's. They moved past the counter with its round stools and the booths with worn vinyl seats. Noah always felt like he was stepping back in time when he entered Griffin's. It had been a cop hangout for as long as Noah could remember. With more boutique-type stores and luxury high-rises taking over the neighborhood, Griffin's looked like a dinosaur.

Customers who weren't regulars at Griffin's craned their necks at the dogs. Some of the women made ahh sounds as Oscar pranced through the establishment with his head up. The people who ate at Griffin's all the time didn't even look up from their food.

Lani and Noah entered an area of the eatery set apart by a big sign that said The Dog House. The owners of Griffin's, Lou and Barbara, had always been supportive of law enforcement and especially the K-9 unit. Even more so since their daughter Violet had married Zach, Noah's younger brother and also a K-9 officer.

They hit the diner after the lunch rush, so only one other K-9 officer sat at a table in the corner. Gavin Sutherland recently had put in for a transfer out of the unit after getting engaged to Brianne Hayes, another officer, and word was that he was slated for a promotion to chief of a new K-9 unit that would be starting up in Brooklyn. Gavin offered them a wave as he sipped his coffee. His springer spaniel Tommy sat at his feet.

She glanced around the diner. Even for the off-hour between lunch and dinner, the number of customers seemed unusually low.

Lou Griffin set two menus down for Lani and Noah. "No Cobb salad today. Delivery messed up on the blue cheese order. The Philly cheesesteak is to die for."

Noah pushed the menu across the table. "Sounds good to me. And one of your chocolate shakes."

Lani flipped through the menu. "I'll have coffee, black, and the chicken sandwich."

"How's everything, Lou?" Noah hadn't had much of a chance to talk to Lou since Zach and Violet's wedding.

Lou shrugged his shoulders. He had dark circles under his eyes. "You know, the same old same old."

Lou and Barbara had been through a great deal in the last few months. A bomber had set up an explosive device in Griffin's to harm K-9 officers, but the owners had done the repairs and reopened. Last month, they'd closed temporarily due to health issues for both Lou and Barbara. Lou still favored the arm that had previously been in a sling.

Even if Griffin's did look out of place with all the new development going on, Noah could not imagine the neighborhood without it.

"You take care of yourself, Lou." Noah's heart went out to the man. "You look tired."

Lou waved his weariness away with his hand. "Ah, you Jameson boys. You are part of the family now." He clamped a hand on Noah's shoulder. "I suppose that means you can nag me about my health."

Noah nodded. "For sure."

Lou swiped the menus off the table. "Your order will be up in just a few." The older man sauntered away and disappeared behind the counter into the kitchen.

Lani took a sip of her water. "He seems really worn-out."

"Lotta pressure on him to sell this place," Noah said.

"Being a police officer in Queens wouldn't be the same without Griffin's," she said.

"I agree." Noah watched as Lani took another sip of water and then played with her silverware.

She sat back in her chair and stared at the ceiling for a moment before looking directly at Noah with her soft blue eyes. "I guess we have to talk about the attacks."

Noah nodded. "I know this is hard to think about, Lani, but is there someone who might have a vendetta against you, maybe someone you arrested?"

Lani tugged at her collar as a patina of sweat formed on her forehead. Thinking that the attacks might be personal quadrupled the fear that plagued her. Oscar, sensitive to the drop in mood, licked her hand.

After stroking Oscar's soft head, she cleared her throat. "I haven't been on the force long enough or made that many arrests. Most of the arrests I made before getting into the K-9 unit haven't even gone to trial yet."

"So you just can't see anyone angry enough to attack and stalk you like that?" Noah ran his fingers through his brown hair. "And why is this happening now? Maybe one of the arrests you made is seeking revenge while he's out on bail."

She shook her head. "There were some drug arrests, but they were all small-timers, not smart guys. Following us to the refuge and lying in wait, knowing my schedule of walking the dogs, all of that takes some planning and intelligence."

"So not a criminal that you dealt with. Maybe some other part of your life, huh?" Noah threw up his hands. "The boyfriend of a rival model."

His tone was half-joking, but the comment cut deep.

"I used to be a trained actress and dancer." She could not hide the hurt in her voice. "I was never a model."

Noah leaned toward her from the opposite side of the table where he sat. "I'm sorry. I was trying to be funny." Regret clouded his expression. He reached across the table and squeezed her hand. "I was totally out of line."

She pulled her hand away, still hurting from the remark. "You know what my nickname is, don't you?"

"Here we go." Lou appeared holding two plates. He glanced at Lani who stared at the table and then at Noah whose gaze was downcast as well. "Looks like the food got here just in time."

They ate in silence for several minutes. Since the attack at the refuge, she had started to see a different side to Noah Jameson. He had seemed sensitive and caring. His hurtful comment blew all of that out of the water though. She salted her french fries and ate one in two bites.

"I know that some of the other officers think I can't cut it as a K-9 cop."

Noah put down his sandwich. "It's not that, Lani."

"It is that." She had started to think Noah had the same confidence in her abilities that she had. She knew she could be a great K-9 officer.

"Look, every time we step out onto the streets, our lives are on the line. The joking and the nicknames happen because of fear."

She shook her head. "I don't follow."

"Other cops just want to know you have the skills in a tight situation. Your résumé isn't exactly the normal path a cop takes." He took a sip of water.

She nodded. Her irritation over his comment softened. "So the other officers wonder if I would have their backs in a tight situation or if I would just break into song and dance." She smiled.

Noah laughed, almost spitting his water out.

Lani laughed too. All the tension she'd felt melted away.

"What you did today in finding that kid, your tenacity in chasing the suspect at the refuge. And I know you shot a suspect in your own house when you were off duty. You are cop material, Lani."

Lani looked into Noah's green eyes, feeling a connection to him. She'd waited to hear those words for months.

Noah said, "I'm going to let it be known that the nickname is not funny." He smiled. "I am the chief, you know. I do have some say over what kind of atmosphere is set for the unit."

"Thank you." She took a bite of her sandwich. "Maybe we can speed up the process of assigning me a dog."

"Yeah, I just don't think it's going to be Oscar."

She laughed and petted the pup's head. "How is your milkshake?"

He sipped some through his straw. "Wonderful as usual." He tilted the tall glass toward her. "It's thick enough to eat with a spoon. Help yourself."

She scooped out a spoonful. She allowed the creamy sweetness of the ice cream to melt in her mouth.

It was nice to be with Noah in an informal setting. Both of them seemed to relax as they finished their meal and talked about inconsequential things.

As they left with their dogs, Lani caught a glimpse of Lou and Barbara in the kitchen. Both of them looked tired. They'd been through so much in the last few months. She'd heard that a real estate developer had offered them a great deal of money for Griffin's. But it wasn't Griffin's he wanted, it was the lot. If Lou sold, Griffin's would no doubt be torn down. And something more in line with the gentrification of the neighborhood would take its place. That possibility made her heart heavy.

Noah kept pace beside her as they skirted around the clusters of people on the sidewalk. Both of them fell silent when they walked past the abandoned building where the air conditioner had been pushed out a window.

Her gaze traveled upward as a shiver traveled down her spine. Oscar sat back on his haunches. Was the puppy remembering the trauma that had taken place? Lani tugged on Oscar's leash.

Noah edged a little closer to her, so their shoulders were nearly touching while Scotty remained on the other side of him, alert and standing. Unlike Oscar, Scotty was unfazed by the people swarming around them.

Noah must have picked up on her fear. He was pretty adept at reading her even though they hadn't spent that much time working together closely.

"So what do you got on the agenda for the rest of your shift?"

With Oscar still squirming at her feet, she turned to face him. "It's a split shift. I'm going home to get some rest and then I will be riding with Brianne and Stella for the night patrol."

Noah's expression changed. He wasn't a man who showed much emotion. Maybe she was reading too much into the crease between his eyebrows and light dimming from his green eyes, but she thought she detected concern for her in his features.

"You be safe out there," he said. "I've got to get back to my desk. I'm sure things have been piling up." He glanced around. "Why don't you walk the rest of the way with me back to headquarters?"

Her car was actually several blocks from headquarters, but she needed to see that Oscar got back into his kennel. Even if she didn't have a dog to return, she would have said yes. There was something nice about being with Noah Jameson.

As they walked with the late-day sun warming her skin, she felt light-headed. Her heart fluttered a little when she cut a glance toward Noah, who offered her a smile. She shut down the feelings of attraction as quickly as they had risen to the surface. He was her supervisor and she was probably reading all kinds of things into his vague expressions that were her projection.

As police officers, they'd had a good shift. Any day where a kid was returned safely to his mom was a good day. That's all they were to each other. Two cops who wanted to keep the people of New York safe.

Lani said goodbye to Noah, watching him head toward his office, before returning Oscar to the kennel. He'd go home to his foster family in the evening and be returned for testing the next day. Though Noah didn't seem to have much confidence about his abilities.

Traffic back home was a bear this time of day and she found the fatigue settling into her bones as she waited several cars back at a light. When she got home, there was a note from Reed saying he was having dinner with Abigail and then taking in a movie. Jessie was with Dominic so they could bond more. Dominic was the teenage boy who Abigail and Reed intended to adopt once they were married.

The note said that he probably wouldn't be home until after ten. Reed was spending more and more time with his fiancée, which was how it should be. Yet she felt the emptiness of the house with both Reed and Jessie gone. Just weeks ago, the house had seemed so full. Abigail and Dominic had stayed here for a bit because both had been in some danger. In addition to all the people, a female pup of Stella's named Midnight had stayed with them. Now Abigail was fostering the puppy at her apartment. Lani stood at the kitchen sink staring out the window at the empty yard in a quiet house. The upstairs tenant wasn't even walking around.

Still full from the late lunch, she had a snack of almonds and blueberries and set her alarm. As was part of her routine, she made sure the doors were locked and latched before she lay down for a nap. Her last thought before she drifted off was of Noah's quiet demeanor and soft smile. If today had proven anything, it was that her initial impression of him, that he was the cold one amongst the Jameson brothers, had been wrong. Noah was one of those men who warmed up to people slowly. He was slow to trust and open up, and maybe that was a good thing. Until their lunch together, she hadn't realized that he had a sense of humor.

She let out a heavy sigh. Why was she even thinking about Noah and his green eyes? What she wanted more than anything right now was to prove that she could be a great K-9 cop. She felt like at least Noah had more faith in her now. He had seen what she was capable of. She remembered what Noah had said about the other members of the unit having confidence that she would have their backs in a tough situation. She needed to show them that was true.

She awoke several hours later to what sounded like someone moving around in the kitchen but trying to remain quiet. Reed. Maybe he had decided not to go to the movie with Abigail.

She rolled over and closed her eyes. It was only a little after eight. She could get a few more hours of much-needed sleep.

The noises in the kitchen stopped and she heard footsteps approach her door and then pause outside.

The ticking of the clock seemed to grow louder as she waited for Reed to walk past.

Lani sat up. Fully alert and staring at the door. Reed would not be lingering outside her door. She reached for her gun which she'd put on her nightstand like she did every night. The last thing she wanted to do was shoot her brother by accident, but she didn't want to take any chances either.

Heart pounding, she opened her mouth to say her brother's name. Her throat constricted. No words came out.

The footsteps resumed and headed back toward the living room. Lani took a deep breath before rising to her feet. Still gripping the gun but holding it by her side, she stepped toward her bedroom door and turned the doorknob slowly.

She moved down the hallway. She took a deep breath and found her voice again. "Reed, is that you?"

Silence.

Her heartbeat drummed in her ears as she crept lightly down the hallway. She raised her gun, prepared to fire. She stepped into the dark kitchen seeing only shadows. She flicked on the light switch. Everything seemed to be in its place.

But her heart wouldn't stop pounding. Had the attacks made her so hypervigilant that she was imagining her stalker was in the house?

As she entered the living room, she kept her gun aimed. She checked behind the couch and anywhere else someone might hide. Nothing.

And still, there was a faint unfamiliar smell in the air. Not cologne or Reed's soapy clean smell, more like sweat.

Lani dropped her arm that held the gun, so it hung by her side. She shook her head. She cleared the rest of the house, checked that the doors were still locked and was headed through the living room to try to get some more sleep when her eyes fell on the photo wall.

Her breath caught. The photo of her posing in a dance costume was gone.

A wave of fear crashed over her as her knees went weak. She turned a half circle in the living room, took a deep breath and moved through the house a second time.

How could someone have gotten in with all the doors locked? She examined the bathroom window closer to find the latch had been forced, which would have taken substantial strength. She stood on the toilet to peer at the ground below where a stack of bricks that must have come from the remodel two houses down had been piled.

Lani sat down on the closed toilet, feeling as if all the wind had been knocked out of her. She placed her gun on the sink counter. Of course she'd have to file a report, but that could wait. If Noah found out, he might put her on desk duty and she'd miss out on the valuable in-field experience and a chance to show the other officers what she could do. She could call Reed and let him know.

She wrapped her arms around herself and waited for her heartbeat to slow down.

Why me? Why am I being targeted?

Ever since Jordan Jameson's murder, the entire K-9 department had been on edge. Not only because they wanted to catch whomever had killed Jordan, but because anytime an officer died in such a premeditated way, the whole department wondered if they were dealing with someone who might go after other cops.

She was the obvious target. The least experienced. The rookie. The taking of the photo did suggest something more personal. Yet her stalker had had the chance to do her harm in her own home and hadn't. Almost as though he enjoyed the psychological torture. She shivered, clenching her teeth against the terror that raged through her.

Her thoughts were interrupted by a tapping on her front door that caused a new wave of terror to wash over her. Why was the person knocking so lightly?

Grabbing her gun, she stepped into the living room but remained paralyzed, not sure what to do given what had just happened. Certainly, the stalker wouldn't come to her door.

SIX

Noah hoped his knock on Lani's door wasn't too loud. If she was still sleeping, she wouldn't hear it at all. He wiped the sweat from his brow. He couldn't say exactly why he'd changed up his jogging route so it ended at Lani's house. Just a feeling he'd had, concern for one of his fellow officers' safety. Scotty sat beside Noah, panting from their run.

He leaned close to the door, tapping it with his knuckles. "Lani, it's me. Noah."

What was he going to say to her? That he was in the neighborhood and thought he'd stop by. How cliché. Before he'd gotten off shift, he'd overheard Reed talking about his date plans with Abigail. That meant Lani was alone for most of the night until she went back on duty.

While he'd been on his jog, he couldn't let go of the worry that she might be in danger. He just needed to make sure.

He heard the peephole slide open and then shut. The dead bolt and the lock released and Lani swung the door open.

He knew immediately from the spasm of a smile she offered him that something was up. Her face was pale, and her gaze seemed to dart everywhere and she was holding her gun in her hand.

"Noah." Relief came into her voice when she said his name.

His heart fluttered.

"We were jogging, and I thought I'd check on you." He pointed at the gun.

"Guess I'm a little freaked because of the attacks." She stepped to one side so he could enter the living room. "I can protect myself." She placed the gun on a table.

Noah and Scotty came inside. He took Scotty off of his leash so he could explore with his nose. He studied Lani for a moment. She massaged the back of her neck, not making eye contact.

He stepped toward her. "Everything okay? I didn't wake you, did I?"

She shook her head. "No, I was up."

Why did he feel like she was keeping something from him? He angled his body so he could peer into the kitchen.

But there was no one in the kitchen.

"I'm alone here," she said.

"You seem uncomfortable, I thought maybe you had a boyfriend or someone over for a bite to eat before you went to work."

She shook her head. "I'm not seeing anyone. I haven't dated for a long time." Her tone took on an edge to it.

Was that pain he detected beneath her words?

All the same, he was glad to see her. The tightness through his chest deflated like a balloon to know that she was safe. Why was he relieved that she wasn't see-ing anyone? Her personal life was just that, personal.

He was here at her doorstep over concern for a fellow officer, wasn't he?

Satisfied, Scotty stopped sniffing around and came to sit at Noah's feet.

"Tell me again why you stopped by." A look of confusion crossed her features. The blue in her eyes intensified and her mouth drew into a flat line.

"I, um…we." He patted Scotty's head. They were in this awkward moment together. "Well, it was sort of on my jogging route."

Scotty adjusted his stance and made a grunting noise.

Lani laughed. "Scotty does not agree with you."

Noah could feel the heat rising up in his cheeks. He held his palms out to her. "Okay, I was out jogging and I knew that Reed would not be home tonight and given what happened to you in the last couple of days, I thought I should check on you."

Her expression brightened. "You were worried about me."

"Yes, I don't want anything bad to happen to one of my officers."

All the light seemed to leave Lani's face. "Oh."

Scotty grumbled again.

Mentally, Noah kicked himself. Why were they doing this strange dance? Why couldn't they just admit their attraction to each other and acknowledge that nothing could come of it?

"Anyway, I suppose I should go. Scotty and I need to get tucked in for the evening." He turned then pivoted back to look at her. "Everything is okay here, right?"

Her lips parted slightly as though she were going

to say something, and then she turned away from him and started to straighten the pictures on the wall and sweep her hand over a shelf that held more photos and ballerina figurines.

The soft lighting in the living room made her look even more attractive. He wasn't used to seeing her with her long blond hair flowing freely. Her cheeks held a rosy glow. She was beautiful inside and out. He stepped toward her as though there were some sort of magnetic pull between them.

"Lani, is everything okay? I know you have been through a lot in the last couple of days."

She planted her feet and turned to face him. "Everything is good. I'm sure if we put our heads together we can figure out who this guy is, and I can get on with my training. That is what I want."

Noah nodded.

She picked up one of the figurines and turned it side to side. "I keep wondering. With what happened to Jordan. What if it isn't personal? What if someone is targeting the K-9 unit?"

Noah let out a heavy breath. That thought had occurred to him too. "It's hard to figure out motive at this point. Let's just focus on catching the guy."

"I suppose you're right." She stepped back toward the door. "I need to get ready for my shift."

"Yes, well, Scotty and I are going to enjoy an evening of popcorn and a John Wayne movie," he said.

"I love John Wayne."

"Maybe sometime you'll have to come over and watch one with us. Scotty and I are doing movie night alone a lot more since Carter got engaged and Zach got married."

"I know the feeling. Since Reed met Abigail, we spend a lot less time together, which is how it ought to be but still, it leaves a hole."

He met her gaze. Looking into her eyes sent a spark of electricity through him. "Well, that's something we have in common." He stepped toward the door.

She leaned toward him. "I'm glad you stopped by to check on me."

"Everything is okay, right?"

"Yes."

He studied her for a moment. It was as if a veil had fallen across her eyes when she answered him. "Hope your shift goes good."

"Yeah, I better get moving." She ruffled Scotty's head. "I'll take you guys up on that movie offer some time."

She closed the door. Noah stood for a moment staring at the door before clicking Scotty back into his leash and jogging toward his house.

Though it was clear that she was all right, he couldn't help but feel that Lani was hiding something from him.

Before she headed out for her night shift with Brianne, Lani gave her brother a call to let him know what happened. She hated interrupting his time with Abigail. Reed as always sounded glad to hear from her.

She let him know about the break-in and the stolen photo.

"I'll grab Jessie from Dominic's place and come right home," he said.

"No, Reed, it's okay. I'm headed out for a shift in a few minutes. I just need for you to make sure the place is secure when you get home. I'll be fine once Jessie is able to sound a warning bark and you're here."

"Sis, this is serious, why didn't you call the department and file a report?"

Lani squeezed the phone and closed her eyes. "I will file a report. I didn't want to miss out on my shift tonight. It's a valuable learning experience to shadow a more experienced female officer. I'm just afraid when Noah finds out, he's going to put me on desk duty."

"Maybe, Lani, but it would be for your own safety."

Tears warmed Lani's eyes. "I don't like setbacks. It's been hard enough to deal with the delay in matching me with a K-9 partner. I know I sort of took the long way around, but I want to be a part of this K-9 unit more than I've ever wanted anything else. This whole thing feels like an obstacle to that."

"Look, Lani, I know you. Whatever you set your mind to, you accomplish."

A tear trickled down her cheek. Until now she hadn't realized how much the attacks were affecting her. "Thanks, Reed. If you could just make sure the home is secure when you get back from your date. Say hello to Abigail and Dom for me and tell her I'm sorry for interrupting your time together."

"I'll do better than that, sis. I'll wait up for you."

"Thanks, but just having you home will be enough. And can you look at the latch on the bathroom window. I think it will need to be repaired." She had come to depend on the sense of safety she felt when he was around. "I'll be fine while I'm on this shift. There's no safer place to be than on patrol with a K-9 and her handler, right?"

"Right."

"I'll catch up with you later. Take care, Reed." After he said goodbye, she ended the call. A set of headlights went by on the street outside moving slowly. A moment of panic gripped her until she saw under the streetlamp that it was a patrol car. Brianne Hayes was looking for a parking space.

Already in uniform, Lani grabbed her utility belt and hurried to the bathroom to place her gun in the holster. Before leaving the house, she took in a deep breath and stepped outside making sure the door was locked behind her.

Brianne eased past the house. She must have seen Lani because she double-parked. Lani ran to the passenger side of the car, and Stella whimpered from the backseat when Lani got in.

Brianne offered Lani a bright smile. Her straight auburn hair was pulled back into a ponytail. Brianne had always been kind to Lani. "Ready for some night patrol?"

Lani nodded. She reached back and ruffled Stella's head. "How's my girl? I was just working with one of your pups."

"Ah yes, Oscar. What a cutie. Gavin said he saw you at Griffin's with him, Noah and Scotty." Brianne lifted her chin. "He said you looked very cozy." Gavin and Brianne had recently become engaged.

"Cozy?"

"Like you'd known each other forever."

Lani felt the heat rise up in her cheeks. "We were

just trying to figure out the motive for the attacks on me. I'm sure you've heard."

"Yes. I heard." Brianne turned onto a street that led to a freeway exit. "Everyone gets uncomfortable when a fellow officer is attacked."

Tension invaded the patrol car. "We still don't know if this is personal or because I'm a cop."

Brianne let out a nervous laugh. "Maybe we should talk about happier things."

"I agree. How is Stella doing with her training?"

"Stella's coming along," Brianne said. After signaling, she pulled back out into traffic. "Unless we get another call, we're headed over to some abandoned warehouses. We've had several calls of suspected drug activity. We'll see how Stella does with her drug detecting training."

Lani felt a surge of excitement at the prospect of working with Brianne and Stella to make the city safer. Even with everything that had happened, she loved police work. "It's nighttime. There might actually be some activity there."

"Maybe. If we find or see anything drug related, the detective division might set up some stakeouts to see who the players are and what the level of activity is." Brianne picked up speed once they were on the freeway.

She took another exit and wove through an industrial part of Queens. They passed parking lots that had only a single car parked in them, probably belonging to a security guard. Some of the multistory buildings had a light or two still on.

They came to a chain-link fence, the gate of which hung open. Brianne eased the vehicle inside. The tires crunched on gravel. "A few days ago the trustee for the property got a call that the chain that held the gate had been cut. Someone also reported seeing a car go in here."

Most of the buildings inside the fence were one or two stories and metal, with the exception of a square brick one that must have held the administrative offices.

Lani's heart beat a little faster as she stared out into the darkness. "What's the story on this place?"

"I think the report said it used to be a textile factory. They imported lots of fabric too, so some of these buildings were for storage and warehouse sales. Hasn't been used for at least ten years."

Stella let out a single excited bark.

"You're ready to work, aren't you?" Lani pushed open her door. "Me too."

Once they were out of the car, both women pulled their flashlights from their utility belts. Brianne attached the leash to Stella's collar. "Let's head toward that first building and see what we find."

Lani shot her flashlight in an arc taking in her surroundings. There was no sign that anyone had been here. No tire tracks or empty soda bottles, not even any trash. Stella darted toward the first long narrow building. Maybe the witness had been mistaken about a car coming in here.

As the two women raced toward the first building, Lani asked, "Is there another way out besides that front gate?"

"The report didn't say." Brianne was breathless as she ran to keep up with Stella. They searched the area all around the three buildings. Though it was hard to see in the dark, it looked like there might be another entry point on the other side of the property. In the distance, cars and trucks whooshed by on the highway, a million tiny bug-like lights. Beyond that, the tall buildings were dark shadows with only a dot of light here and there. Lani pictured a lawyer hunched over his desk in that lighted room or maybe it was a late-night cleaning crew.

In searching the property, Lani had gotten separated from Brianne and Stella. She could hear Brianne giving words of praise and commands to Stella who yipped from time to time. There were no excited barks indicating Stella had found something.

Lani thought she saw movement on the far end of the fence. Heart racing, she ran toward it. The flashlight illuminated her path. She stopped twenty yards from the fence and aimed the light all along the fence. Was that the glint of metal? A parked car maybe? She stepped closer to the fence.

A noise by the square metal building, something banging against something else, caused her to pivot. Fear invaded her awareness. She had a moment of wondering if her stalker had followed her here. She shone the light just in time to see a dog racing for the cover of a pile of wood pallets. The animal turned and looked in the flashlight beam, its eyes glowing red. Her breath caught. It wasn't a dog, it was a coyote. The animal disappeared into the darkness.

Footsteps behind her caused her to swing around. Brianne's light bobbed up and down as she came toward Lani.

"I'm not finding anything. Let's see if we can gain entry to any of the buildings. We have permission."

Lani hadn't gotten a chance to search the remainder of the fence to see if there was a car there.

They hurried back toward the long narrow building.

Lani shone her flashlight on the door, which held an open padlock. She checked the bottom of the padlock where the key went. Scratches around the keyhole indicated someone had picked the lock.

Lani pushed open the door and it screeched on its hinges.

Stella let out a nervous whine. With only a little moonlight shining through the small high windows, the building was dark.

Both of them stood on the threshold for a moment before stepping across. The eerie quiet made Lani's heart pound.

Once inside the building, Brianne let Stella off her leash so she could sniff around. She shone her light wherever the dog ran. "Even if she alerts to something, we'll probably have to get a more experienced K-9 out here to confirm."

Lani shone her flashlight into the dark corners of the building. There were huge metal vats that must have been used for dying fabric. A conveyor belt took up most of the center of the room nearly touching each of the far walls.

There was no sign of occupants after the factory closed. This place was too out of the way to be appealing to the homeless or even teenagers looking for a cool hangout.

Though she continued to sniff, Stella hadn't alerted to anything. Lani strode to the end of the building taking the rickety stairs up to peer inside the giant metal bowl. It looked like there was some sort of object in the vat. She stood on tiptoe and raised her flashlight to get a closer look.

On the other side of the building, Stella barked incessantly. Brianne screamed and dropped her flashlight. Lani's heart squeezed tight with fear as she ran across the factory.

SEVEN

Lani dashed toward the ruckus Stella was making. She stumbled over a pile of metal, catching herself before she hit the floor.

Stella had gone ballistic with her barking. Racing back and forth and then alerting to something high up.

Brianne crawled across the floor to recover her flashlight, which was still on but had rolled beneath a table.

Lani pulled her weapon.

Stella's barking was relentless, which only fueled Lani's excitement mixed with some fear.

Brianne rose to her feet. "No need for the gun." She spoke above Stella's barking. "Stella, back, quiet."

Stella obeyed, sitting but shifting her weight and whining.

Brianne shone the light up toward where Stella had focused. Tiny black eyes stared back at them, a cornered raccoon, probably as scared as they were. The raccoon skittered away across the high shelving and through a hole in the roof.

Brianne shivered and shook. "Critters give me the heebie-jeebies." She reached out and touched Lani's forearm. "Don't tell anyone I screamed and dropped my flashlight. I can just imagine the nicknames that will come from that."

"I know all about nicknames."

They both laughed.

"I think Stella freaked just because she's never encountered a raccoon," said Brianne.

A screeching noise from the other end of the dark building alerted them. They both darted toward the sound, which had come from the far side of the vat Lani had peered into. Stella ran alongside them.

Lani circled around the metal vat, which had a hinged door on it. She swung the door open. The package she'd seen inside earlier was gone. Noise like footsteps above them caused Brianne to shine her light just in time to see a man moving along the high shelving and out the same hole the raccoon had gone.

They raced toward the door. Brianne and Stella went in one direction toward where the hole in the roof was while Lani went in the other. They'd be able to get the suspect regardless of what direction he ran. Lani radioed for back up.

The far side of the long building was dark. Lani shone her light toward the ground where rubble and debris created a sort of obstacle course. She ran as fast as she dared. When she came to the end of the building, she shone her light all around the property. She caught an occasional bark and yip from Stella some distance away but nothing else.

Her chest felt like it was in a vise making it hard to get a deep breath. She stood paralyzed for a moment. The silence was oppressive. Again, she wondered if her stalker had followed her out here. She shook off the fear and continued to search.

It didn't matter if the stalker was here or not. He was inside her head now. She would always be wondering if he was close, watching and waiting.

The inflection of Stella's bark changed, becoming more frantic. Lani moved toward the sound, shining her light in an arc across her path. She saw shadows, a man running with Stella at his heels. But Brianne was nowhere in sight.

The man yelled in pain as Stella jumped and wrapped her mouth around his upper arm. Lani raced toward where Stella had taken down the suspect. She pulled her weapon. What had happened to Brianne?

"Get this dog off of me," the suspect yelled.

Lani gave the command for Stella to let go. Stella backed off but stood alert, emitting a small growl.

The suspect held his hands close to his upper body probably to protect himself. "Look, I'll do whatever you want just don't let that dog attack me again."

Lani dared not take her gun off the suspect to look around for Brianne. She heard the sirens in the distance. Backup was on the way.

Footsteps pounded behind her and she caught a glimpse in her peripheral vision of Brianne running and holding her arm.

"Took a tumble back there. Glad you and Stella were here to back me up."

"He must have dropped that package somewhere," said Lani.

"I know about where. We'll find it. My guess is it's not a box of chocolates. It's probably drugs, and he was the pickup man."

As the sirens drew near, Lani gripped her gun, letting a realization sink in. Tonight had turned out good.

They'd gotten their suspect. But she knew now she wouldn't be able to give a hundred percent to her police work as long as the stalker was out there. If she was distracted and fearful wondering when the man would make an appearance again, she was a risk to herself and others. Like Noah had said, the other officers needed to know she had their backs.

She'd have to tell Noah what had happened and agree to go on desk duty. As the sirens for the other police cars drew closer, she vowed to put all her energy into finding the stalker and seeing that he was put behind bars, so she could have her life and future as a K-9 officer back.

As he scrolled through the pages on his computer screen, Noah found himself distracted by Lani's presence as she sat in the desk normally occupied by his newlywed assistant, Sophie, who had gone on her honeymoon with K-9 officer Luke Hathaway.

Noah hit the print button.

He was glad that Lani had come clean with him about the home entry. And that it was probably her stalker. He didn't like there being secrets between them. That the stalker had entered her home was disturbing.

The temp they'd hired to take Sophie's place had not worked out, so it seemed a logical solution to put Lani in the desk where he could keep an eye on her.

After grabbing the pages he'd printed, he stepped toward his open doors with some paper in hand watching Lani as she tossed some crumpled paper toward the wastebasket. She pushed herself back from the desk in her roller chair several times.

Noah smiled.

She had a harder time sitting still than he did.

Patricia Knowles, the receptionist for the K-9 unit, came toward Lani, holding a bouquet of flowers. Lani stood up. Her hand went to her heart and he saw her mouth the words *For me?*

An unfamiliar surge of emotion invaded Noah's awareness. So Lani was getting flowers. Why did that bother him?

He stepped closer to her desk putting the papers on it. "Flowers, huh?"

Smiling, Lani pulled the envelope from its holder. "I have no idea who they're from." She opened the envelope and read the note. She dropped it as though it was on fire.

"Lani?"

She shook her head and stepped away from the desk. Putting trembling fingers up to her face.

He rushed toward her, touching her elbow lightly before turning and picking up the note. He clenched his teeth when he read the note.

I love you and I am watching you always.

Lani slumped down in her chair and put her face in her hands. She looked defeated and afraid.

Uncertain of how to handle Lani falling apart, Noah went into fix-it mode. "Let's find out who dropped these off."

He examined the flowers and the container they came in to make sure there was no camera or bomb or anything that might do harm. After dismantling the arrangement, it appeared they were just dealing with flowers and a note designed to keep Lani afraid.

Lani crossed her arms over her chest and looked off

to the side. Her voice was weak, a million miles away. "He wouldn't be so dumb as to drop them off himself. I'm sure he had a delivery service give them to Patricia."

He hated seeing her so distressed. It made him feel helpless. "We can do a little detective work." The envelope had the name of the florist stamped on it. "After work, we can go to the shop and find out if the clerk remembers who placed the order." She continued to stare into space.

He studied the note. It was typed, probably by the florist. The purchase might even have been called in or ordered online. He was grasping at straws, trying to find a way to get Lani to not shut down.

She shook her head, gazing as though she wasn't really seeing.

Promising solid police work wasn't helping. He kneeled and pulled the chair toward him, forcing her to make eye contact. "Lani?"

She looked down at him. The veil seemed to fall away from her eyes. "Noah, no matter what? He can get to me. I'm sitting at a desk in a building with armed police officers."

Noah glanced at the note again. "Well, he's obviously a liar. He's not watching you right now. There's no way he could get past security. You have to be issued a visitor's badge to get access to this part of the station." He tried to keep his tone light. "Right?"

She lifted her chin slightly. And released a single-syllable laugh. "Is that the bright side of all this?"

"Look, I'll stay close to you. When I can't, we'll make sure another officer is around to check on you. It doesn't have to be official. I'm sure any of these guys would give up some off-duty time to provide protection for you."

"I hate that I need the protection. I should be the one doing the protecting. I want to do my job."

He was grateful that Lani had perked back up. That was the Lani he knew and respected. "Thank you for not giving up."

"The only way I can do my job is if we put this guy away."

Figuring out the guy's psychological profile would help with catching him. "This note sounds almost… romantic…in a twisted way."

"I know. Maybe this isn't because I'm a cop," she said. "I started to wonder if maybe someone had a beef against the department and I was the easiest one to target 'cause I'm the newest recruit."

"Yes, the note implies something different."

She rose to her feet and took in a breath. "Guess I better do my job." She pushed some forms toward him. "You need to sign off on these. It's just order forms for supplies for the dogs and then I'll take it over to the training center to make sure it's all good."

Noah picked up a pen and signed the forms. "Couldn't you just email it to the supply officer?"

"I like seeing the dogs. It calms me down."

"I'll go with you. Maybe we can brainstorm who might be sending you this kind of note."

"What do you mean?" She gathered up the papers and headed toward the door.

Noah walked beside her as they headed down the hallway toward the stairs that led to the training center. "So if it's not someone you arrested or someone who has a beef against cops, maybe it's someone who liked or likes you in a romantic way, maybe an ex-boyfriend."

She walked a little faster holding the forms close to her chest. "Maybe."

"I'm not meaning to pry, but did you date anyone in the past who struck you as unstable?"

She walked even faster, he had to double his pace to keep up.

"Selfish, yes. Unstable, no," she said. "Give me some credit."

Her tone was almost defensive.

They entered the training center where Tony Knight was working with his chocolate Lab, Rusty, running him through an obstacle course on the AstroTurf flooring. A look of concern crossed Tony's face when he saw Lani.

"Okay, so maybe someone who might want revenge," Noah said.

"It's really hard for me to talk about my dating life. I haven't been out in over a year by choice." She met his gaze, her eyes rimmed with tears. "Honestly, if anyone had cause for revenge, it would be me for the way I was treated, not the other way around." She walked away toward a door where the supply person probably was.

Noah shook his head. He could kick himself. He'd only wanted to get to the bottom of who was after her so she would feel better, safer. Instead he'd struck a nerve and made her sad. He remembered something his mother had said to him that men, especially Jameson men, always wanted to fix everything and sometimes women didn't want things fixed. They just wanted someone to listen.

Maybe he should just try to be her friend. She'd talk

if and when she wanted to. As much as he wanted the
stalker behind bars, pressuring Lani would only back-
fire. She had enough to deal with.

Lani returned, running toward Noah, her face etched
with worry. Tony Knight was right behind her with an
equally concerned look on his face.

"What's up?" A sense of dread settled into his bones.

"It's Oscar. Someone has snatched him."

Tony came up behind Lani. "It was my turn to walk
him and work with him out on the street. I made him
sit and stay while I went into a store. When I came out,
he was gone."

EIGHT

Lani clicked through the screens on her computer, then hit the print button for the forms she needed to leave on Noah's desk before she quit for the day. It had been two days since Oscar had gone missing, presumably stolen, and her heart was heavy from the loss. It was so easy to get attached to the dogs. Another of Stella's puppies, Midnight, had been at the Branson home quite a bit since Abigail was fostering her during her training.

She'd checked the website of local shelters as well as ones where missing pets were posted. The other officers had put up lost posters around the city. Still, no one had phoned in about the puppy.

Oscar's disappearance brought back the emotional impact of the loss of another dog. Snapper, Jordan Jameson's K-9, had been missing since the former's chief's murder. The German shepherd had been spotted around the city, and then Dominic had admitted that someone had given him a dog that matched Snapper's description, but the shepherd had run off. Snapper was alive somewhere. And one of Stella's other puppies, Cocoa, had been taken briefly as well but was now home safe. She didn't see any that resembled Oscar or Snapper.

Lani closed the website containing postings of found

pets. She had to believe that Oscar was alive as well. Someone probably took him for a pet because he was so cute. Or thought he was valuable because he wore a vest that said he was a K-9 in training.

She left the forms on Noah's desk. His meeting with other precinct chiefs must be running late. The preparatory meetings for security at the Columbus Day Parade required coordination between all the boroughs. Plans were being made for some of the K-9s and their handlers to march in the parade as well. She had no idea what her role would be for the big event. Maybe she wouldn't be permitted to help at all. The confinement of sitting behind a desk was taking a toll on her.

What she liked about police work was how active it was. But now, she couldn't jog or ride her bike in the park alone anymore. Though Noah and Reed both offered to go with her, she missed the alone time when she could clear her head and pray.

The one bright spot about feeling like a prisoner because of her stalker was that she and Noah had spent more time together. She found herself looking forward to being around him. She was glad he hadn't asked her about her dating history again. The whole thing was so painful. Men tended to see her blond hair and blue eyes and nothing more. She was a whole person, and she wanted to be loved for who she was inside and out. It was better to be alone than with someone whose attraction to her was only skin-deep.

She placed the forms on Noah's desk and gave Scotty's head a pat from where he lay on his dog bed. She kneeled so the dog could lick her face.

"What a good boy," she said. "And your boss isn't a bad guy either."

After texting Noah that she was leaving for the day,

she grabbed her purse and headed out of the building toward the parking garage. The text was a courtesy. She was a trained officer, she didn't need an escort to the parking garage. The police lot was for NYPD vehicles only. Her personal car was in the parking garage not far from headquarters. Her feet seemed to echo on the concrete as she walked toward the elevator that would take her to the third story where her car was parked.

She watched the numbers light up. The door slid open and she stepped out onto the concrete. As she walked toward her car, she heard the sound of a car pulling out and racing down the ramp to the exit.

Some people were just anxious to get home on a Friday night. She had no plans other than to stay in, make some popcorn and find a movie to watch. The thought that maybe she could take Noah up on watching a John Wayne movie together put a smile on her face.

When she arrived at her car, there was a folded piece of paper on the windshield. She assumed it was some sort of solicitation or announcement of an event. She reached for the paper.

Her breath caught in her throat.

None of the other cars had the paper on them.

A sense of dread fell on her like a lead blanket as she opened the folded paper careful to only touch the edges in case there were fingerprints on it. The note was neatly typed in a squarish font.

I took Oscar because I know you love him. Next time it might be your brother or that other cop you've been hanging around so much. I have that kind of power. Say you love me, and I'll give you back the dog.

Feeling as though she'd been punched in the stomach, Lani turned and leaned against her car for support. She opened her purse, feeling for the gun she always kept there.

She listened to cars on the floor above her pulling out and rolling down the ramp. The sounds from the street, traffic and people, reached her ears.

She took a deep breath to calm herself. With her hand still on the gun in her purse, she pushed off the car and surveyed all around her. The note could have been placed here anytime while she was at work. Maybe her stalker was long gone and maybe he was keeping his promise and watching her always.

She could hear but not see cars pulling out and gaining speed. Footsteps echoed somewhere on the other side of this floor of the parking garage. But she could not see anyone.

Her heart squeezed tight, and the blood whooshed in her ears.

She tilted her head. Maybe the parking garage camera had picked up the stalker when he'd placed the note.

Her phone buzzed. A text. The number was Noah's. She clicked on it. Somehow even a text from him made it easier to breathe.

Where are you?

In the parking garage.

Another text from a different number came in. Out of habit, she clicked on it.

I am watching you always.

Lani's gaze darted all around the garage. She felt light-headed as she took in several shallow breaths. Though he could be texting from anywhere, it couldn't be coincidental that she'd read the note and then the text had come through. He knew what time she got off work and when she would be at her car.

Her phone dinged again.

She didn't have time to answer it, didn't want to answer it. She pulled the gun from her purse and placed it on the hood of the car. She fumbled in her purse for the keys. Her fingers trembled.

She had been as cool as a cucumber dealing with potentially violent people when she'd been on regular patrol and when an intruder had entered their home. But this was different, it was personal.

She pulled the keys out and pressed the unlock button.

Footsteps moving at a rapid pace sounded behind her. She whirled around not seeing anyone.

"Lani?"

The voice was Noah's. Relief spread through her and she was able to take a deep breath. "I'm over here."

More pounding footsteps. Noah with Scotty beside him came into view. Though she remained standing, her knees felt like cooked noodles. She hadn't realized how afraid she was until she saw Noah.

"Hey, I was worried about you when you didn't answer my second text." His voice filled with compassion as he stepped toward her. He must have seen something in her expression despite her best effort to hide the fear that had been like a wave pulling her under.

She cleared her throat. "He found me again." She wanted to crumple the note and tear it to pieces, but knew she needed to keep it pristine if they were to get any DNA off it at all. She lifted it toward Noah.

Noah took the note and read it. His jaw grew tight and hard indicating that he was upset, maybe even angry.

"Then…he…sent a text." Her voice faltered. She couldn't be the hard as nails police officer, not under these circumstances. "I'm sorry. I didn't mean to fall apart."

"Anyone would." He gazed at her with a welcoming softness in his green eyes. "You've been stronger than anyone I've ever worked with Lani."

It felt as though a weight had been lifted off her and she fell into his arms. He wrapped his arms around her. "It's okay," he said. "It's going to be okay."

She relished the warmth and comfort of his arms. How safe it felt to be held by him. Her cheek brushed over his collar and she took in the musky aroma of his cologne. She tilted her head to look into his eyes. "Thank you for understanding." A tear rolled down her cheek. "I know it's not very professional…to lose it like this."

He reached up and swiped the tear away with his finger. His touch was as gentle as a feather brushing over her skin. "I think we are more than just colleagues, don't you?"

Her heart fluttered. "Meaning?"

"I consider you a friend, Lani. I hope you see me in the same way."

What had she thought he would say? And what was this pounding heart and ooey-gooey melting feeling inside her belly all about. "Yes, friends." Even if he was attracted to her, Noah was too much of a man of integrity to ever cross a line. There could never be anything but a friendship between them.

She took a step back trying to escape the magnetic pull being close to him created. It wasn't just the attraction that was a problem. The truth was she felt safer when he was around. She wasn't sure that kind of dependence on him was a good thing.

She studied him for a moment. For his meetings today, he'd dressed in a light blue button-down shirt, khakis and a camel hair coat. She had thought he looked quite handsome when he left the office earlier in the day. She had teased him and now she reminded him of her comment. "You still look like you are ready for the opera."

"Yeah, opera's never been my thing."

Noah was one of those guys who could dress like he was ready for a business meeting, and he could pull off the jeans and T-shirt look just as easily.

Scotty whined and adjusted his stance.

"Well, I suppose I better get home." She turned back toward her car. "I'm glad you showed up when you did."

"Got a big Friday night planned?"

"Not really, just going to go home and find a funny movie."

"I suppose Reed will be out with Abigail."

"Once he gets off duty. That's usually what he does."

"Listen, I have a favor to ask of you since you don't have anything planned." He touched the collar of his coat. "At the meetings today, it became obvious to me that there is an expectation that as chief I ought to be rubbing elbows with—" he made quotations marks with his hands "—the important people of New York."

"You have to attend some kind of event?"

"Yes, at the Bayside Historical Society. A lot of big-wigs will be there." Noah stared at the ground, shoved his hands in his pockets and kicked at nothing. "I've never been good at that sort of thing…schmoozing. You're so articulate and outgoing. It would be great if you came with me."

This was a side of Noah she had never seen, such vulnerability. "I'd like that. It won't take me long to shower and change."

"Great. How about I follow you partway out to your house, before I turn to get to mine. And then if you could text me that you got there safe, I'll come by in an hour."

"That sounds good." She gave Scotty's head a rub, which made his tail wag.

He waved the note the stalker had left on her car. "Of course, we'll take this in to Forensics."

Her mood shifted. "I'm worried about Oscar."

He exhaled through his teeth. "Clearly we are dealing with someone who is not only unstable but not very logical. He says you get Oscar back when you declare your love for him." He shrugged. "How would you even do that? Are you supposed to text him that?"

She shivered. "Maybe he'll communicate further. If he comes out into the open, we'll be able to get him, right?"

He squeezed her arm. "I don't like the idea of you being bait."

"It might be the only way," she said. "I don't get my life back until this guy is behind bars." Her voice sounded strong, but her insides still felt like gelatin.

"Let's not think about it right now." He pointed across the parking garage at where his car must be parked. "Why don't you pull out. Let me and Scotty get back over here and then we'll follow you. I'll drop this note off at Forensics in the morning."

She nodded, got into her own car and exited the space. Soft instrumental music played on her sound system while she watched her rearview mirror until she saw the headlights of Noah's car. She could just make out the outline of Scotty's square head in the passenger seat. She rolled down the ramp and out onto the street.

It got dark around dinnertime this time of year. The city was already lit up. She pulled out into traffic. Every time she checked her mirror Noah was right behind her. She felt a sense of loss when he turned off to go to his house.

Lani circled the block before a space opened up a few blocks from her house. She hurried home, unlocked the door and the dead bolt, and stepped inside the quiet house. After making sure the door was locked behind her, she switched on lights. She was glad Reed had met Abigail, but getting used to being alone was a challenge. Reed and Abigail were always inviting her to their activities, but they were in love and surely wanted time alone. Plus they were becoming instant parents because of Dominic. They had enough on their plate.

She was grateful for Noah's invitation. She liked the idea of being friends with him.

She headed toward her room to pull something from her closet to wear. She'd had to attend galas and fundraisers when she was doing theater and dance, so her wardrobe of evening wear was extensive.

Have gown, will travel.

She smiled and shook her head at her own joke.

She was glad to have somewhere to wear the gowns.

It was nice to have something to do on a Friday night with someone she liked being with. She suspected one of the reasons Noah had invited her was because he didn't want her to be alone in her house.

As she showered and then dressed, a thought weighed heavy on her mind. The stalker had figured out that she was attached to Oscar. Next time, would he go after a person that she cared about, like Reed or maybe even Noah? The note had said as much.

NINE

Noah found a parking space on the street opposite Lani and Reed's house. He walked across the street feeling a sense of anticipation. When he had thought about having to go to one of these functions alone, all he'd felt was dread. He knocked on the door. His shoulder holster dug into his chest when he lifted his arm.

Even when he was off duty he carried a gun, especially now that Lani's safety was under threat. He heard the lock open and the dead bolt click back. Lani opened the door.

Noah nearly fell backward at the sight of her. His knees felt mushy. She wore a long light blue dress that brought out the blue in her eyes. Her hair was pulled up on top of her head in a loose bun with soft curls framing her face. Her skin glowed like she'd put some sort of glitter on it.

He shook his head and managed only a single word. "Wow."

She smiled faintly. "Believe it or not, I've had a lot of practice with this dressing up and schmoozing."

Still not able to catch his breath, he held an elbow out for her. "Shall we?"

She stepped across the threshold and then turned to secure the door, pulling a key out of the tiny beaded purse she held.

As they crossed the street to his car, Noah's stomach felt like it was filled with melting wax. His throat had gone dry. He hurried around to the passenger side of his car and opened the door for Lani. He caught the faint scent of her floral perfume as she got inside.

She lifted her chin and locked him in her gaze, which made him feel like he might fall over.

"This should be fun," she said.

He nodded, unable to form any coherent words. On the walk back around to the driver's side of the car, he gave himself a combination pep talk and kick in the pants.

Come on, Noah, pull it together. This isn't junior high.

Noah got behind the wheel and offered Lani a grin that he hoped didn't look too dorky. He pulled out onto the street. He drove through the neighborhood and then got on the Van Wyck Expressway.

Lani went into her usual hundred mile an hour talk. He was grateful he didn't need to do much talking due to the fact that he'd lost the ability to form words.

She finished her story and then fell silent for a moment. "It's nice to be able to get out and do something social."

"I'm sorry having this stalker at large limits your ability to do things. Maybe if we can figure out his motive, it would be easier to catch him. You never finished answering my question. Do you think an old boyfriend might be stalking you?"

"It would have to be from a long time ago. I gave up on dating."

"Really?" Why would someone like Lani not want to date?

She didn't answer right away. "I don't know how to explain it exactly. It's like all men see is who I am on the outside, and they don't want to get to know me in a deeper way. Even Christian guys."

Hadn't he just been guilty of kind of the same thing? Making assumptions about her because of her background and if he was honest because she was pretty. Images flashed before him of Lani showing so much compassion to the boy with autism at the horse stables. "As your friend, I'm telling you they missed out on getting to know a really great person."

"Thank you."

"Lani, I've underestimated you in a hundred ways. If I ever made you feel like one of those boyfriends, only seeing who you were on the surface, I'm so sorry."

Noah veered onto the Cross Island Parkway. It was about a half-hour drive from Rego Park to the historical society.

He took the exit and drove up Totten Avenue. The parking lot was about half-full when he pulled into it. The building that housed the historical society was also known as the Bayside Castle. With its striking red and white brick structure and turrets it was aptly named. The castle had once been part of a working fort where soldiers stayed.

Noah got out of his car and hurried around to open the door for Lani. She stepped down and straightened the skirt of her dress. Made of layers of sheer fabric, the dress made a sort of whispering rustling sound as they walked toward the double doors of the castle. Light spilled out from within and he could hear the sound of people visiting and laughing.

They entered a long wide hallway with wooden floors. People were gathered in clusters of three and four, sipping drinks and eating from small paper plates.

"So I guess we just wander, right?" Noah said as a note of sadness filled his voice. "My brother Jordy was always better at this sort of thing than me."

She leaned close to him, wrapping her arm around his. "Don't worry, the time passes quickly."

The castle contained rooms for dining, rooms that had rotating displays of art, and some permanent collections of both art and artifacts. He knew from having come here as a kid with his brothers that they had exercise classes and activities for children. They walked past a room where a quartet played classical music.

They wandered into a room that had been turned into a sort of labyrinth because of the way the temporary walls that displayed artwork had been set up. A man with a tray wandered by and Noah grabbed two glasses of water from him.

Lani took her glass.

A man walked toward them with his hand outstretched. "Noah, so glad you could make it." Noah knew he'd met the man previously, but he couldn't quite place him.

"And who is your lovely date?" The man turned toward Lani.

"I'm Lani Branson, I'm with the K-9 unit Noah oversees, Mr. Liscomb."

"Delighted," said Mr. Liscomb.

The three of them exchanged small talk about the

event and food with Lani carrying the conversation before Mr. Liscomb faded into the crowd.

Noah leaned close to her and whispered in her ear. "How did you know his name?"

"I checked the city council website before we came here while I was getting ready. Mr. Liscomb oversees the committee that decides how the law enforcement money gets distributed."

"Yeah, I guess I did meet him. Just don't remember where." He tugged at his collar, which felt tight. His neck was sweaty. He wanted to get out of the tux and into a pair of sweats and a T-shirt. "Honestly, this is not my thing. I'm glad you're here."

She tilted her head, blue eyes shining. "I'm glad I'm here with you."

Noah's heart fluttered. Somehow, he wished he could stay in this moment with Lani gazing at him with such warmth and affection. "We make a good team."

"Yes, we work well together." She laughed. Then her expression darkened, and she took a sip of water, turning to look at a painting.

He felt the drop in mood. He touched her shoulder, wanting to ask her what she was thinking about.

She turned to face him, that sad look on her face. Her lips slightly parted.

"Hey," he said. "Everything okay?"

Was she thinking about the stalker or was it something else?

"I'm fine." The shadow across her face told a different story. For the next half hour, they talked with other city officials and people of influence. With each interaction, Noah was glad Lani was there to make the conversations go more smoothly. She had a wonderful understanding of art, theater and all the stuff he knew very little about.

Instruments being played in an adjoining room rose to a crescendo. "Why don't we go listen to some music?"

"Sure," he said. Again, Lani had that faraway look on her face. Something was on her mind.

He knew better than to press her about what was on her mind. She'd share when she was ready.

They stepped back out into the hallway.

She touched his arm. "I think I'll go find the restroom and then meet you in there." She pointed toward the room where the musicians were playing.

"Sounds good." Noah wandered across the hall just as the violin trilled with intensity. He glanced over his shoulder in time to see the effervescent skirt of Lani's gown disappear around a corner.

Noah gulped his water and set the glass on a side table where a waiter swooped it up. It felt awkward standing and listening. A woman came up and introduced herself as the mayor's wife. Noah chatted with her for a moment, wishing Lani with her easy laugh and knowledge of the arts was standing beside him.

The musicians completed their piece and were well into another when Noah began to wonder what was keeping Lani. Even if there was a line to use the bathroom, she should have been back by now.

A knot of tension formed at the back of Noah's neck. He stepped toward the threshold to go in search of her.

A short man and a woman with a tiny dog in her purse approached him. "Chief Jameson, how good to see you."

"Councilman." He couldn't remember the guy's name. "Good to see you too."

Noah could feel himself growing restless and worried as the councilman and his wife kept him trapped in conversation about nothing. The knot of tension in his neck got even tighter.

He waited for a polite moment to excuse himself. Worried, he hurried down the hallway in search of Lani.

Lani watched the warm water from the bathroom faucet spill over her hands. The line for the downstairs bathroom had been long, so she'd slipped upstairs to find one. All the planned activity was on the first floor. Only a few people wandered the hall upstairs.

She stared at herself in the mirror. Why had Noah's remark about them working together so well hit her so hard? The truth was she was starting to have feelings for Noah, deep feelings.

His remark had caused her to envision having a life together. Such as being a support for him at these gala events that he didn't much like. Somehow when they were together, it ended up being an adventure. She saw them jogging together in the park with Scotty or going to church together. Gripping the countertop, she wiped the pictures from her mind.

She'd closed her heart off to the possibility that she'd ever meet someone special, but now she felt her heart opening to Noah. And he was not available. He was her boss.

Lani grabbed a paper towel and dried her hands. She stepped out into the silent hallway. Laughter, music and party chatter floated up from the first floor. She wasn't ready yet to go back downstairs. She walked down the hallway and stepped toward the window that looked out on the parking lot and the city beyond all lit up like a Christmas tree.

Footsteps pounded behind her. When she turned to see who it was, no one was there.

Lani's pulse drummed in her ears. Her chest squeezed tight with fear. "Hello." The footsteps had been distinct. Could it be that someone was working late and had slipped into one of the upstairs offices? That was the explanation that made the most sense. This was what the stalker had done to her mind. Even when he wasn't close, he had power, control even, over her.

The safety of the crowd was just downstairs. All she had to do was walk to the opposite side of the hallway where the stairs were. Easy-peasy, right? Lani took in a deep breath. She strode past locked office doors. The men's bathroom was at the end of the hall by the window. So whoever was up here wasn't in there. Still, she had heard someone.

She stood before a room not too far from the staircase. The door was ajar, but it was dark inside. She pushed the door open farther and reached a hand inside the room, searching for a light switch. Once the light was on, she eased the door all the way open.

It was a sort of storage room. Framed photographs and paintings were stacked against the walls. There was a suit of armor and a garment rack where costumes were hung. File cabinets and shelves with labeled bins cluttered the chaotic room.

She cleared her throat. "Hello." She reminded herself that the safety of the crowd was just down the stairs. There was a part of her that wanted to overcome her fear. She'd always thought of herself as a strong woman. What kind of officer would she be if she couldn't face the thing that she was most afraid of? But more than anything she just wanted to catch this guy and put him behind bars.

While her heart pounded in her chest, she surveyed the room inch by inch. Sweat trickled down the back of her neck.

A single bumping sound reached her ears before a mass barreled into her and pushed her to the ground. She lay there staring at the ceiling, the wind knocked out of her. The man had on a face mask so she couldn't see his face. He pinned her to the floor by holding her shoulders down.

"Now I've got you."

Terror raged through her.

"Lani?"

The voice was Noah's.

The attacker lifted his head, alarmed by the voice. He bolted up and ran out of the room.

She managed to sit up by the time Noah was by her side. She gripped his arm. "It was him."

He helped her to her feet. "Did he hurt you?"

She shook her head. "I'm okay. I think he knew he would be caught if he hung around." Her head cleared. "I heard his footsteps. There must be a back stairway." She hurried down the hall to the window she had stared out earlier.

She spotted a dark figure moving toward a cluster of trees not far from the parking lot.

Noah dashed toward the stairway. "Maybe we can catch him before he gets to his car."

She hurried after him, grateful she'd worn flats not heels. With Noah in the lead, they sprinted across the grounds toward the parking lot.

"Stay with me." Noah pulled his gun out.

"Wouldn't it be better if we split up to look for him?"

"Maybe but I don't want to risk you being hurt or kidnapped."

Somewhere in the lot, a car door slammed. The sound seemed to reverberate.

Lani stepped toward Noah. They wove through the lot up one row and down another. All the cars remained dark. A couple holding hands came out of the building and headed toward the parking lot.

Noah put his gun behind his back, probably so the man and woman wouldn't be alarmed. They waited while the couple got into their car, pulled out of their space and headed toward the street.

Just as the couple turned onto the road, tires screeched behind them. Lani whirled around to the blare of two headlights charging at her. Noah pulled his gun as the car zoomed toward them.

TEN

Noah wrapped his free arm around Lani and pulled her out of the path of the car. They fell hard on the concrete, his gun dropping to the ground. He rolled off of her, angling his body just in time to see the car turning around to take another shot at them.

He grabbed Lani's arm and pulled her to her feet, then guided her in between cars as the stalker's car barreled toward them. Tires screeched. They came to an open area that led to the next row of cars.

"Let's make a run for my car. You go first. I'll be right behind you."

She sprinted out, the skirt of her dress flying behind her. He was at her heels, aware of the sound of the stalker's car zooming through the lot toward them.

The headlights were only feet away when Noah swung open the driver's side door and jumped in. The car whizzed by scraping the side of his vehicle, knocking off the side view mirror so it hung by a single wire. Another second of delay and it would have torn his door off.

Lani sat in the passenger seat. Her dress was torn. Her hair had shaken loose. She had a dark smear across her cheek. She'd lost her purse in the struggle. She was beautiful still.

He pulled his phone from his pocket.

He tossed the phone toward her. "You want to call for backup?" He shifted into Reverse and pulled out of the space. "Let's give this guy a run for his money."

The stalker had turned his car and was circling back around to come up behind them again.

Lani phoned into the station, gave their location and the situation.

Noah zoomed up the row. He took a turn so tightly the car seemed to be on two wheels. He could see the stalker's car moving through the lot as he pressed on the gas. The plan was to come up behind the guy. Without a gun, he had no recourse but to try to disable the car with his own.

He sped up another row as the stalker turned and headed toward the exit. So the guy knew that he didn't stand a chance if he stayed in the lot.

They raced out onto the road. Noah was concerned about leaving his gun behind but there was no time to go look for it. Once they were on the expressway, traffic was heavy enough that keeping up with the car was a challenge. Though he hadn't lost sight of the stalker's car, several cars had slipped in between them.

"If we can just get close enough. I can at least get a read on his license plate," Lani said. "Everything happened so fast. I didn't notice the plate when we were in the parking lot."

Noah stared straight ahead. "Let's see what we can do." He waited for an opening in the next lane and slipped into it, pulling ahead so they were two car lengths behind the stalker.

Lani shifted in the seat, lifting her head and leaning toward the side window, trying to get a view of the license plate at the odd angle.

The stalker took the next exit without signaling first. There was no time for Noah to switch lanes before they passed the exit. Noah clenched his jaw. They'd lost him.

Lani sat back in her seat. "I couldn't see to get the numbers." Picking up his phone she quietly called off their backup.

They drove on in silence for a while longer. The look on her face nearly tore his heart out. "We'll get him, Lani. Call it in and Forensics can go over where he was hiding."

"There's probably a million fingerprints in that room." The tightness in her voice revealed her frustration. "His car was generic looking. Maybe there were some cameras that will show the plate number."

"Maybe," she said, not sounding very hopeful.

A tension-filled silence invaded the car. He'd do anything to make her feel better, lift her spirits. He felt a connection to her that he didn't quite understand. His mood mirrored hers.

"Sorry about your dress," he said. "You looked really beautiful tonight."

"Thank you." She smoothed over her torn skirt. "We have to catch him, Noah. I want my life back. That's all there is to it."

"I should not have let my guard down back at the castle," he said.

She let out a heavy breath and massaged her forehead. "It's not your fault. I should be able to go to the bathroom alone. Right?" She laughed and shook her head. "Okay, it is a little bit funny."

He was glad she hadn't lost her sense of humor.

Though he still felt the weight of her frustration and fear, the levity was a nice reprieve. "So when does Reed get home?" He liked the idea of spending another hour or two with her even if they just drove around and grabbed a cup of tea somewhere.

"I'm not sure. I can text him." She pressed her palm to her forehead. "My purse. I dropped it. Probably when he knocked me over."

"We can go back and get it." He searched the exit signs calculating how to get turned around. It took a good twenty minutes to get turned around and headed back to the castle. "The celebration is probably just breaking up," he said. Really it didn't matter to him what they did. He just liked being with her.

When they arrived, the lot was less full, but the lights were still on inside.

Noah and Lani searched the lot until they found his gun twenty minutes later.

By the time they got to the building, the cleanup crew was busy pulling tablecloths off of tables and hauling out bags of trash. The musicians packed up their instruments. Only a few people lingered, caught up in some intense conversation.

"The upstairs is closed to the public now." A woman with a clipboard caught them at the base of the stairs. She had small intense eyes and tight lips. "Can I help you?"

"I dropped my purse upstairs."

The expression on the woman's face indicated that she required more information.

"I used the upstairs bathroom earlier this evening. I left my purse up there. I think in that storage room,"

Lani said. She turned toward Noah, touching the lapel of his coat. "We won't be but a minute."

"That room is locked. I'll go up with you," said the woman.

Lani stepped in behind her and Noah followed.

Once they were in the upstairs hallway, the woman opened the door for them, flipped on the light and stood back. "This room should have remained locked during the festivities. There are some valuable artifacts in here. It was an oversight on the staff's part."

The woman with the clipboard seemed like an up-tight, by-the-rules kind of person.

Lani stepped across the threshold and stared at the floor. "It's not here."

"I can tell you right now, no purses were turned in to the lost and found," said the woman with the clipboard.

Noah stepped in as well and surveyed the area. "It looked like an antique. Maybe it just got picked up." He stepped toward a rack of costumes, searching.

"Please don't touch anything," said the woman.

There were several beaded dresses that looked like they were from the 1920s. Lani's purse was hung up with one of the dresses on the hanger. She reached for the hanger. "I can prove this is mine." She said to the woman.

Lani's deference to the woman indicated that she was having a similar reaction to her. Noah felt like he was back in second grade again with Mrs. Pendleton, the meanest teacher he'd ever known.

Lani pulled the purse strap off the hanger and put the dress back on the rack. "My phone and my license are in here." She clipped the purse open so the woman could see.

"All right, then," said the woman. "I've got a great deal to do before we shut off the lights."

Noah held out a hand for Lani. He was anxious to get away from the uptight woman with the clipboard.

Lani stepped toward him but then froze in place. The rosiness faded from her cheeks as she stared straight ahead.

"What are we waiting for, then?" said the woman.

Lani shook her head and rushed toward Noah who wrapped his arms around her. "What is it?"

Lani pointed at a bunch of framed photographs stacked against the wall. Noah followed the line of her gaze.

The photo of Lani as a dancer lay on the floor. The attacker must have dropped it. She stepped closer to peer at it. A red *X* had been drawn over her face.

Lani gripped her stomach, feeling suddenly nauseous. Noah wrapped an arm around her.

The woman, who had struck Lani as a harsh schoolmistress type, seemed to soften. Her voice held a note of tenderness. "You look as though you are going to be sick. Let me get you some water." After setting her clipboard down, she hurried out of the room. Her heels clicked on the hard surface of the floor.

Noah snatched up the picture of Lani, holding it by the corner so as not to contaminate it too much. He flipped it over to where letters had been cut out of magazines.

Lani peered over his shoulder to read.

Say you love me or else.

The words sent a chill down her spine. Something about Noah standing close to her made the fear bearable.

He stared at the front again. "What a mixed message. Find me some sort of bag to put it in. Maybe Forensics can come up with something on it."

Lani doubted it. The guy had been super careful so far. "Yes, and I think we better consult a psychologist to try and understand his motive. He's clearly not a stable human being."

The woman returned holding a paper cup. "Here you go, dear." The woman's whole demeanor had changed to become much more maternal. "Are you not feeling well?"

Lani took a sip of the water allowing the cool liquid to soothe her throat. She glanced up at Noah, finding strength in his gaze. There was no need to share with this woman everything that was going on. "I think we just need to get home. Do you have a plastic bag we could use?"

The woman disappeared again and returned with one. Lani appreciated that she didn't ask any questions.

Lani held her purse up. "Thank you for your trouble."

"I'll walk you two out," said the woman.

Noah placed a protective hand on Lani's back as they headed out to the hallway and down the stairs where the woman said goodbye to them.

"So what do you think that guy was planning?"

The question did not upset Lani. It had been reeling through her mind as well. "I think he saw that I was alone. He made noise on purpose to lure me into that room. He probably wanted to scare me by showing me the photo."

"But he panicked and ran," said Noah.

When they entered the wide hallway, a man in a

waiter's uniform was moving from room to room shutting off the lights.

"Yeah, maybe he heard you coming up the stairs," Lani said. "You got to me pretty fast." She turned to face him for a moment to look into his green eyes. What did she see there? Affection? Admiration?

"I was worried about you." His voice filled with warmth. She liked the way his mouth curled up in the faintest smile. She hadn't noticed before that his eyes had gold flecks in them.

There was a lot she hadn't noticed about Noah before all this happened. He was the quiet, serious Jameson brother. Noah had an integrity and a depth of character that she admired. As she stared into his eyes, she had to be honest with herself. She was falling for him. Feelings that she had locked away in a box a year ago were coming alive.

"Last call, folks, we got to shut this place down." The man in the waiter's uniform turned off the hallway lights.

The waiter's interruption killed the power of the moment between them. Lifting her skirt, she turned. "I just need to get cleaned up a little bit."

Noah looked down at his torn pants. "Me too."

She turned back to face him. "If he wants me to say I love him, why doesn't he tell me how and when?" Her voice tinged with pain. "He said he would give Oscar back if I did." She couldn't bear the thought of anything bad happening to that dog.

"I think he gets some sort of sick thrill out of toying with you. It's about power and control," said Noah.

After both of them retreated to respective bathrooms

to get cleaned up, they stepped outside into the darkness and headed toward the parking lot.

It had been a long night for both of them. Yet, there was something about going through it all with Noah that she could get used to.

There was a small cluster of people still visiting in the parking lot. One of the men broke away from the group and headed toward them.

Noah spoke under his breath. "It's the deputy commissioner. I'm going to have to make nice." He grabbed her hand and squeezed it. "Help me out."

His touch lit a fire inside her. And she liked that he sought out her support.

The deputy commissioner was a tall African American man with a bright smile. "Noah, talk about running into you at the last minute." He held out his hand.

"Good to run into you, John." Noah shook John's hand and then turned toward Lani. "This is officer Lani Branson. She's with the NYC K-9 Command Unit and a close friend."

John offered Lani a nod and then turned his attention back to Noah. "I was actually hoping I'd see you tonight."

"Oh?" Noah drew his shoulders back ever so slightly, body language that to anyone else would have been unnoticeable. But Lani knew it meant he was nervous. They'd been spending so much time together she was starting to pick up on things like that.

The deputy commissioner continued. "Yes, I wanted to tell you what a great job you have been doing as chief. I know when we lost your brother, you stepped up as acting chief. The commissioner agrees that we want to offer you the position on a permanent basis."

"Noah, that's wonderful." Though her voice gave nothing away, Lani felt like she'd been knocked in the stomach. "What a great opportunity." She wanted to be happy for Noah, but if he took the job it truly meant they would only ever be friends.

"Thank you. I'll have to think about it," said Noah.

A woman in a pastel orange colored gown broke away from the group and came toward them. She touched John's arm in a way that indicated they were a couple. "Do we know how to close a party down or what? We should get going, John, we already owe the sitter a small fortune."

"Get back to me with your answer as soon as possible, Noah," the deputy commissioner said before he wrapped his arms around his wife's shoulder and walked toward one of the remaining cars.

Noah turned to face Lani. "Come on, I'll take you home."

Noah escorted her back to his car where he held the door for her. She sat in the passenger seat feeling numb. Of course, Noah should take the job as chief. Why was he even thinking about it?

For a moment, she'd let herself entertain the idea that maybe they could be more than friends if Noah went back to working patrol. She wasn't going to deny the feelings. She just didn't need to act on them and stand in the way of Noah getting ahead in his career.

"It's a great opportunity for you...to be the chief permanently." It felt like she was pulling the words up from the bottom of her toes.

"Sure," he said. He seemed very far away, lost in thoughts of his own.

They drove through the city. She watched the honey-

colored headlights of other cars bleep by on the expressway as the hole inside her grew. The reality was that as
much as she liked Noah, there could not be anything
romantic between the two of them.

Noah slowed down as he turned onto the residential
street that led to her house. He double-parked in front
of her house. The glow of the lights inside indicated
that Reed was home.

"I'll wait until you're inside," he said.

She pushed open the door.

"Thanks for helping me out tonight," said Noah. "I
couldn't have done it without you."

"No problem. I had fun even with everything that
happened." She slipped out of the car and turned back to
face him. "It's what one friend does for another, right?"

He hesitated in answering. She could not read his
expression in the dim light. "Yeah, sure," he said. His
voice sounded a million miles away.

"You have a good night, what's left of it. Get some
sleep." She shut the car door and headed up the walkway to her house feeling like she had been hollowed out
on the inside. She could see Reed through the window
watching television. Jessie lay on the couch resting her
head on Reed's thigh. A welcome sight. Reed waved at
her from inside the house.

She peered over her shoulder at Noah, who hadn't
pulled away from the curb yet. She swung open the
door and stepped inside, feeling as though something
in her life had died.

ELEVEN

Noah watched as the last of Lani's martial arts students shuffled out of the dojo and headed toward the locker rooms. A few parents waited in chairs in the viewing area along with Noah and Scotty while others must have run errands and would pick up their ten-year-olds in a few minutes.

"Great class. See you next week," said Lani as she stood at the front of the room with her hands on her hips. She even looked great in a martial arts uniform. Her long blond ponytail set high on her head.

In the days since their night at the castle, things between them had seemed a little frosty. Lani had been pushing to be back out in the field, arguing that the stalker was going to get to her no matter what. Why did her training have to be stalled? The logic of the argument wasn't lost on him. She even wanted to know why she had to be stuck at a desk with him. Her saying that hurt. Didn't she like being around him? Or was it just the inactivity that was hard for her? Lani was a woman of action. Maybe her coldness had nothing to do with him and was just because she was so frustrated by the confinement and the need for protection.

Still, anytime Reed or one of the other officers was available, she'd chosen them over Noah to be her protection. That did feel personal. Tonight, none of the other officers were free, so he got to see her in action teaching her class. Lani was a natural teaching the kids using humor while still maintaining control.

Noah rose to help Lani put away some of the equipment. She handed him a spray bottle and a cloth. "You can sanitize the mats. I'll put this equipment away and then I got some paperwork I have to do in the office on the third floor."

"Take Scotty with you," he said.

"Sure, no problem." She offered him the faintest of smiles. She commanded Scotty to follow her and disappeared through a door which he assumed led to an office.

It wasn't that she was abrupt or even dismissive toward him, it was just that he could feel distance between them. He sprayed down the mats as the last of the parents drifted away and noise from the locker room died out.

He enjoyed the time he spent with her so much. And yes, he was attracted to her. He admired her compassion and her integrity. When he wasn't around her, he missed her easy laugh and animated storytelling.

He heard a door slam somewhere. His heart squeezed tight as concern for Lani's safety rose up in him. He dropped the spray bottle and hurried in the direction Lani had gone. The door led to a narrow set of stairs which Noah took two at a time. The building must have been a residence at one time, these narrow stairs for servants to travel up and down the floors without being intrusive.

The stairs led him to a door on the third floor that was slightly ajar. He pushed it open. Lani sat at a desk behind a computer. The room was the size of a broom closet. Uniforms and belts of various colors still in their packaging and a file cabinet took up most of the remaining space.

Lani looked up from her computer. Though Noah couldn't see him, Scotty must be on the other side of the desk in the tight quarters.

"Everything okay?" She glanced back at her screen.

The panic that had made his chest tight released its hold on him. "Yeah, I just thought I heard a door slam. Is anybody else in this building?"

"I wouldn't think so at this hour. There are two other tenants on the second floor. I think a bookkeeper and a guy who sells real estate. One of them might be working late."

"Maybe, I'll just have a look around," he said.

"I'll be done here in a few minutes. I've just got to get this letter about the tournament written and sent off," Lani said. She leaned over to pet Scotty. "We'll be fine here."

Noah stepped away from the threshold. "I'll let you know if anyone else is around." He headed down the hallway, opening doors. The office for the martial arts school and several rooms used for storage appeared to be the only thing on this top floor. He knew that the dojo and locker rooms took up all of the basement. But the building was laid out oddly and it wasn't obvious how to access the second floor. The narrow stairs that led to Lani's office had no other doors or exits. He returned to the dojo and found a second more substantial stairway on the other side of the building that led to the other offices.

Both the offices had signs on their doors indicating their respective businesses. He stood for a moment on the silent floor staring out the window at the city at night. Could the noise he'd heard just be a parent returning to grab some forgotten item? In and out so quickly he hadn't seen them?

He hurried back down the large stairway to the dojo. He peered in the now empty locker room and turned to head back up to where Lani and Scotty were.

An object hit the back of his head. Black dots filled his field of vision. He could feel his body falling forward in space as he crumpled face-first to the floor.

The last thought he had before the sensation that lights were being turned out and he was in total darkness was that maybe he should get up and make sure Lani was okay.

Lani finished the letter to the parents and hit the send button. She glanced down at Scotty. "Almost done here, buddy."

The dog looked at her and made a noise only Rottweilers made, somewhere between a groan and a whine. She rubbed the top of his head. "I miss you too, when I can't see you."

Scotty and Noah were sort of a package deal. If being around Noah was just too painful, it meant she didn't get to see the sweet Rottweiler either. She cared for Noah. Maybe it was just because of the danger they had faced together, but her connection to him was so deep. Knowing that they could never be anything more than friends made her feel like the heartache might overwhelm her when she was around him. Maybe that would change with time.

Having to work so closely with him in the confined space of his office put her over the top. She'd been pushing to get back out in the field for more reasons than just to continue her training.

Lani closed down the computer and bent over to get her purse. She rose to her feet and squeezed through the tiny space between the desk and the file cabinet pushing a chair out of the way to get through and then putting it back in place. Her back was to the door when she reached for her coat.

A hand went over her mouth as lips pressed close to her ears. "Now I have you all to myself."

She pulled his hand away from her mouth, but the man's grip around her waist was like iron. "I love you. Are you happy?" She spoke through gritted teeth. "Where is Oscar?"

Her attacker squeezed her even tighter making it hard to breath. "You sound so sincere." He wrapped the arm that had been over her mouth around her, so her neck was in the crook of his elbow.

Scotty jumped up putting his front paws on the desk, going ballistic with his barking. The desk was not one he could slip under to have access to her attacker. Lani had had to move a chair to even let him in behind the desk. Now that chair blocked him.

The man's anaconda-like grip weakened for just a moment. He probably hadn't counted on Scotty being here. Scotty's intense barking filled the tiny space. In the second that the attacker was distracted, Lani tore away from him and turned to face the man who had made her a prisoner.

She saw his face clearly for just a moment before he whirled to run. The arched eyebrows and gaunt features stood in sharp contrast to his muscular body. Now that face would be etched in her memory. Scotty had worked his way around the desk through the same tight space Lani had squeezed through. His paws tapped out an intense rhythm and scratched the linoleum as he made a beeline for the attacker who stepped toward the door and the narrow stairway.

Lani hurried after the dog. The attacker reached the bottom of the stairs in the basement and ran through the dojo. The dog continued the chase, but Lani stopped when she saw Noah lying facedown on the floor just outside the locker room. Her panic ratcheted up a notch at the sight of him not moving.

Knowing that Scotty would go after the attacker, she kneeled to check on Noah. He was unresponsive when she shook his shoulder. Fear washed through her as she rolled him over. His chest moved up and down. She let out a sharp breath. He was alive, but unconscious.

Above her on the second floor, Scotty's bark intensified and then she heard a yipping sound. A door slammed. Had the man been able to get away? She raced up the stairs on the other side of the dojo that led to the second floor and out to the street.

She found Scotty hurling himself at a shut door.

Noah called to her from the bottom of the stairs as he came around the corner. "Did he get away?"

She glanced down at him. He appeared a little wobbly on his feet. His hair was disheveled. His unfocused gaze suggested he hadn't fully recovered.

"Not yet." She swung open the door. Scotty burst through it giving chase. "He hasn't gotten away. Not if we can help it." She hurried after the dog who had stopped to sniff the ground and then took off running up an alley.

Scotty turned a corner. She couldn't see the dog anymore, but she could hear him.

Rain drizzled out of the dark sky. From the look of the shine on the street, it had been raining for some time. She slowed a little in her step, fearing an ambush from her attacker hiding behind something.

Noah came up behind her and touched her shoulder.

She pointed. "He went that way." With Scotty and Noah close by, she didn't fear being kidnapped or worse.

They sprinted up the alley and turned the corner. The street led to an open area. She could just make out Scotty as he raced toward a dark street. Noah lagged behind, probably still recovering from his injury. The attacker must have knocked Noah out so nothing would stop him from getting to Lani. But the stalker hadn't counted on Scotty.

The Rottweiler reached the street just as a single headlight came on. A motorcycle pulled away from the curb. Scotty chased after it, running for several blocks before the attacker gained enough speed to escape. His taillight faded in the distance.

Noah caught up with her and then ran out to get Scotty.

Feeling a sense of defeat, Lani shivered from being cold and wet. There hadn't been time to grab her coat. Noah returned with Scotty heeling beside him.

She reached out to stroke the dog's head. "You did good, boy." She gazed toward Noah, unable to read his expression in the darkness. He probably felt the same level of frustration she was experiencing. "Come on back inside, let's get dried off and warmed up."

The three of them trailed back toward the dark building. Once inside, Lani gathered up some clean towels from the locker room. They toweled off Scotty before drying their own hair and clothes. Her shirt was still damp from the rain, but she wasn't shivering.

"Come on up to the office. I'll make us some tea to warm up before we go," she said.

They trudged up the narrow, twisted stairs. Lani made the tea a cup at a time with the Keurig that rested on top of the file cabinet. She sat behind the desk and Noah sat on the desk since there was no room for another chair even if they had one. Scotty perched on the threshold of the door, exhausted from his run but still vigilant.

Noah blew on his steaming mug. "I'm sorry I let you down."

Lani scooted her chair back from her desk. "What do you mean?"

Noah touched the back of his head. "I was supposed to protect you, and that guy got the better of me."

"He didn't hurt me thanks to Scotty."

The dog let out a huff of air.

"I just wish we could have caught him," said Noah.

"I did get a look at him." Lani bit her lip as the memory of her attacker's face materialized in her head. "I can tell you for sure that he's not a former boyfriend or anyone I arrested. Still, it feels like I've seen him somewhere."

Noah took a gulp of tea. "That's progress. We can have you look through some databases or put together a police sketch." He set his mug on the desk.

Lani finished her tea and set the mugs aside. She could wash them next time she was teaching a class. "You ready to take me home?"

Noah rose to his feet. "Yes, let's go."

Scooting the chair to one side, Lani squeezed through the narrow space between desk and file cabinet.

Noah grabbed her coat from where it hung on a hook. He placed it over her shoulders, and she slipped her arms through the sleeves. He stepped out first so she would have room to stand on the landing and face him.

Scotty rose and moved closer to the stairs.

She stared up into his green eyes. "This is getting old."

He shook his head.

She sighed. "Sometimes it just feels like this is never going to end. That I will be at this guy's mercy forever. Being escorted around."

He leaned toward her. "It hasn't been awful, has it? Being with me." His face lit up with that soft smile.

Here they were again, looking into each other's eyes. She wondered if he was experiencing the same magnetic pull toward her that she felt to him. She wished he would put his hand on her cheek. She wanted to be held in his arms. She longed to feel his touch.

She cleared her throat and took a step back. "No, it hasn't been terrible." *Just heartbreaking at times.* "I enjoy your company, Noah." Lost in the moment, she struggled to tear her gaze from his face.

Scotty whined and wagged his tail. Noah looked away, brushing his hand over the dog's back. "Okay, buddy, let's take this lady home."

They took the stairs to the second floor and out onto the street. Noah had parked the car several blocks away.

They passed only a few people on the sidewalk. This wasn't a part of Queens with a lot of nightlife.

After loading Scotty in the back, Noah opened the passenger side door. "You should probably drive since I was just hit on the head." He tossed her the keys.

Lani got behind the wheel.

Scotty must have sensed the heaviness of the moment. He rested his chin on the seat and made his I'm-here-for-you noise. As Lani pulled out onto the street, Noah reached back and patted Scotty's jaw.

The moment of intense attraction she'd felt back at the office weighed on her. She needed to know what was to be between them. "So have you decided about becoming the chief permanently?" As much as she dreaded the answer, the question had to be asked.

Noah answered. "I suppose the deputy commissioner will want an answer soon. Being with you has given me a chance to spend more time in the field. I do miss it after nearly seven months of mostly sitting at a desk."

Her heart fluttered. So he wasn't sold on the idea of taking the promotion. "Yeah, desk duty makes me restless."

A few blocks later, he spoke up. "It's a tough choice. Lot to think about."

She smoothed her hand over her shirt and stared out through the windshield. The city ticked by in her peripheral vision, dark office buildings, neon, people spilling into the street from restaurants and bars.

Lani took the exit that led to her house. They rode the remaining way in silence. She circled the block until a space opened up close to her house.

Lani grabbed the door handle. "You should make sure there is nothing seriously wrong with your head."

"I should be okay. I'll go in tomorrow."

She turned back to look at him. Light from a streetlamp spilled into the car. She could see the brightness in his eyes and his angular features.

"Don't be bummed about the guy getting away tonight. Being able to ID him is a big step toward catching him."

Lani felt like a balloon that all the air had been let out of. So he thought the reason for her silence was she was thinking about the stalker. "Yeah, hopefully he'll be behind bars soon." She stepped out to the curb and shoved her hands in her pockets. "So I can get on with my life." She shut the door and headed toward her house.

As always, she knew Noah would remain parked until she was safely inside. She glanced toward the street. The cab was still lit up, and Noah had slid into the driver's seat. She could see him as he held his phone to his ear.

She opened the door of her house. Maybe she had read the situation all wrong. The attraction only went one way.

Noah answered his phone. The number came up as his brother Carter.

"What's up, little brother?"

"Where you been? I keep hoping to catch you at home."

Carter sounded anxious. "I've been busy with work and…things." Like being a bodyguard for Lani. It seemed that anytime Noah was home Carter was sleeping.

"I was just wondering if anything new has come up

with Jordan's murder," Carter said. "I figured it would cross your desk first."

Carter had not been on active duty for some months since being shot in the knee. He was doing physical therapy and receiving temporary disability. The injury had been severe enough that the prognosis for Carter coming back on the force was not good. Being out of commission meant Carter had a lot of time to think and worry about Jordan's murder going so cold it was forgotten.

"Nothing new, Carter," said Noah. "'Preciate you checking in." There was a lot going unsaid with Carter's phone call. His call was a way of saying none of the brothers would let this case go cold. Any thread, any morsel of a clue had to be followed up on.

"Okay, thanks, big brother," Carter said. "Keep me in the loop if anything does surface. I have time now. I can make some calls and inquiries in an unofficial way. I'll let you know if I find anything that needs a more official follow-up."

"Can do," said Noah, a note of sorrow echoed through his words, for what Carter was going through with this injury and for the whole Jameson clan.

He glanced at Reed and Lani's brightly lit living room.

From the backseat, Scotty rested his chin on Noah's shoulder. "I know, boy. I like Lani a lot too."

He still wasn't sure what he wanted to do. He missed working the street and being in the field with Scotty and he liked working with Lani. If he stepped down as chief, maybe there could be something more than a friendship between them. If she had the same feelings for him as he was starting to have for her. That was a big if. He'd never been very good at reading women. Criminals he did fine with, but women were a mystery.

He stared at his phone. He could do a lot of good for Lani and the other K-9 officers as the chief. And really he only trusted himself to make sure Jordy's case remained front and center. He felt the heaviness of his responsibilities, and then the memory of Lani's smile flashed through his head. Another time, another place it would be so easy to fall for her. He stroked Scotty's head. "Not everything can be about me or you and what we want. No matter how bad we want it."

Scotty licked the side of his face.

As he pulled away from the curb, he knew that the right decision would be to accept the permanent position as chief.

TWELVE

K-9 officer Tony Knight slapped Noah on the back as he unloaded Scotty from the patrol car.

"So it's all hands on deck," said Tony as his dog Rusty, a chocolate Lab, remained standing and alert. Rusty was trained in search and rescue, but with the Columbus Day Parade about to start, all the K-9s who weren't marching in the parade were on duty.

"Looks that way," said Noah. Scotty jumped out of his kennel in the back of the patrol car and stood at attention.

Up Fifth Avenue, Noah could hear the sound of a marching band warming up. Crowds were already lining the street in preparation for the parade, some of them waving Italian flags. From the police marching band to the motorcycle brigade, NYPD would be well represented. Several of the K-9s would be marching as well with the rest of law enforcement, but most of the K-9s would be on patrol. It would be a long day. Even after the parade, the celebrations would go on into the night in Little Italy. The day had come to be a celebration of Italian culture more than anything.

Another patrol car pulled up. Brianne got out of the

driver's seat and moved to the back of the vehicle to get Stella. Lani emerged from the passenger seat, walking around the vehicle toward Noah and Tony.

"What are you doing here?" said Noah.

"I think you could use every hand you've got. The pickpockets will be out in full force," said Lani. "For starters. We all know the crime level ticks up during this kind of event."

Scotty wagged his tail as Lani drew close. With Sophie back from her honeymoon, Lani had been on desk duty with a different department and spending time in the training facility working with the dogs. Like the rest of the K-9 unit, she had received the news of his acceptance as permanent chief at the morning briefing between shift changes. As Noah had stood at the front of the room to make the announcement, he saw her expression change. What was that he saw in tightened features? Concern? Anger? Maybe even disappointment. After the briefing, he had meant to find her, but she'd disappeared while the other officers were slapping his back and shaking his hand. Since then, she'd made herself scarce. He'd seen her only in passing and there was no time to talk. He missed her.

Lani was right that the presence of the dogs tended to cut down on the muggings and pickpockets. Lani's keen eyes and athletic ability might come in handy too.

She reached down to pet Scotty. "The stalker finds a way to get to me no matter what. I wanted to be a help. I'm used to action and activity, Noah. Desk duty is going to make me feel claustrophobic."

She was right on that account too. Desk duty hadn't kept her safe.

"Okay," said Noah. "Stay close to me."

"Ten-four," said Lani.

The dissonant sound of marching bands warming up grew louder. Several blocks up Fifth Avenue he could see a large balloon of a cartoon character floating in the air. The people lined up ten deep on the sidewalk up to the street where barriers had been set up. This part of Fifth Avenue was one of the places entertainers in the parade would stop to perform.

Brianne and Tony headed south while he and Lani took the other side of the street. The crowd parted for them as Scotty trotted through. Some of the kids wanted to pet Scotty, which Noah allowed. Having the dogs out with all these people provided a PR opportunity.

Lani's shoulder brushed against his. Her presence had a debilitating effect on him and her touch turned his knees to mush. That he had that sort of a reaction when he was close to her, he would just have to accept and keep in check.

The sound of the approaching parade grew even louder as people pressed toward the edge of the street in anticipation.

Lani nodded her head toward a teenage boy who had stepped back away from the crowd toward the store-fronts. His eyes grew wide at the sight of Lani and Noah.

"Something is up with that kid," said Lani. "I think he lifted a wallet."

Scotty quickened his pace. The teenager turned to run, a sign that he was up to something. Lani sprinted after him. The side streets were virtually abandoned. Noah could see her blond head as she burst down the alley after the suspect. Scotty bounded ahead. Noah led him down a side street in an effort to cut the suspect off once he emerged from the alley.

Scotty bolted to the edge of the alley and barked.

Lani stood at the other end of the alley with her hand hovering over her gun. She didn't see any sign that he had a weapon, but training taught her to never assume.

The kid raised his arms. "I didn't do anything. Make that dog stop barking at me."

"I saw you ditch the wallet back there," said Lani. "And I saw you take it from the man in front of you."

"Okay," said the kid.

Noah gave Scotty the command to stop barking and sit. The kid still watched the dog closely with an expression of fright on his face.

"Why don't we walk back to where you dropped the wallet. You can give it back to the man and apologize," said Noah.

The jails were going to be full before the day was over. Taking this kid in would be pointless.

The kid shrugged, glanced at Scotty and then trudged back up the alley. Noah stepped in behind the suspect, keeping Scotty's lead short. The kid acted like he was going to cooperate as long as Scotty was around. Dogs were effective in that way. The teenage boy stopped to root beside a dumpster for the stolen wallet.

Though they were several blocks from the action, the noise of the parade swelled to a crescendo as the first of the marchers went by and the crowd cheered.

On command, Scotty sat while the teen continued to search for the wallet behind the dumpster.

Noah glanced over at Lani who was studying the fire escapes and windows of the apartment building. Was she always wondering if she was being watched?

Even though they had a face to go with her stalker, the search through the databases of criminals had yielded no results. The guy must not have a criminal history. He hadn't had time to find out if Lani had sat down with the police sketch artist.

When she caught him staring, she lowered her gaze and tilted her head to one side, shaking it a little, probably meaning that she was thinking about the stalker, but that she didn't notice anything that indicated the stalker was around. The connection between them was so strong, no words needed to be exchanged.

It was the kind of connection that made two people good partners as police officers, but he had a feeling it ran even deeper than that.

"Here it is. I found it." The teenager stood up waving a wallet.

Noah took the wallet. "Do you remember what the man you took it off of looked like?"

"From behind. He had on a red jacket." The kid stared at the ground. Returning the wallet and apologizing would probably be punishment enough.

Lani came to stand beside Noah. Noah opened up the wallet and showed the kid and Lani the driver's license. "That's who we're looking for."

When they reached the street where the parade was passing by, the number of spectators had grown even more.

Noah with Scotty in tow hung close to the teenager while he searched for the wallet's owner. The crowd always gave wide berth to Scotty.

"There." The teen pointed to a man in a red jacket.

They pressed through the crowd. The boy tapped the man in the red jacket on the shoulder and made his apologies when the man turned around. Noah handed him his wallet.

The man glanced at Noah and then back at the teen, whose tight features and stiff shoulders indicated he was distraught.

"I don't need to press charges," said the man.

The teen melted with relief. His shoulders and his expression softened, and he disappeared into the crowd.

Noah glanced up expecting to see Lani. All he saw was a sea of faces all focused on the passing parade. Panic gripped him. Had the stalker found a way to get to her? He and Scotty squeezed through the crowd, searching. He pushed toward the storefronts still not seeing her.

When he caught sight of the back of Lani's head, he let out the breath he was holding. Even though he'd lost her in the crowd for only minutes, the feeling that something bad might have happened to her and she would no longer be in his life, made him see how much he cared about her.

He rushed toward her. She slipped deeper into the crowd. A wall of people came in front of her and he lost sight of her.

He called out her name. Where was she going? Scotty walked in front of him, parting the crowd. He caught a glimpse of her blond head now half a block away.

He hurried toward her, wondering what had caught her attention.

Though she was shaking with fear, Lani squeezed her way through the throngs of people. She'd seen her stalker, and he had Oscar. She looked over her shoulder hoping to see Noah and Scotty. There hadn't been time to let him know what was going on. She dared not even slow down to radio him.

The man had grinned at her in the most sinister way while he held the puppy, and then he'd been swallowed up by the crowd. She'd probably lost him, but more than anything she wanted to get Oscar back. She doubted he would hurt her as long as she remained where people were.

She hurried around a group of children. The crowd thinned. Up the side street, she saw Oscar's head bobbing as he was pulled on a leash. She saw the back of the man and then he was gone again around a corner.

Someone touched her shoulder.

She whirled around. All the fear left her tense body when she saw that it was Noah.

"Oscar. I saw Oscar."

"Are you sure it was Oscar. There are a lot of yellow Labs in this city."

"He was with the man I saw at the studio. They just went around the corner."

Noah tugged on Scotty's leash. "Let's go." Noah's walk intensified to a jog. "I'm glad I caught up with you. He's probably setting a trap."

They hurried up the street. A few parade watchers were lined up for a half a block on the side street. They broke free of the crowd. Despite street closures due to the parade, there were still people wandering around. None of them had a yellow Lab puppy.

Lani scanned the entire area not seeing the dog or the man. They continued up the street. She heard a faint bark, Oscar's bark.

"He's headed toward the subway," she said.

They hurried toward the stairs that led to the subway.

Noah clicked on his radio. "Got a suspect with the missing yellow Lab headed down the Fifty-Ninth Street entrance. Officer Branson and I are in pursuit."

They hurried down the stairs. Noah flashed his badge and leapt over the turnstile. The platform was busy but not overly crowded. She scanned the sea of faces. It wouldn't be that easy to hide a squirmy yellow Lab.

Noah patted her shoulder. "Scotty and I will check that area around the corner."

Lani hurried up and down the platform searching. Her radio glitched. She clicked her on button. "Go ahead."

The voice was Tony's. "Rusty and I are at the exit. No sign of him."

"Nothing here either. Will continue the search." Lani peered over her shoulder at where Noah had gone behind her. No sign of Noah. "Our suspect is wearing a blue jacket and a baseball hat."

"Got it," said Tony. "I read your description of him in the report you filed. Muscular guy."

She hurried past some buskers playing guitar and violin. She could hear the subway moving through the tunnel whizzing toward the platform. She scanned the crowd again. If the man was in hiding, he might step out to board the subway. Her heart pounded in her chest. He was here somewhere. He had to be.

Up ahead, she saw Tony and his chocolate Lab. When she glanced over her shoulder, Noah had emerged from around the corner. He shook his head. The stalker must know that he was trapped. Where was he hiding?

Screams rose up from the crowd gathering to board the subway. Lani turned one way and then the other, trying to figure out what had caused the panic. The attention of the crowd was directed toward the tracks.

All the air left her lungs when she saw Oscar bounding along the tracks, stopping to sniff something on the ground. The sound of the approaching train pressed on her ears. Lani sprinted toward the tracks to the edge of the platform. Scotty ran out ahead of her and leaped down onto the tracks. Scotty hurried after Oscar and grabbed him by the collar. The weight of the six-month-old pup looked to be almost too much for Scotty to carry.

The train was within seconds of arriving at the platform. Scotty reached the area between track and platform. Lani sprinted the distance to where the dog was at. She reached down and gathered Oscar in her arms.

The sound of the approaching train filled the tunnel. Noah came out of nowhere. All her attention had been on Oscar. Noah jumped down on the tracks and boosted Scotty back on the platform. Lani reached an arm down to help Noah up just as the train came into view. Though it had slowed to make the stop, Noah lay on the platform only seconds before it whizzed past and came to a stop.

A cheer rose up from the crowd. Noah shifted from being on his stomach to sitting. Lani gasped for air while Oscar crawled into her lap.

The doors of the subway slid open.

Still out of breath, Lani bolted to her feet. "He'll use this chance to get away. He probably wanted Oscar to be a distraction."

Noah rose to his feet as well. "Looks like Tony's got the train covered."

Lani glanced down the platform to see Tony and his dog board the subway.

Lani grabbed the leash that was still attached to Oscar. She searched all the boarding passengers and then turned her attention to the people who remained. None looked like her stalker. None bolted for the exit to indicate their guilt. Maybe Tony and Rusty would find him.

Noah patted her shoulder. "He must have slipped out when we were saving Oscar."

Lani nodded. She leaned down to gather Oscar into her arms. "I'm glad I have this little guy back." Oscar licked her face.

"Scotty and I will do one more search up and down," Noah said.

Lani trailed behind pulling the easily distracted Oscar along. The pup stopped to wag his tail at a group of girls in school uniforms. The girls oohed and aahed. Oscar knew how to turn on the charm. Her phone beeped that she had a text. She clicked open the message.

The dog was too much trouble. Next time it will be your boyfriend.

Before, the message might have sent a wave of fear through her. But she was stronger now.

Noah came back over to her. "He got away. I'm sure of it." He stepped a little closer toward her. "Is something wrong?"

"Another message from him." She lifted the phone up so he could take it and read the text.

"That guy has some nerve." Noah's forehead crinkled as he shook his head. He turned his attention to Oscar. "The good news is, sometimes being an obnoxious puppy works in your favor."

Oscar yipped and bounced around Lani's feet.

"Who does he mean, 'your boyfriend'? I thought you weren't dating anyone."

"He must assume it's you since we're together so much," Lani said. "I'm sure if someone were watching from a distance, it might appear that way."

He shrugged. "I guess so."

Tony's voice came through Noah's radio. "We got nothing here. Sorry."

Noah radioed back. "Nothing here either."

"Well, guess we better finish the shift," she said. "I'll put Oscar in your car if that's all right."

"Yeah, I'm sure the celebration will be going on into the night in Little Italy." Noah let go of the radio and straightened his neck to look at Lani. "The Jamesons have their own Columbus Day celebration. Lots of Italian food. You want to come?" His eyes rested on her for a long moment. "Reed is welcome to come along."

Lani felt torn. She missed spending time with Noah, but being around him brought up the pain that there could never be anything between them.

"My mom makes an awesome lasagna." He tried to entice her.

"Can't turn that down, can I?"

"Great, let's go up topside and finish out this shift. Parade has probably moved past, but I'm sure there are still plenty of opportunists working the crowd."

They stepped toward the subway exit and climbed up into the daylight, Lani wrestling with the uncertainty of everything in her life. Could she handle just being

Noah's friend? Would she be able to complete her training with the stalker still out there?

The only thing she knew for sure was that she was glad to have Oscar back. Even if he wasn't police dog material, she'd grown fond of the little guy.

THIRTEEN

Noah lifted the lid on the spaghetti sauce and took in a deep breath filled with oregano and basil. His mouth watered. He reached for a spoon to sample the sauce. As he drew the spoon up to his mouth, he breathed in the heady aroma again.

His mother entered the kitchen. "Get out of there. If you boys keep sampling the food, there will be nothing left for dinner."

His mother tended toward exaggeration. She had cooked enough to feed an army. Ivy Jameson's blue eyes held a sparkle that had faded a little since the death of her son. Her dark hair was pulled up in a topknot. Even though she dressed in jeans and a blouse, she always carried herself with a certain elegance.

Noah licked his lips and put the spoon down. "It could use just a smidgen more garlic."

Ivy wagged a finger at her son. "Too many cooks spoil the soup, and the same could be said of spaghetti sauce. Now go on back into the living room. I'm sure your guest will be here any minute. What did you say her name was?"

"Lani."

"Yes, I've met her. Pretty girl, blonde. Nice lady." Her voice dropped half an octave and she gazed out the window. "I remember her from Jordan's funeral." Ivy studied her son for a moment. The jovial tone returned to her voice. "You like her, don't you? I noticed you cleaned up and put on a fresh shirt."

"Can't a guy take a shower without being accused of ulterior motives?" said Noah.

Ivy laughed and shook her head while she stirred the sauce and checked the lasagna in the oven. "I know my son."

Noah rested his hand on the counter. "Okay, I like her...as a friend. I'm her direct supervisor, so nothing is going to happen."

"Too bad. Your brothers have all met such nice women."

"I know, Mom. One of us has to be the forever bachelor, right?"

Ivy shut the oven door and placed her hand on her hip. She reached over and squeezed Noah's chin. "I want you to meet a nice girl. If not Lani, then maybe one of those sweet women from the Sunday school class your father and I teach."

It was his turn to stare out the window. "Yeah, maybe." The phrase "if not Lani" echoed through his head. The truth was he had dated a couple of the women from church. All of them were nice, but kind of ordinary.

The doorbell rang. By the time Noah made it into the living room, his niece Ellie had answered the door. Ellie was Carter's daughter by his first wife who had died. His brother Zach sat on the couch with his wife, Violet. Carter and his fiancée, Rachelle, stood by the window watching the dogs play outside through the sliding glass door. And Katie, Jordan's widow, sat by herself. Her tunic length blouse covered her bulging belly. The family had learned of her pregnancy after Jordan's death.

Alexander, the family patriarch, rested in his easy chair, arms folded over his chest, half dozing. He wore a Mets sweatshirt and baggy pants.

Ellie opened the door. Lani stood holding a casserole dish. Her brother, Reed, was behind her. Katie pushed herself to her feet. "Let me take that."

As the two women stood by each other, he was struck by how much they looked alike. Both were blonde, similar hairstyles, tall and slender.

"It's my contribution to the festivities. Just some brownies. Not very Italian, I know."

Noah was impressed that she'd managed to throw anything together in the short time they'd gotten off shift.

Zach rose to his feet. "All the food in this house gets eaten." He held a hand out to Lani. "Good to see you. I've been in the field so much. I guess our paths haven't crossed much lately."

"Yeah, Noah pretty much has me at a desk for now," Lani said.

A little tension entered the room. Of course, his brothers knew about the stalker. But they had a rule about not bringing work into family celebrations. Noah diverted the conversation to the Mets.

Lani and Reed stepped into the living room. The group engaged in small talk until Ivy called them all to the large dining room table which overflowed with food. Zach opened the sliding glass door so the dogs could come in. Frosty, Eddie and Scotty lay down just on the threshold between living room and kitchen. The two foster pups of Stella, one black and one yellow, whom Carter referred to as Mutt and Jeff pranced around the older dogs before settling down.

After Alexander said grace, dishes were passed around and plates filled up with food. The conversation was about the parade, which Ellie had attended with Carter and Rachelle.

Lani shared about getting Oscar back.

"So where is he now?" Zach asked.

"He's back at the kennels for now. The vet is making sure he wasn't harmed while he was being held. I know he needs to be returned to his foster family. I just am fond of the little guy. He's not K-9 material."

Reed laughed. "Yeah, he's kind of hyper. He gives Jessie a run for her money. She's not used to that kind of energy."

Lani tore apart a piece of garlic bread. "Speaking of missing dogs. Have you made any progress in finding Snapper? I was thinking you should look on the website I checked when I was trying to find Oscar."

Noah glanced nervously at Katie. Lani didn't know they didn't talk police business at meals. He tensed, worried that bringing up anything about Jordan's death would be upsetting to Katie this late in her pregnancy. Snapper was his brother's K-9 who had gone missing after Jordan's murder.

Reed shook his head. "No progress far as I know even with that sketch Dominic helped us put together of the man who gave Snapper to Dominic."

Katie set her glass down. "There was a sketch made of the man who took Snapper?"

Noah glanced at his brothers, feeling a rising tension. Dominic was a foster kid from Brooklyn who'd taken care of Snapper for a while before the dog had run off. Dominic claimed that a man had given him the German shepherd, and everyone hoped that finding the guy would result in Jordy's murderer being put behind bars. Reed and his fiancée, Abigail, were working on adopting Dominic. "We weren't trying to keep you out of the loop, Katie."

"We just wanted to protect you and your baby," said Carter.

Lani cleared her throat. "I'm sorry. I think I may have spoken out of turn."

Noah placed a hand over hers. "You had no way of knowing."

Katie sat across the table from Noah. She put her napkin on the table. "I want to see that sketch." She rested a protective hand on her stomach.

"I can probably pull it up on my computer after we eat."

Alex raised his glass of lemonade. "Yes, later. Now let's enjoy the meal."

Noah glanced at Carter and then at Zach. Katie had a right to know what was going on with the investigation, but with the baby due in three weeks, he didn't want to add stress to her life.

After dinner, Noah went upstairs to retrieve his laptop. He sat on the back porch watching the dogs play while Katie and Lani leaned in close to see his screen. The trees had turned shades of gold, rust and yellow and a cool autumn breeze whirled around them. They all had put on their fall jackets while they sipped the cider Ivy had offered them.

Noah typed in his password to access the official files. He clicked past a long list of documents before the sketch came up on-screen.

Katie sat back in a lawn chair. Her voice grew cold. "I know who that is."

Breath caught in his throat. This could be the break-through they needed to catch Jordy's killer. Noah glanced at Lani.

"Can I have a closer look?" Lani asked.

Noah handed her the laptop and then drew his attention to Katie.

Noah tilted his head toward the computer. "So who is he?"

Katie rose to her feet and stepped to the edge of the porch. "His name is Martin Fisher. I knew him from church. We dated briefly before I met Jordan. I hadn't seen him at church in ages. But he came to Jordan's funeral and gave his condolences."

So this Martin Fisher might have killed Jordy out of jealousy.

"What did he seem like at the funeral?" Noah stood up and stepped closer to Katie, who gripped the railing of the porch. "I'm sorry I have to ask you these questions."

"It's all right. If this will get us closer to catching Jordan's killer—" she turned to face her brother-in-law "—I don't mind thinking about it." She smoothed her hand over her belly. "The two of us will be all right."

"Did he act peculiar in any way?"

She shook her head. "He was perfectly nice. And seemed really concerned about me." Katie looked down at the ground, still resting her hand on her tummy. "He came by about three weeks ago to check in on me. He wanted to take me out to dinner. I said I wasn't ready to date."

"How did he react to that? Was he angry?"

Katie shook her head. "One of the reasons we only went out a couple of times was that he came on a little strong, in kind of a smothering way. When I turned him down three weeks ago, I could tell he was upset, but he was still polite."

"Can you tell us anything else about him?"

"We only went out a couple of times. He worked construction and stayed in good shape for that."

Katie turned back toward the house, shaking her head. "Why would Martin have taken Snapper? You don't think…"

Her voice trailed off, but Noah knew what she was thinking. Was Martin Jordan's killer? It looked that way. But he could not draw a conclusion without solid evidence. Still, this felt like a huge step in the right direction. Noah shook his head. "I don't know anything for sure."

Ivy opened the sliding glass doors. "Come on inside, people. We've got gelato and Lani's brownies." Ivy closed the door and disappeared back into the kitchen.

"I think I might need to lie down for a bit," said Katie. "If there is any progress in the case, I want to know from now on, okay?"

He nodded. His sister-in-law went inside to head up the stairs.

Noah shook his head. He hated putting her through all this, but she was a strong woman. If they had kept her in the loop in the first place, they would have been able to ID the man in the sketch sooner.

He turned back to face Lani who had closed the laptop. Her features were taut. And her face had gone pale.

She tapped her finger on the laptop. "I think this is the same man who has been after me."

Noah reeled from the confusion. "But how?"

"I barely glanced at the sketch when it was shown in a briefing. We look at half a dozen of those a week. But now that I look at it and his face is burned in my mind... I think it's the same guy."

Noah sat down beside her. "If his connection is to Katie, why is he after you?"

"I don't know either. We kind of look alike. Katie said he was a little over-the-top with his affection when they were dating."

"Like he is using you as some kind of substitute." Katie and Lani were both blonde and blue-eyed, but their personalities were miles apart. Katie was quiet and thoughtful and Lani was outgoing and talkative. Noah stared at the sky. "I think we need to talk to a psychologist. I'm going to get a patrol unit to go to Martin Fisher's last known address right away."

"I agree. I'm with Katie that I want this all to be over with. Not just for me but for her."

Noah could feel his body tense from all the questions that hung in the air. Martin connected to Katie and he'd had Jordan's dog at one point. Did that mean Martin had killed Jordan? The evidence wasn't in yet, but he clearly had motive if he thought Jordan's death would help him be with Katie. But why bring Lani into it?

Lani walked up and down the hallway of the commercial high-rise searching for the address Noah had given her. They had agreed to meet Dr. Brenda Benchley, a private psychologist who often consulted with the police. It was Lani's day off and Noah had taken a long lunch to meet her here.

His text had come in a moment earlier saying he was delayed.

And now she couldn't find the office. Martin Fisher was still at large. Officers had been dispatched to his last known address as soon as they had his name, but Martin's landlord said he'd moved out three weeks ago.

Half the building was undergoing a remodel. Plastic was drawn across some side corridors and she could hear the sound of tools being used and men barking orders and questions at each other.

Her heart squeezed tight. Katie had said that Martin was a construction worker. Of course, that didn't mean he was here. She took in a breath to calm herself.

A man drew one of the plastic curtains aside and stepped out.

It wasn't Martin. But she had tensed all the same.

The man had dark hair that was graying at the temples. "Lady, are you lost?" He rested his hand on his tool belt.

"I'm trying to find an office." She showed him the address on her phone.

"Don't know it."

"It belongs to a psychologist."

Light came into the man's face and he nodded. "That's up a floor. You must have her old address. She moved her office when all the remodeling started."

Lani thanked the man, who disappeared behind the plastic curtain. She headed toward the door marked Stairs, walking slowly so she could text Noah about the change of address. She heard footsteps behind her but when she looked up and turned around, no one was there. Her heart beat a little faster. She searched the area, which had connecting hallways where someone could have gone. The corridors appeared to be unoccupied.

Maybe the stairwell wasn't such a good idea. She searched for the elevator and got on. Lani found the psychologist's office which had "Dr. Benchley" typed on a piece of paper and taped to the door.

A receptionist with short candy apple–red hair and cat-eye glasses looked up from her computer. "Yes?"

"I'm here to see Dr. Benchley, but I'm waiting for someone." She found a chair and sat down and tried to take in a deep breath. She hated the way Martin Fisher had a hold on her mind even if she couldn't prove he was around.

When Noah walked through the door, she could feel the tension leave her body and the air fill her lungs. His warm smile was a nice bonus.

"Sorry I couldn't get away faster," he said.

"Just through that door," said the receptionist.

Lani had always thought of herself as a free spirit and an independent woman. The only other men who made her feel safe when she was around them were her brother and her father.

She pushed open the door. Dr. Benchley sat at her desk with her laptop open. "Noah, it's always good to see you. Both of you have a seat." The doctor was maybe in her fifties. Her voice was soft, and she had a grand-motherly quality about her.

She closed her laptop. "So Noah explained the situation to me over the phone. It sounds to me like Martin Fisher may have a sort of transference taking place, and that's why he's been stalking you."

"But his attraction is toward Katie," Lani said.

The doctor shrugged. "Obsession is a funny thing. Maybe he sees her as unattainable. The fact that he has been both violent toward you and done things that suggest romantic attraction is what intrigues me the most. He can't acknowledge that Katie rejected him, but he has anger about that. Katie is sacred, untouchable, so he takes his anger out on you."

The doctor rose to her feet and put her hands in her pockets. "He may also not be able to process the rejection. He might have some sort of rich fantasy life that he and Katie are in a relationship. When reality creeps in, he feels anxious and he takes it out on you. I couldn't tell you for sure until I question him."

In the days since they had a name to go with the face, Noah had kept Lani in the loop about the challenge of trying to bring Martin in. It was too much to hope for just a simple arrest. The man had made himself all but invisible.

"We know he moved out of his place three weeks ago." Noah added, "Three weeks ago was also when he lost his job for giving the receptionist at the construction company unwanted attention."

"So the job loss might have triggered the instability into high gear," said Brenda.

Lani cleared her throat. "That's when the attacks on me started."

Noah's forehead crinkled as though he were thinking deeply. He squeezed Lani's shoulder. "We should get going. I have to get back to the office."

Though his touch was intended to be friendly, it still sent a spark of energy through her. Years from now, would she finally be able to be around him without having that kind of response? She had to accept reality. Noah was her boss. Her dream was to be an NYPD K-9 cop. The less she nursed the feelings of attraction, the sooner they would fade. Noah was a handsome man. Sooner or later he'd meet someone and get married. They would both move on with their lives.

Lani and Noah rose to their feet, thanked the doctor and left the office, then got into the elevator.

Noah stared at the elevator doors as they closed. "That was illuminating."

She watched the numbers flash by. "Yes, but it doesn't get us any closer to bringing him in."

Once they were outside, Noah spoke up. "Where did you park? I'll walk you to your car."

After scaring herself over what was probably just in her imagination in the high-rise, Lani was grateful for the escort to her car.

Noah opened the car door for her. "I'm parked in a lot up the street."

She got into her car but left the door open so she could talk to Noah. "Okay, let me know if anything breaks with the Martin Fisher case."

"You got it."

She shut the car door, resting her hands on the steering wheel but not ready yet to pull out. A day off gave her too much time to think about Noah. She did better when she was on duty.

She heard the screech of tires. She couldn't see anything in her rearview mirror. She jumped out of her car and stared down the ramp where a motorcycle was barreling toward Noah as he sprinted to get out of its path.

FOURTEEN

With the motorcycle coming straight for him from behind, Noah ran toward the protection of the parked cars. The roar of the motorcycle engine seemed to surround him. Before he could get to the cars, a blunt object hit him from behind. He fell to the ground and rolled. His vision blurred as he looked up at the taillight of the motorcycle and the man, Martin Fisher, no doubt, holding a crowbar. Pain shot through Noah's back where he'd been hit when he tried to get to his feet.

The motorcycle did a tight turn and headed toward Noah once again. He had an image of the tires running over his back. Again, he tried to get to his feet but the pain was too severe. He crawled toward the safety of the cars, which were still five yards away.

He heard the screech of car tires and the thump of brakes being pushed with force. Lani had pulled up beside him. He reached up for the passenger side door and crawled into the front seat.

Behind Lani's car, Martin swerved around them and then headed up the ramp. Lani hit the gas before Noah had even closed the door. Still dazed, he struggled to click his seat belt into place.

She turned the wheel and her car barely missed the parked vehicles. Martin whizzed by on the down ramp. Though her car was not as nimble as the motorcycle she hurried after him down the ramp and out into the noonday traffic. By the time she got through the exit and out on the street, the motorcycle was not visible.

"Valiant effort. I'll call it into dispatch. Maybe they can catch him." He made the call offering a description of the motorcycle. He spoke into the phone. "Also if they don't catch up with him, put an officer on pulling the footage in the parking garage to see if we can get a plate number."

She slammed her hand on the steering wheel. "This has gone too far. Now he wants to take out the people I care about. The other times he hurt you to get to me."

"Thank you. I care about you too." Noah felt his smile turn to a grimace as pain shot around his torso.

"I'm taking you to the ER," she said.

He wasn't in a place where he could argue. At the very least, he was badly bruised.

Lani drove looking straight ahead. Her jaw had turned to stone.

So this is what she looked like when she was angry. Still as pretty as ever, but the intensity of her rage seemed to suck all the oxygen out of the car.

"Thanks for saving me before I got run over."

"This never should have happened." She spoke through gritted teeth. "We have to do something."

"We're making progress. We have a name to go with the face. He's got to be living somewhere."

Lani didn't respond. She wove in and out of traffic, taking risks that she normally wouldn't take.

"I'd like to get to the ER alive."

She let up on the gas. "Sorry."

She took the exit that led to the hospital, rolling through several streets before pulling into the parking lot by the ER entrance.

He leaned forward to unfasten his seat belt. The radiating pain made him wince, but he didn't make any noise.

Lani unbuckled quickly. "Stay put. Let me get you out."

"I can handle it." Now he was the crabby one. He didn't like needing help. The level to which she was tuned in to his emotions stunned him. He thought he was hiding his pain, but she'd picked up on it.

By the time Lani got around to his side of the car, he'd opened the door and swung his legs out. He raised a palm to her. "I don't want your help." He braced his hand on the door frame and pulled himself up. His lips were pressed together and the pain seemed to be twisting all the way around his rib cage, but he got to his feet.

"You don't need to be a superhero. He hit you pretty hard." He thought he saw just a touch of amusement cross her face.

Grateful for the change of mood he smiled as well. "Sorry, I have to act like such a tough guy." Time to swallow some of that Jameson pride.

"This has upset both of us." She held out an elbow so he could grab her arm for support, which he took. Once they were inside, Noah was taken in for an exam that revealed cuts on his hands and knees and bruised ribs. The X-ray of his back didn't show any damage to vital organs though he had a feeling he was going to be sore for a few days.

The doctor, a man who didn't look like he was more

than twenty, came in after the nurse had wrapped his
ribs. "You are free to go. You need to rest for a few
days at least and I've written you a prescription for
painkillers."

Noah slipped off the exam table and grabbed his
shirt. He shook the doctor's hand. "Thanks. I sit at a
desk most of the day, so I should be okay."

"Actually, I'd take a couple of days off and really
rest," said the doctor.

Noah felt like the doctor was speaking in a foreign
language. Jamesons worked, that's who they were. A
couple of days off would drive him up the wall. He'd
seen how Carter had struggled after being shot. Doing
nothing was not in the Jamesons' vocabulary.

"At least take your work home with you and sit in an
easy chair," said the doctor.

Noah picked up his paperwork and found Lani sitting in the waiting room. She rose to her feet when she
saw him. Something in her expression was different.
She wasn't angry anymore, there was a look of resolve
in those blue eyes.

"What did the doctor say?"

"Rest…tall order for me."

"Noah, I've been thinking. What if we lure Martin
out by setting a trap for him using me as bait," she said.

The words seemed to echo through Noah's brain. He
couldn't risk Lani being hurt or worse.

"We know he watches me enough that he's figured
out my schedule and routines. He's not working, so he
has all kinds of time on his hands. If there was some
way to provoke him to come out into the open, to come
after me while I was wearing a wire and a team was
set up. We might be able to get him to confess to Jor-

dan's murder. We can definitely file charges for his attacks on me."

Noah wasn't sold on the idea, but maybe there was a way to make it work that ensured Lani's safety. "We know he's provoked when he thinks you and I are an item. Maybe we can get him to come after me again and this time I'll be ready for him."

"But you're in no kind of shape to get into a fight," Lani said. "I'm assuming he waits for me to leave my house in the morning or he hangs in the shadows around headquarters then follows me."

"This is going to take a while to plan and set up. I should be feeling better in a week or so. But yes—you and I should make it look like we're seriously dating since he thinks I'm your boyfriend."

Lani blinked as though the remark had hurt her. "What do you mean exactly?"

"I'll pick you up. We'll go out someplace in public where if he's following you, he'll see us. He's watching from a distance. He's never getting close enough to hear our conversation and know that we're not involved. You're right, he probably does have a way to watch you leave your house."

"What's to stop him from going after either one of us before we're ready?" she said.

"He's never attacked with people around. He only taunted you at the parade. I'm sure I can talk Zach and maybe another officer into standing by in case something does go down."

"Reed would lend a hand too." She was silent for a moment. "So we stay in public places until he's good and angry. Then maybe I can go for a bike ride or a jog.

I'll wear a wire and go to an area where there aren't many people but the team can be in place watching."

Noah knew Lani well enough not to argue with her now, but he hoped it didn't come to her being the bait. Next time Martin came after him, Noah intended to be ready.

Before she entered the living room, Lani took one more glance at herself in her full-length mirror. She had gone to way too much trouble for her pretend date with Noah. The pastel purple dress and sapphire necklace brought out the blue in her eyes. She'd braided her blond hair into a French braid.

Reed, Abigail and Dominic were in the living room playing a board game.

Reed smiled at her. "You look great."

"Like a princess ready for the ball," said Abigail.

"Hardly," said Lani. "Just another day on the job."

"Are you sure they have enough officers covering you?" Reed asked, concern etched on his face.

"Noah knows what he is doing." Reed had so little free time to spend with Abigail, she didn't like making him feel like he had to give up even more of it for her. "Enjoy your night off."

The doorbell rang. Lani walked over and opened it. Noah stood dressed in tan pants and a button-down shirt.

They got into his car and he pulled out onto the street.

"I picked a restaurant that has outdoor seating. Zach and Tony are already in place. One at the bistro and one across the street."

"Sounds like you have everything set up." Almost

like a real date. She had to admit to the sadness she felt over it not being real.

"Both Zach and Tony have a photograph of Martin. Chances are, he'll stay out of sight but if they see him, we can grab him. And this will all be over."

Both of them kept checking traffic through the windows and the mirrors. There was no sign of the motorcycle or the dark sedan. Though Martin was clearly unstable, he wasn't stupid. He may have rented or borrowed a car.

Once they were at the bistro, Noah requested a table close to the sidewalk. Lani spotted Tony Knight immediately. He was at the bar sipping a soda. A baseball hat covered his brown hair. Lani didn't know that much about Tony. She hadn't worked with him much. She did know that he'd been Jordan's best friend.

It wasn't until they had ordered that she noticed Zach on the other side of the street standing at the window of a bookstore that stayed open late. A moment before, Zach had been seated at a table inside the bookstore, his face hidden behind a magazine.

Lani glanced around not seeing anyone with Martin's build. He could be peering at them through any one of the windows of the high-rise across the street.

"We should make it look like you and I are really enjoying each other's company," said Noah.

"Who would have thought my acting skills would come in handy?" The only problem was, she wasn't acting. She leaned her head closer to him, resting her chin in her palm and gazing into his eyes. "How's this?" That spark of attraction caused a flare in Noah's eyes. She wasn't imagining things, he must feel it too. She pushed aside the intense feelings and opted for humor. "See, I'm acting like I'm hanging on your every word."

"If only." Noah snorted a laugh, which made her laugh too.

He bent his head as well and continued to laugh. They talked through the meal and a cup of tea. Lani loved hearing the stories of the pranks the Jamesons had pulled on each other as kids.

Once the meal was over, Lani rose to her feet. Zach had repositioned himself on the same side of the street as the bistro. He stood beside a food cart holding a hot dog. Tony still sat at the bar.

When she turned to step out to the sidewalk, Noah put his hand on her back and leaned close to her. Anyone watching would think they were on a date.

Noah glanced at the windows of the high-rise and then up the busy street. She turned to face him. He leaned in and kissed her on the cheek. The kiss, though brief, melted her feet in her shoes. His hand lingered on her neck.

"So it looks like a real date?" Her voice held a note of bitterness. "That's what the kiss was about, right?"

He nodded, and she thought her heart would break. It was all just part of the job. And Martin hadn't even made an appearance. They both got into the car. No one could see them in here.

Noah stared at the steering wheel. "Lani?"

"Yes?"

He turned to face her, his eyes filled with warmth. He leaned closer to her. His Adam's apple moved up and down.

Feeling the pull of his gaze, she leaned toward him.

He covered her mouth with his. His hand rested on her neck and she scooted even closer to him.

He pulled his hand away from her neck. "You deserve a real kiss, not something for show." He lowered his head. "Sorry if I crossed a boundary." His forehead creased, and he leaned toward her, his eyes searching. "Lani, I care about you so much. This is such an impossible situation. The unit needs me as chief."

"I know." She nodded even as the tears warmed her eyes. She was still light-headed from the power of his kiss. She touched her palm to her chest. Her heart was racing. "I suppose we did cross a line. But I don't regret it." She was glad she knew what a real kiss from Noah was like. Even if it could only be this one time.

Noah put the key in the ignition as a faint smile graced his face. "Yeah, me either. But now we have to go back to being just friends."

Her stomach twisted into a knot. "Agreed."

While Noah healed from his injuries, they spent more time together out in the open at the park and in other high-profile public places with no sign of Martin for days. He sent her no texts or notes. She was beginning to wonder if maybe after injuring Noah, Martin had skipped town. Somehow, she didn't think he would give up his obsession that easily.

Once Noah was back to a hundred percent and authorization had been given to put a team in place, they made plans for Lani to ride her bike to a remote part of Flushing Meadows Corona Park. The decision was made to set things up in early evening when there would be fewer people in the park and Lani would look more vulnerable.

The team, which consisted of Reed, Noah, Tony and Lani, met in Noah's office where Lani was fitted with a wire. Noah brought up a map of the park and pointed out each man's position in relationship to where Lani would fake an injury on her bike.

Noah pointed to the spots on the map. "I'll have visual on her up here from this gazebo. Tony and Reed, you'll be able to hear her. If we need to shift positions, I will radio you. Wait for my signal before we move in."

Reed gave Lani a hug before he and Tony took off to drive to the park and get in position. So there was no chance of Martin knowing what was going on, Lani and Noah would leave in separate vehicles.

Once Tony and Reed were gone, Noah closed out the program that had the map of the park. "Give us a half hour before you take off."

"Okay."

"I'm not wild about this plan," he said. "I'm concerned about the level of danger it puts you in. You're still new to being an officer."

"Noah, I want this to be over with. If this doesn't draw him out, nothing will." A knot of tension formed at the base of Lani's neck. Her chest felt tight. She'd be lying to herself if she said she wasn't afraid. "I could use a hug."

He gathered her into his arms. She relished the warmth and safety of his embrace. They lingered for a long moment before he pulled back and gave her a smile that warmed her to the marrow. She'd settle for being Noah's friend if that was all he could offer.

Scotty let out a little protest groan from the corner of the room where he rested on his bed.

Noah laughed. "He hates it when he's not part of the

hug." Noah kneeled. "Come here, boy." Scotty trotted over to him and Noah rubbed his ears.

Lani kneeled as well. "Who's a good boy?" Scotty licked her face.

Noah locked her in his gaze. "Take him with you... for my piece of mind. Scotty will protect you until I can get there."

Lani continued to stroke Scotty's square head. She petted his back and he leaned against her. "Okay."

Noah opened a drawer and pulled out his shoulder holster with his handgun. He slipped into a jacket. He squeezed her shoulder. "Let's do this." He stepped out of the office. She stood at the door and watched him walk past Sophie's desk and then disappear down a hallway.

Lani turned her attention back to Scotty. "Okay, I guess it's just you and me." Lani left headquarters with Scotty. Her mountain bike was already loaded on top of her car. She drove out to the park. At one point while she switched lanes, she thought she caught a glimpse of a motorcycle several lanes over before a car blocked her view.

A van without windows was parked on the far end of the lot. The techs were in there listening to all the communication. The other three officers had probably parked in a different lot. Another car with a bike on top of it pulled into the lot. She didn't have a clear view of the driver. Her heart pounded all the same.

Lani turned her head sideways speaking into her shoulder where the microphone had been placed. "I'm in place. ETA to the spot on the trail is about ten minutes." She unloaded her bike. Earlier in the day, she had parked where her car could be seen from the street so that if Martin was watching her, he would know she had plans to go for a bike ride. The trail she would be going on was one she frequented.

Scotty would run beside. If he was in the habit of doing that with Noah, he'd probably get the idea.

She stared out at the Unisphere, a giant metal globe which was the central feature of the park, visible from almost anywhere. The park had a museum, zoo and amusement rides for kids, but she would be avoiding those for a quieter spot. Flushing Meadows Corona Park was big, the second largest after Central Park, providing lots of places for Martin to make his move.

Her heart was pounding from a mixture of excitement and fear by the time she got on her bike and headed toward the trail. She called over her shoulder. "Come on, Scotty." Scotty ran after her while still on the leash.

In fading light of day, she encountered only a few other bicyclists and walkers. When she looked over her shoulder, Scotty was bounding behind her. She pedaled, watching the trail up ahead. Other side trails intersected with this one. She came to a crossroads, still seeing no other bicyclists in either direction. When she slowed, she could hear Scotty panting.

She arrived at the spot where she was to wait to see if Martin showed up. She lay down her bike, gave a little yell as though she were injured and sat down. Scotty came up beside her.

She listened to the rustling of the fall leaves. A gust of wind pulled some from the trees and sent them swirling through the air. Her heart pounded in her chest.

She tuned her ears hoping to hear the whirring of bike pedals or the pounding of feet on the trail. She knew that Reed was about fifty yards down the hill and Tony was positioned even closer on the other side in a large grove of trees. Up the hill, the gazebo where Noah waited hidden from view was barely visible through the rust- and red-colored bushes.

Pounding footsteps caused her to turn her head back around. In the twilight, she saw a female jogger with reflective gear on coming toward her.

When the woman got close to Lani, she stopped, still jogging in place. "You okay?" She was out of breath.

"Yes, just resting," said Lani.

The woman nodded and disappeared down a side trail. Her footsteps fading into silence.

Scotty hunkered over to her and sat down beside her, pressing his solid muscular body against her side.

Lani turned her attention back to her surroundings. She glanced back up to the gazebo. Her breath caught in her throat. A shadowy figure was moving toward Noah's hiding place.

FIFTEEN

Noah peered through the lattice of the gazebo using small binoculars. He could see Lani's bright purple workout suit as well as the reflective gear she wore on her feet and headband. Scotty's reflective collar was visible as well in the gray light of evening.

He let out a heavy breath. So far nothing.

His chest squeezed tight over the anxiety he battled about putting Lani in this kind of danger. He understood her frustration and that she wanted to get on with her life and her training as a K-9 cop. Rookies always felt like they needed to prove themselves. That had to be part of it.

He could see her blond ponytail bobbing as she petted Scotty who had come to sit beside her. He cared about her so much and wanted more than a friendship with her. He knew it would be out of place for him to ask her to transfer to a different unit in the NYPD. She had her heart set on being a K-9 cop.

He heard a scuffle behind him. Noah turned just as a huge muscular body came down on him like a ton of bricks. Martin Fisher had found him. Though he was caught off guard, and he was in a kneeling position,

Noah managed to angle slightly away so he didn't take the full impact of Martin falling on him.

Tech support and the other men couldn't hear the sound of the fight unless he radioed them. Only Lani was wired.

Martin placed all his weight on Noah's shoulder, pinning him in place. He raised a fist to deliver a blow to Noah's neck.

Noah gasped for air from the impact.

Martin grabbed Noah's hair on the crown of his head and pressed his face close to Noah's.

"You stay away from her. She's mine."

Even in the dim light, Noah could make out the arched eyebrows and gaunt features. Martin's eyes held the glazed quality of a man who was living in his own world.

Even as he fought for breath, he raised his free hand and managed to get a punch into Martin's side and then his stomach.

The man groaned from the pain of impact but remained in place. Martin's strength was stunning. Martin landed more blows to Noah's face and then to his solar plexus.

Again, Noah fought for breath.

He used his knee to pummel Martin's back. The move seemed to take Martin by surprise. The weight on Noah's shoulder lessoned.

Noah struggled to twist free.

Martin hit him again. This time in the head. The blows left Noah dazed.

Martin shifted so both of his knees shoved into Noah's stomach. Reaching for his gun was not possible.

Martin pulled a needle from his back pocket. Uncapped it and held it up.

Noah fought harder to break free using his knees again to throw Martin off kilter before he could stick the needle in Noah. Jordan had died from a drug injection. More evidence that Noah was in a fight with Jordan's killer.

The distant bark of a dog, of his dog, reached the gazebo. The barking grew louder and more intense. Lani must have seen Martin enter the gazebo and was headed up the hill with Scotty.

Martin's eyes grew round. He looked one way and then the other.

"Lani and the dog are on their way," said Noah.

"She's got quite a hike up the hill," said Martin. The inflection in his words gave away that he was afraid.

He grabbed Noah's radio off his shoulder and tore it free. Noah reached for Martin's shirt collar and yanked hard enough to put Martin off balance. Martin clawed at Noah's face and then slammed his fist back into Noah's chest. Noah released his grip on Martin as he wheezed in air. He felt like he was breathing through a straw.

Martin hit Noah a couple more times. Noah feared he would pass out. Fueled by mental instability, Martin's strength was almost superhuman.

In the seconds when Noah was trying to orient himself and regain focus, Martin bolted from the gazebo.

Still dizzy, Noah leaped to his feet and took off after Martin, who disappeared into some brush. He must have dropped the needle somewhere. It would be too dangerous to hold on to an uncapped needle. He glanced around as he hurried after Martin. Finding the needle would be close to impossible. Now he wished Scotty was with him. The dog would have no trouble tracking Martin.

Noah ran after him, still not at full strength. Keeping his eyes on the shaking branches that indicated which direction Martin had gone, Noah willed himself to move faster.

He took in as deep a breath as he dared. His ribs still hurt from his injury.

Noah saw a flash of color. Martin had veered off the path into the thick of the trees. There was still enough brush and foliage on the trees to conceal him.

Aware that he risked hitting an innocent bystander if he wasn't careful, Noah pulled his gun.

Scotty's bark persisted, dying off now and then when he must have been sniffing the ground. A fearful person on the run emitted a scent that was easy for dogs to track. Noah dashed into the trees, he turned one way and then another, studying the landscape for any sign of movement. He had to assume that Reed and Tony would move in as well. Lani could communicate with them.

A squirrel ran up a thick oak tree and he could hear the traffic on the expressway far in the distance. He turned in a half circle, still looking. Martin was dressed in neutral colors, tan and browns, that would make it hard to spot him. He saw a jogger in bright colors on another path.

Noah stepped deeper into the trees. Though he could not say why, his cop instinct told him that Martin was close. He could feel the weight of a gaze on him. The brush got thicker and more overgrown as he got farther from the trail. His pulse drummed in his ears. He pushed a tree branch out of the way. He had to bend his knees and almost crawl to get through.

Somewhere off to the side a tree branch broke. A woman on a bicycle dressed in neon colors whizzed by on a parallel trail.

A weight landed on Noah's back and pushed down on his shoulders. Noah fell forward when Martin jumped him from behind. He fell on a bush that collapsed beneath him. Branches scratched his face.

Martin wrapped his hands around Noah's neck. The move meant Noah's arms and legs were still free. Martin's he-man grip around Noah's neck had the potential to be lethal. Noah's vision filled with black dots as he tried to twist free. Firing his gun would put innocent people at too great a risk.

He needed to break free before he lost consciousness or couldn't breathe anymore. He could feel Martin's breath on his ear as he stood behind Noah and suctioned even tighter around Noah's neck. Noah jabbed an elbow into Martin's stomach.

The blow didn't even seem to faze Martin. He continued to cut off Noah's air. Noah knew the light-headedness meant he was about to pass out. He struggled for breath. With the final bit of energy and focus he had left, he jabbed Martin three times with his elbow. Martin let up on Noah's neck and stepped back.

Noah choked and gasped for air even as he lunged at Martin. The attack had left Noah weak.

The sound of Scotty working his way toward them grew even louder. He heard sirens in the distance. Lani must have called in reinforcements. Tony and Reed must be moving in as well. Martin's eyes grew round with fear, and he dashed into the underbrush.

Still unfocused and stumbling around from nearly being choked to death, Noah spotted the purple of Lani's outfit moving through the trees. Scotty ran up ahead of her. Reed and Tony were close behind her.

"Boy am I glad to see you. He went off this way."

Scotty had already picked up the scent and was pushing through the underbrush like a four-legged bulldozer. They raced after Scotty as he led them toward a trail. Scotty bolted along with Lani and Noah at his heels. The dog stopped, sniffed the ground and then left the trail. Noah couldn't see Martin anywhere, but he trusted Scotty's nose.

The sirens grew louder. No doubt, officers would be in all the parking lots that surrounded the park. When he glanced through the trees, he saw Reed and Tony searching as well. Martin wasn't going to get away this time.

Lani spoke into her hidden radio. "I think we're in the northeast corner of the park. I'm with Noah."

They continued to work their way through the trees. Scotty lost the scent when they came to an open area where there were several sleeping bags stuffed in the brush and evidence that a fire had been built.

They came toward a busier part of the park where parents watched their children on the carousel. Martin could easily fade into the crowd.

Scotty continued to sniff the ground. All the human smells were making it hard for him to find Martin's scent.

"Let's keep looking. Uniformed officers are going to be in all the parking lots, so he won't go back to his car if he parked in one of them." Noah commanded Scotty to follow him. They searched the area where the crowds were coming to the street that bordered the park.

The sound of New York coming alive at night

reached his ears as they came to the edge of the park. A sea of faces. Martin was smart. He'd stop running and blend in with the crowd.

Scotty heeled beside Noah while Lani walked on the other side of him.

They searched up and down several streets before giving up. If Scotty picked up on Martin's scent at all, he would alert. The dog remained close to Noah, sniffing the air and the ground but not giving any sign that Martin might be close. Noah tried to not give in to the sense of defeat that he felt.

They walked for several more blocks before Lani spoke into the radio. "This is Officer Lani Branson and Chief Noah Jameson. Could you come pick us up? We're headed back toward the northwest entrance to the park."

Maybe one of the other officers was able to nab Martin. Maybe Reed or Tony had caught up with him. From the sound of the sirens, NYPD had pulled out all the stops to try to catch the guy. Somehow, though, he doubted they'd gotten him. Martin was slippery. And he and Lani were the ones who had gotten the closest to him. Noah was 90 percent sure Martin had eluded them.

The only thing that was clear to Noah was that as long as Martin was on the streets neither he nor Lani was safe.

As Noah drove Lani back to her house, she could feel a weariness settling into her muscles. Once again, Martin had escaped them only to fade into the crowd of people. News had come over the radio that a stolen car had been left at one of the parking lots surrounding the park. Martin had probably arrived in that.

Noah had not spoken much since he had offered to

take her home. She didn't feel too talkative herself. Now it felt like this thing with Martin would go on forever. Would she be free of him if she moved out of the city? The thought caused her pain; she'd have to leave everything she cared about. Her job, her brother, her home and Noah.

From the backseat, Scotty nudged against her cheek and groaned. The dog was amazing in how he picked up on her mood. She stroked Scotty's square jaw. The thought of not being a K-9 officer would break her heart. The truth was she felt like she was in her element when she worked with the dogs.

Noah cleared his throat. "So you texted Reed?"

"Yes, he just made it home." Noah and Lani had hung around the park to see if there was any sign of Martin and to wait until the vehicle that probably belonged to Martin had been located, which ended up taking a couple of hours. The forensic team was still going over it.

Not catching Martin had triggered a restlessness in Lani. She couldn't stay in limbo for much longer. Something needed to change in her professional and personal life. Reed and Abigail were talking more about wedding plans and finalizing adopting Dominic. Maybe she could look into being a K-9 officer in another borough. Maybe then her intense feelings for Noah would fade. She turned her attention to him.

"Martin attacked you too," she said. "He might do it again."

"I'll be all right," Noah said. "I live in a house with a bunch of Jameson men."

Lani suspected Noah was saying that to keep her from worrying. His father was still in good shape but older. Carter was injured and Zach no longer lived in the house since he'd gotten married.

"I suppose you've got Scotty to protect you, and the other dogs," she said.

"Don't worry about me, Lani." Noah drove a few more blocks before speaking up. "This will go in my report tomorrow, but when Martin attacked me he had a needle with him. Jordan was killed by drug overdose administered with a needle, remember? We have Forensics working with the dogs to find the needle."

"Criminals usually use the same methods most of the time. That certainly makes it more likely that Martin did kill Jordan."

"We don't know anything yet for sure. We need evidence. Katie sometimes comes into headquarters to have lunch with Sophie. If you see her, please don't say anything."

Noah double-parked in front of the house where the glow from the lights in the living room and kitchen indicated that Reed was home.

Noah leaned toward her. "Don't worry about me."

Though she didn't feel it on the inside, she gave Noah a faint smile and reassurance. "You have a good rest of your night, Noah."

Lani hurried up the sidewalk. As she unlocked the door and stepped inside, she heard Noah pulling away from the curb. From the moment she stepped inside her home, something felt wrong. Reed wasn't on the couch or in the kitchen.

"Reed?" No answer.

From inside the garage, Jessie's muffled baying reached Lani's ears. Reed never left the bloodhound in the garage. It was reserved for the upstairs tenant. Lani hurried to her bedroom to grab her gun, pulling her phone out so she could call Noah. He couldn't be more than a few blocks away.

The lights in the house went out. Someone had thrown a breaker. She fumbled with her phone to click on the flashlight. She didn't hear the upstairs tenant walking around. He must be out.

Hands grabbed her from behind jerking her back. She dropped her phone. Before he even spoke, she knew it was Martin.

"You're coming with me. You were meant to be with me."

Lani struggled to twist away. She kicked Martin in the shin, one of the vulnerable parts on the human body. Martin didn't so much as groan in pain. His grip remained locked tight on her. She couldn't get the leverage to try for Martin's knees or his stomach. The other vulnerable parts of the body.

He dragged her across the floor, swinging her around to face the garage door where Jessie was still putting up a fuss. Certainly, the neighbors would begin to wonder what all the noise was about.

"Now open the door," said Martin.

He released her from his grasp. She felt something hard and solid press against her back, a gun.

"Where is Reed?" Her voice trembled. Had Martin killed her brother in order to get to her?

"Open the door," Martin said, his voice filled with rage.

She twisted the knob. Jessie whined when she saw Lani and lunged toward her. The dog was tied up in a corner on a short rope unable to move more than a few feet.

"Doesn't that dog ever shut up? Thought if I put her out here she'd be quiet."

"Not when she's distressed." Lani looked around the garage for something to fight Martin with. The tenant's tools were on the far wall.

Exhausted, Jessie lay down but continued to whine.

"Now go to the outside door and open it." Martin shoved the gun in her back as a reminder of who was in control.

She swung open the door. Martin had parked his car in a side street where no one would see it.

"Put your hands behind you."

Lani hesitated, trying to figure out a way to get the gun from Martin.

"Do it now!" Martin's voice filled with rage.

Reluctantly, she did as she was told even as she looked around for an escape route. The next-door neighbor had a high fence in his backyard. No one would be out at this hour anyway.

Martin secured her hands.

She felt a pinprick in her left shoulder and then the sense that some venomous substance was moving through her veins.

"Just to make sure you don't try to get away." Martin opened the back car door and shoved her in.

Lani had a fearful moment of wondering if whatever Martin had given her was going to kill her. As they rolled through the streets, she realized it was probably just meant to weaken her so she wouldn't fight back. She remained conscious, but it would take all her strength to even sit up in the car, let alone find a way to escape.

She was trapped in a car with a volatile man who had probably already murdered once before.

SIXTEEN

The phone call awoke Noah from a deep sleep. It was his brother Zach. Noah still felt groggy. "Yes?"

"Reed just phoned in. Martin came to their house and disabled Reed so he could kidnap Lani. Reed got away and was able to get the license plate number of the sedan as he chased Martin down. Reed lost him, but Patrol spotted the sedan at the marina. We think he has her on the boat."

Noah's head felt like it might explode from the news Zach delivered. His stomach turned to a hard rock. He was still trying to wake up, still trying to process what Zach was telling him.

He threw back the covers, swung his legs to the floor and bolted to his feet in one swift motion. "Get the coast guard involved. I'm going to commission a chopper. We need to find that boat."

"Ten-four."

"Keep me posted," said Noah. "Tracking dogs and search and rescue on standby. I'm taking Scotty with me."

As he dressed, his heart squeezed tight. He bent over from the fear that washed through him. Lani was in

Martin's clutches. There was no telling what Martin might do. He straightened and took in a breath. He had to stay strong for Lani.

He headed toward the door. "Come on, Scotty, we got work to do."

Scotty trailed behind him.

Within half an hour, he was at the police helipad. Reed met him there with a scarf that had belonged to Lani. It had her scent on it in case they had to track her that way.

With the blade whirring, creating a tremendous wind, he loaded Scotty into the backseat, and he got in the front with the pilot. He put his headset on. His stomach lurched as they rose into the air. He'd been in a chopper dozens of times. The tightening in his stomach was about Lani. His world would fall apart if something happened to her.

When Noah glanced over his shoulder, Scotty sat firmly in the seat, his head held high and alert. Something about seeing his partner ready to work and face whatever lay ahead gave him strength.

News came from the coast guard that they thought they had spotted the boat headed toward the East River but the boat had evaded them. The helicopter pilot headed in that direction. Noah stared down below to search the water. There were no flashing lights indicating a boat down there. Maybe Martin had turned off the lights on the boat to avoid detection.

Noah commanded the chopper to fly lower. His eyes searched everywhere. For Lani's sake, he would not let his fear overtake him. He needed to remain cool and focused if he was to find her and save her from Martin.

He thought he saw shadows that looked different from the rest of the water.

He gave the pilot the signal to lose elevation.

"Any lower and I'm going to end up in the water." The pilot spoke through his headset. "Night vision goggles in that compartment by your seat."

Noah put on the goggles and continued to survey the water. He leaned out of the chopper even more. Then he saw it. It was not that an outline of the boat came into view, but he saw the effects of a boat on the water, the triangular shaped ridges created in the wake of a boat pushing through the current.

"Can you angle off toward there and shine the light?" he spoke to the pilot.

"Gonna have to get a little elevation first," said the pilot.

It took a few minutes for the chopper to get higher and then switch on the light. It was a boat all right, headed toward North Brother Island, an abandoned island between the Bronx and Rikers Island.

"Back off. I don't want him to know we're using the chopper to search for him. Make it look like we're moving away from him." If Martin figured out he'd been seen, it could endanger Lani even more. "You've got to put me down on the other side of North Brother where he's not likely to see or hear that we landed there."

"That's a tall order," said the pilot. "I'll do my best."

The pilot gained elevation and angled away, making it look like they were headed toward the Bronx. Martin would just think the chopper was on a regular patrol or was a private hire for a tourist. It looked like Martin was taking the boat to dock on the north side of the island. The pilot came in low on the west side. There were numerous buildings that would block the view of his landing. The buildings, most of them brick, were crumbling and overgrown with plant life.

Before the turn of the last century, the island had housed people with infectious diseases. After that it had been a home for veterans and heroin addicts. But no one had been on the island since the early 1960s and it was illegal to go there. It was a perfect hiding place for someone like Martin.

The pilot brought them down in an open area and killed the motor.

"Wait here for me," said Noah to the pilot as he jumped out and commanded Scotty to get out as well. Once the noise of the chopper died down, Noah phoned Zach and let him know where he was. Zach promised that backup was on the way. It would take them a while to get there.

Noah pulled the scarf Reed had given him out of his jacket. He held it to his own nose, drinking in the light floral scent of Lani's perfume. His heart filled with longing. He had to find her. He put the scarf away.

They would need to get over to the other side of the island where Martin had docked before Scotty could pick up a scent. He pulled his flashlight out. Once he got close to where Martin had Lani, he'd have to navigate in the darkness. He tugged on Scotty's leash.

"Let's go find her."

The dog took off running. Noah kept up with the steady pace that Scotty set.

Martin finally kidnapping Lani instead of just tormenting her probably indicated that something inside of his obsessed brain had snapped.

Yes, backup was on its way, but Noah knew that right

now Lani's life hung in the balance. It was up to him and his K-9 partner to bring her home safe.

Lani could feel the waves hitting the boat as it chugged through the water and finally came to a stop. She'd been in such a weakened state from the drugs that Martin had had no trouble lifting her onto the boat from the car. Only now as the boat was docking did she feel the drugs wearing off and her strength returning. She had no idea where he'd taken her. Lying on her stomach with her hands tied behind her had not given her much of a view of her surroundings.

Martin pressed his foot on her calf. "Don't try anything. I need to tie the boat off."

She heard his feet pound across the deck and then onto the pier.

She attempted to roll over and to sit up. Even that took substantial effort. All she could see were shadows on the landscape and stars twinkling overhead.

Martin climbed back on the boat. He crossed his arms and stared at her. "Well don't you look pretty in the moonlight. My beautiful Katie girl." His voice held a slimy quality.

His words sent a new wave of fear through her. So in his twisted mind, Martin had become convinced that she was Katie. If she broke the news to him that she wasn't Katie, what would the effect be? Would it put him over the edge? She knew he was capable of violence. Or was the lie so entrenched in his mind that reality could not get in?

He stomped over to her. "Let me help you to your feet, my dear." He cupped her elbow.

The boat rocked in the water as she stared around at

what looked like an end-of-the-world scene. Buildings crumbling and leaning to one side, piles of rubble everywhere, the plant life was consuming what men had built. This had to be North Brother Island. She'd seen pictures but never been here. Though it was illegal to step onto the island, urban adventurers and teenagers on a dare still came here from time to time.

"Why have you brought me here?"

"It's my hiding place, my sanctuary. We won't be here for long. Just until the heat is off of us. Then I'll take you to someplace nice for our honeymoon." He tugged on her elbow. "Come, I'll show you."

He led her to the edge of the boat. Lani steeled herself against the encroaching panic. It did not appear that he intended to harm her...at least not for now.

He climbed over the railing of the boat. "I'm going to have to lift you out."

"I think I can crawl over." She still felt weak from having been drugged. It would be a balancing act with her hands tied behind her back, but the thought of Martin touching her sent chills all over her skin.

"I said, let me lift you." A note of rage had entered his voice.

So that's what it took. If she was at all disagreeable, if she didn't do exactly as he requested, he might turn on her. Was he capable of murder? If he *was* Jordan Jameson's killer, then the answer was yes. She had to assume so.

"Okay, Martin, have it your way."

He wrapped his strong arms around her middle and lifted her like she was made of paper. Again, she was reminded of how she was no match for him physically. Her best hope was to try to outwit him. Maybe if she played along with his bizarre fantasy, his defenses would go down.

He sat her on the dilapidated pier which squeaked from the weight of two people. Some of the wooden floorboards were missing, offering a view of the dark water flowing below.

Again, he cupped her elbow with his hand. "Follow me." He pulled a flashlight out of his pocket and turned it on.

Even if she could get away from him and back to the boat, she'd never operated a boat before. Though she'd watched other people. He led her past a brick building of Victorian design. They stepped through the thick brush and overgrown plant life.

They walked past theater chairs that looked like they were set up for an outdoor program though the chairs were more moss than wood. They entered another brick building. Holes in the roof allowed some moonlight to illuminate the area. Part of the wall had crumbled. She could see an iron bed frame leaning to one side due to a broken leg, and a sink and tub in the far corner.

"This way," said Martin.

Beside a spiral staircase, Martin had made a sort of camp. He had a propane stove, two cots with sleeping bags on them, a supply of canned goods and some other personal items. He gestured toward one of the beds. "Have a seat?"

When she sat down, one of the items on the bed looked like a photo album.

"I'm going to build us a fire to keep us warm," said Martin. He rubbed his hands together.

"Could you untie me, please, Martin?" She tried to sound sweet instead of demanding.

Martin didn't answer right away. He turned and stared at her. It was too dark to read the minute details of his expression. His body language suggested he was relaxed.

"I suppose it wouldn't hurt. Tonight is a special night." He pulled a knife from his shirt pocket. She shifted so her bound hands were toward him. He sawed away at the rope. "You have to promise me, you'll sit still."

"I promise." She sounded sugary sweet. Who would have thought her acting skills would come in handy yet again?

She saw then that he had placed some rocks in a circle and had a supply of wood already stacked and ready to go. While Martin's back was to her as he built the fire, she flipped open the photo album.

Shock spread through her as she turned the pages. Martin had clipped the news stories of Jordan's death. There were photos of Katie at the funeral and standing in the driveway of the Rego Park house. All taken from a distance. There were also drawings of Katie and a poem written to her.

Lani remembered what the psychologist had said about obsession being a twisted, unpredictable condition. The object of desire can just as quickly become the object of hate.

As he built the fire, Martin's shirt rode up to reveal he had shoved the gun in the waistband of his jeans.

She closed the photo album softly, debating if she should try to grab the gun while he was distracted with building the fire. If she failed, he might become violent. Rage would only make him stronger.

Once the fire was going, he turned to face her. "Why

don't you rustle up something for us to eat." The shadow of flames from the fire danced across his face and in his dull, dead eyes.

"Sure, Martin, I can do that." Every muscle in her body felt tight as she rose to her feet and stepped over to where the cookstove had been set on a makeshift table fashioned from bricks and a board.

Somewhere in the distance a bird made a sound that resembled a scream. The brutality of the noise startled her. She remembered reading that North Brother Island was a bird sanctuary.

Her heart pounded as she grabbed a can of beans and the can opener. She lit the stove, raising her gaze slightly to assess her surroundings. Her only hope would be to get to that boat. If she could disable or restrain Martin, she had some chance of figuring out how to operate it and escaping. The only way she could make that happen would be to surprise Martin, and she needed some kind of weapon. He was stronger than her, but she was quicker and understood how to use his strength against him because of her training.

"I know what you are thinking about." His voice pelted her back like tight, hard balls of hail.

She turned slowly to face him.

He held the gun on her. His lip curled up at one end of his mouth.

She swallowed to get rid of the lump in her throat. "I was only thinking about you, Martin." Not a total lie. He continued to stare at her in a way that unnerved her. She had to find a way to reassure him, so he would relax and let his defenses down. If his paranoia went into overdrive, there was no telling what he would do.

"I'm just going to cook us a nice meal here and we can enjoy it…together."

He let the gun fall by his side. Her little act of compliance had relaxed him.

She turned her back, put the pan on the stove and stirred the beans. Her stomach was in a tight knot, but her voice had given nothing away.

As she stirred, watching the beans bubble from the heat, she wondered what had happened to her brother. Was Reed alive? Her heart squeezed tight with angst. She massaged her sternum, trying to take in a deep breath. She couldn't get distracted by such dark thoughts. She needed to stay in the moment. No one was coming for her. If she was to escape, it was up to her.

She wondered too if she could get Martin to talk, would he confess to killing Jordan? That was dicey territory. She knew from having witnessed police interrogations that with a stable person, the desire to confess was almost overwhelming. But with Martin, it was hard to know what his response would be. Martin might want to brag about what he'd done…if he had killed Jordan. Or making him face reality might send him over the edge.

She prayed for guidance.

God, show me how to get away.

SEVENTEEN

Noah and Scotty moved silently through the thick un-derbrush. He'd commanded Scotty not to bark. Though the barking often intimidated and paralyzed a criminal on the run, Noah thought the better strategy would be to surprise Martin.

He heard the lapping of the water before he saw the shoreline and Martin's boat.

Noah could see Martin's boat bobbing at the dock. He hurried over to it where Scotty picked up a scent right away, jerking on the leash.

From the pace that Scotty was setting with his nose close to the ground, Noah knew the scent was hot.

They hurried past dark buildings overtaken by plant life, past piles of bricks and through thick brush.

Scotty stopped abruptly and sat back on his haunches, a hard alert. Noah kneeled beside Scotty, stroking his head and his back. Noah didn't see anything, but if Scotty said they were close, he'd trust his dog's nose over his own senses anytime.

He heard birds feeding in the distance and waves hitting the shore and then…the faint sound of voices.

Crouching, Noah moved in toward the sound. He

signaled for Scotty to follow. The dog trailed behind
as they approached, padding softly. Scotty seemed to
instinctually know he needed to be quiet.

They pressed against the brick wall. On the other side
just feet away, Lani spoke in soothing tones to Martin.
Above him was a rectangular opening that must have
been a window at one time in the brick building.

"I see that you put together a photo album of Katie."
There was a long pause. "You know that I'm not really
Katie, right, Martin?"

More silence.

Even though a wall divided them, Noah could sense
the tension and hear it in Lani's voice.

Lani prompted. "Martin?"

"Shut up," Martin shouted.

Martin was wound as tight as a coil. Noah could hear
pots and pans being banged together. His feet stomped
the ground.

Was Lani trying to bring Martin back to a lucid moment with her question?

"What happened to Jordan, Martin?"

He still wasn't sure what she was doing. Was Lani
trying to get a confession out of Martin? Or she might
be trying to push him over the edge to create an opportunity for escape. If he knew anything, it was that
Martin was volatile and unpredictable. All of it was
dangerous. Lani still thought she was on her own and
had no other choice but to take such a risk.

It was time to move closer and wait for the chance to
jump in and extract Lani and, hopefully with Scotty's
help, subdue Martin. Noah gave a hand signal for Scotty
to follow. He couldn't wait for backup. They circled

around the building using the thick brush as cover. Part of the wall where Martin had Lani was deteriorated.

Scotty pressed in close to him as Noah raised his head and assessed the situation.

"You ruined our nice dinner. I know what you are trying to do. You're not going to get away." Martin was in the process of tying up Lani. He bound her wrists in front of her. "I was meant to be with Katie. You're not Katie. I know you're not Katie. Katie is soft and quiet. I don't want anything to do with you. You are a betrayer."

Martin had a gun shoved in the waistband of his belt. A blazing fire crackled. A pan was overturned in the dirt and beans had been spilled.

Once Lani was tied up, Martin paced, rubbing his hands through his hair, his fingers stiff and clawlike.

He continued to pace and get more and more worked up. "You talk. You talk way too much."

Scotty was so close Noah could feel the dog's breath on his cheek. Noah inhaled deeply and pulled his gun. There was never going to be an exact right time. He rose to his feet and aimed his gun knowing that Scotty would jump in at the right moment if needed.

"Put your hands up, Martin."

Both Lani and Martin looked surprised. Martin reached around to his back but then grabbed Lani, yanking her to her feet and holding the gun to her temple.

"Come one step closer and she gets a bullet in her head," said Martin. "I don't care about her anymore. It's Katie I want."

Noah tensed. The last thing he wanted was for Lani to be in danger like this.

"Put the gun down, Martin," said Noah, taking a step toward him, weapon aimed at Martin's chest. Noah didn't want anyone to die here tonight, but sometimes a police officer had no choice. He just wasn't sure if he could pull the shot off without risking Lani's life.

"Come on, Martin, if you kill me—" Lani spoke between jagged breaths "—we can't be together."

Martin jerked Lani around. "I don't want to be with you. I see that now. It's always been Katie. Only Katie."

Noah was afraid Martin's gun would go off accidentally. He was clearly unhinged.

Scotty lunged out of the brush and started barking at Martin. Martin aimed his gun at Scotty.

"No," Lani and Noah shouted at the same time.

Heart racing, Lani slammed against Martin by swinging her bound hands against him. The bullet he'd fired at Scotty went wild.

Noah commanded Scotty to back off.

Martin whirled around and aimed the gun at Lani. "You're coming with me." Then he turned, pointing the gun at the dog and then at Noah. "Try anything and she dies. Put your hands up. Drop your gun."

Scotty growled but stood his ground.

As if to make his point, Martin grabbed Lani by her collar, jerking her back. The cold metal of the gun pressed against her temple. Sweat formed on her forehead, and she took in shallow breaths.

"It's all right, Noah, do what he says." She nodded. Scotty had almost died for her. She couldn't face losing either of them. She'd find a way to get away. And she knew Noah and Scotty wouldn't give up either.

"Drop it now. Toss it toward me," said Martin.

In the seconds that Noah hesitated to respond, she

could tell he was strategizing, trying to figure out the best way to get them out of this situation.

Martin wrapped his free hand around the back of her neck, squeezing tight. He spoke through gritted teeth. "Drop it now."

Noah tossed the gun in Martin's direction. Martin kicked it hard, sending it sailing into the brush. No way would Noah be able to find it quickly.

"If you or that dog comes after me, she is dead, do you hear me?"

Noah nodded. Despite his seeming surrender, Lani knew that he was probably already trying to come up with a plan of attack.

"Now go." Martin pushed on Lani's shoulder to get her to turn and then pressed the gun in her back. Martin craned his neck to check on Noah. "I meant what I said. Try anything and she dies."

Lani dared not turn to see Noah. She'd never been so happy in her life when he and Scotty popped up from behind the rubble. She wasn't in this alone.

"Run," said Martin. "Back to the boat."

Lani took off at a jog slowed by her hands being tied in front of her.

She had every confidence that Noah and Scotty would be after them as soon as Martin couldn't see them anymore. She also sensed that Martin was serious about killing her. Whatever attachment he'd had to her was gone, now that he had experienced the reality of being with her.

Her foot caught on a root and she fell. She twisted to one side to avoid the full impact of falling on her face.

"Get up," said Martin.

"I'd have better balance if you would untie me."

"Quit trying to trick me. I see now you are nothing like my Katie girl." He glanced around nervously and then pointed the gun at her. "I said, get up."

She managed to stand by anchoring her hands in front of her and pushing up with her legs. Still off balance, she swayed when she straightened her torso.

They took off at a steady pace. Once they were free of the tangle of undergrowth and rubble, Lani broke into a jog. She could hear the waves hitting the shore as they drew closer to the boat. Martin's footsteps pounded behind her.

They arrived at the dock.

"Get on the boat." Martin glanced around.

Lani didn't see Noah anywhere but that didn't mean he wasn't right behind them. He and Scotty were probably hidden in the shadows. Once Martin took off in the boat, there was no chance for Noah to get to her. She had to stall for time.

Lani lifted her hands. "I can't step over that rim with my hands tied."

Martin seemed distracted. He stalked toward some trees, aiming his gun at one point and then at another. He turned and stared up the path where they'd just run.

"Martin, you have to cut me loose so I can get into the boat."

He turned back to face her as though seeing her for the first time. He stalked back over to the dock. "I know your game." His wild eyes seemed to burn right through her. Her heart beat faster, and her throat went dry. He lifted her up and put her on the boat as if she was a feather.

She knew in that moment, he would only keep her alive as long as she was of use to him. Holding the gun to her head and threatening to shoot had been enough to make Noah hold back to keep her from being killed. Once Martin was away from the island and there was no danger of being caught, she suspected he'd shoot her and toss her body in the East River.

Frantic, she glanced around again hoping to see some sign that Noah was close.

After unwinding the rope that kept the boat attached to the dock, Martin got onto the boat as well.

She sat on the deck with the autumn breeze making her skin prickle.

Martin got back on the boat and started the engine.

She leaned forward, praying that she would find a way to escape. Praying that Noah would get to her before it was too late.

EIGHTEEN

Noah shivered as he treaded water underneath the dock in the East River. Had he made a mistake to plan his attack this way? He'd gotten to the boat only seconds before he heard Martin coming with Lani through the brush. They had been slowed by Lani being tied up and she had stumbled. There hadn't been time to climb on the boat and hide.

Martin seemed to have a sixth sense about when he was about to be caught. Noah wanted to wait until Martin's defenses were down. There would be no place for Martin to run once the boat was in open water.

He could hear Martin walking around on deck and the boat engine roared to life. As it backed away from the dock, Noah grabbed rope that wrapped around the boat. He'd left Scotty hidden on the shore. He knew he could trust Scotty to stay put until he could come back for him.

The boat putted along. Martin couldn't go very fast in the shallow water.

Behind him, Noah saw a blinking light descending not too far from where Scotty was hiding. He heard the distant whir of a helicopter. Backup was here, but they would not get to the boat fast enough.

Martin cursed at the sight of the helicopter.

The boat picked up speed.

Noah pulled himself up and peered above the rim of the boat. Both Lani and Martin had their backs to him. Lani was tied up. Martin's gun was still in his waistband.

He shivered. The wait in the cold water had left his muscles weakened.

The boat was out in the open now, bumping over the waves. It was now or never. The engine was loud enough that Noah thought he could pull himself in without being heard. He gripped the rim of the boat and hoisted himself on deck. He'd been quiet but Lani must have sensed something, because she turned her head slightly sideways.

Still feeling the effects of having been in the water, Noah got to his feet and bolted the short distance to where Martin stood steering the boat. When he was about two feet away, Martin reached for his gun and turned to face him, raising the gun with his finger on the trigger.

Lani kicked at Martin's legs. He didn't fall down, but the move was enough to set him off balance.

The gun went flying across the deck.

Martin turned his attention back to steering. He drove like a wild man, zigzagging and tilting the boat from side to side. The gun moved back and forth across the deck, and Noah plunged to his knees. Lani slid across the deck as well.

The gun was on the other side of the deck when Martin stopped the boat engine.

Still on his knees, Noah crawled toward the gun. Lani's stalker rushed toward him and kicked him hard in the jaw. Pain radiated through Noah's head and he tasted blood.

The boat continued to sway back and forth. Martin edged toward his weapon.

Noah reached out and grabbed his leg at the ankle and yanked him down. Martin flipped over so he was on his back. He dove toward Noah, who dodged out of the way as Martin, with his almost superhuman strength, came down on him.

Meanwhile, Lani was trying to scoot toward the gun even though her hands were tied.

Noah scrambled to his feet and managed to get a kick into Martin's ribs before the other man could stand up. Once he was on his feet, the terrible unbridled fury that was Martin Fisher dove toward Noah. Noah knew he could not match his strength. He'd have to use his agility and quickness to save himself and Lani.

Noah stepped out of the way. Lani was within inches of being able to pick up the gun. Martin backed him up to the railing of the boat and clutched his neck beneath his chin, squeezing hard and pushing Noah backward.

Noah gasped for air, trying to find a way to break free and keep from being shoved overboard. He let go of the railing with one hand to get in a punch to Martin's stomach, which only caused a minor letup in the pressure on his neck.

Martin released his hold and landed a blow to Noah's stomach and then two to his shoulder in rapid succession. That assault weakened Noah, and Martin pushed him overboard. Noah reached up for the railing as he fell backward.

A gunshot went off on deck. Lani must have recovered the gun. The shot had gone wild. She probably couldn't aim with much accuracy with her hands tied.

"You." Martin stomped across the deck. No doubt to snatch the gun from her.

Noah caught the railing as his feet skimmed the surface of the water. He attempted to pull himself back up on deck. He felt weak from fighting and from having been in the cold water. He managed to get back in the boat flopping like a caught fish.

Martin had yanked the gun from Lani and was aiming it at her. Noah summoned up all the strength he had and charged at Martin's back. This time Martin's stomach pressed against the railing. He heard the gun fall in the water.

Noah had had enough. He was weak and tired, but more than anything, he was tired of Martin tormenting Lani.

He let up pressure on Martin's back. Martin swung around, ready to fight. This time Noah was prepared. His opponent tended to go for the stomach or the head. Noah blocked the punch and landed two to his head, which seemed to stun him.

Martin lunged at Noah, but he dodged out of the way and then brought his clenched fists down on Martin's back. He fell on the deck. Noah landed a final blow to his head, which left him dazed but still conscious.

"That rope over there," said Lani, who was trying to scoot toward some cording.

Noah kept his weight on Martin's back while he struggled to get away and cursed at Noah, but his voice was weak from the struggle and having been hit in the head. Lani dragged the rope across the deck until Noah could reach it. He tied Martin's hands and his feet with the single length of rope. He didn't want any chance of him getting away. After Martin was secure, Noah drew his attention to the island. He saw light everywhere, searchlights and flashlights bobbing. A helicopter hovered over the debris and buildings.

"Why don't I get this boat turned around and we can go get Scotty? Looks like there is plenty of help to deal with Martin," said Noah.

"That sounds like a plan," she said. "Noah, is Reed okay?" Her words were drenched in fear.

"Yes, he's the one who was able to track Martin's car to the dock."

"I was so afraid that...you know."

He could hear the fatigue in her voice as well. He moved across the deck so he could untie her hands. His fingers brushed over her palm as he worked the knots free. He clamped his hand on her shoulder and whispered in her ear. "It's over."

She turned toward him, and he gathered her into his arms while she cried. He held her until she pulled away.

She took in a breath and brushed her hair off her face. "I'm okay."

He touched her cheek with the back of his hand. "You sure?"

She nodded.

He hated destroying the tender moment between them. He rose to his feet, restarted the boat and headed toward an open area where he could get turned around. Lani came and stood beside him, squeezing his arm and then leaning against him so their shoulders touched.

It was over. Together, they'd defeated Martin. He'd be locked up, unable to torment anyone anymore.

He liked being this close to Lani. He only wished it could last.

* * *

Once Noah got the boat turned around, Lani watched as they drew closer to the shore of North Brother Island. It looked like the NYPD had gone all out to catch Martin. As they docked, she could hear men shouting at each other and dogs barking. One bark though was distinct. Even before they docked, she saw Scotty bounding toward them. Once they were on the pier, Noah and Lani gathered Scotty into their arms. Scotty licked Noah's face and then Lani's. "Boy, am I glad to see you."

Tony was the first to arrive at the boat with Rusty. He radioed that Noah and Lani had Martin in their custody. A swarm of other officers showed up to haul him away. The rope was taken off Martin and he was handcuffed and led away.

Lani and Noah stood beside Tony while Scotty and Rusty sat at attention.

"So I imagine he's headed to the psych ward," said Lani.

"For starters," said Tony. "They will double lock the doors so he can't hurt you or Katie. Yeah, I saw that photo album he made…weird."

Lani crossed her arms. "I don't think I'm the object of his obsession anymore. I shattered that fantasy when he actually got to spend time with me."

"Well, we'll make sure he can't come near Katie. That guy will be locked up for a long time," Tony said before stalking over to where some of the police officers were gathered.

Lani collapsed on the shore and Noah sat beside her. "I imagine that boat needs to be taken in for evidence."

"I can take it in to dock and make sure the techs

know where to find it." Noah turned to face her. "That way I can give you a ride home in style."

"I'd like that," she said as a feeling she couldn't quite name permeated her awareness. After Noah let the others know what he was doing, he and Lani loaded Scotty onto the boat.

The sun was coming up as they made their way along the East River past Rikers Island, the site of its namesake prison complex. Once they were docked and off the boat, Noah hailed a taxi. He held the door for her.

"For once, I don't have to escort you all the way to your door and make sure Reed is home."

"Not ever again," she said. Her words caused a sadness to flood through her. With Martin in custody, she and Noah would have no reason to work together so closely.

As they stood there facing each other with the sun warming her skin, she wished he would kiss her. It was an unrealistic longing, she knew, but all the same, it was what she wanted.

He touched her cheek lightly. "Get some sleep. We'll see you on duty later."

She nodded and got into the car. She stared through the window at Noah as he spoke on his phone. He probably had hours of work left to wrap up everything related to Martin. As the taxi pulled out onto the street, Lani swiped at her eyes where tears were forming.

She rested her head against the back of the seat letting the sadness wash through her.

NINETEEN

Noah paged through the website that featured pets for adoption, a website different from the Queens shelter website that they had been checking. Lani had suggested it weeks ago, when Oscar had been missing, as a method to find Snapper, Jordan's missing dog. With Martin in custody, Noah finally had a moment to do a search. He could have asked Sophie to do it, but he liked feeling like he was doing something to find Snapper.

They knew the dog was alive. Once in custody, Martin had confessed to Jordan's murder and admitted to keeping Snapper for a while. The psychologist who had conducted the intake interview with Martin assured them that whatever obsession Martin had had with Lani had been broken. Katie had become Martin's only focus.

Noah paged through the pictures. Almost all were mixed breeds or pit bulls. He stopped on a picture of a German shepherd. A double click provided more pictures and the story behind why the dog was available for adoption through a privately-run shelter.

The dog had been found wandering the streets. He was thin and dirty. The description said he had on a black collar, which is what Snapper wore. The shelter had cleaned him up. Noah clicked on the pictures hoping to see Snapper's markings. His heart stopped when a headshot of the dog showed the distinctive horizontal black lines that came out from each of his eyes. This had to be Snapper.

Noah picked up the phone.

A woman with a chipper-sounding voice answered.

"I'm Chief Noah Jameson of the NYC K-9 Command Unit. I have some questions for you about one of the dogs you have on your website, the German shepherd with the dark lines by his eyes."

"You're not going to believe this, but he was adopted less than two hours ago. I handled the adoption myself."

Noah's heart sank. Though recovering Snapper would not bring his brother back, it would provide some healing for everyone affected by his death. "Can you give me the name of the person who adopted him?"

The woman did not respond right away. Such information was probably somewhat private.

"I think that dog might be a highly trained missing police dog," Noah said.

"Oh, I understand. I can look up the information for you." He heard computer keys clicking. "We tried to detect a chip in the dog's shoulder but couldn't find one. It must have migrated. I'm so sorry we couldn't get him back to you. I have the information here on my screen." She read the name and address slowly.

Noah wrote down the information the woman gave him. When he looked up, Lani was standing in his doorway.

After Martin had been taken into custody, she'd requested three days off. Though it was what Noah would have suggested, it seemed a break in character for Lani.

She was all about working no matter what. She hadn't returned any of his texts in the three days she'd been gone.

Today she was dressed in jeans and a kimono-style jacket. She still wasn't ready for duty. With Martin finally locked away, he had assumed she would return to her training with a vengeance.

"You look like you've heard good news," she said.

"Maybe, I got a lead on where Snapper might be."

"That is good news." There was something about her that was different. "Look, I've been busy with…some things. Sorry I didn't return your texts. I was going to invite you out to coffee at Griffin's but when I went by there, there was a sign on the door. It looks like Lou has finally given up trying to keep the place open."

Noah put his hand over his heart. "That is a loss… a big loss."

The phone rang. Noah picked it up. "Chief Jameson."

"Noah, it's Tony. I just got a call. Martin overpowered a guard at the mental hospital and escaped. I'm with Katie right now. We think he might come after her. I'm making sure she's safe."

Noah's throat went dry and his chest felt like it was in a vise. "Any visual on him since his escape?"

"A patrol unit thought they spotted him back at Flushing Meadows. A BOLO has been issued and all patrol units are on alert."

"I'll head over there and have a look myself. This is personal at this point." He hung up the phone.

Lani took a step toward Noah. "It's Martin, isn't it? He's escaped. I'm going with you and Scotty. Let's finish this."

"You're not in uniform."

"You have an extra gun, don't you?"

Noah knew it was an act of futility to argue with her. He unlocked his drawer and pulled out his Glock. His own gun was nestled in the leather shoulder holster he had hung on the coat tree. He grabbed it and commanded Scotty to follow.

"We'll take my car," said Noah.

With Scotty trotting alongside them, Lani and Noah raced out of headquarters to the parking garage where Noah had his car. They drove through Queens to the park. He and Lani circled the park and then took Scotty out on foot patrol to question people. Several people had seen a man matching Martin's description.

After searching for another hour, they turned up nothing. Noah and Lani stood in the parking lot by his car.

Lani pointed toward a high-rise that was under construction. "I thought I saw a shadow in one of the windows." It was Sunday, so no construction workers were around. "People tend to go toward places they are familiar with."

Noah studied the dark building. "You think he's hiding out in there?"

"He's got to know there is an all-points bulletin out for him. He's probably laying low until the heat is off," she said.

Noah shrugged. "It's worth a shot."

The building had three floors that looked like they were mostly complete and the fourth floor was only steel framing. The place was probably locked up. That didn't mean Martin hadn't found some way in.

There were signs posted on the fence that indicated which construction company was doing the building.

Noah looked up their number and got a recording of where he could call in case of emergency. Noah phoned the number, identified himself and got permission to enter the premises.

"If Martin is hiding in here, he didn't get through that locked door. He must have snuck in." They circled the building with Scotty until they found a part of the fence that had been cut away.

It didn't mean Martin was there for sure. Anyone could have slipped in there to hide out for any number of nefarious reasons. The only lead they had was that the last place Martin was spotted was the park next to this building under construction.

Both of them had their weapons drawn as they circled the outside of the building and Scotty followed them. They found a ladder propped against the back of the building leading up to the second floor where a hole for a window had been cut but no glass was in the window.

"Like old times, huh?" said Noah. "Climbing around." So much had happened between them since the training exercise at Jamaica Bay and then climbing around the abandoned building chasing Martin.

Lani's expression seemed to darken. She shook her head and smiled. "We've been through a lot together." He had the feeling she wanted to say something more, but there was no time.

Noah stared up the ladder. "I'll go first." Just in case Martin was waiting for them. Entering the building this way was hardly from a position of strength. He called for backup before going up the ladder into a room that was framed but lacking drywall.

Lani's excited voice from down below reached him.
Scotty barked. "I see him, Noah. I see him."

"What?" Noah poked his head out. Lani was already
running across the construction site toward a backhoe
parked by the other heavy equipment, with Scotty right
behind her.

Martin's head bobbed up and then back down in the
cab of the backhoe.

Lani had drawn her weapon and was racing toward
where Martin was hiding.

Noah swung his leg around to get down the ladder.
The rumble of the backhoe starting up surrounded him.
His heart stopped when he looked for where Lani was.
She'd fallen into a hole that must have been covered
with a tarp.

Dirt cascaded around Lani as she rolled over and
stared up at the sky. The spitting and hum of the backhoe engine grew louder. Above her, Scotty ran back
and forth barking.

She scrambled to find her gun and get to her feet.
The hole was maybe seven feet deep, probably the start
of a trench to lay some pipe that led to the building.

She clawed the dirt and struggled to get a foothold
that would allow her to escape. She looked up to see the
arm of the backhoe above her with a full bucket, lifting so it could release and open, dropping dirt on her.
When that happened, she'd be buried.

She dug her fingers into the loose dirt and tried to
climb.

Noah was above her. He shot at the backhoe which
must have delayed Martin. He held his hand out to pull
her free. She clamored to get on level ground even as

the backhoe charged toward them. Noah pulled her to her feet just as the dirt filled the hole. Scotty turned and barked at the backhoe.

Martin turned the backhoe, so it was headed straight toward Scotty. The front windshield was shattered where Noah's bullet must have hit. The dog stood his ground and continued to bark.

Noah drew his gun and shot at the cab of the backhoe. Martin kept the machine running but came to a halt. Noah stalked toward the backhoe with his gun drawn commanding Scotty to back down. The first shot had shattered but not broken the glass in the cab.

Scotty let out one more threatening bark before falling in place beside Noah.

Lani raised her own gun to back up Noah.

Martin swung the machine around and lumbered toward the edge of the construction site. She fired a shot that didn't reach its target.

They raced after him as he crashed through the fence, flung the cab door open and jumped out. Martin bolted away with Lani, Noah and Scotty at his heels. Lani pushed harder to run faster, closing the distance between her and Martin. Up ahead was a street bustling with people and cars.

Martin stepped onto the sidewalk and raced across the street while the light was still red. Cars honked and brakes squealed. Out of breath, Lani reached the sidewalk and stared across the street.

Martin's head disappeared into the crowd.

Noah and Scotty caught up to her just as the walk sign flashed. They crossed the street searching the sidewalk for several blocks. No sign of Martin anywhere.

Across the street, patrol officers were getting out of their cars. That must be their backup.

A heaviness like a weight on her chest caused Lani to sit down on a bench outside a shop. She continued to scan the sea of faces. Once again, Martin Fisher had eluded them. As if sensing her mood, Scotty pressed against her.

Hours ago, she had come into Noah's office to tell him what she had been doing on her days off. Lani had made a decision to apply for a transfer when she heard that a spot had opened up in a new K-9 unit starting up in Brooklyn. With a newer unit, there was a better chance she'd get a dog sooner.

One of the officers radioed that there still was no sign of Martin.

"I think he got away." Lani rested her elbows on her knees and placed her palms on her cheeks.

"At least you're not a target anymore. I don't think Martin will come after you now that he doesn't associate you with Katie anymore." Noah rose to his feet, placing his hands on his hips and staring out into the street. "I'm worried for Katie's safety though."

"It sounds like Tony is staying pretty close to her."

Now with Martin still on the loose, the moment to tell Noah about the transfer felt awkward.

Noah sat back down. He pointed toward a coffee kiosk. "Weren't you going to buy me a cup?"

"Won't be as good as Griffin's, but sure." Noah must have sensed something was up. They bought their coffee and carried it back to the park. More news came via the radio that Martin was still at large.

They walked through the park watching red, gold and rust colored leaves twirl through the air. Still stinging from the defeat of Martin being on the run, Lani could not find the right moment to tell him about her transfer.

The truth was that she was afraid of what his response might be. Yes, she'd applied for the transfer to get a dog sooner, but more than anything, she'd hoped that if Noah wasn't her direct supervisor he might be open to them being more than friends.

Noah tossed his empty coffee cup into a trash can. "I've got to get back to work."

He turned to face her.

She stepped over to the trash can and threw her cup away as well.

He put a finger beneath her chin to lift her head. "Something up?"

She took in a breath. "Noah, I requested a transfer."

He let his hand drop to his side. "A transfer? Out of state?"

She thought she detected fear in his voice.

"No, there was an opening in the new Brooklyn K-9 unit. There's a better chance of getting a dog sooner there. I'm tired of waiting for one here in Queens."

Noah had a stunned look on his face. "Don't you like working in Queens…with me?"

"Brooklyn isn't the moon. I'll still see you." What had she expected? That he would declare his love for her.

"Yeah, I hope so." He sounded hurt. "Well, come on, I'll give you a ride back to headquarters. I'm sure you'll say your goodbyes." He trudged toward the parking lot then turned to look at her. "I still have to approve the paperwork. It hasn't come across my desk yet. I'm sure you'll be around for a few more days." She detected the note of sadness in his voice.

"You will sign the paperwork?"

"Of course Lani. I wouldn't keep you from your dream," he said.

She stared at his back as he walked away. "Noah Jameson. Stop right where you are. Turn around and tell me what you're thinking." Fear made her throat go tight. He had at one time admitted his attraction to her. Had he moved on emotionally already and gotten over her?

He stepped toward her and locked his eyes on her. A light breeze ruffled his brown hair. "Lani, I'm happy for you. I think the new unit will be a good career move."

"Really, that's all you're thinking."

"No, I was thinking this too." He gathered her into his arms. His mouth covered hers.

She wrapped her arms around his neck while he drew her close and deepened the kiss. As he pulled away, the world seemed to be spinning. He rested his hand on her cheek.

"Well, look at that. Lani Branson speechless." Amusement danced in his eyes.

As she stared into his eyes and relished the softness of his fingers on her face, she still could not find words to respond.

He leaned in and kissed her lips again and then drew her to his chest. She closed her eyes, listening to his heart thud.

He brushed his hand over her hair and kissed the top of her head. "Did you take the transfer…for this? So we could be together?"

She still could not find words. She lifted her head and nodded.

He picked her up and twirled her around. "You have made me so very happy." He set her down.

He beamed as he gazed down at her.

She reached up to rest her hand on his face, to brush her fingers through his hair at the temple. "I love being here with you in this moment."

"And I love you," he said.

He gathered her into his arms and hugged and kissed her. Lani buried her face against Noah's neck, loving the warmth and the musky smell of his skin. Her heart flooded with good feelings, knowing that they could truly be together, getting to know each other as more than friends. She looked forward to many more real kisses from Noah.

* * * * *

Aside from her faith and her family, there's not much **Shirlee McCoy** enjoys more than a good book! When she's not hanging out with the people she loves most, she can be found plotting her next Love Inspired Suspense story or trekking through the wilderness, training with a local search-and-rescue team. Shirlee loves to hear from readers. If you have time, drop her a line at shirlee@shirleemccoy.com.

Books by Shirlee McCoy

Love Inspired Suspense

Hidden Witness

FBI: Special Crimes Unit

Night Stalker
Gone
Dangerous Sanctuary
Lone Witness
Falsely Accused

Mission: Rescue

Protective Instincts
Her Christmas Guardian
Exit Strategy
Deadly Christmas Secrets
Mystery Child
The Christmas Target
Mistaken Identity
Christmas on the Run

Visit the Author Profile page
at Harlequin.com for more titles.

SWORN TO PROTECT

Shirlee McCoy

Whither shall I go from thy spirit?
or whither shall I flee from thy presence?
If I ascend up into heaven, thou art there:
if I make my bed in hell, behold, thou art there.
If I take the wings of the morning, and dwell in the
uttermost parts of the sea; Even there shall thy hand
lead me, and thy right hand shall hold me.
—*Psalm* 139:7–10

To the men and women in our armed forces,
the true heroes of our world.

ONE

Once upon a time, Katie Jameson could have sprinted up two flights of stairs, raced down a hall and corralled twenty-five fifth graders with ease. She could have finished her workday, gone to the gym, worked out, made dinner and had a smile on her face when her husband returned home. Once upon a time—when Jordan had been alive and Katie had not been nine months pregnant—she had been energetic, enthusiastic and filled with hope.

Now, she was just tired.

Her mother-in-law's constant chatter wasn't making her any less so. Katie loved Ivy. She appreciated how much she and her husband, Alexander, had done since Jordan's death. But, she had not been sleeping well these past few weeks. The pregnancy was nearing its end. She felt huge and unwieldy, her body uncomfortable and unfamiliar.

And, Jordan was gone. Murdered. The reason for it was as shocking as his death had been. Martin Fisher, a man Katie had gone out with twice before she had begun dating Jordan, had become obsessed with her and decided that getting Jordan out of the way would clear a path to the relationship he longed for.

The guilt Katie felt over that was almost overwhelming.

No matter how many people told her that it wasn't her fault, that she couldn't blame herself for Martin's insane bid to win her love, she couldn't help thinking that if she had turned down his invitation when he had asked her out to lunch a few years ago, Jordan would still be alive.

She swallowed down tears, refusing to let her mother-in-law see her sorrow. Ivy had lost her son. That grief had to be almost unbearable. Somehow, though, she had managed to pull herself together and focus on her three remaining sons, her granddaughter and, of course, Katie and the impending baby.

Ivy had done everything she could to make certain Katie didn't feel alone during the pregnancy. If she had not been able to attend obstetric visits with her, Ivy had one of Jordan's brothers go. Someone was always there, sitting in the waiting room.

But, no amount of in-law love could make up for the fact that Jordan was gone. Over seven months now.

She missed him every day.

Today, she missed him even more.

They should have been at home, checking the hospital bag to make sure everything was packed for the big day. They should have been putting the finishing touches on the nursery, putting away baby diapers and bibs, and making certain that their daughter's home would be warm, welcoming and ready.

"Are you okay, dear?" Ivy asked, her voice echoing through the quiet corridor of the medical center. Unlike other obstetric patients, Katie had not been ushered to an exam room. She was being taken to Dr. Ritter's office—a corner room in the far reaches of the medical building. This wasn't a normal appointment. This was an appointment designed to put Katie at ease, to make sure she felt comfortable and confident as she reached her due date.

"Just a little tired," she replied.

"Are you sure? Alex and I both feel that you've been pensive these last few days. More quiet than usual. We don't want to pry, but we also don't want to miss cues that you need more help."

"You've given me plenty of help, and I'm fine. The baby is getting big, and I'm getting uncomfortable. That's all there is to my pensiveness." She kept her voice light and offered a quick smile.

"We thought maybe…"

"What?"

"I hate to even bring it up." Ivy glanced at the nurse who was leading them down the hall, her voice little more than a whisper as she continued. "But, Martin Fisher's escape from the psychiatric hospital has to have put you on edge."

"It has. I'm not going to lie. I feel nervous, but the police and K-9 team are working hard to find him. They aren't going to let him get to me. And, God is still in control." The last one was what she was clinging to. Knowing that God was in charge. That He had a plan. That no matter what, He would work things out for His good.

"Yes. He is. And, you're right—the NYPD is doing everything in its power to bring Martin in. I just… I don't want you to worry. Not now. Now, with the baby's birth so close."

"I'm trying not to," she said, pasting on another phony smile. She wanted to relax and enjoy the last days and weeks before the baby arrived, but how could she not worry? Martin Fisher was out there somewhere. So far, he had stayed away, but she knew that might not last forever. He might be biding his time, waiting for the right opportunity to come after her. She was the object of his obsession, the reason he had killed Jordan and, maybe, the purpose behind his escape. If he did come after her, there were three possible outcomes.

He could kidnap her and hide her somewhere she'd never be found. In his twisted mind, the baby would be his.

He could kill her—in the classic "if I can't have you, no one can" scenario.

He could try either of the above, and the NYPD would get to him first.

She was counting on the third option. Jordan had been the chief of the NYC K-9 Command Unit. His three brothers were all cops. They were committed to apprehending Martin before he could cause more harm.

She would be safe. Her baby would be safe. Katie had to be believe that.

"Here we are," the nurse said, pushing open a door at the end of the hall. Young, with a bright smile and eyes the color of dark chocolate, she knew why Katie was being seen in the doctor's office rather than an exam room. Everyone who worked at the clinic was aware of the circumstances surrounding the pregnancy—that the baby's father had been murdered, that he had been one of New York's finest.

What they didn't know—what they couldn't—was how loved Jordan had been. How kind. How good of a father he had planned to be.

"Thank you," Katie murmured, blinking back tears.

She hated crying in public.

Just like she hated the pity she could see in the nurse's eyes.

"Is there anything I can get you while you're waiting?" the nurse asked.

"I'm good." Katie stepped into the doctor's office, took a seat on one of the leather chairs that faced his desk and dropped her purse on the floor near her feet. She had been in this room before. Just a week after Jordan had died, she had attended her first prenatal appointment. Dr. Ritter had met with her here before taking her to the exam room.

"Okay. You let me know if you change your mind. Dr. Ritter will be with you shortly. He's just delivered a baby, but he'll arrive at the clinic soon. Your next prenatal exam is scheduled for next week, right?"

"Yes."

"Who knows?" The nurse smiled. "Maybe the baby will be here before then."

"Wouldn't that be lovely!" Ivy exclaimed, her cheerfulness a little too bright and a little too brittle. The previous day, she had been talking excitedly about the Thanksgiving meal she was planning. Ivy was the consummate hostess. She loved to cook and entertain, and she had invited a dozen people to join the family for Thanksgiving.

The house would be full.

But, one Jordan-sized space would remain empty.

Ivy was as aware of that as Katie.

The nurse smiled again and departed.

For a moment, the room was silent except for the soft hum of the heat blowing through the floor vents.

Ivy cleared her throat and settled into the chair next to Katie. "It's going to be okay," she said.

"I know," Katie lied.

She didn't know.

No matter how much she wanted to trust God's plan, she couldn't stop worrying that she wouldn't be enough for the child she was carrying. Good enough. Smart enough. Strong enough. Loving enough. *Parent* enough to make up for the fact that the baby didn't have a father.

This wasn't the plan, God.

This wasn't what was supposed to happen.

How am I going to do this alone?

How many times had she prayed those words since Jordan had died?

Too many.

And, there was never any answer. Never any clear direction as to how she could be all of the things the baby would need.

"You don't look like you know it," Ivy replied. She had aged since Jordan's death; lines that had not been there before bracketed her mouth and fanned out from her eyes. She was a beautiful woman. Strong. Determined. But, losing her son had cost her.

"Like I said, I'm tired. It's hard to sleep with this one kicking me in the ribs all night." She patted her belly. No fake smile this time. She was too tired to try.

"I remember those days," Ivy said with a soft smile. "Jordan was especially prone to keeping me up. It's not surprising that his child is the same." She reached out and laid her hand on the swell of Katie's abdomen.

When she pulled away, there were tears in her eyes. "He would have loved this."

"Yes, he would have."

"And, he would have been a great father. He was always so good with children."

"The kids at school loved him," Katie agreed.

Jordan had been born and raised in Queens, and he had had a passion for mentoring the youth there. He had often visited schools with his K-9 partner, Snapper. He had also taught self-defense classes at the local YMCA. He had been Katie's instructor when she had moved to New York and taken a self-defense class. Just in case.

A year later, he had visited the school where she was teaching. They'd bumped into each other in the hall. The rest had happened fast. Long conversations. Walks in the park. Jokes. Laughter.

Love.

Marriage.

They should have had their happily-ever-after.

Instead, Katie was alone. Getting ready to give birth to their baby.

"I wish I'd asked the nurse to bring me something to drink," she murmured, her throat tight with emotion.

"They have water in the waiting room. And, coffee. Would you like me to bring you something?" Ivy offered.

"Would you mind? I'd love a cup of water."

"Of course, I don't mind. Should you stay here alone, though? The boys would have my head if they thought I'd left you unattended even for a minute."

"I'll be fine, Ivy," Katie assured her. "Don't worry. You'll be back in five seconds."

Ivy looked unsure, but then stood and hurried from the room.

Just as Katie had hoped she would. She didn't want to talk about Jordan. Not now. Not when she felt exhausted and emotional. She wanted to keep focused on the birthing plan, on staying safe, on making sure she did what her brothers-in-law and the police asked her to. Since Martin's escape, the Jameson brothers had been escorting her almost everywhere. Today, though, they were attending a training seminar in Manhattan. They'd asked fellow K-9 officer Tony Knight to run patrols past the medical clinic. They'd told her to be careful and aware. To stay close to their mother. To listen to her gut.

Right now, her gut was saying she was exhausted. That she needed to sleep. That she didn't want to think about the danger or the tragedy.

Someone knocked on the door.

"Come in," she called, bracing herself for the meeting with Dr. Ritter.

The door swung open and a man in a white lab coat stepped in, holding her chart close to his face.

Only, he was not the doctor she was expecting.

Dr. Ritter was in his early sixties with salt-and-pepper hair and enough extra weight to fill out his lab coat. The doctor who was moving toward her had dark hair and a muscular build. His scuffed shoes and baggy lab coat made her wonder if he were a resident at the hospital where she would be giving birth.

"Good morning," she said, feeling unsettled. She had been meeting with Dr. Ritter since the beginning of the pregnancy. He understood her feelings about the birth. He probably suspected a lot of the fear and trepidation she tried to hide. She never had to say much at her appointments, and that was the way she liked it. Talking about the fact that Jordan wouldn't be around for his daughter's birth, her childhood, her life always brought Katie close to the tears she despised.

"Morning," he mumbled.

She could see his forehead and his brows but not much else. That seemed strange. Usually, doctors looked up from the charts when they entered the exam rooms.

"Is Dr. Ritter running late?" she asked, uneasiness joining the unsettled feeling in the pit of her stomach.

"He won't be able to make it," the man said, lowering the charts and grinning.

She went cold with terror.

She knew the hazel eyes, the lopsided grin, the high forehead. "Martin," she stammered, jumping to her feet.

"Sorry it took me so long to get to you, sweetheart. I had to watch from a distance until I was certain we could be alone."

"Watch?" she repeated.

"They wanted to keep me in the hospital, but our love is too strong to be denied. I escaped for you. For us. And, I've been so close to you these past few weeks. It's been torture." He lifted a hand, and if she had not jerked back, his fingers would have brushed her cheek.

He scowled. "Have they brainwashed you? Have they turned you against me?"

"You did that yourself when you murdered my husband," she responded and regretted it immediately.

He grabbed her arm and dragged her the few feet to his side. "We're leaving here, Katie. We're going to a quiet place where we can be together."

"I'm not going anywhere with you," she replied, trying to yank her arm away, but his grip was firm, his fingers digging through the soft knit fabric of her sweater.

"Katie? I brought juice and water." Ivy appeared in the doorway, a paper cup in each hand.

Her eyes widened as she saw Martin, her gaze dropping to his hand, then jumping to Katie's face. "What's going on?"

"Nothing you need to worry about," Martin responded, pulling a gun from beneath the lab coat.

The cups dropped from Ivy's hands, water and juice spilling onto the tile floor, her screams spilling into the hall.

"Shut up!" Martin screamed, yanking Katie forward as he slammed the butt of the gun into the side of Ivy's head. She went down hard, her body limp, eyes closed.

Katie clawed at Martin's hand, trying to free herself and get to her mother-in-law. She had taken self-defense classes. She should know how to do this, but panic and pregnancy made her movements clumsy and slow.

"Stop!" he said. One word. Uttered with cold deliberation. The barrel was suddenly pressed into her stomach. She could feel the baby wiggling and turning.

She froze.

Just like he had commanded. Everything in her focused on keeping the baby alive.

"That's better. You wouldn't want the baby to get hurt in the scuffle," he growled, yanking her away from the office. Several nurses were racing toward them, one of them yelling into a cell phone. A doctor barreled around the corner, eyes wide with shock as she saw what the commotion was about.

"Everyone just stay cool," Martin said, the gun still

pressed into Katie's abdomen. "I'm not here to hurt anyone. I'm just here for my wife."

She stiffened at the word but was too afraid to argue.

"I've called the police," the nurse with the cell phone said. "They'll be here any minute."

"Good for them," Martin responded. "Everyone get out of our way." He pushed open the stairwell door and dragged Katie down two flights of steps. She was stumbling, trying to keep her feet under her, terrified that she'd fall and hurt the baby, that the gun would go off, that he'd get her outside and take her wherever he intended.

"Stop." She gasped, panicking as they rushed into the lobby on the lower level of the building. "I can't breathe."

"You're breathing just fine, my love," he murmured, smiling tenderly into her face as he pressed the gun more deeply into her stomach.

"Martin, really. I can't."

There were people all around, shocked, afraid. Watching but not intervening, and she couldn't blame them. Martin was armed and obviously dangerous, his eyes gleaming with the fire of his delusions.

"Hey! You! Let her go!" A security guard raced toward them. No gun. Nothing but a radio and a desire to help.

Martin moved the gun, and Katie had seconds to shove him sideways, to try to ruin his aim, save the guard and free herself.

The bullet slammed into the wall, and a woman shrieked.

For a split second, Katie was free, running back to

the stairwell, clawing at the doorknob, trying to get back up the stairs and away from Martin.

He grabbed her jacket and dragged her backward, nearly unbalancing her. She felt the barrel of the gun against the side of her neck.

"Don't make me hurt you, Katie," he whispered, his lips brushing her ear.

She froze again.

"That's my girl. Now, let's go." He grabbed her hand, the gun slipping away from her neck, and dragged her outside.

Tony Knight had been a police officer for enough years to know how to stay calm in the most challenging of circumstances.

The current situation demanded every bit of the discipline he had learned during his years on the force.

He watched as Martin Fisher dragged Katie across the crowded parking lot. She wasn't fighting or protesting, and Tony couldn't blame her. Martin was swinging the firearm in the direction of anyone who dared to call for him to stop.

Katie had to be terrified.

Katie.

His best friend's *widow*.

The word still made his chest tight and his jaw clench. Jordan should be alive, getting ready to celebrate the birth of his first child.

Martin Fisher was responsible for his death.

That was reason enough to take him down.

But, Tony came from a long line of police officers. He believed in the criminal justice system. He believed in due process and trial by jury. He did not believe in vigilantism. To get Katie safely away from Martin, Tony would use whatever force was required. But, he also didn't believe in risking the lives of innocent civilians—Katie and the big crowd watching. The moment Tony pulled the trigger, so would Martin—with the gun pointed at Katie's heart.

Tony also didn't like the idea of firing his weapon when he was aiming at a target so close to Katie.

"Let her go, Martin," he called, his service weapon aimed at the killer's head, his police dog, Rusty, by his side. The chocolate-colored Lab growled quietly. Trained in search and rescue, he had a powerful build and split-second reaction time. If asked to, he'd go after the perp and attempt to take him down.

Tony didn't want to ask him to. Martin would shoot Rusty and have the gun aimed back at Katie in a heartbeat.

"Or what?" Martin asked, his yellow-green eyes focused on Tony.

"I don't think you want to find out," Tony responded, trying to keep him talking and buy some time. Backup was on the way. A 911 call had been placed moments before he had arrived at the medical center. He had been running his regular patrol route through Queens, detouring past the four-story brick building every few minutes. Worried, because he knew that none of Jordan's brothers had been available to accompany Katie to her appointment.

"You're a big talker, Knight," Martin snapped, yanking Katie backward. Of course, he knew Tony's name. He was obsessed with everyone and everything that had anything to do with Katie's life.

"I'm also big on action. Let her go."

Martin scowled. He was moving Katie to the edge of the paved lot. A few feet of lush grass separated the medical clinic's property from the edge of Forest Park. Tall oak trees marked the eastern edge of the public area.

"But, you won't risk Katie's or the baby's life," Martin said. "For the sake of your buddy Jordan, if nothing else."

He was right.

Tony couldn't take a chance. He was confident in his ability to hit his mark, but if Katie moved, if Martin yanked her at just the wrong moment, she or the baby could be injured.

Or, worse.

He couldn't allow that to happen.

"Put your gun down, Martin. Let her go. We'll get you the help you need."

"I don't need help. I need my family." He pulled Katie into his chest, pressing the gun against her side. The barrel was hidden by the soft swell of her abdomen, but Tony could see her face, her blue eyes and her blond ponytail snaking over her shoulder.

"Please, Martin," she said, her voice shaking. "Just let me go. We can talk things out after you've gotten treatment."

"Treatment for what?" Martin asked coldly, his eyes blazing hot in his impassive face.

He was delusional and dangerous, and he was stepping into the grass, dragging Katie with him.

Tony needed to stop him before he made it into the park.

"You were in the hospital," Tony pointed out, stepping closer, his gun dropping to his side. He wanted

Martin to be off guard and vulnerable, unprepared for what was going to happen. "And, from what I heard, you were doing well there."

He hadn't actually heard much, but Martin would do just fine locked up in a mental health facility for the remainder of his life.

"I didn't ask for your opinion. Or, the opinion of anyone else," Martin snapped, but the gun had fallen away from Katie's side, and he was glancing back, eyeing the sparse growth of oaks that heralded the beginning of parkland.

The proximity of Forest Park might make it more difficult to apprehend Martin. Tony was determined to get Katie away from the guy, but if Martin managed to disappear into the park, there would be plenty of footpaths and several roads that he could use to make a quick escape.

"Get back in your car," Martin said coldly. "I would never hurt Katie, but Jordan's kid means nothing to me." He jabbed the gun into Katie's stomach, and she winced.

"You can't hurt the baby without hurting the mother," Tony reminded him.

"I'm not as stupid as people think I am. I know a lot of tricks." Martin moved backward, away from Tony, his K-9 vehicle and the parking lot.

Tony unhooked Rusty's lead from his collar so he could release him. Normally the chocolate Lab wouldn't attack. He was a placid, easygoing house companion and a die-hard worker when it came to search and rescue, but he hadn't been trained to unarm dangerous criminals. He did, however, have a fierce desire to protect his pack.

Right now, he was barking, sensing the tension and

anxiety and ready to do what he had to in order to make certain his people were safe.

"And don't even think about releasing that dog!" Martin screamed, the gun shifting away from Katie as he focused on Rusty.

Katie slammed her elbow into his stomach.

Martin gasped and dropped the gun from his hand.

"Go!" Tony shouted, releasing Rusty as Katie darted away.

TWO

Fight. Free yourself. Run.

Jordan's words echoed through Katie's head as she sprinted away. He had said them dozens of times when he had taught the self-defense class she had signed up for a few weeks after taking the job teaching in Queens. The neighborhood had been safe, but she had grown up in the suburbs, and the hustle and bustle of the city had been disconcerting.

Plus, she had been a young woman, alone.

She had wanted to know that she could defend herself.

She had not been thinking about defending an unborn child.

She hadn't been thinking about being a wife or a mother. She had been thinking about living life on her terms. That was something she had not been able to do when she had been a teenager moving through the foster-care system.

Rusty growled and snapped as he dashed by.

She ran in the opposite direction, darting off the curb, her ankle twisting. She tried to right herself, but the pregnancy made her ungainly, her body front-heavy and cumbersome.

She tripped and went down, hands and knees skidding across asphalt. Someone grabbed her arm and pulled her to her feet. It had to be Martin!

She fought the way Jordan had taught her.

Elbow to the stomach, pushing back into his weight.

"Katie, stop. It's me," Tony said.

She knew his voice.

If she had not been so panicked, she'd have known his gentle touch—his fingers curving lightly around her upper arm.

He had done the same at the funeral, standing beside her as Jordan's coffin was lowered into the ground.

Ashes to ashes. Dust to dust.

She stopped struggling and whirled toward the park. "Where did he go?"

There was no sign of Martin, but Rusty was nearing a copse of trees, still barking ferociously. He was trained in search and rescue and had no business going after a deranged and dangerous man.

"Rusty is going to get hurt," she said, her voice shaking. "You need to call him back."

"He'll be okay," Tony responded. He was tracking the dog's movements as he relayed information into the radio.

If he was worried, she couldn't hear it in his voice.

But, then, he was one of New York's finest. Just like Jordan had been. He had great training, a good head on his shoulders and the ability to stay calm even in the most challenging circumstances.

He and Jordan had been best friends.

My fourth brother.

How many times had Jordan said that?

And how often had Katie set an extra plate at the dinner table? How often had she watched as the two men tossed balls for their K-9 partners in the yard behind the three-family house they'd shared with the Jameson clan? Countless times. She and Jordan had lived on the second level of the home. His parents just below them. His brothers and young niece above. They were the family she had longed for after her parents had died. They were the connection she had prayed she would have during the years she had spent drifting from one foster home to the next.

She had thought life would keep going in the same positive direction. She had thought—wrongly so—that the tragedy of losing her parents in a car accident when she was ten was enough for a lifetime.

She should have known better.

There was nothing in the Bible about life being easy.

There were no promises made to the faithful.

Except that God would be there. Guiding. Helping. Creating good out of bad.

The problem was Katie couldn't see how anything good could come of losing Jordan. Or, of being stalked by a deranged man.

She shuddered, then her eyes widened. "Ivy! My mother-in-law. He hit her with the gun. Is she all right? I need to know that Ivy is all right!"

Word came over the radio just then that the building was secure, the suspect was on the loose and one victim, Ivy Jameson, had come to and was being treated for a minor head injury.

"Thank God," Katie said, the breath whooshing out of her.

"It's going to be okay," Tony murmured, his hand still on her arm. "We'll get him."

"I hope so," she replied.

His gaze dropped from her face to her belly.

There was a smudge of dirt on her shirt.

"Are you hurt?" he asked, meeting her gaze again.

He had the darkest eyes she had ever seen. Nearly black, the irises all but melding with his pupils.

"I don't think so," she responded. The baby was turning cartwheels, little elbows and feet and hands jabbing and poking. She would be an active child, and Katie wondered if Jordan had been that way.

It bothered her that she didn't know.

They'd known each other for only a few years. They'd met, dated and married so quickly, people had probably wondered at their rush.

"You aren't sure?" Tony released her arm and turned her hands over, frowning as he eyed the scraped and bleeding flesh.

"I'm fine. I just… I'd be better if you were going after Martin. I want him caught."

"We all do," he replied. "I called in the direction Martin took. Police are all over Forest Park, looking for him." He held her gaze for a moment, then motioned at a small group of medical personnel that had emerged from the building and were standing near the clinic's door.

"We need some help over here," he said.

A nurse rushed over.

That was no surprise.

Tony had a way of getting people to do what he wanted. He wasn't manipulative. He wasn't demanding. He simply had an air of confidence that people responded to.

"Mrs. Jameson!" the nurse cried. "I'm so glad you're safe!"

"Me, too," she murmured, suddenly faint, her heart galloping frantically. She couldn't catch her breath, and she sat on the curb, the edges of her vision dark, sounds muted by the frantic rush of blood in her ears.

"Katie?" Tony said, his voice faint, his palm pressed to her cheek. She realized he was crouching in front of her, his face filled with concern. The nurse was beside her, checking the pulse in her wrist.

"I'm okay. I just want Martin caught."

"Me, too." He glanced toward the parking lot's entrance. Several patrol cars were pulling in, with their lights and sirens on.

"You can go, if you want," she said. "There are dozens of people around. Martin would never try to…"

She stopped, because she knew he would try anything to get to her. There was no telling what he might do. No one had imagined that he'd enter the clinic and go after her there, but he had. He had killed Jordan. He'd kill again to get what he wanted.

And, what he wanted was Katie.

Her pulse jumped at the thought, and her abdomen cramped with such surprising intensity, she gasped.

"Hun, are you okay?" the nurse asked, laying a hand on Katie's stomach as if she knew exactly what was happening.

"Yes," she replied, but she wasn't certain.

"Feels like you're having a contraction," the nurse said.

"A contraction?" Tony frowned. "As in the baby is coming?"

"No. We're a couple weeks out from that," Katie managed to say.

The nurse smiled kindly. "The baby will come when he or she decides it's time. If today is the day, there's not a whole lot you can do about it."

"Today can't be the day," Katie said.

"If it is, you'll be fine and so will the baby. You're at what? Thirty-six weeks? That's early, but we deliver thirty-six-weekers all the time. They do remarkably well." The nurse straightened and turned back toward the building. "I'll get a wheelchair, and we'll bring you back into the clinic, hook you up to a fetal monitor and see what's going on."

"Today can't be the day," Katie repeated, but the nurse was already hurrying away.

"She's right," Tony said quietly. "You and the baby will be okay. Even if she arrives today."

"I don't want to give birth until after Martin is caught."

She didn't want to give birth alone, either, but she didn't tell him that. She hadn't told anyone how afraid she was to go through this without Jordan.

"Like the nurse said, the baby will decide." He smiled gently. "Noah just arrived. I'm going after Martin."

He touched her cheek, then stood.

When he moved away, she could see her brother-in-law, the new chief of the K-9 Command Unit, rushing across the parking lot, his rottweiler partner, Scotty, bounding beside him.

"Katie!" Noah shouted, his expression and voice only hinting at the fear she knew he must be feeling. The baby she was carrying was the Jameson family's last link to Jordan. She knew Jordan's parents and three brothers cared about her, but the baby was blood.

"I'm okay," she assured Jordan's brother. "And so is your mother."

She wasn't sure if he heard.

The police sirens were loud. An ambulance was screaming into the parking lot. A large crowd had formed, the murmur of panicked voices drifting beneath the cacophony of emergency sirens and squawk of radio communications.

There were dozens of people around.

But, somehow, Katie felt completely alone.

Katie and the baby would be fine, Tony told himself as he jogged along the railroad tracks that cut through Forest Park. Rusty was in front of him, following a scent trail through oak leaves that partially covered the railroad ties that stretched between the rails. The Lab had an exceptional nose. They'd spent countless hours together training in wilderness-air scent and urban recovery. They were a team, partners in a way people who have never been dog handlers couldn't understand.

Jordan had understood. Just like he had understood the desire to go into law enforcement, the deep-seated need to see justice done. They had been best friends for years. Jordan's death had been a blow that Tony was still trying to recover from.

Martin Fisher was a cold-blooded killer—evil. When Tony thought about the horrific lengths Martin had gone to… Threatening to kill Katie via a bomb he'd said he'd rigged, Martin had forced Jordan to write his own suicide note, then had given him drugs to simulate a heart attack. The "suicide" had seemed plausible to some, but not to the Jameson clan or to Tony.

Jordan had been happily married, excited about life and enthusiastic about the future. He'd had everything to live for.

The discovery that Jordan had been murdered had not surprised Tony. He *had* been taken by surprise by the reason for his best friend's murder. Every police officer understood the dangers of the job. Tony and Jordan had discussed what would happen if one of them were killed in the line of duty. Jordan had promised to always be there for Tony's family; Tony had, of course, promised to always be there for Jordan's. During Jordan and Katie's wedding reception, Jordan had pulled Tony aside and reminded him of that promise.

If anything happens to me, you'll make sure she's okay, right?

You know I will, but nothing is going to happen to you, bro.

Something had happened, but not in the way either of them had imagined. There had been no gunfire during a robbery, no ambush during a response to a domestic incident. As far as Tony could ascertain, Jordan hadn't even had a chance to fight. He had been murdered by a man who was obsessed with Katie, and he'd seemed to have been taken as much by surprise as the rest of the team had been.

Jordan's German shepherd partner, Snapper, had been missing since the day the suicide note had been found. Recently the team had learned that Snapper had been picked up by an animal shelter not too long ago and adopted out. The once-majestic canine had been a stray on the streets for so long that he had become unrecognizable. The NYC K-9 Command Unit was attempting to contact the man who had adopted Snapper. So far, they'd had no success.

Jordan would want Snapper home.

He would want Martin prosecuted and tossed in jail.

He wouldn't want anyone on the K-9 unit to circumvent justice and mete out punishment without due process.

Tony knew that. He had been working hard to keep his emotions in check and not allow anger to skew his perspective, but he *was* angry. Jordan had been one of the best. Not just at his police work but at his friendships and his life. He had been loyal, brave and devoted. He should have had decades of service left to the community. He should have grown old with Katie, raised a bunch of kids with her and retired into a life of leisure. Tony frowned, stepping over a downed tree that had fallen next to the tracks.

He had grown up in Queens and still lived there, renting a one-bedroom floor unit in a multifamily house right on the edge of Forest Hills. He and Rusty spent their downtime in this park, walking the trails and hiking through the oak woods. They both knew the area, and Rusty was confident as he loped ahead. After Tony had freed Rusty from his lead, the dog had circled back to find Tony in the park and then led him here. Like any well-trained search dog, he knew his job. Find the subject and return to the handler again and again, until the handler and the subject were in the same place.

With backup arriving and fanning out across the five-hundred-acre expanse of trees and trails, it wouldn't take long to find Martin if he had stayed in the park. Based on the direction Rusty was heading,

Tony didn't think he had. There was a crossroad ahead, dirt and gravel that cut through the park. Vehicles were prohibited, but that didn't keep teens and young adults from driving through.

Rusty sniffed an area in the center of the road, circled around and headed east. Tony followed. Tire tread marks were clearly visible, all of them sprinkled with leaves and debris. They had been there awhile. From the look of things, Martin wasn't in a vehicle.

"Find!" Tony called, encouraging the Lab to keep searching.

Rusty made another circle, sniffing the ground and then raising his head. He had caught the scent again. Tony followed him off the road and into the woods.

The day had the crisp edge of winter, the bright sunlight filtering through a thin tree canopy. From his position, Tony could see a trail that wound its way through the trees.

If Martin knew the area and the park, he would know that the trail led to a busy road and an easy escape. Tony had every reason to believe Martin was familiar with the area. He had been renting an apartment just a few miles away before his arrest for Jordan's murder.

A murder Martin had tried to make look like a suicide. Tony shook his head, unable to stop thinking about it, what Martin had done. *Tried* to do. If he had gotten away with it, Jordan's family would have spent a lifetime trying to understand how they had missed signs of Jordan's depression. They would have wasted energy on unfounded regrets.

The thought still filled Tony with fury.

Again, he had known immediately that Jordan would

not have taken his own life. His friend had had too much respect and appreciation for all that God had given him.

There were others who had doubted, though. People who had whispered that Jordan might have had secrets or addictions or relationship troubles that had sent him into a spiraling depression.

Those whispered rumors had only compounded the tragedy of Jordan's death.

Somewhere in the distance a dog barked, the sound carrying on the breeze. Another joined the chorus, the wild baying of a hound on the scent. This was Tony's music, his symphony. He loved the sound of working dogs doing their thing. He loved being part of the NYC K-9 Command Unit. His father had wanted him to follow in his footsteps and become a homicide detective, but Tony enjoyed pounding the pavement, interacting on a daily basis with the community he served. The fact that his job choice had led him into K-9 work was something Tony was constantly grateful for.

He loved what he did.

He loved the life he led.

But, a piece of his soul seemed to have disappeared the day Jordan died.

They had been as close as brothers.

Losing him had left a giant hole in Tony's life.

He had been trying to fill it with work, but even that had begun to feel hollow. There had to be more than long days stretching into long nights and a quiet apartment.

He frowned.

He hadn't been sleeping well lately. That had to be the reason for his melancholy mood. Nearly eight months after Jordan's death, and he was still burning the candle at both ends. In the first few months, he had been trying to figure out exactly what had happened to his friend.

Now, he was desperately trying to get a step ahead of Martin.

He was close. Tony could feel it.

Rusty growled softly, and the warning made the hair on the back of Tony's neck stand on end. He knew his canine partner better than he knew the park or Queens or New York City. Rusty only growled when he sensed danger.

Tony whistled to call the dog back, then stood still, listening to the sudden silence of the park. A bird took flight, zipping away from a tree a dozen yards away. Leaves rustled. Branches snapped. Someone was coming, and he wasn't being quiet about it.

Tony pulled out his gun and aimed it in the direction of the sound. Martin had dropped his gun near the clinic, but if he'd been able to get his hands on one firearm, he could certainly have another.

Seconds later, a teenager stumbled from the woods, his face ashen. Thin and gangly, his entire body trembling, he looked to be thirteen or fourteen. Probably a kid playing hooky from school who had run into a lot more trouble than he had expected.

"Hold it! Hands where I can see them," Tony shouted.

The kid whirled in his direction, his eyes wide with fear. "Some guy has got my friend. He has a knife to his throat."

Tony didn't need to ask who. He knew. This was exactly what a coward like Martin would do. Find an innocent bystander and use him as a shield during his escape.

"Which way did they go?" Tony asked.

"That way!" The boy pointed through the trees.

"Stay here. Rusty, find!" The Lab plunged into the undergrowth. Tony followed, branches snagging his clothes. Rusty bounded ahead, ears flapping, tail high. He knew where he was going, and he shot straight as an arrow toward the scent pool.

He disappeared into a thicket.

Tony raced after him, radioing in his location and hoping backup would arrive quickly. Martin had already committed murder; there was no reason to believe he wouldn't do it again. The teenager he'd kidnapped could be as easily disposed of as he had been abducted.

Rusty barked, and the sound reverberated throughout the woods.

"Call your dog off!" a man shouted, the voice high-pitched and filled with anger and fear.

Tony plunged into the thicket, pushed through the heavy bramble and thick vines and shoved his way into a small clearing.

Martin was just ahead, his arm around a young teen's waist, a knife held against the boy's throat. Rusty was snapping and growling nearby.

"Let the kid go, Martin," Tony said calmly.

"Call off your dog," Martin responded, the knife nicking flesh, a tiny bead of blood sliding down the kid's throat.

He didn't flinch, didn't cry out. He just stared into Tony's eyes, silently begging for help.

"Rusty, off," Tony commanded.

The Lab continued to growl as he backed off and took his place next to Tony.

"That's better," Martin muttered, stepping backward, the knife blade still pressed against the boy's neck. "Now, put your weapon down, and we'll all be just fine."

"You know I'm not going to do that, Martin."

"Then, I guess this kid is going to die. Just like your buddy." Martin's eyes were cold, his tone emotionless.

"Put the knife down, let the boy go and we'll get you the help you need."

"I don't need help. I need to get back what your friend took from me." Martin nearly spat the words, his gaze suddenly sharp with rage.

"Please let me go," the teen gasped, his eyes wide with fear, the thin trickle of blood staining the collar of his jacket.

"Once we're out of the park and away from the police, you can go on with your day. *If* you cooperate." Martin dragged the boy to the edge of the clearing, his focus on Tony. "None of this needed to happen. *None of it.* Jordan could have had any woman. He didn't have to go after mine."

"Katie was never yours, Martin. You know that." Tony followed Martin across the clearing, Rusty close to his side.

"She was always mine. She will always be mine. She knows that. I know it. It is just the rest of the world that needs to understand." Martin's knife hand slipped away from the boy's neck.

Tony lunged toward Martin, grabbed his wrist and dragged it away from the boy's throat. The teen twisted free, shoving into Tony as he tried to run. He tripped, sprawling on the ground, his shoulders knocking Tony's arm. Tony's hand slipped, and the knife slid across his shoulder, slicing through fabric and flesh. There was no pain. Just the desperate need to regain control of the weapon.

Martin jerked back, the knife still in his hand. He swung, the blade arching through the air inches from Tony's face.

"Back off!" Martin spat as he raised the knife again.

This time Tony was ready.

He gave Martin a two-armed shove backward, pulled out his firearm and aimed for Martin's arm. He didn't want to kill the man. He just needed to stop him. "Freeze!" he yelled, as the teen jumped to his feet and darted between them.

It was the second of opportunity Martin needed.

The knife blade dropped again, this time slicing across the boy's cheek. He darted away, pushing through a patch of brambles and darting from the line of Tony's gunfire.

Blood spurted from the wound in the teen's cheek. He wobbled as Tony shoved past, ready to follow Martin.

"Stay here!" he shouted at the boy.

But, the kid didn't seem interested in listening.

He followed Tony, rushing after him as he shoved through the patch of brambles and called in his location.

"I said, stay put!" Tony repeated, concerned for the boy, but more concerned that Martin would escape again. He had proven to be cunning and dangerous, and he needed to be apprehended before he hurt someone else.

"I'm not staying there waiting for him to come back for me," the teen responded, his voice muffled and faint. One minute he was running behind Tony. The next, he was falling, his scrawny body knocking into Tony as he went down.

"You okay?" Tony asked, still moving. When the teen didn't respond, he glanced back. The kid was lying prone, blood seeping from his cheek, eyes closed. He was clearly unconscious.

Tony itched to go after Martin, but he couldn't leave an injured and unconscious teenager lying in the park alone.

Frustrated, he jogged back, crouching near the young man and feeling for a pulse. Every second he spent there was a second more of distance Martin put between them, but this wouldn't be the end of the chase. As soon as backup arrived, Tony and Rusty would return to the hunt.

I'll get you, Tony vowed. For Katie. For Jordan. For himself.

THREE

Katie didn't like hospitals. The scents and sounds brought back memories she'd rather forget. She had been ten when her parents died. An only child being raised by only children, she had had an idyllic childhood—a pretty house in the suburbs, nice clothes, good food and parents who'd loved her.

That had changed the night of her parents' fifteenth wedding anniversary. She had been at home with a babysitter when a drunk driver had blown through a red light and hit her parents' sedan. Her father had been killed instantly. Her mother had lived for nearly a week. Katie had visited her every day, standing alone in the ICU and listening to the *whoosh* and *beep* of the machines keeping her mother alive. She'd had no grandparents, uncles or aunts to support her as she grieved. Just strangers who had meant well but who had not been able to give her the only thing she had wanted—her parents.

Even now, all these years later, hospitals made her stomach churn.

She touched her abdomen, her fingers skimming across the fetal monitor that was strapped there. The baby was moving, her rapid heartbeat filling the silence of the room. The contractions had ended as abruptly as they'd begun, and for the past two hours, she had been lying in the hospital bed, watching the clock, wondering how Ivy was doing and if Tony and Rusty were all right. Worrying about what Martin might be doing.

He'd tracked her here earlier. Walked right into the clinic, donned a lab coat and fooled everyone he'd passed. He could do it again. Had he managed to circle back to the building? Was he inside right now?

Breathe, she told herself. *An officer is stationed outside your room. Martin can't get you. Or, hurt the baby.*

She wanted the thought to be comforting, but Jordan had been tough, strong and smart. Somehow Martin had managed to get to him. If that could happen, anything seemed possible.

She had not heard anything from her father- or brothers-in-law since she had insisted they stay by Ivy's side. They had left reluctantly, but they *had* left. Katie hadn't expected or wanted anything else.

That didn't mean she liked being alone.

For the first hour, regular contractions had distracted her.

Now, with the pain gone, her mind was spinning, her thoughts jumping from one thing to the next. She had spent nearly nine months preparing to give birth without Jordan, but the threat of an early labor, even just by a couple of weeks, had made her realize how desperately she still wanted him there.

He'd promised her a lot of things before they had married.

He had promised her even more when they'd stood in front of friends and family and spoken their vows. He had said he would love her always, that she would be first in his life after God, that he would put her needs in front of his own and be the family she longed for. That he would always be there for her.

She had believed him. But, even in the first few months of their marriage, she had known that her needs were secondary to the needs of the K-9 unit and the community. Jordan had taken his responsibilities to both seriously. He had worked long hours and devoted himself to justice. She had admired that more than she had resented it, but there *had* been a tiny bit of jealousy—a small part of herself that had wondered how they would both feel in a decade or two, after his job had pulled him away from anniversaries and holidays and birthdays a few too many times.

She frowned, shoved aside the blanket that covered her legs and got to her feet. She unhooked the monitor and set it on a table near the bed.

Lately, she had spent too much time looking at the past through a microscopic lens. As if, somehow, that could change all of the things that had happened.

But, of course, no amount of dwelling on her decisions, on the things she had believed and expected, could change the fact that Jordan was dead, that she was alone, that a man who had seemed as innocuous as a buttercup in a field of daisies had killed her husband and nearly kidnapped her.

Martin was deranged.

A dangerous man with a twisted obsession.

And, she was the target of that obsession.

She was the reason Jordan had been murdered.

No matter how much she wanted to, she couldn't forget that, and she couldn't forgive herself.

If she could go back to the days before she and Jordan had met, she would. Instead of being open to all of the new people in her life, she would have ignored Martin when she saw him at the church they had both attended. She wouldn't have chatted with him when they ran into each other in the parking lot after service. She certainly wouldn't have accepted his invitation to coffee the following Sunday morning. Nor would she have had lunch with him the week after that.

To Katie, those had not been real dates. They had been opportunities to get to know a nice guy in her new church community. Martin had been charming. He had also been a Sunday school teacher, a deacon, a man who quoted Scripture and lived a seemingly upright life. Katie hadn't seen any harm in saying yes to his invitations.

If she could go back, she would have known the truth about what lurked beneath Martin's charming exterior. She wouldn't have spoken to him. She wouldn't have gone out with him. She wouldn't have unwittingly sparked the obsession that had cost Jordan his life.

She swallowed a hard lump of grief.

Her clothes were folded neatly and set on a chair near the door. Her purse had been retrieved from Dr. Ritter's office and was sitting on top of them. She grabbed the purse and her clothes and ducked into the bathroom to dress. She wanted to be quick, but pregnancy made her once-athletic body cumbersome and clumsy. By the time she managed to get out of the hospital gown and back into her clothes, a nurse was knocking on the bathroom door.

"Katie? Is everything okay?"

"Fine." She opened the door and smiled as she sidled past the nurse and slid her feet into her shoes.

"We were worried when the fetal monitor stopped reading your baby's heartbeat." There was an unmistakable note of censure in the nurse's tone.

"I haven't had a contraction in a couple of hours. The doctor said the baby's heart rate is great, so I thought I'd go see how my mother-in-law is doing."

And, then, she was going to ask one of her brothers-in-law to arrange for an escort home. She would call Tony on the way there and make sure he and Rusty were all right. She hoped they were. The last thing she wanted or needed was more blood on her hands.

She frowned, hiking her purse up on her shoulder and trying to shove the thought and the guilt away.

Maybe one day she would stop feeling as if she were responsible for the horrible things Martin had done.

Today was apparently not that day.

"We need to clear that with the doctor and with…" The nurse's voice trailed off, her gaze darting to the now-open door.

"The police?" Katie offered. "I know they're standing guard, but I'm not a criminal and I can go where I want."

"We still need to clear things with the doctor," the nurse argued. "You had quite a scare this morning, and Dr. Ritter wants to be certain you and the baby are healthy."

"I'm as concerned as he is, but he has already assured me the baby looks great," Katie responded, anxious to get back to the quiet home she and Jordan had shared. Sometimes, if she allowed herself, she could still hear him walking up the steps and sliding his key into the lock.

Despite the long hours he'd spent on the job and the

weekends she had often spent alone, she had always run into his arms when he returned home.

She missed that.

She missed him.

"Is everything okay in here?" A uniformed officer peered into the room.

"Everything is fine, but I would like to visit my mother-in-law. If you wouldn't mind escorting me there, I would appreciate it."

"I'll have to check with the chief," he responded. She recognized most of the men and women in the NYC K-9 Command Unit. He wasn't one of them.

"Noah Jameson is my brother-in-law," she said. "I'm sure he wouldn't mind."

"Currently the chief is out in the field." Another officer stepped into the room, a yellow Lab on a lead beside her. Katie recognized her immediately. Brianne Hayes was new to the K-9 team. One of the few female officers in the unit, she had proved herself to be a top-notch handler when she had helped apprehend a bombing suspect a few months back.

"Can you contact him? I'm anxious to see Ivy."

"I can try, but…" Brianne hesitated, the look in her eyes reminding Katie of the one she had seen in the faces of the officers who had informed her of Jordan's death.

"What's going on?" she asked. "Did something else happen to Ivy? Is she…worse than they originally thought?"

"She's fine," Brianne answered hurriedly.

"Did something happen to Tony?" Katie asked, her mind rushing in a direction she had been trying not to allow it to go.

She had been married to a police officer.

She knew the risks.

Every time Jordan had left the house, she had known there was a possibility he wouldn't be coming home. Over the past few months, that nagging worry had transferred to the other men in Katie's life—her brothers--in-law and Tony.

Brianne hesitated, her gaze jumping to the other officer. "He's fine."

Her answer was about as reassuring as the concerned look on her face.

"Then, why do you look like he's not?"

"You need to relax and not worry, okay?" Brianne responded.

"I would worry less if someone would tell me what's going on."

"There isn't much to tell. Martin Fisher hasn't been apprehended. The chief is out searching for him with other members of the team. Until I hear something different, I'd rather you just sit tight and wait here."

"The NYPD have been hunting for Martin since he escaped the mental hospital. There's no guarantee he'll be found tonight or tomorrow, and I can't remain in the hospital indefinitely. Besides, I'm not asking to leave. I'm just asking to visit Ivy." She wanted to leave, though, and if she could talk one of her brothers-in-law into bringing her home, that's exactly what she planned to do.

"I have to check with the chief, but if I can get in touch with him, I'll see if I can clear it. Just give me a few minutes, okay?"

"Sure," Katie conceded. She was too tired to argue. Even if she weren't, she would have allowed Brianne to do her job. She had too much respect for law enforcement to make trouble for any of the officers.

"Thanks." Brianne smiled, her eyes shadowed with fatigue, her auburn hair tucked behind her ears. Like everyone on the K-9 team, she had been burning the candle at both ends, trying to locate and apprehend Martin.

"I'll contact Dr. Ritter," the nurse added, walking out of the room as the officers left.

Katie waited until they closed the door, then dug through her purse until she found her phone. She scrolled through text messages from friends who had heard about the attempted kidnapping on the news and were worried about her. Former colleagues had called, and she had gotten a call from her pastor. She didn't listen to the voice mails. She'd do that later. For now, she had the information she wanted. Tony had not tried to contact her. That wasn't surprising, if he was still out searching for Martin.

But, she couldn't forget Brianne's hesitation.

Something was wrong.

She was sure of it.

She swung open the door, determined to get the truth.

Tony was there, hand raised as if he'd been getting ready to knock. His jacket and uniform shirt were off, and a thick bandage was showing beneath the short sleeve of his T-shirt. There were specks of blood on his forearm and a smear of it on his cheek.

But, he was on his feet and alive, Rusty standing beside him.

She was so relieved, she threw her arms around him, pulling him close before she realized what she was doing.

* * *

Tony had been hugged hundreds of times, and he'd given plenty of hugs. At Jordan's funeral, he had stood beside Katie, his arm around her shoulders, offering support, because he had known that's what his friend would have wanted.

Now, though, she was nearly nine months pregnant, her belly pressing against his abdomen, her arms wrapped around his waist. He felt the baby move, the tiny life demanding attention.

He had made a promise to Jordan, and he meant to keep it. He would make certain Katie and the baby were safe. Even if that meant going out to hunt for Martin with a bandaged arm.

Katie stepped back, eyes dark in her pale face. "Sorry."

"For what?"

"The hug." Her gaze jumped to Brianne.

"No need to apologize. We're family."

"You and Jordan always did call each other brother," she said, offering a half smile.

"We did," he agreed. She was obviously self-conscious about what had been a completely platonic hug.

"I was worried about you." She touched the edge of the bandage that covered his cleaned and sutured wound. "Are you okay?"

"Fine. I would have been here sooner, but Martin grabbed a teenager in the park, and he was wounded."

"Oh no! Will he be okay?"

"He has a cut on his cheek and is shaken up, but he'll be fine."

"And your shoulder?"

"Also fine, but Noah insisted I get checked out at the hospital and take a couple of days to recuperate."

"That doesn't sound like a bad idea."

"It wouldn't be, if Martin weren't still running free." He took her arm and led her back into the room. The less time she spent out in the open, the happier he'd be.

"I was hoping to avoid returning to the hospital room," she murmured, stopping just over the threshold.

"It's best if you stay here."

"So everyone keeps telling me, but I'd prefer to go check on Ivy."

"I spoke with Carter a few minutes ago. Ivy is doing well. She broke her wrist and has a mild concussion. They plan to keep her for observation, but she should be able to return home tomorrow."

"Poor Ivy. This is all—"

"Don't say it," he cut in.

"What?" she asked, raising one light brown brow and eyeing him with a look she had probably used on her fifth-grade class when she was teaching.

"That it's your fault."

"If I hadn't—"

"Katie, we could all spend our lives thinking about what we could have done differently, but none of us can go back. You and I go to the same church. I've spoken to Martin a few dozen times, and I never would have imagined he was capable of murder."

"You're right. I know that."

"Then, stop feeling guilty for the actions of a sick individual. There is nothing you could have done to keep him from becoming fixated on you. Even if you hadn't gone out with him, he may still have stalked you. He's unhinged."

"Maybe so." She smiled, but her eyes were sad. They'd been that way since Jordan's death.

"Exactly so," he replied, and some of the sadness left her eyes.

"You're always a cheerleader, Tony, and I appreciate it. But, I'd appreciate it a lot more if you would bring me to see Ivy and then drive me home."

He should have refused.

Noah had already told him to get treatment and to return home to rest. There'd been nothing in his directives about visiting Katie or taking her home. But, Tony had never been one to blindly follow someone else's lead. He was off the clock, and he knew how to protect Katie.

He'd bring her up to see Ivy, and then he'd check in with Jordan's brother Carter, who was still recovering from being shot several months ago and had only just returned to the office part-time. The other two Jameson brothers, Noah and Zach, were hunting Martin while Carter stayed at the hospital with Ivy and their father.

"All right," he agreed.

Her eyes widened, and she offered the first real smile he had seen in months. "Really?"

"Did you think I'd refuse?"

"Everyone else has."

"I'm not everyone else."

He touched her shoulder, brushing aside a thick strand of hair. She looked exhausted, her cheeks hollow, her eyes red-rimmed. In the few years that he'd known her, she had always seemed energetic and enthusiastic, her outlook optimistic. She had a clear-eyed, pragmatic view of life that had attracted Jordan and intrigued Tony. He had grown up in a family filled with silence and unspoken resentment. His mother had gone to the grave bitterly resentful of his father's career. An NYPD homicide detective, Dillard Knight had devoted his life to law enforcement. He'd had little time for his wife or his only child. Even when Tony's mother had been dying of cancer, Dillard had spent more time working than he had at home.

Jordan and his family had been Tony's escape from that, and when Katie had entered the picture, the joy she took in the simple things in life had captured his attention. That may have dimmed after Jordan's death, but she had kept her focus on the future and tried hard to stay positive.

He didn't want that to change.

Not because of someone like Martin.

"It's going to be okay, Katie," he said.

"Ivy told me that right before Martin showed up," she responded, stepping away and walking into the hall.

He followed, staying close as they walked to the bank of elevators that would bring them up to Ivy's room.

Jordan had never been one to ask for much.

He was more likely to give than to expect to receive help.

Tony once again thought about how Jordan had pulled him aside on the morning of the wedding and asked him to look after Katie if anything happened to him.

She's strong. She can go it alone, but I don't want her to have to. I know my family will be there for her, but I want to know that she'll have someone on her side who knows what it's like to grow up without a firm support system in place. She's like you, man—just looking for a place to belong. You two will understand each other better than any two people I know.

Tony remembered the words as if they'd been spoken seconds rather than years ago, and he remembered his response. That he'd be there if Katie needed him. Always. For a lifetime. If that's what was necessary.

Right now, she needed him.

Whether she realized it or not.

For as long as that was true, he'd be there, ready to do what Jordan couldn't—keep her and the baby safe.

FOUR

Ivy looked better than Katie had anticipated. Head bruised and arm in a cast, she was holding court in the hospital room, Alexander and Carter sitting on one side of the bed, the pastor and two friends on the other.

"Katie! What are you doing here?" Ivy cried as Katie and Tony walked into the room.

"I wanted to make sure you were okay," she responded, bending down awkwardly to kiss her mother-in-law's cheek. Her belly seemed to grow bigger every day, the baby's elbows and feet jabbing into her sides so often, she had begun to wonder if she was carrying a future dancer or gymnast. Jordan would have been happy with either of those choices.

Whatever our children decide to be will be fine with me, as long as they're happy, he'd whispered in her ear the night she had told him she was pregnant.

He had been ecstatic.

She had been, too, but she had also been worried about how soon after the wedding the pregnancy had happened. She had wanted another year or two of teaching before she had kids, but Jordan had been gung ho to begin a family. She had also wanted to work until right before the baby was born, but Jordan had thought it would be best for her to give her notice before the new school year began.

In retrospect, she had compromised a lot in the short time they had been married. She wasn't sure how she felt about that. She was certainly glad to be pregnant and happy she would be bringing Jordan's child into the world, but without teaching and Jordan, the days since his death had been long and empty. Time had stretched out, and it seemed to be taking eons rather than months for the baby to arrive.

"You wanted to see how *I* was doing? *You're* the one who is about ready to have a baby," Ivy exclaimed, laying a hand on Katie's abdomen.

She tried not to tense.

She loved Ivy. She understood the gift the baby was to the Jameson family, but she wasn't used to having a mother in her life, and the attention often made her feel awkward and uncomfortable.

Tony might have sensed that.

He stepped up beside her and leaned down to kiss Ivy's cheek, distracting her from Katie and the baby bump.

"How are you doing, Mom?" he asked.

Ivy smiled just as she always did when he called her mom. "Better than you, I'd say. What happened to your shoulder?"

"I had a run-in with the sharp end of a knife. Nothing a few swipes of antiseptic and a bandage couldn't fix."

"That's an awfully thick bandage for something that only needed a little attention." Carter stood stiffly, grimacing.

He had the same blue eyes as Jordan and a similar

smile. Katie had not seen much of it since he'd been shot. He had recently gone back to work part-time, but the doctors weren't sure if he would ever be able to return in his full capacity.

That had to be weighing on him.

Like his brothers, he loved the work he did with the K-9 unit. Katie had no idea what he would do if he couldn't return to it full-time. He had his daughter, of course, and his fiancée, Rachelle. It wasn't like his life was empty, but she knew Jordan would have been devastated to lose his ability to work in law enforcement. She imagined any of his brothers would feel the same. She hadn't asked Carter. As wonderful as the Jamesons had been to her, she had not known any of them for very long. At least not long enough to ask deeply personal questions.

"I was thinking the same thing," Alexander Jameson said, still seated beside Ivy, his hand resting on her shoulder. The patriarch of the Jameson clan, he had a good head on his shoulders, an abundance of loyalty to his family and a calm demeanor that all four of his sons seemed to have inherited. "I take it you got that from Fisher."

"Unfortunately, yes."

"Does Noah know?" Carter asked.

"He's the one who insisted I get treated at the hospital. I wanted to keep searching for Fisher. Rusty and I almost had him." He patted the Lab's broad head and scratched behind his ears.

Rusty seemed to smile in return, his head cocking to the side, his mouth open, tongue hanging out.

"There is an entire K-9 unit hunting for him. We'll get him. It's just a matter of time." Carter sounded confident. There was no reason why he shouldn't be. Martin couldn't stay hidden forever. Eventually, he would show himself again.

She shivered, crossing her arms over her stomach.

She had been trying not to dwell on what had happened that morning, refusing to allow her mind to go to the darkest places. The places where Martin was successful in his kidnapping attempt and hurt the baby.

"You're exhausted, Katie," Carter said, his voice filled with concern. "You should go back to your room."

"I'd rather go home. I still have a lot to do before the baby arrives."

"The baby won't know if pictures are hung or if all the baby stuff is put away," Alexander pointed out.

"I know, but I'll feel better if I get things done." And, she would feel better away from the hospital and the four sets of eyes that were watching her intently.

"Going home is probably not a good idea. Fisher knows where you live, and based on what happened today, he's been watching your movements," Carter said.

"He got to me in a medical center. I don't think I'll be any safer here than I will be at home."

"She has a point," Tony said, unexpectedly coming to her aid. "If guards can stand outside her hospital room, they can stand outside her house."

"That's true," Ivy agreed. "And, if I were in Katie's shoes, I would want to be home. As a matter of fact, maybe I'll follow her lead and get myself checked out of here."

"No, you won't," Alexander said calmly. "You have a head injury, and you need to stay here for observation."

"I believe I make my own decisions about where I'm

going and what I'm doing," Ivy retorted, her gaze sharp. Her words sharper. She ran a tight ship at the Jameson house, keeping the five Jameson men in line.

Four.

There were only four Jameson men remaining.

Grief washed over Katie like it had hundreds of times since Jordan's murder, and she swallowed back tears.

"You do. Unless you have a head injury. In which case, I make the decisions." Alexander pressed a kiss to Ivy's hand and smiled. "I don't know what I would do without you, Ivy. So, how about you let me have my way this time? If you don't, I'll be pacing our bedroom all night, checking on you every fifteen seconds to make sure you haven't fallen into a coma."

Ivy's expression softened, and she touched her husband's cheek. "Fine. For you, I'll stay."

The exchange was brief and sweet, the simplicity and beauty of their love evident in the gaze that passed between them. They'd been married thirty-five years and had weathered many storms together.

That is what Katie had imagined having with Jordan.

Martin had taken that from her.

"I'm assuming you plan to escort Katie home?" Alexander asked, his gaze shifting from his wife to Tony.

"I'll escort her there, and I'll stick around until one of you arrives."

"That's not necessary," Katie began, but it was. She knew it. They knew it. "What I mean is you're injured. If you'd rather me stay here so you can go home, I'll understand."

"I would rather you be somewhere that feels comfortable and safe. If that's home, then I'm all for you being there. Ready?"

She nodded, kissed Ivy's and Alexander's cheeks, waved to Carter and the other people in the room, and followed Tony into the hall.

Neither of them spoke as they took the elevator to the lobby. When they reached the hospital's exit, Rusty nosed the ground near the door and sniffed intently.

"Do you think he smells Martin?" Katie asked, suddenly wondering if she were making the right choice. Maybe the hospital *would* be safer than her house.

She almost told Tony she had changed her mind, but he opened the door and gestured to a police officer who was standing near the curb. Long and lean, the man had a narrow mustache and coal-black eyes.

"What's up?" he asked, his hand resting on his utility belt, the leather creaking as he moved.

"I need another set of eyes while I'm walking to my car," Tony replied.

"I can be that." The officer smiled and moved in beside Katie. Neither man touched her, but she felt cocooned between them.

It took seconds to cross the parking lot and reach Tony's SUV, the police K-9 logo emblazoned on the side. She waited while he opened the passenger's side door and moved a bloodstained shirt and jacket from the seat.

"That's a lot of blood," she said as she tried to pull the seat belt across her lap. Her hands were as clumsy as the rest of her, trembling as she attempted to snap the ends of the belt beneath her belly.

"Not really." He brushed her hands away and snapped the belt into place, his knuckles skimming her abdomen. Her cheeks heated at the intimacy of it. Tony leaning in, his head bent close to hers, his hair tickling her chin.

She had never thought of him as anything other than

Jordan's best buddy. Tony had been beside her since his death, offering help, support and comfort. She had appreciated that, and she had thanked him for it, but she wasn't sure she had realized until just that moment how much it had meant to her.

"Tony?" She touched his wrist before he could close the door. "Thank you."

"For the ride? Thanks aren't necessary." He smiled and would have closed the door, but she had learned a valuable lesson from the deaths of her parents and her husband: always say what needs to be said to the people you care about.

"Not for the ride. For everything you've done since Jordan's death. You've been a rock. I don't know what I would have done without you."

"You would have been just fine."

"Maybe."

He didn't reassure her. He didn't offer platitudes. He studied her face, his gaze skimming across the curve of her cheek and down the flushed column of her throat. "Based on what I have seen the past few years and what Jordan told me about you, I don't think you have nearly enough confidence in yourself."

"I have plenty of confidence."

"Then, don't sell yourself short. You would have been fine, Katie. You're tough and smart. Even if you had no one but yourself to rely on, you would be okay." His fingers skimmed her cheek as he tucked a few loose strands of hair behind her ear. Warmth she hadn't expected or wanted seeped into her blood.

She thought he must have felt that strange and unsettling spark of heat. His eyes narrowed and his hand dropped away. He stepped back quickly and closed the door without saying another word.

She rested her head against the seat's headrest, closing her eyes and telling herself she was overtired and overreacting. What she had felt was a product of stress and trauma. Of course, she would have strong feelings for the person who had saved her life. It was a normal and expected thing.

Plus, she was nearly nine months pregnant.

Hormones were raging. Emotions were heightened.

That was all there was to the heat in her cheeks and in her blood.

Cold air swept into the vehicle as Tony opened the back hatch and let Rusty in. The Lab huffed quietly as he settled down for the ride. When the driver's side door opened, Katie kept her eyes closed and her body relaxed. She was too tired to talk, and too confused to want to.

The engine started, and the vehicle pulled out, the soft purr of the motor soothing some of the tension from her shoulders and neck. The heat in her cheeks faded, the country music Tony had playing a pleasant backdrop to the quiet rumble of tires on pavement.

"You're a country music fan?" she asked. She had had no idea. Now that she thought about it, there were a lot of things she didn't know about him. He had spent a lot of time with Jordan and, by extension, Katie, but she had never asked him where he lived or what he enjoyed beyond dogs and criminal justice. She knew he liked fishing and hunting. He and Jordan had taken a few long-weekend trips to Maine to hike trails and track game.

She had never joined them.

Tony had invited her once, but Jordan had told him that she wasn't much of an outdoors person. It wasn't true, but she had not corrected him. Not in front of Tony and not later when she had had the chance.

Like so many other things in the past, that hadn't seemed problematic. She had been newly married and in love. She had assumed she and Jordan would have all the time in the world to learn about each other.

Funny how life was.

All of the things that were planned so carefully often coming to nothing, and all of the unexpected things taking their place.

The SUV bounced over a pothole, and she almost opened her eyes, but she didn't feel like talking. The baby had finally quieted, and all she wanted to do was be quiet with her.

Katie wasn't asleep, but Tony let her pretend to be.

Her relaxed muscles were a nice change from what he had grown used to seeing these past several months. Since Jordan's death, she had been tense and nervous, her skin pale and her face gaunt. Aside from the baby bump, she had grown thin; her once-athletic body had become almost too lean. Like everyone else who knew her, Tony had been worried. Once he had realized exactly what had happened to Jordan and why, his concern had grown exponentially.

He should have apprehended Martin today.

He *would* have apprehended him if not for Martin's using that scared teenager as his personal escape plan. Rusty shifted in the back of the SUV, his head popping into view and then disappearing again. The Lab knew work had ended for the day. His K-9 vest had been removed and he had been allowed plenty of attention and pets from hospital staff. Like any good working dog, Rusty knew what was required. He didn't seek attention while he was on the job, but when he was off duty, he was a typical goofy, happy-go-lucky Lab.

Traffic was slow in the city, as always, and it took nearly forty minutes to drive to the Jameson house. A three-level home on a pretty lot in a quiet Queens neighborhood, the multifamily dwelling was exactly what Jordan and his family needed. Like so many other New York City dwellers, they coveted fenced backyards. From what Jordan had said, it worked out well. The dogs had a place to run, family was close, but not so close there wasn't privacy.

Tony found a spot just a few doors up from the house. He'd park in the driveway, but he wanted to leave that available for Alexander and Ivy. As soon as the car engine died, Katie straightened, her long blond ponytail sliding over her shoulder as she reached for the door handle.

"Thank you for the ride, Tony," she said, as if she thought he would let her out and then drive away.

"I was hoping for an invitation to coffee," he said, not wanting to remind her of the attempted kidnapping or the fact that Martin was still on the loose.

"From what I've seen, you're not much of a coffee drinker, so I think it's more likely that you want to check the apartment and make sure Martin isn't waiting for me there."

"You're right—on both counts," he admitted.

"You could have just said that. It's not like I'm not aware of the danger I'm in, and it's not like talking about it will break me." She reached for the door handle again.

"Wait until I'm out, okay?"

"Sure." Her hand dropped to her belly. She still had specks of blood on her knuckles. Her jeans were torn. Her hands were scraped raw. The fact that Martin had gotten so close to kidnapping her filled Tony with fury and with fear.

He jogged to the hatchback and released Rusty. The dog was as familiar with the Jameson house as he was with his own, and his tail wagged happily as Tony opened Katie's door and offered her a hand.

"Thanks." She allowed herself to be helped out of the vehicle, her gaze scanning the exterior of the house, the driveway, the sun-dappled shrubs near the corners of the yard.

"If it makes you feel better, I don't think he is brazen enough to show up here."

"Did you think he was brazen enough to show up at the medical clinic?"

"I hoped he wasn't, but I was worried that he might." He and Noah had agreed it was a possibility, which was why Tony had been driving past the medical center every few minutes. "The fact is Martin is mentally ill and unpredictable because of it. We're using every bit of man power and caution we can to—"

"Tony," she cut in tiredly. "I know all that. I've been told the same thing by every member of law enforcement I've spoken to."

"Sorry. Sometimes I forget to take off my law-enforcement hat when I clock out for the day." He smiled to try to lighten the mood, but Katie was digging keys from her purse and didn't seem to notice.

"I didn't realize the hat ever came off," she commented as she led the way through the front door and up the stairs to her apartment.

"If a police officer wants to have a pleasant home environment and a happy family, it should," he replied.

"Interesting." She tried to fit the key in the lock, but her hand was trembling, and she kept missing the mark.

"Why?" He took the keys from her hand and unlocked the door.

"I don't think Jordan had a hat. Either that or it was always on." She would have entered the apartment, but he pulled her back.

"I'll send Rusty in first. He'll know if anything is off." He released the dog, watching as the Lab trotted inside and paused in the small entryway. He sniffed the floor, then raised his head and scent-checked the air. When he plopped down on the carpet in the living room, Tony knew the place was empty.

"Looks like he's making himself at home," Katie murmured as she stood in the doorway, her arm pressed against his, her body leaning just a little in his direction.

Before Jordan's death, she had seemed perpetually optimistic, her cheerful good nature making her a favorite with the K-9 unit. She had been the spouse who had brought Christmas cookies and holiday candy to the station, who had bought treats for the dogs and remembered everyone's birthday. She seemed to have faded since Jordan's death, her glossy hair brittle, her eyes shadowed and red-rimmed. Tony wasn't sure if it was Jordan's death or the pregnancy that had sapped so much of her energy.

"This is like a second home to him." He nudged Katie into the apartment, walked in behind her, locked the door, and then peered into all of the rooms and out each window, focusing particularly on the backyard below. The late afternoon sun had finally broken through the cloud cover, painting the grass with gold highlights. There were no footprints pressed into the earth near the fence line, no sign that anyone had been lurking near the property while the Jamesons were away.

Still, Tony felt uneasy, and he stood by the window for a moment longer, waiting for someone to step around the side of the house, for a shadow to move where one shouldn't, for Martin to show himself.

"Is everything okay?" Katie asked, and he finally turned away and walked back toward her.

"Fine, but you look exhausted. Why don't you go lie down? I'll put the crib together."

"With a bandaged shoulder? I don't think so." Her hands settled on her hips, and she looked like a Victorian schoolmarm, hair just a little messy, eyes blazing as she tried to take control of an unruly student.

"Your inner teacher is coming out."

She blinked and then, to his surprise, chuckled, her hands falling away from her hips. "Jordan used to say that to me every time I put my hands on my hips when we were...discussing things."

"Discussing? Is that the same as arguing?" he asked as he walked into the galley-style kitchen and opened the fridge. There wasn't much in it. Orange juice. Eggs. Milk. Cheese.

"Not when you're a newlywed," she replied. "If you're looking for a meal, you may have to go elsewhere to find it. Ivy and I planned to go grocery shopping after my appointment today."

"I'll go for you, after the Jamesons get home. For now, how about I make you an omelet?"

"I'm not hungry."

"The baby might be."

"The baby is sleeping." She pulled out a chair and sat at the kitchenette table, her stomach bumping the wood.

It wasn't his responsibility to get her to eat, so he poured a glass of juice and set it in front of her.

"Thanks for not pushing the food issue. Everyone I know seems to think a good meal will solve my problems."

"Maybe they just don't know what else to offer you," he suggested, taking the seat across from her.

"Probably not. There really are only so many things a person can say to a twenty-six-year-old pregnant widow. I suppose *eat this* is one of them." She smiled and took a sip of the juice.

"*I'll put together the crib* is another."

She chuckled again. "You're good at that, Tony."

"What?"

"Making me laugh." She pushed away from the table and stood. "Seeing as how I am exhausted and don't have the energy to do it myself, I'm going to do what Mrs. Henderson was always telling me and *not* look a gift horse in the mouth. If you want to put the crib together, I'll be happy to let you do it."

"Mrs. Henderson?"

"My last foster mother. I lived with her until I turned eighteen. She was a retired schoolteacher. Tough but kind."

"I didn't realize you were in foster care." He felt like it was something he should have known. Jordan had said a lot of things about Katie. He'd spoken about her intelligence, her caring nature and her optimistic outlook, but Tony couldn't remember him ever mentioning Katie's past.

"It's not something I talk about much."

"Is there a reason for that?" he asked, curious despite himself.

"There's not much to say. My parents died in a car accident when I was ten. Neither of them had any surviving family, so I was shuffled into the foster system." She shrugged as if it didn't matter, but he knew it did. He had lived through his own rough childhood. He knew how hard it was to break the old habits of silence and self-protection.

"That is a difficult thing for a kid to go through."

"It could have been worse. None of my foster homes were horrible or abusive. I wasn't mistreated. But, it was...lonely." She shrugged again. "When I found out I was pregnant, I prayed that God would allow Jordan and I to be around for our child through all the ups and downs of her life. Through the tough things that happen during childhood and adolescence. Through the chaotic teenage years. On into adulthood, because I miss that. Not having parents to turn to for the big things and the small ones. I don't want my child to ever feel alone. Maybe God was sleeping that day." She smiled, but the sadness was still in her eyes. Only, now, he understood it a little bit better.

"God never sleeps, but sometimes He has reason to say no. Maybe this is one of those times." He knew she didn't need the reminder. From what he had seen, Katie's faith had remained rock-solid after Jordan's murder.

"I've been reminded of that a few dozen times recently. But..."

"Like the omelet, the reminders aren't something you need right now?"

"Something like that. I'm exhausted. I'm going to lie down. Thanks again…for everything."

She walked down the hall that led to three bedrooms and a bathroom. Tony waited until he heard her door shut before following. The door to the guest room was open. He walked past without looking in. He had stayed at the house a few times before Jordan and Katie married. He knew the layout. The nursery was just across the hall from the master bedroom.

He moved silently, while Rusty's paws clicked against the hardwood floor behind him. Photographs lined the walls on both sides of the wide hallway, muted sunlight streaming through a window at the far end. As far as Queens apartments went, this was a good-sized one. The bedrooms were small but not tiny, and the living room was large and functional. The kitchen was narrow but still had an eat-in area. Jordan had once told Tony he would be content to stay there for the rest of his life. He had loved the city, and he had loved working for the NYPD.

If his life had not been cut short, he would have continued on his career path, striving to make a difference in the community he loved.

"This shouldn't have happened, brother," Tony murmured as he walked into the nursery. Jordan had not been around to choose the paint color or the bedding. He had had no part in picking the crib, which was still in a box in the middle of the floor. It didn't seem fair or right that a good, honest man was dead and his murderer was alive and free.

God's plans were always best, but that didn't mean accepting them was always easy.

Tony sighed, pulling his utility knife out and using it to open the box. It shouldn't take long to put the crib together. When he was finished, he'd go online and find a grocery-delivery service to have food delivered to the house.

He couldn't change the past, and he couldn't bring Jordan back, but he could do that.

FIVE

Despite the discomfort of her pregnancy, Katie fell asleep. She woke to darkness and the soft sound of someone snoring. She reached across the bed to wake Jordan. She had done the same dozens of times before. Only now, instead of encountering Jordan's warm, muscular shoulder, her hand met empty air.

Because, of course, Jordan wasn't there.

Of course, his side of the bed was empty.

She was alone, yet she could hear someone snoring. She flicked on the bedside lamp, her heart pounding frantically. Someone was in the room, and the only person she knew of who might wander into her house and fall asleep like he belonged there was Martin.

He was *that* delusional and, if he had found his way into the house, she needed to find a way out.

Now!

She jumped from the bed and stumbled over something that was lying beside it. She went down on her knees and tried to jump up again, but her body was heavy, her movements uncoordinated.

She would have screamed, but her mouth was dry with terror.

She struggled to her feet, tried to take a step forward, but the thing that had tripped her blocked her path. Chocolate fur, dark eyes and a fuzzy face, Rusty watched her expectantly, his doggy grin chasing away her fear.

"Rusty! What are you doing in here? Did your handler leave and make you stay here to protect me?" She scratched his broad head, and his tail wagged happily.

Tony appeared in the doorway. "Actually, he was whining at your door. I knocked, but you didn't respond, so I opened the door to check on you. He slipped in and made himself comfortable by the bed." Tony stood on the threshold, his hair mussed, a five-o'clock shadow giving him a rugged, outdoorsy look. She had seen him like that before. He and Jordan had often watched football together or tossed balls to their dogs out in the yard on the weekend. She had loved sitting in the kitchen, sipping tea and watching through the window. Jordan's K-9 partner, Snapper, had enjoyed Rusty's company as much as Jordan had enjoyed Tony's.

The apartment had been too empty since Jordan's death. Snapper had gone missing the same day, and Katie had felt the absence of the loyal dog almost as keenly as she had felt the absence of her husband.

Her life had been full.

Now it seemed barren, every day stretching into the next with nothing but a few visits from friends and family to fill them. She tried to stay positive, to look toward the future and the birth of the baby with excitement and joy, but even that was tainted by the loss of the only man she had ever loved.

"Are you okay?" Tony asked.

"Fine," she murmured, kneeling ungracefully so she

could run her hands over Rusty's warm coat. His tail continued to thump, and her eyes burned with tears.

She wanted her life back. The one she had so carefully planned and prayed about. The one that she had been so eager to step into. She wanted to go to bed at night knowing she wouldn't wake up alone in the morning. She wanted to make enough coffee for two and set the table for more than one. She wanted the things she had dreamed of during the long years of moving from foster home to foster home.

"Katie," Tony said quietly, crossing the room and crouching beside her. "You don't have to pretend to be okay."

"I'm not pretending," she lied, her focus still on Rusty.

He touched her chin, urging her to look at him. "Then, why are there tears in your eyes?"

"Because this wasn't the dream," she admitted. "This wasn't the answer I wanted to my prayers as a kid."

"I'm sorry," he said, staring into her eyes as if he could read her sorrow and heartache, and as if he understood it.

"I know," she said, that feeling she had had in the SUV welling up again as she continued to look into his eyes.

The air seemed to fill with it—a palpable tension that he must have noticed.

He stood, offered her a hand and then pulled her to her feet.

No more staring into her eyes.

He was all business, walking to the window to close the shades. "It's probably best to keep the shades drawn for a while."

"I guess that means they haven't apprehended Martin?"

"Unfortunately, it does." He ran a hand over his hair, smoothing the thick strands. "Noah called about an hour ago to say they were calling in the teams and regrouping. We'll meet tomorrow to discuss a plan of action. In the meantime, you'll have twenty-four-hour protection."

"Provided by the K-9 unit?"

"Yes. Currently, keeping you safe and apprehending Martin is our top priority."

"I'll have to thank whoever Noah sends to play bodyguard. Hanging around the house, waiting for something to happen, isn't going to be fun for someone who is used to being on the move."

"You can thank me by keeping the shades closed and staying away from the windows. I don't think Martin would harm you, but the less he knows about which room you're in and what you're doing, the happier I'll be."

"You?" She wasn't quite able to hide the surprise and uneasiness in her voice.

"It makes the most sense. I'm off on medical leave for a couple of days because Noah insisted, but my shoulder is fine. So, I'll take the first few shifts while other members of the unit pound the pavement and see if they can locate Martin."

"But…you're not supposed to be working," she protested.

"It sounds like the idea of me being here bothers you," Tony said, studying her face, probably seeing all kinds of things she would rather he didn't.

"Of course, it doesn't," she lied.

"You don't have to worry about what people will think, if that's what's bothering you."

"Think about what?" she hedged, because she *was* worried. But, not about that.

When Jordan had been alive, Tony had been the trusty sidekick. The guy her husband relied on when he needed help with home-improvement projects or yard work. The die-hard bachelor she had enjoyed setting a place at the table for when he came for a visit.

She had never looked at him as anything else.

Now, though…

Something was changing; their relationship was shifting from one that orbited around Jordan to…what? Friendship? Mutual respect? Affection?

She wasn't sure, but in the nearly nine months since Jordan's death, she had stopped seeing Tony as his bachelor buddy and begun to see him for who he was—a strong, driven, compassionate man who would do anything for the people he cared about.

She wasn't sure how she felt about that.

Disloyal? Alarmed? Worried.

"I thought you might be worried about what your neighbors will think if your deceased husband's best friend suddenly begins spending too much time at your place," he responded.

"I've never cared about what the neighbors think," she murmured, turning away and walking into the hall.

He followed. "Then, what are you worried about?"

She couldn't tell him the truth—that she was worried about the way she had felt when he had touched her cheek and when he had looked into her eyes.

"Everything. Ivy. Martin. All the K-9 handlers who are trying to find him. You." She added the last because it was true, and because she knew he would misunderstand the reasons for her concern.

"I can take care of myself, Katie, so don't waste any energy worrying about that."

"I'm worried about Snapper, too," she responded, glad to have the conversation on safer ground. "Has anyone been able to get in touch with the man who adopted him from the shelter?"

"Not yet, but we spoke to a neighbor who is taking in the mail and watching the house while he is out of town."

"If he's out of town, that would explain why he hasn't been in touch." She walked into the kitchen and put the kettle on to boil. She had given up coffee during her first trimester, when just the thought of it had turned her stomach. Now, she relied on tea to fuel her energy.

"It doesn't explain why he was able to adopt a microchipped police dog," Tony replied, a hard edge to his voice. Like everyone else on the K-9 unit, he had been putting in extra hours to search for the German shepherd. The dog had been spotted in Queens after Jordan's death, and Tony had scoured neighborhoods close to where he had been seen.

He had come up empty, and Katie knew that had bothered him.

"Did the shelter check for a microchip?" she asked. She had been so focused on Martin's escape, she hadn't asked many questions when Snapper had been spotted on an adoptable-pets search engine that the canine team had been perusing in the months following his disappearance.

"They are supposed to check every animal that comes in, but there is no record of that happening in

Snapper's case. Which makes me wonder if someone knew who he was and skipped that part of the process on purpose."

"Why would anyone do that?" She opened the fridge to get milk for her tea and was shocked to see the full shelves and drawers.

"It costs a lot of money to train a dog like Snapper, and there are plenty of underground operations that would love to take advantage of his very expensive education."

"You're talking about someone who works at the shelter alerting one of those operations that a police dog had come in?" She was still staring at the contents of the fridge, her mind half on the conversation, half on trying to figure out how the empty shelves had suddenly filled.

"It's possible. Could be a volunteer there for just that purpose—to scout out high-value dogs. It's also possible that Martin somehow got rid of the chip or corrupted it."

"I hope you're wrong about someone at the shelter being shady." Jordan would have been devastated if the dog he had worked with for countless hours were being used for criminal activities.

"Me, too, and I probably am. More than likely, there was just a mix-up when Snapper was brought in. The microchip was overlooked, and he was adopted out before anyone realized it. He's a great dog, and if I had seen him in a shelter, I would have taken him home in a heartbeat." He stepped up behind her, his hand resting on the still-open refrigerator door. "Looking for something?"

"Trying to figure out how my empty fridge became full."

"I had a delivery service come bring a few things."

"You didn't have to do that, Tony," she said, grabbing the milk and moving away.

"Yes, I did. The night of your wedding, Jordan asked me to promise to look after you if anything ever happened to him. I never break a promise."

She withheld a gasp. She hadn't known that Jordan had asked such a thing of his best friend. She hadn't thought he would have had the foresight to be concerned about what might happen if he were killed in the line of duty. He had been a man who had liked to live in the moment, and he had lived each moment fully.

Now, that she knew, she understood Tony's constant attention since Jordan's death. The fact that he had been by her side so often, checking in and making sure that she was doing okay? It was part of the obligation he felt to his best friend.

No wonder Tony was here.

And, no wonder he'd ordered groceries and put them away. He was stepping in and doing what he knew Jordan would want him to.

Knowing that shouldn't make her feel disappointed. She should be pleased that Jordan had been thinking about her future on their wedding day, that he had been preparing for whatever might come.

She was pleased.

But, that…awareness she'd noticed—*felt*—between them…? It was really just Tony Knight feeling the weight of the promise he had made. Understanding that didn't change anything. At least, it shouldn't. He was still Jordan's best friend. They still had their love for Jordan in common. He had still been there for her through the hardships of the past few months.

"Always is a long time," she murmured, refusing to meet his eyes. She didn't want him to see her confusion or her…disappointment? Maybe she did feel that. Just a little.

"I realized that when I made the promise," he said.

"Maybe, but I doubt you realized he would die. None of us were expecting that."

"I didn't expect it, but that doesn't mean the promise isn't valid."

"Tony, you don't have to feel obligated to me." The kettle was boiling, and she lifted it, poured steaming water over a tea bag and then added some milk.

Her hands were shaking again, the thought of Jordan pulling his best man aside to ask for such a huge favor making her heart ache. They had never discussed what would happen if he were killed in the line of duty. It wasn't something she had wanted to think about. Let alone discuss.

"Helping you isn't an obligation," he countered.

"Then what is it?"

"It's friendship."

"I know how close you and Jordan were, but he wouldn't expect you to stand by a promise like that. You have a life to live that doesn't include his widow and child."

"I'm not talking about my friendship with Jordan. We're friends, too, Katie."

She met his eyes and could read the sincerity in his face. "We are, but I don't want to be your obligation. I don't want to be the reason you work too hard and spread yourself too thin."

"You're not an obligation," he said, stepping closer, his hands settling on her shoulders. "You're a reminder that life goes on after we're gone, and that the legacy we leave behind really does matter."

He was staring into her eyes again, and she could feel warmth spreading across her cheeks.

She wanted to look away, but she was caught in his gaze, remembering all of the times Tony and Jordan had sat on the couch, watching television while she worked on lesson plans at the kitchen table. Tony had always been the one to ask if the volume was too loud. He'd been the one to offer to bring her a soda or cook her a meal. If she were honest with herself, she would admit he had been more concerned for her needs and comfort than Jordan had been.

Rusty barked, and the sound was so unexpected, Katie jumped, hot tea sloshing over her knuckles. She nearly dropped the mug, her scalded fingers burning as she set it on the counter. Rusty was barking ferociously. Hackles raised, tail stiff, he stood near the living room window, his head between the curtains and the glass.

"You okay?" Tony nearly shouted to be heard above the dog's frantic warning.

"Fine. It's nothing some water won't cure," she responded, putting her hand under the faucet and running water over it. "What is Rusty barking about?"

"I'm not sure, but how about you go in the bathroom to do that?" he suggested, tugging her away from the sink and the window above it.

"You don't think Martin is out there, do you?" she asked, her attention jumping to the darkness beyond the window. The sun had set hours ago, and all she could see was the shadowy outline of the six-foot privacy fence that surrounded the yard. It would be difficult for someone to climb but not impossible.

A light flashed, and the small storage shed that abutted the fence burst into flames, the blaze shooting outward and lapping at the branches of an old elm that stood in the center of the yard.

Shocked, Katie jumped back, and Tony's arms wrapped around her as she stumbled and nearly fell.

"Get your cell phone, go in the bathroom, lock the door and call 911. Don't open the door until I get back." He gave her a gentle nudge toward the hall, hooked Rusty to the leash and walked to the door.

She was still standing at the end of the hall, feet planted on the floor, heart galloping.

"I'll lock this door. You get your phone and call 911," he said again. "I'll be back as soon as I can." Tony stood with his hand on the doorknob, his dark eyes staring into hers.

He wouldn't walk out the door until she moved, and the longer she stayed where she was, the more likely the fire would burn out of control and that the person who had set it would escape.

Someone *had* set it.

There was nothing in the shed that would have spontaneously combusted. And, there was no one who would have set it except for Martin.

She swallowed down her terror and forced herself to nod.

"Be careful," she said, and then she turned and ran for her phone.

Tony didn't wait.

There wasn't time.

He knew exactly what had happened, and he knew why. Martin had set the fire, hoping to draw Katie out of the apartment. He wasn't going to get what he wanted. But, if Tony was quick, Martin might get what he deserved—a trip back to the psychiatric hospital and a trial before a jury of his peers.

He looked out the peephole, scanning as much of the exterior landing as he could. There was no sign of Martin. That didn't surprise him. Martin was unbalanced, but he wasn't stupid. He knew how to keep a low profile. He also knew New York City. He was good at using public transportation to move quickly through the city. He had escaped the mental institution. He had escaped the attention of the police for weeks.

Tony didn't want him to escape again.

"Find!" he commanded, unhooking Rusty from the lead.

Rusty took off, bounding down the stairs, barking wildly.

Firelight flickered on wooden fence posts as the dog jumped at the gate, trying to open it and get into the backyard. Tony had the key to the lock that held the gate closed, but he knew Martin had not entered the yard that way, and he doubted he would exit there.

"This way," he commanded.

Rusty loped after him as he raced to the corner of the fence and plunged through the thick hedges that surrounded the neighbor's property.

He could hear someone crashing through the foliage ahead of him, and he picked up speed as he called out for the perpetrator to stop. Rusty flew past, his dark coat gleaming in the exterior lights of the neighboring houses.

A dozen yards ahead, a dark figure clambered over a wrought-iron fence and darted toward the street.

Rego Park wasn't the suburbs; the yards were small, the houses packed close. Tony couldn't risk taking a shot at the fleeing figure. Not until he was sure there weren't any innocent bystanders nearby.

"I said *stop*!" he called, the faint sound of sirens joining the quiet rumble of neighborhood traffic as he and Rusty followed the perp.

The man reached the road and darted toward a light-colored four-door Ford. He stopped when he reached it, the streetlights illuminating his familiar face. Tall and muscular with a rock-solid build he had earned on construction sites, Martin Fisher didn't look anything like the staid, suit-wearing guy Tony had seen at church.

He scowled as he met Tony's eyes, reaching under his jacket and pulling out a gun. "You need to stay away from Katie," he growled.

"Or what? You'll murder me the same way you murdered Jordan?"

Martin didn't speak. Didn't blink. Just aimed the gun and fired.

But Tony was already diving to the side, calling Rusty back as the bullet slammed into a car parked a few feet away.

"Martin! Put your weapon down and give yourself up," Tony commanded, Rusty pressing close to his side, both of them prone near the edge of the street. Tony had his gun in hand as Martin jumped into the car and slammed the door.

He gunned the engine as Tony took aim at a back tire.

It exploded, bits of rubber flying as the car fishtailed, straightened and accelerated. Not forward as Tony had expected. Backward. Straight at him.

He rolled to the side, scrambling out of the way, Rusty stuck to his side like glue. The Lab might be a search-and-rescue dog, but he was trained to function in volatile, dangerous situations involving firearms. Currently his most important job was staying out of the line of fire.

They moved in sync as Tony ducked behind a parked vehicle and aimed for the back window of Martin's car. He fired a round, as Martin reversed direction again and sped away. Glass shattered. The car fishtailed again, but Martin kept going. He was escaping, and that was something Tony couldn't allow to happen.

Martin needed to be stopped.

Before he made good on his plans to abduct Katie.

He called for Rusty to heel as he sprinted into the middle of the road and followed the damaged vehicle down the street. He lost sight of it as it turned the corner, but he didn't think Martin would be able to keep going on the blown tire. He'd have to stop eventually. When he did, Tony planned to be there.

SIX

Sirens and smoke.

If Katie forgot everything else about the evening, she thought she would still remember the faint whirring of the sirens and the acrid scent of smoke that seemed to be filling the bathroom.

She pressed her palm against the door, checking for heat because of the fire. It was cool to the touch, and so was the old-fashioned metal doorknob. Tony had been gone for twenty minutes. She doubted that was long enough for the fire to spread from the shed to the house, but the yard wasn't large, and the leaves of the elm would make perfect tinder for the flames. A few errant sparks, and who knew? The house could catch fire, and she could be trapped.

She had already called 911.

Based on the sound of sirens, help had arrived.

Martin wouldn't stick around with so many first responders outside.

Would he?

Tony had been right when he'd said that Martin was unpredictable. There was no way to know what he might do, but sitting in a burning building was a more certain death sentence than getting out of one and running into Martin.

She unlocked the door and eased it open, listening for any movement in the apartment. When she heard nothing, she stepped into the hall, her heart sloshing in her ears as she eased along the wall and made her way to the living room. The scent of smoke was thicker there, as the wood frames on the windows that looked out over the backyard were warped enough to let cold air seep in during the colder months.

She flipped off the kitchen light and walked to the window. A half dozen firefighters were there, holding a hose that was spraying the smoldering remains of the shed. The elm seemed untouched, its wide trunk and broad branches dark against the evening sky.

A dog barked, and when someone knocked on the front door, she hurried to answer it, looking through the peephole first.

Her brother-in-law Noah.

She yanked open the door. "Noah. What are you doing here? I thought everyone was still at the hospital."

"We were on our way back when the call came in. I sent Mom, Dad, Carter and Ellie to a hotel and came straight here to pick you up. Zach is outside with Eddie. We have a team looking for and collecting evidence. I wanted to take you over to the hotel before I join the team."

"I'm fine here," she said. "Tony was with me, but he left when the shed lit up to try to catch Martin."

His gaze dropped to her abdomen, and she knew exactly what he wanted to ask.

"The baby is fine, too. No more contractions. Go do

what you have to do and stop worrying. Tony will be back up soon."

"It's tough not to worry when the guy who killed my brother is wandering around Queens, causing trouble." He ran a hand down his jaw and shook his head. "We're going to find him, Katie. I promise you that. And when we do, we're going to make sure he is punished to the full extent of the law."

"I know." She tried to smile, wanting to reassure him because she knew how much he and his family had suffered these past few months. They were grieving just like she was. Yet somehow they continued doing their jobs and seeking justice.

"Okay. Sit tight for a little longer. Try to relax. I'll check in when we're finished." He opened the door and called for Scotty as he stepped onto the landing. He looked tired; his eyes were shadowed, and a few fine lines were starting to show near them.

"Noah," she said, stepping into the doorway and touching his arm. The cold fall air carried the stench of smoke and a hint of moisture that could turn into rain or snow.

"You need to stay inside. We have no idea where Martin went after he drove away. Until we find him, you're going to be under twenty-four-hour guard."

"Tony told me that, and I appreciate everything the K-9 unit has done to keep me safe. I also want you to know I appreciate you and your brothers on a personal level. You have done more than I ever could have asked or expected, and it means a lot to me. It's hard knowing Jordan won't be here for his child, but knowing that you and your brothers will be…" She swallowed a lump of grief and forced herself to keep going. "That makes it a little easier."

"Jordan chose well, Katie. We all think that, and we're glad you're part of the family." He pulled her into a quick bear hug and then stepped away. "Close the door and lock it. Stay inside."

She did as he had asked, then walked back into the living room, her body humming with useless adrenaline. She was a good friend, a good teacher and a good cook, but she wasn't a police officer. She had no training when it came to dealing with men like Martin, and she knew the best thing she could do—the smartest thing—was to stay where she was and wait for the experts to do their job.

She had never been good at waiting, though, and she walked back into the kitchen and looked out the window. The hose had been turned off, and there was nothing but a blackened carcass where the shed had once been. The grass all around it was burned, the ground a black scar where it had once been.

She had done this.

Not intentionally.

Not with her own hands.

But, with her actions and her choices.

No matter how many times she told herself it wasn't true, no matter how many people told her, she couldn't make herself believe it.

"Stop it," she muttered, walking away from the window and out the kitchen. She needed to stop dwelling on things she couldn't change. She needed to trust that God's plan was working out. She needed to move into the future. No matter how faltering and slow her steps.

And, that meant getting ready for the baby's arrival.

She had been avoiding it for weeks, but the hint of smoke in the air, the knowledge that tomorrow could bring more troubles, was enough to spur her to action.

She stepped into the nursery, her pulse jumping in surprise as she saw the crib put together and standing against the far wall. Tony had unpacked boxes of baby clothes and put them in the dresser. The diapers were in the drawer of the changing table. A small basket hooked to the side contained baby wipes and lotions. He had taken the cardboard boxes out to recycle and carried the rocking chair from the guest room, where she had stored it.

Stored it?

Hidden it. The antique rocking chair had been in Ivy's family for three generations. She had rocked her sons to sleep in it. She had rocked Carter's daughter, Ellie, in it. Two months after Jordan's death, she had asked Alexander to carry it up to Katie's apartment with a note that said they were redecorating the guest room, and she was hoping Katie would accept the chair as a gift for the baby.

Katie hadn't wanted to.

She had argued that one of the Jameson men should have it, but Ivy had been insistent. Noah, Carter and Zach were crowded enough in their apartment with all of Ellie's things; they didn't need to add more. Plus, Ivy wanted Jordan's child to have it. A reminder that Jordan had once been young and lively and loved.

Just thinking about that had made Katie's eyes burn with tears.

She had put the rocking chair in the guest room, closed the door and left it there, because she hadn't wanted to think about what it would be like to talk to her child about the father who would never be there to read a book, watch a game or give advice.

Now, the rocking chair was in the corner of the room, the standing lamp Zach and his wife, Violet, had purchased for the nursery beside it. She had bought a three-shelf bookcase months ago, and Tony had assembled that, too. He'd even slid all of the books she had been given by friends and church members into place there.

The room looked like what it was—a space for a baby. One who would be well loved and well cared for by an entire tribe of family and friends.

That was what she needed to think about.

Not what wouldn't be, but what would.

"It's going to be enough," she whispered, lifting a children's Bible that was sitting on top of the bookcase. She had clung to her faith through a lot of hard times, and she wasn't going to give up on it now.

But, lately, it was hard to see God in the details of her life.

Her cell phone rang, and she pulled it from her pocket, glancing at the caller ID before she answered. She didn't recognize the number, but Ivy and Alexander had gone to a hotel. It was possible they were calling from there.

"Hello?" she said breathlessly, dropping into the rocking chair, the baby wriggling around as if the phone had woken her.

"You're going to have to forgive me, darling," Martin said, his voice as smooth and cold as a snake's skin.

"What did you do?" she asked, jumping up from the chair and rushing to the back door. She opened it and looked down into the backyard, hoping to see a police officer or one of her brothers-in-law.

The yard was full of officers.

"Go back inside, darling. It's too chilly to be out without a coat," he said, and her blood ran cold, her body numb.

"Where are you?"

"Not far. I tried to get to you, but there are too many people around. I would ask you to come to me, but I don't want you to tire yourself when you're so close to giving birth to our child."

"Where. Are. You," she repeated, her heart racing so fast, she felt light-headed and woozy.

She lowered herself to the floor of the deck, afraid she might pass out and fall down the stairs.

"Close enough to know you're safe, but too far to help you escape. I'm sorry, my love. I should have planned the fire better. I thought it would burn slowly and that your…friend would come and investigate."

"Martin, you need help," she murmured, her head still spinning, her ears ringing.

She had never passed out before, but she had the horrible feeling that she might.

"I need you. I need our child. I need the life we planned together."

"We didn't plan anything. This isn't your child. It's Jordan's. You know that. Just like you know that there is nothing between us. There never has been. There never will be."

"You have obviously been listening to Jordan's family. They've brainwashed you," he snapped, his tone hard. "Once you're with me, you'll remember how much we love each other."

"Please. Turn yourself in. Get help. Stop stalking me."

"*Stalking?* Is that what you call my devotion? You're

an ungrateful wretch. You know that? If you're not careful, I'll take our child and leave you behind." He ended the call, and she sat where she was, holding the phone to her ear.

"Katie?" Tony called.

She glanced down and saw him jogging toward the stairs to the deck, Rusty on heel beside him.

"What are you doing out here? Noah said you were in the house, waiting for him to return."

He hurried up the stairs, but she didn't stand to greet him. She was still clutching the phone, her throat so tight with terror, she didn't dare try to speak.

She was afraid that if she did, she would start screaming and never stop.

"Katie?" he said again, dropping down beside her and taking the phone from her hand. "What's happened? What's wrong?"

She shook her head, because she couldn't get the words out. Couldn't tell him the threat Martin had made. The thought of a madman kidnapping her child made her feel physically ill.

"Come on. Let's get you inside." He helped her to her feet and ushered her into the apartment.

"Sit. Before you pass out." He held her arm as she lowered herself to the couch. Then, he patted the cushion beside her.

"Place," he said, and Rusty jumped up and settled his warm head on her knee.

Tony set the phone on the end table and disappeared for a few minutes, returning with the guest-room comforter in his arms. He wrapped it around her shoulders, then bent so he could look into her eyes. "Tell me what happened. I'll take care of it."

If anyone else had said it, she would have brushed it off, but she was looking into the darkest eyes she had ever seen, reading sincerity and concern in them, and she knew that, if he could, he really would take care of things.

"I'm probably overreacting," she finally managed to say, because she thought she probably was.

There were dozens of firefighters and police officers on the property. Martin wouldn't be able to get to her. But, it wasn't what could happen now that had her terrified. It was the future—the unborn baby who would make an entrance into a world where Martin was wandering free.

"You aren't the kind of person who overreacts to things."

"I didn't used to be. The pregnancy has changed me."

"Don't do that, Katie," he said, wrapping the comforter tighter around her shoulders, his fingers skimming the sides of her neck. She could imagine—if she let herself—leaning into his warmth, allowing herself to find comfort in his arms. Just the thought made her heart ache with guilt and sadness.

She had loved Jordan.

She didn't expect to ever love anyone else.

She certainly had no intention of filling the empty spot he had left with his best friend.

"Don't do what?" she murmured, focusing her attention on Rusty. That was easier than looking into Tony's eyes.

"Downplay your experience. You're levelheaded and smart. Pregnancy hasn't changed that. If you're worried, then I have every reason to think I should be, too."

"I'm not…" She stopped herself. She was worried,

and Tony was right. She had never been the kind of person to blow things out of proportion or make mountains out of molehills. Being in foster care had forced her to be resilient, to take each day as it came and to hold her emotions in check. "Okay, I *am* worried. Martin called."

"Your home phone?"

"My cell."

"You gave him your number?"

"No, but it's in the church directory."

"We'll try to trace the call. If he called from a landline, that should be easy. If it's a disposable cell phone, it will be a lot more difficult."

"I'm sure it was a cell phone. Unless he broke into a house somewhere nearby."

"Nearby?"

"He said he could see me. He even told me to go back inside because it was too chilly to be out without a coat."

His eyes flashed, his jaw tightening. Unlike Jordan who had had a perpetual smile, Tony tended to look gruff and a little unapproachable. "Stay here. I'm going to talk to Noah."

"There's something else, Tony," she said as he opened the front door.

"Go ahead."

"He said that if I didn't cooperate, he would take my baby and leave me behind." Her voice broke on the words, the fear she had finally gotten under control threatening to escape again.

"He's not going to get the baby. He's not going to get you. We're going to keep constant watch and make sure of that." He stepped out of the apartment, into the hallway, signaling for Rusty to stay.

The Lab settled down next to Katie again.

She patted his head, her heart still beating too rapidly, her stomach hollow with anxiety.

She wanted to believe that things would work out.

She really did.

But, her track record for losing people she loved was high, and she didn't think she could count on anything other than things happening exactly how they were going to.

Outside, people were still calling out to each other. Men. Women. All of them working as a team.

Inside, though, it was just Katie and a dog that belonged to someone else.

Loneliness wasn't a state of being; it was a disease, and it could destroy a person if allowed to.

She wouldn't allow it.

She had a life to live and dozens of years of memories to make with the child she and Jordan had created together.

She wouldn't let Martin take that from her.

She wouldn't let him destroy the one thing she still had.

She touched her belly as the baby kicked and squirmed.

"Don't worry, sweetie," she said. "It's going to be okay. I promise."

The K-9 unit fanned out across the neighborhood, searching yards, outbuildings and vehicles for Martin. If what Katie had said was correct—and Tony had no reason to doubt it—the escaped murderer was close enough to see the Jameson house, to see what Katie had been wearing and to know exactly where law enforcement was. That put him at a decided advantage.

But, the K-9 unit had dogs and manpower on its side, and Tony had no intention of sitting idle while the rest of the K-9 team hunted for the very dangerous and deluded man.

Despite his shoulder injury and orders to take a few days off, he had teamed up with Officer Reed Branson and his bloodhound, Jessie. Reed had used a pillow taken from Martin's room at the mental hospital after he had escaped as a scent article, allowing Jessie to sniff it until she knew exactly what trail she should be following.

"Where's Rusty?" Reed asked.

"Staying with Katie for now," Tony explained. "Rusty will alert Katie to any danger faster than she would be able to notice anything on her own. I feel better with that safeguard."

Reed nodded, and they got to work.

Nose to the ground, Jessie followed the fence line and made her way into a neighbor's yard. She stayed there for several minutes, nosing a large rosebush that sat close to the neighbor's house. The earth beneath it was obviously disturbed, recent rain making it soft enough for footprints to be left in the soil.

Tony flashed his light on the area, his heart jumping when he saw a clear footprint between the house and the bush. "He must have been here for a while," he said. "The print is deep."

"Agreed. And, look at this." Reed pointed to what looked like blood on one of the branches.

"Not a smart idea to hide in a rosebush."

"Not smart, but it gave him a great view of the street and the side of the Jameson house. He may have been hoping Katie would return home alone. Or, with someone who wouldn't be able to help if he made another attempt at kidnapping her." He put in a call for the evidence team, then set a flag near the rosebush. "Martin is smart, but his delusions are causing him to make mistakes. His mistakes are our opportunities."

"Agreed," Tony said, standing back as Jessie began following the scent trail again. Nose to the ground, ears brushing grass and fallen leaves, she covered ground quickly with her long, muscular body. Like most bloodhounds, Jessie didn't give up on a scent once she had it. She moved quickly as she followed it across the neighbor's yard and out into the street where Tony had confronted Martin. She stopped there, circling a few times before she found the scent again.

She trotted along the road in the direction Tony knew Martin's vehicle had gone. "Do you think she's catching scent from his car?" he asked.

Reed shrugged. "It's possible. She's got a great nose, and the scent is fresh. She'll lose it if he's gone too far, though."

"He didn't. I blew out one of his tires."

"Yeah. I thought I heard that over the radio. You think he abandoned the car and circled back?"

"I can't think of any other way he would have been able to see Katie."

"He really *is* making mistakes. This neighborhood is crawling with police. There is no way he's going to escape the dragnet we've set for him."

"He's escaped the other ones. The subway station isn't that far from here. All he has to do is make it there, and he's gone," Tony pointed out.

"All we have to do is stop him," Reed responded, picking up speed as Jessie barreled around the corner of a street three blocks from the Jameson place. She trotted across a lawn and up a driveway that led to the back of a three-level house that had been turned into apartments. Like many in the neighborhood, it had a small paved area in the back for tenant vehicles.

Tony spotted the car immediately, parked bumper-to-bumper with a sporty Toyota. Its back tire was missing, its rim was bent and its back window was shattered.

Jessie made a beeline for it, baying loudly as she jumped up against the side of the car to look inside.

"Off," Reed commanded, and the bloodhound fell back, taking her place beside Reed as he pulled his firearm and moved in.

Tony moved in tandem with him, easing toward the car, watching for any sign that Martin was still there.

The area was still and quiet but for the muted sound of traffic that drifted between the old houses. The air was tinged with smoke. It was still early, and lights were on in neighboring properties—a television was visible through the open curtains of the next-door neighbor's house. People were in their homes, going about their evening rituals, unaware that a deranged killer had been feet away and might still be close by.

Tony reached the car and glanced inside, knowing before he checked that Martin wasn't there. A jacket was lying on the front seat, with a flip phone sitting on top of it.

"I would venture a guess that that's the phone he used," Reed muttered, his tone reflecting the frustration the K-9 unit had been feeling for nearly a month. Martin had murdered their chief, been captured and somehow escaped. The fact that he was still free was both frustrating and infuriating.

"He must have parked the car and walked to an area where he could observe the Jamesons' house, then returned after he made the call. He left the jacket purposely," Tony added. "To draw the dogs here."

"And left the phone to let us know he was one step ahead," Reed added. "But, leaving the jacket was another mistake. We can use it to get Jessie started again. She can track him from here."

"I have a feeling she'll scent-track straight to the subway station."

"I do, too, but Martin seems to be getting more delusional and less rational. It's possible he's staying close." Reed snapped a photo of the car's interior, called for the evidence team and set another flag. Then, he lifted the jacket with gloved hands and held it for Jessie to sniff.

When she had the scent, he placed it back in the car and gave the signal for her to search.

She took off, racing through the backyards of several houses before darting across a driveway and out into the road. She had the scent, and it was a strong one. Whether or not they would reach Martin before he escaped Rego Park remained to be seen, but Tony had never been a quitter. From the time he was young, he had gone after what he wanted with single-minded determination.

Right now, what he wanted—*all* he wanted—was to apprehend Martin Fisher before he had a chance to go after Katie again.

SEVEN

The walls were closing in, and there wasn't a whole lot Katie could do about it. In the week since Martin had set fire to the shed and called her cell phone, she had been housebound, as requested by the K-9 Command Unit, her brothers-in-law, Ivy, Alexander and Tony. The Jamesons had refused to stay at the hotel once they knew the house was sound and that Katie had insisted on staying. Everyone who knew anything about the case had begged her to stay inside, where she could be guarded and protected.

She hadn't needed convincing.

She would do anything to protect her unborn child. Even stay inside for long days and long nights.

Now, though, she was restless, pacing the living room, the shades drawn, the door locked and bolted, her overnight bag sitting next to it.

Just in case.

She had kept her appointment with Dr. Ritter the previous day. Accompanied by Noah, Zach and their dogs, she had arrived at the medical center and departed from it without incident.

She *had* felt watched, though; the skin on the back

of her neck had tingled as she maneuvered her ungainly body into Noah's SUV. Martin had called a few minutes after they'd pulled out of the parking lot.

You are glowing, my love. Carrying our child suits you, he had said. *What did Dr. Ritter think? Will the baby be coming soon?*

She had been terrified.

Just like she was every time her phone rang.

She had tried to keep him on the phone, stretching the conversation out in the hopes that it could be traced. When he abruptly disconnected, she had felt drained.

The K-9 unit had converged on the clinic, combing the area for signs that Martin had been there. They had found nothing except a scent trail that had led from the clinic to a queue of taxis waiting in front of a hotel.

As far as Katie knew, they still had not found the taxi driver who had given Martin a ride.

She sighed as she walked to the kitchen and opened the fridge. It was nearly midnight. She wasn't hungry, but she felt restless and lonely and a little afraid.

Even knowing there were two armed police officers watching the house and that her brothers-in-law were in the apartment above her couldn't ease her worry and fear. Martin had threatened to take the baby. No matter how many times she told herself he would never have the opportunity, no matter how many people reassured her, she couldn't shake the feeling that he would make good on his threat.

She was trying to give everything over to God. She really was, but it was difficult to trust that He wouldn't let anything happen to the baby when He had allowed something terrible to happen to her parents and to Jordan.

It's all part of God's plan. You just have to have faith.

How many well-meaning people had said that to her?

And, how many times had she stopped herself from telling them that her faith had not saved her parents and it had not saved her husband, and she had no reason to believe it would save her child?

God's plans and His ways were a mystery she couldn't solve. She knew He was good. She knew He had her best interest at heart. She knew she could count on Him to guide her steps. But, she did not know if He would spare her baby, if He would keep Martin away or if He would give her the peaceful life she so desperately craved.

The home.

The family.

The future she had prayed for.

Her phone rang, her pulse jumped and the baby shifted as the sudden spurt of adrenaline hit. The stress couldn't be good for either of them, and she tried to calm her breathing and slow her heart rate as she glanced at the caller ID.

It was an unknown number, but she knew who was calling.

It was nearly midnight. Everyone else she knew was either asleep or working. Even if they weren't, they would assume she was tucked in bed, resting for the upcoming birth.

"Hello?" she said, bracing herself for the smooth, slimy voice of the man she had grown to despise.

"Tell him to leave!" Martin screamed, his rage palpable.

"What are you talking about? There's no one here," she responded, taking out a cell phone Noah had provided and then hitting the quick-dial function to contact the precinct and let the dispatcher know Martin was on the phone.

"You know who I'm talking about, Katie. Don't play dumb."

"No. I don't." The baby twisted and squirmed, obviously as distressed by the conversation as Katie.

"Knight. He is trying to steal you from me the same way Jordan did. I don't want to murder someone else. I'm a peaceful guy. One who just wants to marry the love of his life, raise a family and enjoy the beautiful things God has provided for him."

"Tony isn't trying to steal me—" Katie attempted to say, but Martin started ranting, his words filled with bitter fury.

"And, if anyone tries, the same thing will happen to him that happened to Jordan. You tell Knight that, you hear me? Tell him!" He disconnected.

She was so shocked, she stood where she was, phone still pressed to her ear, heart hammering against her ribs.

She had known he was mentally ill. She *had*.

But, she had not known just how deep his delusions went.

She finally disconnected and shoved the phone into the pocket of the suit jacket she had put on a few hours ago. The pinstriped blue suit was one of the few items of Jordan's clothing she had kept. He had worn it the night he had proposed, and she had not been able to let it go.

She lifted the second cell phone to her ear and spoke to the dispatcher for the first time since she had made the call.

"Were you able to trace it?" she asked, her voice shaking.

"We have a ping from the cell phone that originated the call," the dispatcher replied. "I've already contacted the chief. He's gathering a team. Stay where you are until he contacts you."

"Okay. Thanks," she said, glancing at the ceiling as the floor joists above her head creaked.

Carter was awake. Noah and Zach were at work.

Ivy and Alexander were away for the weekend, spending a few days with friends before the baby arrived, so Carter would stay with his daughter, Ellie, while his brothers went to hunt for Martin.

Please keep them safe, she prayed silently.

She didn't know what she would do if another Jameson brother was killed by Martin.

Someone knocked on the door, and she hurried to answer it.

Or, *tried* to hurry.

She was moving more slowly than ever, the pregnancy heavy and cumbersome, her belly huge. Rather than running, she waddled, reaching the door breathless and tired, a stitch in her side making her pause before she peered through the peephole.

She expected to see Noah or Zach, returning from work and coming to check on her before they retired for the night.

Tony was there. Dark hair gleaming in the hallway light, jaw dark with five-o'clock shadow.

She unlocked the door and stepped back. Something in her chest went soft as he walked inside, Rusty padding along beside him.

"You look tired," she said without thinking.

"Three twelve-hour shifts in a row will do that to you," he responded, closing the door and sliding the bolt into place. "I was on my way home and decided to bring coffee for the guys pulling guard duty and to check on you. I heard the call go over the radio while I was talking to them. Martin called again."

It wasn't a question, but she nodded. "He knew you were here. He told me to tell you to leave."

"He's going to be disappointed to discover that I haven't."

"You should, Tony," she said, the cramp in her side worsening.

"Because you want me to go?"

"Because I don't want you hurt. Martin said—"

"Let me guess—you're his. He won't let anyone get in the way of the two of you being together. He already murdered Jordan, and he will murder again if anyone tries to take you away from him."

"Something like that," she replied, bending over as another, sharper cramp shot through her abdomen.

"You okay?" he asked, taking her arm and leading her to the couch.

"I tried to run to answer the door. The baby didn't like it," she responded, easing onto the cushions, the jacket billowing out as she sat.

She suddenly felt self-conscious for wearing it, as if it were tangible proof that she wasn't healing and moving on.

"Jordan wore this the night he proposed," she said, smoothing her hand down one of the too-long sleeves.

"I know. I was there—remember?"

"How could I forget? You wore a tux and a frilly pink apron while you served dinner from the gigantic picnic basket you somehow carried into Central Park." She smiled at the memory, because it was a good one. The way the fading sunlight had washed the grass and trees in a golden haze and the late-summer air had wrapped around her as she had walked hand in hand with Jordan. Her surprise when he had taken her to a small clearing where a blanket had been spread on the soft summer grass. Her laughter when Tony had appeared wearing a well-fitted tux and a pink apron.

"I rented the tux, and I didn't want to get anything on it. When I mentioned that to Ivy, she offered the apron. I wasn't going to wear it, but Jordan was a nervous wreck and I thought it might lighten the mood." He smiled, his gaze soft with the memory.

"Jordan nervous? That's hard to believe," she replied, her breath catching as another cramp made her stomach spasm.

"You two hadn't been dating that long when he proposed. He was worried you might say no."

"That definitely doesn't sound like the Jordan I knew."

"No? What was he like? The Jordan you knew, I mean." Tony's attention was focused on her rather than on his phone or the television or one of the dozen other things Jordan had spent his time looking at when she had tried to talk to him. He had always been tired from long days on the job, and she had always made excuses for him, because they had been newly married and she had not wanted to think that the pattern of behavior was one that would follow them throughout their marriage.

She hadn't been happy, though. Not with that part of their relationship.

The thought made her feel disloyal, and she shoved it away.

"Too confident to be worried about being turned down by one of the dozens of women he had dated in his life." She kept her tone light, not wanting Tony to think she was criticizing the man they had both loved.

"He loved you, Katie. He wanted to spend the rest of his life with you. The proposal and your answer meant everything to him," he said quietly. "I hope you know that."

"Of course, I do," she lied, pushing up from the couch and walking into the kitchen. "Are you hungry? Do you want me to make you something before you leave?"

"You're changing the subject," he pointed out.

"Because there is nothing more to say."

"I have a feeling there is. Was there trouble between you and Jordan before he died?" he asked bluntly.

She shouldn't have been surprised.

As caring and compassionate as Tony was, he had always been a straight shooter. From what she had seen, he didn't play games, didn't beat around the bush and didn't mince words.

"No. Of course not."

"But, something *was* bothering you."

"What if something was? Jordan wasn't perfect, and neither was I. We both did things the other didn't like."

"Such as?" he asked, refusing to let the subject drop.

A dog with a bone was how Jordan had described Tony. *And the perfect cop because of it.*

"I worried too much about what his family thought of me, and he… He was more focused on work than on building our relationship. At least, that's how it felt to me." She shrugged, and the nagging ache in her side swelled with pain again.

She rubbed the area but refused to look away from Tony's searching gaze.

"I can see how you might have thought that," he finally said. "Jordan was devoted to his job, and he had a difficult time breaking away from it. My father was a police officer, and he was the same way."

"Your mother didn't mind?"

"She hated it. By the time she died of cancer, I'm pretty sure she hated him, too. But, my father was also mean. He didn't care that Mother was lonely. He didn't care that he never saw me. All he cared about was looking good to his buddies on the police force."

"I'm sorry," she said, touching his arm, feeling firm muscle beneath his jacket and knowing she should let her hand drop away.

Instead, it rested there as he tugged her a step closer, her belly bumping his abdomen as he continued to look into her eyes. Something sparked between them, a hint of attraction that could have meant nothing or everything.

"I can't tell you that Jordan wouldn't have stayed committed to his job, but I can tell you this—he was also committed to you. You would have made it, Katie. The two of you would have raised a bunch of kids and grown old together, and I would have been the sidekick, looking on and wondering why I hadn't ever had the guts to give love a go." His gaze dropped to her lips, and his jaw tightened.

He stepped back, putting space between them that she should have wanted but didn't.

"Is there a reason why you haven't?" she asked, hoping he didn't notice the huskiness of her voice or the reluctance with which she moved away.

"I don't ever want to be to another person what my father was to me and my mother," he replied, the honesty of his answer making her want to reach out to him again.

And, that scared her.

Her stomach cramped again, and she grabbed the counter.

"Are you sure you're okay?" he asked, taking a step toward her.

"Fine. It's just been a long week, and I need some rest. Drive carefully on your way home," she responded.

"I told Noah I would stick around until he and Zach returned. Go ahead and lie down. I'll be here if you need anything."

She nodded, grateful he'd be here—at a distance, while she rested in her bedroom. There was a lot about Tony Knight she hadn't known. Sides to him. His past. Including the promise he'd made to Jordan to watch over her. He was doing just that. Making good on the promise to his late best friend. Following orders from his chief. Maybe the awareness she kept feeling between them was all in her mind.

But, she didn't think so.

"All right. Thanks." She would have hurried away, but she had learned her lesson. She moved slowly instead, making her way down the hall and closing herself in her room.

She sat on the bed, waiting for the cramp to ease.

She had been in false labor the previous week. She knew what contractions felt like. These weren't them, so she lay down, still fully clothed and wearing Jordan's suit jacket, closed her eyes and tried to sleep.

Tony knew he needed to be careful.

Katie was a beautiful and intelligent woman, and he wasn't going to pretend he hadn't noticed. But, she was also his best friend's pregnant widow. That made her off-limits.

The truth was she would have been off-limits anyway. He never dated "forever" kind of women. He dated women who were as interested as he was in keeping things light. No expectations. No commitment. Just nice evenings out and pleasant conversations. That had always been enough for him.

Although, lately...

Lately, he had been wondering if his hard-core opposition to marriage had been built on faulty reasoning. As he had watched one member of the K-9 unit after another find love, he couldn't help thinking that he had as good a chance as anyone of making a lifetime commitment work.

He wasn't his father.

He had always known that.

As committed as he was to his job, he made time and space for the people he cared about.

The fact was he was getting older. His friends were married or getting there, having children or planning to. And, he was still living a bachelor's life, sitting down for meals alone or with families that weren't his.

He frowned, lifting a framed photo from one of the end tables. Jordan smiled out at him, arm around Katie, blue eyes alive with happiness. Jordan had never believed that Tony would remain single forever.

You'll meet your happily-ever-after, he had said a few weeks before his murder. *And, when you do, I'll be the first one to say I told you so.*

"I wish you could," he murmured, setting the photo back in place, grief a hard knot in the middle of his chest.

He walked over to the living room window and looked out, hating that Martin was skulking in the bushes somewhere, watching. Probably right now. The guy was likely getting more furious that Tony hadn't heeded the warning to stay away from Katie. Furious and delusional were not a good combination. Tony always watched his back, but he'd be vigilant now. Both for Katie's sake *and* his own.

Martin's last call had come in three hours ago. Tony had received no updates on the team's search, which meant there had been no changes. No sightings and no capture. He wanted to be out there, searching with Rusty, but Katie's well-being was everyone's top priority. Leaving her alone—even when she had two officers stationed outside—was not an option.

Her bedroom door opened, the soft creak of the old hinges warning him seconds before she appeared at the end of the hallway. She still wore Jordan's suit jacket, but her hair had come out of its ponytail and was spilling over her shoulders.

"Everything okay?" he asked, moving toward her.

"I'm not sure," she replied, her eyes dark blue against pale skin.

"Did Martin call again?" He hadn't heard a phone, but she might have had her cell phone's volume turned down.

"I think I'm in labor," she responded, the words so surprising it took a few seconds for them to register.

"Labor?" he asked. "As in the baby is coming?"

She grinned, some of the tension easing from her face. "You've known this baby was coming for a while. Why are you acting so surprised?"

"It's early."

"Only a couple of weeks."

"And, you have three brothers-in-law and two very concerned parents-in-law who were supposed to be on scene when the big day arrived," he responded.

She laughed. "Don't sound so horrified, Tony. I can have one of the officers—"

"No." He grabbed her coat from the closet.

"You didn't let me finish."

"Because you don't need to have them do anything except follow us to the hospital. I'm driving you there, and I'll be there with you until you tell me to leave or until one of your family members shows up and boots me out." He dropped the coat around her shoulders and grabbed his jacket.

"Carter is upstairs. I can call him. Ivy and Alex are out of town, visiting friends, but Carter can probably find someone to sit with Ellie," she said, and he stopped frantically searching for his phone just long enough to meet her eyes. Despite her smile and laughter, she looked scared.

"If that's what you want, I'll be happy to sit with Ellie."

"What I want is for Jordan to be here," she replied.

"I wish I could make that happen for you." He tugged the edges of her coat closed and pulled silky hair from beneath its collar. "Do you want me to call Carter?"

She shook her head. "Ellie keeps him busy, and

he needs his sleep. We can call him when I'm further along."

She reached for the small bag that sat near the door, and he took it from her hand.

"I'll leave Rusty here. He's good at the hospital, but he already worked a full shift today and I'd rather let him rest. Do you need anything else?"

"Courage?" she responded.

"I can be that for you," he said, dropping his arm around her shoulders and ushering her out of the apartment.

EIGHT

The baby arrived three hours after Katie checked into the hospital, the labor so quick, there was barely enough time to breathe let alone think about how nervous she was. True to his word, Tony had stayed with her, sitting beside the bed and holding her hand as things progressed. When it was time to push, he had asked if she wanted him to leave, but she had been gripping his hand too tightly to let him go.

She was glad for that.

Her daughter had not been born into the world with an audience that consisted only of medical staff. She had been born into a room that contained two of the people who had loved her father most.

Even now, an hour after Jordyn Rose Jameson had arrived, Katie's eyes filled with tears when she thought of that.

She blinked them away, not wanting Tony to ask questions.

He was still beside her, talking quietly to one of her brothers-in-law, his voice a soothing rumble that made her want to close her eyes and sleep.

She shifted Jordyn in her arms and ran her hand over

the baby's soft brown hair. "You're beautiful, Jordyn Rose. Your daddy would be so happy if he were here."

"Yes, he would," Tony agreed, leaning closer so that he could look at Jordyn's face. "Noah is asking for a picture to show people at work. I said I would ask you."

"That's fine, but I'm a hot mess. Just take a picture of Jordyn." Even though she wouldn't be in the shot, she still smoothed her hair and straightened the collar of the cotton nightgown she had changed into after Jordyn was born.

"He would love that."

"Who?"

"Jordan. He would love that you gave your daughter his name. And, you aren't a hot mess. You two are the most beautiful mother and daughter I have ever seen." He lifted his cell phone and snapped three quick pictures.

"I'm pretty sure I told you not to take a picture of me." But, she didn't care that he had. Not really. Her daughter had been born alive and healthy. Ten fingers. Ten toes. Chubby cheeks and a rosebud mouth. Fine brown hair and a tiny button nose. Katie could not have asked for anything more than that.

"One day Jordyn Rose is going to be very happy that you have these photos, but if you would rather me not send the one with you in it to Noah, I won't." He smiled, and she felt that thing in her chest melt again, the solid mass of anxiety and grief that she had been carrying for so long seeping away.

"Go ahead and send them. I know everyone in the K-9 unit has been praying for a healthy and safe delivery. I'm happy for them to see that their prayers were answered."

Please, God, keep answering, she prayed silently. *Keep protecting my daughter.*

"You look nervous," he commented as he sent the photo. "Worried about being a new mom?"

"Worried about Martin doing what he threatened and kidnapping Jordyn Rose," she admitted, kissing the baby's downy cheek.

"I'm not going to let that happen. The team isn't going to let it happen."

"I know." But, she was still afraid. "I just wish he had been apprehended."

"Me, too. Unfortunately, the dogs lost his scent at a bus stop. We're obtaining surveillance footage from the one we think he boarded, and we're hoping to discover where he got off. For right now, dogs and handlers have returned to the precinct."

"I know how much work everyone is putting into finding Martin. I wouldn't want anyone to think I'm not aware of it and grateful. It's just hard knowing that the man who murdered Jordan is still out there."

"I know." His fingers skimmed her shoulder, and his hand rested on her upper arm. She could feel the warmth of his palm through the thick cotton of her nightgown, and it felt so right and so comfortable that her eyes drifted closed.

"You're exhausted," he said quietly. "How about you let me hold the baby while you rest? I won't leave the room with her. I promise."

She forced her eyes open and looked at his familiar face. How had she never noticed the flecks of gray in his dark eyes, or how long his lashes were?

"Have you ever held a baby?" she asked, shifting her gaze before she could notice more.

"Not that I can remember, but there's a first time for everything, right?"

"You're not boosting my confidence in your ability," she murmured, kissing Jordyn Rose's head.

"I promise you, in as much as I am able, I will never let anything happen to her," Tony said solemnly.

And she knew he meant every word. That for as long as he could, he would be around to make sure that Jordyn Rose was safe.

"Okay," she said, because Tony had always been someone she could rely on. Even before Jordan's death, he had been there for her, rushing to the rescue anytime Jordan wasn't available.

Which, she had to admit, had been often.

She supported Jordyn Rose's head as she held the swaddled infant out for him.

His large hands slid across hers as he shifted the baby's weight and pulled her to his chest. He stayed there, the baby held closely, her head cupped by one of his hands, her body by the other.

"You look terrified," Katie said, oddly touched by the picture they made—tiny infant and large, gruff man.

"She's delicate, and I tend to be a bull in a china shop when it comes to delicate things."

"I watched a documentary that tested that idiom once," she said, something warm and a little alarming filling her chest.

"Did you?" He was staring down at Jordyn Rose as if she were as delicate as a gossamer thread.

"Yes, and they discovered that a bull isn't all that destructive when let loose in a china shop."

"Good. Great. This little one and I should be just fine, then." He settled into his seat, Jordyn Rose close to his chest. "Man, she's beautiful," he whispered. "Jordan would be over the moon with love for her."

"I know." Her voice broke, and she closed her eyes, willing the tears away. This was a happy time. Not a sad one, and she didn't want to waste a second of it crying tears of sorrow.

"It's okay to cry, Katie. There isn't anyone who wouldn't understand why you're doing it."

"I know, but I don't want to cry tears of sorrow on the day of my daughter's birth. Maybe on her first Christmas or first birthday or the day she gets married. But, not today."

"That's a big jump from first birthday to wedding," he commented, and she knew he was trying to lighten the mood and take her mind off the one thing that was missing from this day.

The one person.

"I hear it goes by in a flash—all those years," she responded, her eyes still closed, exhaustion finally winning the war against her desire to stay awake.

"You blink and then she's grown," he agreed.

"Hopefully not that fast of a flash." The words were slurred, her body heavy with fatigue.

She thought she felt Tony's fingers skim across her cheek, but before she could decide if she had, she fell asleep.

Tony had never been part of something like this, and the miracle of the tiny life he was holding filled him with awe. He had heard from friends who had children that newborns were incredibly beautiful, but he had figured blind love had skewed their perspectives. He'd seen photos of their babies. The red faces, misshapen heads and squished noses had not been his definition of beauty, but he had oohed and aahed anyway.

Jordyn Rose, though… She was about as perfect as a human being could be. Tiny little fingers and toes. Cute little nose and chubby cheeks, she had stolen his heart the second the doctor had placed her on Katie's chest. He had been holding Katie's hand, her fingernails digging into his palm, his face so close to hers, he could see the blond tips on her brown eyelashes. He had not expected the baby to be plopped down, naked and pink and still speckled with blood, but that's exactly what had happened. One minute, Katie was red-faced with effort, and in what seemed like the next, a baby was lying on her chest.

"You're something else, sweetheart," he whispered, not sure if he was talking to the baby or to Katie. Both, in his admittedly exhausted opinion, were amazing.

Katie's cell phone rang, and he grabbed it from the table, answering before it could wake her. "Hello?" he said quietly, holding the phone with his shoulder so that he could keep two hands on Jordyn.

"Who is this? Why do you have Katie's phone?" a man said, his familiar voice sending a jolt of fury through Tony.

"Martin?"

"I asked who this is," Martin spat, hatred seething beneath the words.

"Tony Knight."

"I told her to tell you to go home. I know she doesn't want you around, so I suggest you do it."

"Here is what I suggest—go to the nearest police station and turn yourself in. That will make things a lot easier for you."

"For you, you mean?" He laughed, and the sound sent chills down Tony's spine.

"I'm not concerned about what is easy for me. I'm concerned about making sure you pay for what you did to Chief Jameson."

"Be careful, Knight. If you're not, your police buddies might wind up trying to make me pay for what I do to you." He disconnected, and Tony dropped the phone on the table again, frustrated by the helpless rage that filled him.

Martin should never have been able to escape the high-security mental institution where he had been held after his arrest, but he had knocked the guard over the head and made a run for it. If he had been a typical criminal, he would have kept going until he had put plenty of distance between himself and the law. Martin was anything but typical; he was unhinged and so obsessed with Katie, he had returned to Queens and begun stalking her.

So far, the NYC K-9 Command Unit had not been able to stop him. Public transportation made it too easy for Martin to move from location to location. Patrol officers had searched his apartment but found no hint that he had been there recently. Since then, foot and bike patrol had been making the apartment complex a regular stop during shifts. They had not seen the fugitive, but that didn't mean he hadn't slipped past them. He still had a key to the apartment, and the lease was paid up until the end of the year. That was unusual, but Martin had probably wanted to make sure he'd have access to his apartment even if he was caught. He'd clearly always planned to escape custody.

Jordyn Rose wriggled in his arms, her tiny fists batting the blankets that swaddled her. She looked like Katie, her features delicate, her skin pale, but she had Jordan's dark hair. The fact that she would never meet her father, that she would know him only through the stories that others told, made Jordan's death even more tragic.

Someone knocked softly, and the door swung open.

Two officers were stationed outside the room, and Tony knew there was no danger of Martin getting past them. He stood anyway, the baby cuddled to his chest.

Ivy and Alexander Jameson walked in, and he motioned for them to stay quiet. Katie needed to rest, and he wanted her to sleep for as long as she could.

Ivy nodded and rushed across the room, tears streaming down her cheeks as she stared at the baby. "She's gorgeous," she whispered as Noah and his fiancée, Lani, Carter and his fiancée, Rachelle, and Zach and his wife, Violet, entered the room.

"I was just thinking the same," he admitted.

"How is Katie?" she asked, her gaze shifting to the bed.

"Exhausted."

"It's been a rough nine months," Alexander said quietly, standing beside his wife, his arm around her waist, his gaze on Jordyn. "Noah said Katie named her Jordyn Rose."

"She did."

"It's a lovely name," Ivy murmured. "Do you think Katie would mind if I held her?"

"Of course not," he said, but he felt reluctant to let her take the baby from his arms. Odd considering he had never in his life imagined holding a newborn. He had never had a desire to do so. When friends had babies, he visited but kept his hands to himself.

"I can't believe she is finally here," Ivy said, brushing aside her tears and reaching for Jordyn Rose. "Ellie is going to be so happy to hear that her baby cousin has arrived! She'll want to buy *all* the frilly dresses and pink bows."

"She begged me to bring her this morning," Carter said, stepping close to his mother and taking a picture of her holding the baby.

Rachelle snapped a few photos of Carter standing next to Ivy and Jordyn Rose. Then Lani and Violet insisted on photos of their Jameson men beside Grandma and their newest niece.

Tony moved back, giving the Jameson family a chance to coo over its newest member. Katie was still sleeping, her hair tangled beneath her head. He tugged the blanket up around her shoulders, concerned by her pale skin and the violet shadows beneath her eyes.

Since Katie was sleeping, Violet, Rachelle and Lani decided to head to the cafeteria for coffee and took orders. Tony could definitely use some coffee.

"Thanks for being here for her," Noah said, joining him beside the bed.

"That's what family does," he responded.

"I know, but I still wanted to tell you how much we appreciate it."

"You know what would be better than appreciation?"

"Martin locked up in a cell, facing a life sentence?"

"Exactly. He called Katie a few minutes before you arrived."

"And?"

"He wasn't happy when I answered. I have a bad feeling about things, Noah. The guy is totally unglued, and he has his sights set on a woman who has just given birth."

"You're not telling me anything I don't already know. We've put as much manpower on this as we can. The department is already stretched thin, and I can't devote the entire K-9 unit to Martin's arrest. If I could, I would."

"I know. You're talking to a member of the unit, remember?"

"Yeah." Noah ran a hand down his jaw and sighed. "I want him caught yesterday, Tony. He killed my brother. He's trying to kidnap his widow. He needs to be stopped, but he seems to always be a step ahead of us."

"He's getting cocky and making mistakes. He won't stay ahead of us forever."

"You're right. I just want this over. For Katie's sake and my parents'. For all of ours."

Katie stirred and her eyes opened as quickly as they had closed.

"The baby!" she cried, shoving aside blankets as if she intended to jump out of bed.

Tony touched her shoulder, gently holding her in place. "Hey, slow down. The baby is fine. Ivy has her."

She finally seemed to take in the room and the people who were standing in it. She sagged against the pillows, her skin so pale he could see every freckle on her nose and cheeks. "I was dreaming that Martin had taken her."

"We aren't going to let that happen," Noah said, taking a seat beside her as Ivy put the baby back in her arms.

"I know you're not. I know it was just a dream, but I don't know what I would do if it came true." Her voice broke, and the tears she had said she didn't want to shed slid down her cheeks.

"Don't cry, honey," Ivy exclaimed, rushing to wipe her face with a tissue. "Everything is going to work out. God will make certain of that."

Katie nodded, her gaze finding Tony's, her eyes filled with worry and heartache and hope. He wanted to tell her that Ivy was right and that everything really would be okay, but words weren't nearly as effective as action when it came to achieving a goal.

He motioned for Noah to follow him across the room. Carter and Zach joined them.

"I've been thinking about Martin and how easily he's been able to elude us," he said.

"Public transit, crowded streets, overabundance of scent pools with millions of scents mixed in," Zach said. "Even the best dog may struggle under those circumstances."

"I agree, but I don't think that's the reason Martin is able to stay hidden. He has to be going somewhere he doesn't think we'll look for him."

"Agreed," Carter and Noah said in unison.

"I think the most likely place for him to do that is his apartment."

"We've checked there," Noah reminded him.

"Immediately after he escaped. Since then, I don't think anyone from the precinct has been in."

"You may be right, but his landlord agreed to keep an eye on things and let us know if Martin showed up. We've also had patrol officers driving by the complex several times a day. Do you really think Martin would risk it?" Noah asked.

"The fact that we're asking that question makes me think he would. The way I see things, Martin tries to anticipate what we'll do and how we'll act. He has to know that we've been in the apartment, and he may assume that we won't go back unless someone tells us he's been there."

"His apartment *is* on the ground level," Zach said. "And there are plenty of windows in his unit. If he managed to break the lock on one, it would be easy enough for him to slip inside."

"I'll send someone there to check things out," Noah said.

"I'll go," Tony offered. "I need to get back to your place. Rusty is in Katie's apartment, and he's past ready for breakfast and a walk."

"You're not on shift today," Noah reminded him.

"I can be. If it means we find Martin more quickly."

"All right. Get Rusty, go home and eat, take a few hours to rest, and then go to the apartment. The superintendent should be able to let you in. If you find anything, let me know."

"I will." He glanced at the bed. Katie was nursing Jordyn Rose, her attention focused on the newborn. As if she sensed his gaze, she looked up and smiled, her expression open and inviting and soft.

"Are you leaving?" she asked, and he nodded, his throat tight with something that felt an awful lot like longing.

"Rusty is still at your place. I don't want to leave him there alone too much longer."

"You don't have to explain, Tony. You've been here for hours. That's way above and beyond the call of friendship."

"Not even close," he replied and then dropped a kiss on the top of her head. Her hair smelled like baby powder and flowers, and he wondered why he had never noticed that before.

"Do what the doctor and your family tell you, okay?" he murmured, his fingers grazing Jordyn Rose's downy head. He didn't want to leave. He wanted to stay right where he was, guarding Katie and the baby and watching as the mother and daughter bonded.

"I'm too tired to do anything else," she replied, smiling as he stepped away. "Be careful, Tony."

"I will be. I'll come back this evening. Just to make certain Jordyn Rose hasn't sprouted into a young adult and gotten engaged while I wasn't looking."

She chuckled, her laughter drifting into the hall as he walked out of the room.

NINE

By early evening, Katie could barely keep her eyes open. She and Jordyn Rose had had a string of visitors. Friends from church, coworkers from her former school, officers from the K-9 unit. The Jamesons had stayed close; Jordan's brothers and parents had made sure she had anything and everything she might have needed.

Currently all she needed was sleep.

Her pallor, lethargy and high heart rate had alarmed the nurse, and Dr. Ritter had been called. He'd ordered blood tests, and when they showed severe anemia, she'd had a blood transfusion.

Guests had been shooed out, and Katie had insisted the Jamesons go have dinner while she was examined and treated.

Now she was alone, the baby lying comfortably in her arms. Jordyn Rose had not cried once since her birth. When she was awake, her eyes opened wide as if she were trying to take in every detail of the odd world she had suddenly found herself in.

Katie had known love before.

She had loved her parents. She had loved Jordan. She loved her in-laws. But, the love she felt for her daughter

was something she had no words for. The strength of
it had taken her by surprise. Even now, when she was
so tired that she thought she might pass out, she didn't
dare rest for fear of what might happen while she was
sleeping.

Her phone rang, and she grabbed it, checking the
caller ID before she answered. She had no desire to
speak with Martin. The day had been eventful, and she
wanted it to end as wonderfully as it had begun.

When she saw the caller was Ivy, she answered
quickly. "Hello?"

"It's Ivy, dear. We got caught in rush-hour traffic and
just now found a place to get some dinner. It's crowded.
You know how Friday nights in the city are."

"Yes. I do," Katie said, stifling a yawn.

"I told Alexander that I should take a cab back to the
hospital. I can stop in the cafeteria and grab something
that we can share."

"Ivy, don't do that. Enjoy your family dinner."

"Honey, you're family, too."

"What I mean is that I don't want you to give up
your plans to sit in the hospital and watch me and the
baby sleep."

"Is our darling Jordyn sleeping?" Ivy asked, her
voice soft with affection.

"She ate like a champ fifteen minutes ago, and now
she's sleeping like one."

"Wonderful! And, what about you? Did the doctor
find the reason for your anemia?"

"Nothing that he could put his finger on. Probably
just the pregnancy."

"I'm glad to hear that, but I still think it would be a
good idea for me to return to the hospital."

"Ivy, I would feel horrible if you did that. Your sons are always so busy. A family dinner is rare. Please just stay and enjoy yourself."

"Are you sure?"

"Absolutely."

"All right. We'll see you when we're finished here. Give Jordyn Rose a kiss for me."

"I will," she promised, ending the call and setting the phone on the bedside table. She could have agreed to Ivy's return. Her mother-in-law would have been thrilled to hold the baby while she slept, but Katie might need help when she returned home and she didn't want to be a burden to the only family she had.

She stared at her daughter's face, and she couldn't help thinking about her parents and how excited they would have been to welcome their first grandchild. They would have been just as thrilled as the Jamesons. Maybe more so because Katie was their only child.

A tear dropped onto Jordyn Rose's face.

Katie brushed it away, sniffing back more that were threating to fall.

Someone knocked, and the door opened, the shift nurse bustling in with a tray of what looked like soup and juice. "Dr. Ritter ordered you a liquid meal. I told him you hadn't been hungry today, and he wants you to eat."

"I'm still not hungry," Katie said, holding Jordyn Rose closer as the nurse set the tray on the table.

"If you want to be released tomorrow, you need to get your blood count up and some food down."

"Will soup keep my blood count up?" she asked, eyeing the bowl of soup. It looked like chicken noodle. Any other time, she would have been happy to eat it.

Currently, she was so tired, she couldn't imagine lifting a spoonful to her lips.

"No, but rest might. You're exhausted. Your body has been through a lot. *You've* been through a lot. Not just today. We're talking months of stress."

Of course, she knew Katie's story.

It seemed everyone Katie met did.

"I think I need sleep more than I need food."

"Take this from a woman who has had six children— you need both. When you get home, you're going to be doing the late-night and early-morning feedings on your own. You'll be burning the candle at both ends, trying to keep up with the baby's appetite while you also try to keep your house in order. Tell you what—we don't have regular nurseries like they did when I had my children, but when a mom is really tired, we can take the baby to the nurses station—"

"No. I don't think that's a good idea," Katie said, her heart pounding frantically at the thought.

"Hear me out, hun," she responded. "No one is allowed on this floor without checking in downstairs. We've got guards posted at the elevator, checking visitor identification. Little Jordyn Rose won't be more than six inches from a nurse at any given time. As a matter of fact, she'll probably be held the entire time she's with us. We love newborns." She smiled reassuringly, and Katie's resistance began to fade.

She knew that everything the nurse said was true. She had been assured by the doctor and the nursing staff, as well as by the Jamesons and Tony, that every precaution was being taken.

And, if Martin did find a way onto the floor, he would assume the baby was with Katie and try to gain access to her room. If she was asleep and he walked in, he could take the baby and she would be none the wiser.

The thought terrified her.

"You're sure she won't be left unattended?"

"I have been working here for thirty years. In all that time, we have never left an infant unattended. Nor have we lost one."

"All right," Katie agreed reluctantly, afraid if she didn't, she would fall asleep and wake to find the baby gone. "She ate twenty minutes ago. She'll probably want to eat again in a couple hours."

"We'll bring her back as soon as she starts fussing. Don't worry about that."

"Okay." Katie kissed Jordyn Rose's head and her cheek. "Love you, sweetheart. Mommy will be right here if you need me."

She handed the baby to the nurse, her body humming with nervous energy as she watched the woman place Jordyn Rose in the bassinet and roll it away.

"She'll be fine," Katie whispered to the empty room.

She told herself she believed it as she ate a few mouthfuls of soup, drank a couple sips of juice and finally let her eyes drift shut.

After visiting Martin's last known address, Tony had received a call from dispatch with information regarding an apartment owned by Martin's great-aunt. She had died several years ago, and probate court records showed that she had left the apartment to Martin. It was an unexpected lead and one Tony was anxious to follow up on.

It was dark by the time he arrived at the apartment complex—a tall brick building surrounded by large homes that had been there since the 1920s. Tony walked the perimeter of the building, letting Rusty sniff the ground. The Lab tugged impatiently at the leash, pulling Tony to a ground-level window on the west side of the building.

Rusty stopped there, nosing the ground and huffing gently, his ears and tail nearly quivering with excitement.

"What is it, Rusty?" Tony asked, studying the window and the ground beneath it.

Rusty whined, his scruff raised, his dark eyes focused on the window. He wanted inside, and Tony was going to get him there.

He walked back to the apartment entrance and rang the buzzer. Several minutes later, the super appeared.

"What can I do for you, Officer?" he asked as he opened the door.

"I'm investigating the murder of—"

"That police officer? Heard about it on the news. Don't know what that has to do with this apartment complex, but I'm happy to help, if I can."

"We're looking for a guy by the name of Martin Fisher. We have reason to believe he owns a unit here." Tony pulled out a photo of Martin and handed it to the super.

"This the guy who shot the cop?" the super asked.

"Yes."

"Can't say I've seen him around. Most of the residents here are older folks who bought long before I started working here."

"His great-aunt owned the unit." Tony offered the name and, the super's eyes lit up.

"Her, I know of. Apartment 115. Ground floor. Quiet

lady, but nice. Always had a kind word when she saw me. She passed a few years back. Figured the estate would sell the apartment, but it never happened."

"Mind if I take a look in the apartment?"

"You don't think that Fisher guy has been here?"

"I would like to rule out the possibility."

"I've got no problem with that."

"I appreciate your cooperation."

"Come on then. Just—"

"Tony!" someone shouted.

He turned and saw Zach running toward him, Eddie, his beagle, loping beside him.

"Hey, bro. What are you doing here?" he asked as Zach stopped beside him.

"Noah got a call from the precinct. A taxi driver says he remembers picking Martin up from a bus stop last night. He dropped him off two blocks from here. I figured you might need some backup."

"You cleared it with Noah?"

"Don't I always?"

"Probably not."

Zach grinned. "You may be right, but this time I did. I'm not going to do anything that might jeopardize the case against Martin."

"You two coming in or staying out?" the super asked, spitting a wad of gum into the bushes beside the property. "Because I don't want to wait here all day while you chat about life."

He walked into the building.

Tony and Zach followed.

As apartment lobbies went, this was a nice one. Marble floors. Neutral paint. Modern paintings of the New York skyline decorating the walls, but it felt like what it was—an art deco-style apartment complex built nearly a century ago.

"Do you have security cameras?" Zach asked as the super led them through the lobby and into a well-lit hall.

"Nah. We haven't had problems. Like I said, most of the residents are older. Quiet. They do their thing and leave each other alone. The apartment you want is down here. End of the hall."

He stopped at apartment 115, knocked and then unlocked the door.

It swung inward, revealing a small living area. A couch covered in floral-patterned fabric sat against a wall. Dark wood end tables flanked it.

"Place looks like it's been cleaned recently," the super said, running his finger over the coffee table. "Came in and checked on the unit a few weeks ago, and there was a layer of dust on everything. Thought it was a shame. What with how hot a commodity apartments in the area are. Maybe the family is finally going to put it on the market. Go on and do what you need to. I've got a faucet leaking in another apartment that isn't gonna fix itself. You need anything, you'll find me there. If you don't need anything, just close the door when you leave. It'll lock automatically." He walked into the hall, hands shoved in his pockets, bald head gleaming in the overhead light.

"What do you think?" Zach asked as he and Eddie moved through the room. The beagle's tail was wagging, his head down as he sniffed the old Turkish carpet that nearly covered the living room floor.

"I think he's been here," Tony responded. "Rusty led me to one of the windows on this side of the building. It's a nice building, but—"

"Security isn't great?" Zach scratched the beagle behind the ears and walked into a kitchen that opened off the living room. Granite counters, white cabinets and stainless-steel appliances made the small space seem larger. There were no dishes in the sink. No dish soap. Nothing to indicate Martin had been spending time here since his escape.

"Right."

"He's not here now. If he were both our dogs would be going nuts."

"Right." Tony used gloved hands to open a couple of drawers and cupboards. He counted two sets of silverware and two sets of fancy china. A small trash can was tucked beneath the sink. Unlike most of the drawers and cabinets, it was full.

"Look at this," he said, pulling it out and setting it on the floor.

"Anything interesting?" Zach asked, standing beside him as he pulled out a few crumpled receipts.

Tony scanned the first. "Dinner at a café two nights ago."

"So, he has been here."

"Someone has," Tony responded, scanning the next. It was longer and the items on it made his blood run cold.

"What's wrong?"

"Look at this. Baby crib. Diapers. Formula. Baby clothes. Pacifier." He jabbed at the bottom of the receipt. "He purchased this at nine o'clock this morning."

"He knows Katie had the baby," Zach growled, his eyes dark with worry and anger.

"And, he's bought everything he needs for her arrival." Tony strode down a small hallway, slamming the palm of his hand against a door that was partially open. The room beyond was small and filled with everything necessary to bring a baby home. Crib. Set up and ready. Changing table. Small dresser. Tony checked the drawers. They were filled with clothes and diapers.

He walked into the second bedroom. Like the living room, it was furnished, the bed and dresser dated, the small closet opened to reveal men's clothes hung from wire hangers. A map of Queens and a highlighter lay on the bed. Rusty sniffed both, his hackles raised. He knew the man they had been chasing had been there.

"Tony," Zach called. "What do you make of this?"

He walked into the room, carrying what looked like a set of blue scrubs. "They were hanging in the closet in the other room. Check out the tag."

He did, and his heart stopped as he read the name of the hospital where Katie had had the baby.

He didn't think about what he was doing, didn't have any plan in mind aside from making sure Katie and Jordyn Rose were okay.

"Call Noah. Let him know what we've found," he said, yanking out his cell phone and dialing Katie's number.

It rang three times before she answered, her voice groggy with sleep. "Hello? Tony? Is everything okay?"

"Sure," he lied. "I just wanted to check in. Make sure you and the baby are getting the rest you need."

"We are. Well, I am. Jordyn Rose has been with the nurses for..." She paused, and he could picture her looking at the time on her phone, her silky blond hair falling around her shoulders. "Nearly three hours! Wow! I really did need some sleep."

"You said she's with the nurses?" he asked, his pulse rate jumping as he realized the two weren't together.

"Yes. I was so exhausted, the shift nurse offered to take her to the nurses station and keep her until she needed to be fed. Which should be soon."

He could hear bedcovers shifting as she sat up.

"Why? Is something going on that I need to know about?"

"No," he lied again, and despised himself for it. He made a habit of speaking the truth, of being a straight shooter who wasn't afraid to say difficult things.

But, he couldn't tell Katie what he and Zach had found. Not without filling her with panic. "Are your in-laws back?"

"No, but they should be soon. Are you sure there's nothing wrong? You sound…worried."

"I *am* worried."

"Tony, please just tell me what's going on," she begged, and he knew he had to. That keeping the information from her wouldn't keep her or the baby safe.

He gave her a brief overview.

When he finished, she was silent.

"Katie," he began.

"I need to make sure she's okay," she replied, and then the call went dead.

She pushed it went back..........obviously

TEN

She didn't bother with shoes.

She didn't put on a robe.

She ran from the room, her head spinning, her pulse racing.

"Ma'am." A police officer grabbed her arm, and she shoved him away.

"Mrs. Jameson," he tried again, following her as she hurried through the corridor. "You need to stay in your room and stay in bed."

"I need to find my baby."

"She's with the nurses. I checked on her twenty-five minutes ago. She was fussing a little, but they were getting her back to sleep."

"You're sure?" She swung around, knowing she looked crazed and wild-eyed, but she didn't care.

He nodded, grabbing her arm again when she swayed with relief.

"You need to get back in bad. You're white as a sheet."

"I want to see my daughter first." Because her mind was running through what he'd said, picking apart his words and finding reason to be concerned. "If she was fussing, she needs to eat. They should have brought her to me already."

"She probably went back to sleep," he said, obviously trying to reassure a woman whom he thought might be on the verge of tears.

And, maybe she was.

Her eyes burned. She felt physically ill, her stomach churning, her head spinning. She pressed her hands to her abdomen, praying this was all a bad dream, that she would wake in a moment with Tony beside her, brushing hair from her cheek and whispering that everything was okay.

"Newborns need to eat every couple of hours. It's been nearly three. She did not go back to sleep. Where is she?" she nearly howled.

"Katie, you need to calm down." A second officer appeared at her side, cupped her shoulders and looked into her eyes. "You're going to pass out if you don't start breathing."

"I am breathing."

"Not enough," the officer said kindly, her eyes rich chocolate, her hair a short Afro beneath her uniform cap.

"Please stop worrying about me and go find Jordyn Rose," she begged, feeling so dizzy, she had to lean against the wall to keep from falling.

"She needs a wheelchair," the first officer said, a note of panic in his voice.

"I need to see my daughter."

"That's not going to happen if you're out cold on the floor," the second officer said gently. "Calm down, okay? I'm going to get a wheelchair. I'll have the nurse bring Jordyn Rose to you."

She walked away, her confidence easing some of Katie's panic. Of course, Jordyn Rose was with the nurses. Of course, she was okay. The baby had been checked on twenty-five minutes ago. She had been fine then, and she was fine now.

But, the couple of minutes it should have taken the officer to return stretched into five and then ten.

"Something is wrong," Katie said, pushing away from the wall and taking a shaky step in the direction the officer had gone.

"You're still in no condition to take a walk down the hall," the first officer said, trying to pull her to a stop. She met his eyes and saw her own fear reflected there.

"You know it's true. If things were fine, she'd have returned by now."

"It can take a while to find a wheelchair. Even in a hospital. How about we just walk back to your room? It's not that far."

She didn't respond. There was nothing she could have said.

Instead, she took another shaky step and then another.

Please, God. Please let her be there.

The prayer ran through her head over and over again, a silent, desperate mantra. When she finally reached the end of the hall, she could see the counter that surrounded the nurses station and the monitors that sat on desks there. A whiteboard with patients' names. Hers was there. And Jordyn Rose's.

She could see the bassinet sitting between two chairs. Empty. The nurses were congregated near one side of the counter, faces pale, eyes wide. The female officer stood with them, holding a radio in her hand, her expression dark. Noah was beside her, and his father and brother Carter were flanking him. Ivy was a few feet away, collapsed on a chair near the waiting room, Violet, Rachelle and Lani hovering around her, their own expressions full of worry.

She was the first to see Katie, and when their eyes met, her face crumbled, tears sliding down her cheeks, a sob escaping some deep, dark place inside.

At the sound, the Jameson men rushed to her side.

Ivy must have said something to them, because all three turned in Katie's direction.

"Katie," Noah began, but whatever he planned to say was drowned out by a voice on the PA system calling for a Code 1 lockdown of the facility.

And, Katie knew, even though the prayer was still running through her head, even though she was telling herself that she was having a nightmare. She *knew* that Jordyn Rose was gone.

Suddenly, Noah was in front of her, trying to pull her into his arms. She stepped back. She didn't want his comfort; she wanted her baby.

"We're going to find her," he said, the words tight with emotion.

She turned and walked away. Stiff. Hollow. Ancient.

She could live to be a thousand and never feel so worn and aged again.

Someone called her name, but she didn't look back and she didn't stop. She walked to her room, stepped inside and closed the door. Her overnight bag was sitting on the floor near the window. She grabbed it and pulled out onesies, diapers and a tiny pair of baby shoes.

The sight made her retch, her empty stomach heaving as she imagined her daughter being held in Martin's murderous hands.

"No," she said, as if that could make it less real and less true. "No."

She took leggings, a T-shirt and a flannel button-down from the bag, not thinking about what she was doing, not thinking beyond that moment.

"Katie?" Noah knocked. She didn't answer.

He could come in or not.

"Katie?" This time, Ivy called through the closed door. "Honey, we're coming in, okay?"

She grabbed her cell phone, ducked into the bathroom and locked the door.

They meant well, but they couldn't give her what she wanted.

They couldn't open the door, hand her the baby and say it had all been a misunderstanding. She knew that just as surely as she knew that if Jordyn Rose were going to be saved, she was the one who would have to do it.

She heard them talking in hushed tones as she changed into her clothes. If she left the bathroom, they would surround her with their love, offering her a million words of comfort that none of them really believed. They would reassure her and plan and explain how they were going to go about rescuing Jordyn Rose, and she would listen to their words and hear the heartbreak beneath them and know that she was responsible for it.

They had lost their son and brother because of Martin's obsession with her.

Now they had lost his daughter.

If not for her, they would still be a family of six.

She couldn't face them. Not yet. And, she wouldn't

be able to slip out of the hospital with all of them there. That was her one and only plan: get out of the hospital. She wasn't sure what she would do once she managed to leave. She had no idea where to start searching, but maybe she wouldn't have to. Martin had proved to be extraordinarily gifted at finding his way into her world. All she needed to do was give him an opportunity to kidnap her.

Because wherever he was, that's where Jordyn Rose would be.

Her legs went weak, and she collapsed.

She sat where she was, leaning back against the door and staring at her phone. She willed it to ring the same way she had willed Jordan to be alive the day he had failed to show up at the K-9 graduation ceremony the morning he'd been killed. She had willed him to life, but she had known, even while she hoped it wasn't true, that he was gone.

She didn't feel the same about Jordyn Rose.

Her daughter was alive, because Martin had no reason to kill her. She was the perfect pawn in the game he had been playing—an easy means to control Katie. He had to know that.

So, why hadn't he called?

"Ring," she muttered, her voice shaking, her body numb with terror.

The phone remained silent, and she realized the hospital room had gone silent, too. Had they moved into the hall to discuss things? If they had, was it possible she could sneak past them and make it to the stairwell?

Probably not.

Even if she could, the hospital was on lockdown.

If she tried to leave, she would be stopped. She was trapped by the concern of the people around her.

And, her daughter was trapped in the arms of a madman.

"Katie!" Tony called. "I'm coming in."

Something scraped the doorknob. It jiggled and then the lock snapped open.

"Katie?" he repeated, the door bumping her back as he tried to open it.

"Scoot over a little, okay?" he said.

She didn't think she had the power to move, but she found herself sliding sideways until her back was against the cool tile wall. The chill of it made her think of the November air and her tiny baby, wrapped in a thin blanket as she was carried through the streets of New York City.

Her head spun, and she leaned it against the wall, trying to keep herself from spinning away with it.

Tony stepped into the bathroom and closed the door. "I asked everyone to go into the waiting room, to give you some time and space right now. We're all beside ourselves, but we're going to get Jordyn Rose back, Katie. We will."

Katie couldn't speak.

He sank down beside her and pulled her into his arms. She sat stiffly, her body rigid with fear.

"I'm sorry, Katie," he murmured, stroking her hair, his calloused fingers catching in the tangled strands.

She started sobbing.

"Shhhhh. You're going to make yourself sick," Tony said, his lips against her forehead, his hand flat on her back.

Katie couldn't stop crying. The sound that ripped

from her throat was filled with every bit of the agony that was in her heart.

"I'm breaking into a million pieces," she sobbed.

"Shhhhh," he repeated, pulling her into his lap and wrapping her in his arms. "I'll hold you together."

She didn't think he could, but her arms slipped around his waist and her head dropped to his chest, the agonizing cries of her broken heart muffled by his shirt.

Tony had known rage before.

He had known fear.

He had even, on a few occasions, known helplessness.

But, nothing compared to the emotions racing through his blood as he held Katie and listened to her cry.

Jordyn Rose was gone, somehow taken right out from under the noses of half a dozen nurses. Noah and Zach were questioning the nursing staff, while Carter tried to comfort his parents, Violet, Rachelle and Lani, assuring them that the K-9 unit would find the baby.

And, Tony was here, trying to hold himself and Katie together.

He smoothed her hair, his hands tangling in the long strands, his mind jumping back to the moment after Jordyn had been laid on her chest. Her joy. Her contentment. Her triumph. In that moment, she had seemed like the strongest woman he had ever met. Now she was broken and defeated; her body had gone limp once her sobs had finally faded.

Martin was responsible for this, and for the first time in his career in law enforcement, Tony understood the rage and grief that drove some people to take the law into their own hands.

"I am going to find him, and I am going to make him pay for this," he muttered, his muscles tight, his jaw tense. He wanted to jump up and rush outside with Rusty. The scent trail was fresh. They couldn't be more than forty minutes behind Martin.

But, Katie was holding on to him as if she were drowning and he were her lifeline.

He couldn't leave her. Not like this.

"I want you to find him, and I want you to get my daughter back," Katie said, her voice shaky, her face pressed against his chest.

"I will," he promised, praying he could do what he said.

She nodded, her warm breath seeping through his shirt as she took a deep, shuddering breath.

Finally, she lifted her head and looked into his eyes.

Her face was pale and streaked with tears, but there was fire in her eyes. "He already took my husband. He can't have my baby, too."

"He won't."

"He does, and it's my fault. I never should have—"

"Stop blaming yourself for things you had nothing to do with," he said, wiping the tears from her cheeks, his palms resting there.

"I should have kept her in my room. I should have—"

"Known that Martin could somehow get past several levels of security? You couldn't know. None of us could, so instead of beating ourselves up, let's go out, find her and bring her home."

She nodded solemnly, swiped a few more tears from her cheeks and stood.

"I'm ready," she said, as if she had girded herself for battle and planned to ride into the fray.

"You need to stay here. We're going to have patrol officers escort you home as soon as the doctor clears it. If Martin got into the hospital once, he may be able to do it again."

"If he does, maybe he'll have Jordyn Rose with him."

"Don't even think about sacrificing yourself to free your daughter," he said, worried about the look in her eyes—the stoic determination he read in her face.

"Wouldn't you?"

He didn't answer, because he wouldn't lie.

"That's what I thought." She wrapped her arms around her waist, and he could see the soft curve of her belly where the baby had once been.

Somehow, that hurt almost as much as seeing the grief and fear in her eyes.

"Promise me you'll stay here until the doctor releases you," he said, his hands settling on her shoulders, his fingers resting on the jutting ridges of her scapula.

"Tony…"

"Promise me, Katie. I can't concentrate on finding Jordyn Rose if I'm worried about where you might be or what kind of trouble might be finding you."

"All right. I promise I'll stay here until the doctor releases me. But, remember, I'm counting on you to find Jordyn Rose and bring her back to me." Her voice broke, and he pulled her close, pressing a kiss to her forehead and then her cheek.

Without forethought, without planning, his lips brushed hers. Gently. Barely a touch, but they both froze, staring into each other's eyes, breaths mingling, lips millimeters apart.

It would have taken no effort at all to kiss her again. Kiss her like he meant it.

Like she was everything he had never realized he wanted and everything he could ever need.

He stepped back, let his hands fall away. "I'll bring her back to you," he said.

She nodded, and he turned away, opened the door and stepped into her room. He expected it to be empty, but the family had returned from the waiting room. Carter and Ivy were sitting beside each other, Rusty lying at their feet. Violet, Rachelle and Lani all looked worried. And, he wasn't surprised that they hadn't stayed away. They were one of the strongest, tightest-knit families he knew. They would stand beside Katie and support her through this. In the midst of their own grief and fear, they would still offer her the comfort she needed.

Ivy stood when she saw Tony. "How is she?"

"About like you'd expect," he responded. "I need to find Martin and get her baby back."

"Tony!" Zach barreled in, Eddie beside him. "The precinct just got a call from the super at the apartment complex we visited. He said he thinks he saw Martin at the back entrance."

"Did he have Jordyn Rose with him?" Katie stepped out of the bathroom, her face paper-white.

"The super wasn't sure. He wasn't absolutely certain it was Martin, but he was suspicious enough to give us a call," Zach said. "You doing okay, sis?" he asked.

"No. Where are my shoes? I'm coming with you." She tried to step past Tony, but he grabbed her hand, pulling her to a stop.

"You promised, Katie."

"That was before Martin was spotted."

"You promised," he repeated, and she pressed her lips together and nodded.

"You're going to let me know, right? If you find them there, you'll call?"

"I will," he agreed, calling Rusty and hooking him to his lead.

He offered Katie what he hoped was a reassuring smile and headed out the door. He was just over the threshold when she called, "Tony!"

He turned, and she tried to smile.

"Be careful, okay? I want you back, too."

"I will be."

"Ready?" he asked, meeting Zach's questioning eyes.

"Sure," Zach responded, his gaze shifting to Katie before he walked out the door.

He didn't ask questions as they jogged through the hospital corridor and barreled down the stairs. There wasn't time. Something that Tony was grateful for. Because he didn't have answers. He had no idea what to call the thing that seemed to be blooming between him and Katie.

He certainly didn't want to call it love.

That would feel like too much of a betrayal of the man he had once called brother.

He scowled, opening the hatchback of his SUV so Rusty could hop in.

He slammed it shut and jumped in the driver's seat, using sirens and lights to navigate afternoon traffic as quickly as possible. It still seemed to take too long. By the time he reached the apartment complex, several other K-9 vehicles and NYC police cruisers were parked there.

He jumped out of his vehicle, freed Rusty and joined the group.

K-9 officer Luke Hathaway motioned him over, his cadaver dog, Bruno, sniffing the ground nearby.

"How's everyone holding up at the hospital?" he asked.

"Not good," he answered honestly.

"Any idea how Martin managed to get the baby? Hospital security is pretty tight."

"We found scrubs at the apartment. Tagged with the name of the hospital where Katie gave birth," Tony responded.

"I made some inquiries about that," Zach cut in. "According to the nursing supervisor, they had to bring in a few temporary hires to fill in for a couple of nurses who were out on maternity and medical leave. One of them was an RN named William Spears. He was placed by a health-services temp agency that works with the hospital a lot."

"I don't think I like where this is heading," Tony said.

"Yeah. I don't much like it, either, but that doesn't change the fact that Spears was scheduled to work today. He showed up with his ID and credentials at his scheduled time. The staff supervisor said he was tall, very muscular and talked a lot about his wife and newborn daughter. She also said he didn't look like the photo we distributed. He had blond hair, a beard and mustache, and blue eyes."

"Hair and eye color can be changed easily. Beards and mustaches can be bought at any costume shop. It was Martin," Tony said, sick with the knowledge of how far ahead the kidnapping had been planned. Martin must have accessed Katie's medical records at the clinic soon after he escaped the mental institution.

"Noah is accessing hospital security footage, but it sounds like it. The nurses had no reason to be suspicious. He had worked a few other shifts and there had never been a problem. As a matter of fact, the other RNs liked him. When Jordyn Rose started fussing, he offered to take her to her mother. He hasn't been seen since. He used his access card to open the stairwell door five minutes later. Two officers think they saw him walking through the lobby with an empty car seat in hand and a duffel slung over his shoulder. They didn't stop him, because he was wearing scrubs and had an ID."

"This guy needs to be stopped. Today," Luke spat, his dark eyes flashing with anger.

"I think it's best if we don't tell Katie about the duffel bag," Tony responded, his fists clenched, the force of his rage nearly blinding him.

If Jordyn Rose was in the duffel…

"Here's the rest of it," Zach said. "We sent patrol officers to talk to taxi drivers in the queue outside the hospital. One of them gave a ride to a man who had a newborn in a car seat."

"Where did he drop them off?"

"A few miles from here. At a bus stop."

"So, he could definitely have come here," Tony said, his gaze shifting to the apartment building. He could see Martin's apartment windows. That meant Martin could see them.

If he was inside.

"What's the plan?" a patrol officer asked, her gaze sharply focused. "You want us to stay or fall back?"

"If he's in there, he could have a newborn with him.

We don't want her hurt. Fall back, and we'll see if we can make contact."

"We'll park in the lot behind the building across the street and spread out on foot. If he's in there and manages to escape, I don't want him slipping through our fingers."

She jogged to her cruiser, calling several other patrol officers to follow.

"What do you think?" Zach asked as their cruisers pulled out of the lot. "Is he in there?"

"My opinion?" Finn Gallagher said as he walked over with his yellow Lab, Abernathy. "He is."

"Why do you say that?" Tony asked.

"I think I saw the shade on that back window move." He pointed to the small window that Tony had found unlocked previously.

"That's the window in the kitchen. The door opens into the living room. No clear line of sight from there to the kitchen," Zach said.

"I don't think we're going to need one," Luke responded grimly as another of the apartment windows slid open and Martin appeared.

He had cropped his hair short and lightened it, but he still looked like the same guy Tony had seen at church dozens of times. Only, now he wore a wild grin that made him look like the madman he was.

"Hey! This has been a fun ride, huh?" he called out, his eyes blazing in his tanned face.

"Where is my niece?" Zach shouted, taking a step toward the window, his hand on his firearm.

Tony pulled him back. "Stay cool," he hissed. "He's trying to rile us up. It gives him a thrill."

"It would give me a thrill to see him locked up for the rest of his life," Zach growled.

"That's going to happen, but first we need to make sure the baby is in a safe location."

"Your niece?" Martin crowed. "Is that what you think? She's not Jordan's baby—she's mine."

"Where is she?" Tony demanded, taking a step closer to the building, trying to distract him from the fact that Finn and Luke were taking their dogs around to the front.

"Not here." He laughed coldly. "My daughter deserves better than a place like this."

He could have been lying. It was possible Jordyn Rose was sitting in the car seat, right beside her kidnapper, but Tony had a sinking feeling he was telling the truth.

"Your daughter is a newborn. She needs to be with her mother," he said, hoping to tap into Martin's delusions and use them against him.

"Don't try to play mind games with me, Knight. It won't work, and your friends coming around the front of the apartment won't work, either. I didn't come here with the baby. I came because this has all been a setup. The crib. The changing table. The diapers. I knew one of you would show up here eventually, and I wanted to prove to you, once and for all, that you can't beat me at this. Only I know the rules of the game, because I'm the one who wrote them. Now, back off before things get ugly." He pulled a gun and pointed it straight at Tony's head.

The guy was delusional enough to risk coming here, maybe to pick up some baby supplies. He had to know the entire K-9 unit was searching for him and Jordyn

Rose and that this apartment was the first place they'd look. Martin clearly wasn't thinking straight, and that would work in Tony's favor.

Or it would get him killed.

"Put that down, Martin," Tony demanded.

"I don't think so. I think you're going to have to make a choice—let me go or kill me. Of course, if you kill me, your precious Katie won't ever see her baby again."

"Katie isn't mine," he said, keeping his voice calm as he moved closer. Rusty was beside him, pressed against his leg and growling low in his throat. He would attempt to disarm Martin if Tony gave him the command, but there was too much risk involved in that.

"You want her to be, and I don't like that." Martin climbed through the window and stood with the building to his back, his gun still pointed at Tony. "She's mine. I won't let anyone take her from me."

"Don't you think she should have some say in that?" Zach asked.

"If she hadn't been brainwashed by your brother, I might. Step back. Both of you." He wore a backpack that was only partially zipped, a few diapers peeking out of the top of it.

Obviously, his story about coming to the apartment to prove something to the K-9 unit had been a lie. He had taken Jordyn Rose somewhere and realized he didn't have the supplies he needed there. So, he'd risked coming here, even with the kidnapping of the baby already making the news. Martin was definitely not thinking clearly. His delusions were crowding out his ability to plan like the experienced, cold-blooded criminal he was.

"Give yourself up, Martin," Tony said. "You can't get away, and I don't want to have to hurt you."

"You wouldn't dare hurt me. I'm the only one who knows where that little brat is. I left her alone, you know. Without someone to feed her, she'll be dead in a day or two. At most." He spoke with cold precision, his eyes suddenly empty of emotion.

"You call your own baby a brat?" Zach said, moving sideways, so that Martin would have more difficulty keeping them both in his field of vision.

"It's all part of the game, Zach Jameson. I won when I played your brother. Let's see if I win with you." He swung his gun toward Zach, then pressed it against his own head.

"So, here is the deal, boys. I can leave, or I can die. You get to choose. Of course, if you choose me dying, the baby dies, too."

"Back down!" someone shouted from across the street.

Tony didn't shift his focus, but he recognized Noah's voice.

"Good call, Chief," Martin called, sidling past Tony, the gun still pressed to his head.

He might pull the trigger if Tony went for him.

He might not.

But, Tony wouldn't risk Jordyn Rose's life on a fifty-fifty shot. If Martin had come for baby supplies, the baby was still alive.

That was exactly the way Tony wanted things to remain.

He holstered his gun.

"I see you understand the rules now, Knight. Good. Maybe you won't join your buddy in the graveyard.

Don't follow me. If I see one cop, I will pull this trigger. I'm not afraid to die."

Dozens of onlookers had gathered and were recording on their cell phones as Martin backed away, the gun pressed to his temple, diapers sticking out of his backpack.

Tony wanted to shout that the onlookers were in a volatile and dangerous situation and they needed to leave, but he didn't want to do anything to send Martin off the deep end.

As long as Jordyn Rose was alive, there was hope of rescuing her.

That had to be the focus and the mission.

Martin reached the street and stepped in front of an oncoming car, waving the gun at the startled driver, who swerved and jumped the curb.

Half a dozen people jumped out of the way, screaming as the car bounced toward them.

Tony ran toward the crowd, stopping when Martin shouted his name. He had already crossed the street and was standing on the corner, the gun pressed to his temple again.

"Give Katie my love when you see her. Tell her we'll be together again soon."

Then, before Tony could respond, Martin shifted the gun, aimed and fired in Tony's direction.

ELEVEN

Katie had watched the video footage at least ten times.

Each time, she flinched when Martin pulled the trigger.

Each time, she expected to see Tony fall to the ground injured. Or, worse.

Each time, she prayed that someone would grab Martin before he escaped and demand that he bring them to Jordyn Rose.

But, of course, that couldn't happen.

The video had been shot nearly ten hours ago. A bystander had sent it to a local news station, and now the entire nation knew just how delusional and dangerous Martin was. He had taunted Tony with a shot that had slammed into a building nearby. Then, he had raced through a shocked crowd of pedestrians, gun in hand, firing shots at a few people who got in his way. For the safety of the crowd that had gathered and was watching, Tony hadn't fired in return.

And, for the safety of Jordyn Rose.

Until they knew where Martin had left her, they couldn't risk killing him. He had known that and used it to his advantage, escaping.

Again.

They also knew that Jordyn Rose was missing, the story of her kidnapping running with the photo Tony had taken—Katie staring down at Jordyn Rose, a soft smile on her face.

It flashed up on the television screen as she scrolled through news stations, her eyes dry from too much crying, her stomach empty.

"Hun, you need to stop torturing yourself," Alexander said, gently taking the television remote from her hand. He and Ivy were staying with her in the apartment while the rest of the Jameson men scoured the city with the NYC K-9 Command Unit. Even Carter was out searching with his German shepherd, Frosty. He had dropped his daughter off at his fiancée Rachelle's apartment. She would be caring for Ellie until Martin was apprehended. Lani, Noah's fiancée, a police officer awaiting the transfer she'd requested so she wouldn't be under the command of her husband-to-be, was acting as a helpful liaison between Katie and the NYC K-9 Command Unit, sharing information even when there wasn't much to report. Zach's wife, Violet, was focusing on Katie and Ivy, bringing them tea and assuring them the team was out there, doing everything to find Jordyn Rose.

"I'm not torturing myself—I'm trying to find some clue as to where my daughter is." Katie stood and walked across the room, still a little light-headed and dizzy. Her milk had come in, and she had no baby to feed, so Ivy had bought her a pump. Each time she used it, she cried.

She had cried so much, she had no tears left.

Please, God, keep her safe, she prayed as she walked

to the window that looked out over the front yard. There were three police cruisers parked there, the officers in them assigned to make certain Martin didn't come for Katie.

She wished he would.

She wished he would find a way in and take her to her daughter.

Anything would be better than waiting for something to happen.

"Sweetheart," Alexander said, clearing his throat and putting an arm around her shoulder. "I never had a daughter, but I always thought it would be nice. I always imagined me and the boys fighting off the young studs who wanted to date her."

"You would have done that for certain," she said hollowly, her gaze focused on the street and the houses beyond it. Martin was smart. Would he attempt to get to her with so many guards around?

"What I'm trying to say is that I love you like the daughter I never had. I hate to see you like this, drawn and scared. Not eating. Jordyn Rose is going to need you healthy when she comes home. If you're sick, how will you care for her?"

"I can't eat until I know she has," she said, because just thinking about food made her stomach churn.

"I understand, sweetheart," Ivy said. She was in the kitchen with Violet, stirring something that smelled like beef broth. "No mother wants to eat if she thinks her child hasn't. But, Martin Fisher is delusional. He is not dumb. He knows he can't have you without Jordyn Rose. If he…doesn't take good care of her, he'll have nothing to bargain with."

"I hope you're right," she said. Her heart thudded in

her ears, the sound nearly drowning out the soft conversation that drifted up from the yard below. Two of the officers were chatting, their voices light and easy.

She didn't want to resent them for that.

They were doing everything they could to protect her, and she couldn't blame them for her sorrows.

But, she wanted a little less sadness and a little more joy. She wanted to recapture that moment when she had looked at her daughter's face and felt as if everything in her life was working out just right.

More than anything, she wanted her daughter in her arms.

She wanted safety, security and the sense of peace that came with those things.

"I made bone broth, Katie." Ivy cut into her thoughts. "I know you're not keen on eating, but all you have to do is sip. It's rich and filled with iron. Something you need if you're going to produce enough milk for your daughter."

"I can't, Ivy," she said. Just the thought of sipping something made her gag.

"Try," Alexander said, the warmth of his tone and the sadness in his voice reminding her that she wasn't the only one scared and grieving.

"Okay. I'll try."

"And, how about we turn off the television and listen to some music? I always find that to be soothing." He took the remote and turned off the news just as another photo of Katie and Jordyn Rose flashed across the screen.

"Okay," she agreed, because her in-laws were doing everything they could to stay strong for her, and she needed to do the same for them. Quiet music filled the room, and Katie settled in the recliner and closed her eyes, letting the soft strains of an old hymn wash over her. God knew. He understood. He was in control.

She needed to remember that.

"Here, sweetie." Ivy pressed a mug of hot broth into her hands. "Just take little sips. You don't want to upset your stomach." There were shadows beneath her eyes and worry lines near her mouth. Katie imagined that, if her mother had lived, she would have looked the same.

"You have some, too, Ivy," she said. "Sit down and rest for a while. It's not like any of us have anywhere to go."

Ivy smiled tiredly. "You're right about that, and this has been a very long and exhausting day."

"Sit down, Ivy," Violet said gently. "I'll get you some broth. And, how about one of those dinner rolls you brought up from the apartment?"

"Just the broth. Thank you, Violet."

Alexander got up. "I'll help you, Violet. I need something to do." He followed Violet into the kitchen.

Ivy settled onto the couch, watching as Katie took a sip of the broth. "Not bad, right?"

"It's delicious. Thank you, Ivy."

"No thanks necessary. I've always loved to cook. Ellie has just started helping me in the kitchen. In a few years, Jordyn Rose will be doing the same."

Katie nodded, swallowing another sip of broth past the hard lump of fear in her throat.

"It's going to happen. I know it. God isn't going to take Jordyn Rose from us. We already lost her father."

Her voice cracked, and Katie set the mug on the side table and reached to touch her arm. "Ivy, it's going to be okay."

"Aren't I the one who is usually saying that to you?"

"We all have the ability to be strong when we need to be. You've been strong for me dozens of times these past few months. Now, it's my turn to be strong for you."

"You're a wonderful young woman, Katie. I was so happy when you and Jordan married. I didn't think there would ever be a woman who could capture his heart enough to tug him away from his work."

She hadn't. Not really. Jordan had loved Katie enough to marry her, but he had been devoted to his job in a way that had not left room for much else. She felt disloyal thinking that. Jordan was gone. His life had been cut short. She wanted to celebrate the love they had shared rather than dwell on the things they hadn't.

"Your family has been a blessing to me. I don't know what I would have done without you these last few months."

"You would have been just fine."

"Maybe, but I'm glad I didn't have to find out," she said, taking another sip of broth because she didn't want Ivy to see the tears in her eyes.

The Jamesons had taught her valuable lessons about family and loyalty and faith. And, no matter what Ivy said, she really didn't think she could have made it through the last nine months without them.

"Tony has been a tremendous help to you, as well," Ivy said as Violet handed her a bowl of broth. "Thank you, dear," she said to Violet.

Katie smiled at Violet, then turned back to their mother-in-law. "Yes. He has."

"He's a wonderful person. Warm. Caring. Loyal. All the things a young—"

"Ivy, now isn't the time," Alexander interrupted,

coming into the kitchen, carrying a small plate with two buttered rolls on it.

"What?" Ivy responded. "I'm simply pointing out some of the good things in our lives to distract us from thinking about the bad."

"I don't think anything could distract me from thinking about the fact that Jordyn Rose has been kidnapped," Katie said, taking her still-full cup to the sink and rinsing it out. "I think I'll go lie down. If you two don't mind?"

"Of course not. We'll be here if you need anything."

She nodded, bending to kiss Ivy's cheek. "You two should get some sleep, too."

"We will," Alexander assured her. He seemed relieved that she was going to her room. She couldn't blame him. She probably seemed ready to shatter.

She *was* ready to shatter.

Again.

Only, this time, she wouldn't let herself. As horrible as the situation was, as terrified as she felt, she had to come up with a plan to get her daughter back.

She went into the kitchen to thank Violet and give her a hug. Violet's cell rang—Rachelle checking in on how Katie was doing. Violet squeezed Katie's hand and assured Rachelle that Katie was holding up.

Barely, Katie thought as she finally went into her room.

Her cell phone rang, and she closed the door quickly, hoping it was Martin. Praying it was him.

"Katie?" Tony said, his voice nearly drowned out by the sound of traffic rushing by.

"Are you guys still outside?" she asked, glancing

at the window and the icy rain that had begun to fall a few hours ago.

"I am standing outside of Griffin's Diner. You know the place?"

"Yes. Jordan took me there a few times when we were dating. He said it was the place to hang out if you were part of the K-9 Command Unit. I heard it was closing this month."

"Next week. The owner, Lou, called the precinct to let us know he was staying open late during our search so we could stop in and warm up."

"That was nice of him."

"He's a nice guy, but that's not why I called. I wanted to check in and see how you were doing."

"I'm okay."

"I wish I believed that."

"I'm not okay," she corrected. "But, I'm not going to break down again."

"There isn't anyone who would judge you if you did," he said, his gentle tone reminding her of the way it had felt to be wrapped in his arms, to have his lips brush her forehead and cheek and mouth.

For the first time in as long as she could remember, she had felt like she was home.

"I'm not worried about being judged," she said, her voice raspy and her throat raw from all of the tears she had shed. "I'm worried about being strong enough to get my daughter back. Breaking down isn't going to help me do that."

He was silent long enough for her to know he was choosing his next words carefully. "Katie, I know it's difficult to sit and do nothing when someone you love is missing—"

"You didn't sit and do nothing when Jordan was missing. And, you're not sitting and doing nothing now," she pointed out. "You're a police officer. Even when you are off duty, you know the system and you can use it to your advantage. All I can do is pray and watch countless replays of you facing off with Martin."

"Prayer is a lot."

"I know, but I still feel like I should be doing something more."

"You staying here and staying safe is the best thing you can do for your daughter," he responded.

"What if…?" She couldn't bring herself to ask, but Tony seemed to hear the unspoken question.

"Jordyn Rose is alive," he said.

"We can't know that, and that's what is eating at me. That's what scares me more than anything," she admitted, her eyes hot and dry, her heart skipping beats. She felt dizzy and sick; the thought of her tiny baby dead at the hands of Martin Fisher nearly stole her breath.

"She is, Katie."

"How can you know?"

"He had diapers in his backpack, for one."

"And, for two?"

"He knows he will never get his hands on you if he doesn't have the baby with him."

"That's what Ivy said."

"We can't both be wrong, can we?" he asked, and she knew he was trying to make her smile. Even now, when he was exhausted and frustrated and working every angle possible to try to find Jordyn Rose, he cared enough about her to do that.

"Yes, but I'm hoping you aren't. I am hoping that, this time, things will have a happy ending."

"We're doing everything we can to make sure that happens, and that is why I called. Don't go maverick on me, okay?"

"What do you mean?" But, of course, she knew.

He had to understand how desperate she was, how willing to do anything to get Jordyn Rose back.

"If he calls you, I want to know it. And, if he tries to get you to leave the house, stay put. We'll trace the call and track him down. He can't move fast with a baby in his arms."

"He didn't have a baby when he nearly shot you," she said, the image of Tony diving sideways as the bullet slammed into the brick building behind him filling her head.

"That was before all the publicity. He can't leave her where someone can hear her crying. He can't ask someone to watch her, and he can't waste time. The entire city is hunting for him. He's going to contact you, Katie. And, when he does, I want you to call me immediately."

"I will," she agreed.

"Good. I've got to go. We're going to regroup and head out to search again."

"Be careful, Tony."

"I will," he said before he disconnected.

She set the phone on the bedside table, flicked off the overhead light and lay down. Ice pattered against the windows, and the hushed whisper of leaves brushing against the side of the house reminded Katie of the first winter she had spent there with Jordan.

If she had known it would be the last, she wouldn't have worried so much about the time he spent away, she wouldn't have resented his distracted attitude. Maybe she would have dwelled in the beauty of each moment rather than in the disappointments.

"If I could do it again, I would be more grateful," she whispered, and she knew if Jordan had been there, he would have told her it was okay. He would have reminded her, as he often had, that no one was perfect. That they were all fallible human beings.

He would have been right, but that didn't make her feel any better about things. Jordan was gone, and any chance she had to appreciate every part of their marriage was gone. She wouldn't spend her life mourning that, but she wasn't ever going to make the same mistake again.

If she got Jordyn Rose back—*when* she did—she would remind herself every morning that the day was a gift to be used and appreciated. Every night she would thank God for the good, the bad and every single moment in between.

"Please, Lord," she whispered. "Let me have my baby back. Please."

She wanted an audible answer, some sign that everything really would be okay. Instead, she felt nothing but the ache in her abdomen where Jordyn Rose had once been.

The floorboards outside the room creaked as Ivy and Alexander made their way through the apartment. She listened as the door closed and the bolt slid home. Minutes later, water ran through the pipes in the walls. She could imagine them in their apartment, making another pot of coffee as they discussed all the things they hadn't dared say when she was nearby.

They had embraced her like one of their own, and she would never forget that.

The apartment went quiet, the old house sighing as it settled for the night. Minutes passed and then an hour, and Katie was still wide-awake.

When her phone rang, she jerked upright and grabbed it without looking at the caller ID. "Hello?" she said, and then realized that the phone was still ringing.

Surprised, she scrambled out of bed, following the sound to the overnight bag she had brought to the hospital. She set it near the closet but hadn't unpacked it yet. The ringing stopped, then began again as she unzipped the bag, dug through the clothes and pulled out a flip phone. Not hers, but ringing.

She answered, her voice shaking. "Hello?"

"Finally, my love. You found the phone I left for you. Our daughter and I have missed you," Martin said, the sweet cooing sound of his voice making her skin crawl. Had he accessed her bag at the hospital? Or had he somehow slipped into the apartment before she had the baby and put the phone there then?

"Is she all right?" she asked, unable to keep the desperation from her voice.

"Don't you trust me to be a good father to our child?" he responded, the hard edge in his tone alarming her more than his sweet talk had.

"Of course, I do. It's just… I was nursing her in the hospital, and it's been hours since she has eaten."

"No worries, darling. I researched everything when I was planning our escape. I got Alison the best baby formula, and she has been eating every three hours."

"Alison?"

"It was my grandmother's name. Do you like it?"

"It's beautiful," she responded, because she needed

to become part of his delusion if she was ever going to see Jordyn Rose again.

"I'm glad you think so. If you didn't, I might consider another option. Although, it is the man's right to make the decisions in the family. Don't you agree?"

"Yes, of course," she lied.

"Have you missed me?"

"I've been waiting for your call," she responded, sidestepping the question because she couldn't make herself say that she had.

"I'm sorry if you were worried, my love. I had to wait until I was sure your guards were asleep. I saw their lights go out a while ago, but you can never tell with people like that."

"Where are you?" she asked, running to the window and staring out into the darkness, hoping she might see him standing there with her baby.

"Not as close as I was. Now, listen carefully. I'm only going to say this once." The steel edge was back in his tone, and she tensed, waiting for instructions and hoping she didn't forget them.

"Are you familiar with the Queensboro Bridge?"

"Yes." It was seven or eight miles away and spanned the East River from Long Island City to the Upper East Side in Manhattan.

"Good. We don't have a lot of time. The city is crawling with police. But, we can do anything together. Even escape them. I hired an Uber to pick you up three blocks from your apartment. That little coffee shop where you and Jordan had your first date."

"How do you know about that?"

"I know everything about you. Now, stop asking questions and listen! The Uber is already waiting. If you're not there in ten minutes, something terrible might happen to our daughter."

"There are three police officers outside. How am I supposed to get past them?"

"You're smart. I have no doubt you'll figure it out. I left a prepaid cell phone under a rosebush at the east corner of the parking lot. Make sure you pick it up before you get in the Uber. My contact information is already programmed in. I want you to call me as soon as the Uber leaves."

"I will," she said.

"Good. You'll be dropped off a few blocks away from the bridge. Use the pedestrian walkway and meet me on the Manhattan side. Leave your cell phone at the apartment. If you have it when you get here, it won't be a very nice trip to our new home."

He disconnected, and she looked around the room, frantically trying to find something that would help her get past the police. She thought about telling them the truth, but she was afraid Martin might still be watching. If he saw her talking to them, he might make good on his threat to harm the baby.

She eased the door open and slipped through the hallway. She didn't dare grab her jacket from the closet, but she had left her shoes near the front door and she slid into them. She glanced out the front window and could see the police officers sitting in their cars, engines idling as they waited for something to happen. She didn't think she could get out the front door without being noticed.

She still had the flip phone in hand, and it buzzed as she switched directions and headed toward the back door and the deck. She glanced at the text message that had come through, her heart nearly stopping when she saw a selfie of Martin holding Jordyn Rose close to his face.

Hurry, my love. We're waiting.

She was terrified of running out of time, but she was just as worried about leaving without letting Tony know where she was headed. She ran back to her room and grabbed her cell phone. She didn't have time to do anything more than that. She was afraid any hesitation on her part, any slow progress on doing what Martin had demanded, and he might harm the baby. She tucked the cell phone in her pocket, shoved the flip phone in with it and eased the back door open. She was breathless and light-headed. She needed to rest, but the clock was ticking and the car was waiting. If she missed it, she would have to find another way to get to the bridge.

She managed to get out the door and down the stairs without being noticed. She headed across the yard and climbed the fence, dropping onto the neighbor's property.

Then, with a quick prayer for protection, she darted through the yard and raced away.

Tony followed Rusty through the lower level of the apartment complex. Noah's fiancée, Officer Lani Branson, was there to help strategize, even though she wouldn't be working the case on the street with a K-9 partner. Lani's request for a transfer hadn't come through yet, but soon she'd be working with another K-9 unit in one of the five boroughs. Last month, Lani had helped capture Martin, her long blond hair and blue eyes giving her enough of a resemblance to Katie to draw Martin's attention.

As far as everyone in the K-9 unit was concerned, Lani had proved her merit when she had gone face-to-face with the man who had murdered their chief. The team was sorry to lose her but understood why she requested a transfer.

"Rusty doesn't seem interested in much here," Lani said as she and Tony walked through lower level of the apartment complex for the second time. They had returned there, hoping that Martin might have done the same.

"We know Martin was here before. I was hoping he came back, and Rusty might be able to catch his scent."

"We're going to find him. You know that, right? He can't stay hidden forever."

"Maybe not, but he's managed to do it for almost eight months."

"He can't do it forever," she repeated. "We're going to find him, and we're going to get Jordyn Rose back."

He glanced at Lani, grateful she was here as a kind of liaison between the police and the Jameson family. "I know," he said.

She nodded, her expression grim but determined.

He walked outside, disappointed that Rusty hadn't found a scent trail to follow but not ready to give up. Martin had been in the area. They knew that. Rusty was a fantastic search-and-rescue dog, and he had scent-tracked Martin enough to know he was looking for someone specific.

"Want to give it another go, Rusty?" Tony asked.

Rusty whined in response.

They crossed ice-coated grass, Tony ignoring the

hail that fell on his head and shoulders. Rusty trotted beside him, head up, tail alert. He loved his job and the game it represented to him. He also loved the tug toy reward he got for a job well-done.

"Ready, boy?" Tony asked, and the Lab strained against his hold. "Find!"

Rusty darted toward the street, his lighted collar glowing orange against his dark fur. An old residential area of Queens, this neighborhood was quiet after dark. Cars lined both sides of the street, bumper-to-bumper, and gleamed in the darkness. Rusty nosed the ground near the curb, rounding one of the vehicles and then returning. He huffed deeply, stacking scents as he continued to try to locate the trail.

Trained in both urban and wilderness air scent, Rusty was one of the best in the country. When he returned to Tony's side and began the process again, it was obvious he hadn't been able to find a scent trail.

"Nothing?" Noah asked, striding toward him, Scotty beside him.

"I'm afraid not."

"Same for every other team that tried." Noah brushed ice from his hair and glanced at the house. "Is Lani still inside?"

He nodded. "I had a rookie call for the evidence team. We found the baby's hospital identification tags in the trash."

Noah shook his head. "I have a bad feeling about this. It's all too well planned."

"I agree."

"Have you been in contact with Katie?"

"I spoke to her while we were at Griffin's."

"How's she holding up?"

"About as well as can be expected. I was hoping to have some good news for her after we cleared the apartment complex."

"I'm sorry we don't."

"Yeah. I'm sure we all are." He called Rusty back to heel, frowning as his cell phone buzzed. He glanced at the text message that he had received, his heart skipping a beat when he realized it was from Katie:

At Queensboro Bridge. Meeting Martin. Can't talk. Please hurry.

His pulse raced, his hand shaking as he swung around and darted toward his car.

"Something wrong?" Noah asked, jogging after him.

"Katie's gone to meet Martin at the Queensboro Bridge."

"What?"

Tony handed him the cell phone, jogged to his SUV and opened the hatchback for Rusty while Noah read the message.

"You're not planning to rush off alone without a plan, are you?" Noah demanded.

"I'm planning to stop him before he kills someone else I care about."

Tony closed the hatch, took his phone and rounded the vehicle.

"We need to come up with an actual plan before we move in." Noah grabbed his arm and pulled him to a stop.

"Did you see the time stamp on the message? She sent it fifteen minutes ago. If we don't get moving, we may be too late. Let me go ahead with Rusty. That way if they leave the bridge, I can follow."

Noah hesitated, then nodded. "I'll agree to that if you agree to this—you're not going to let your heart get in the way of your head."

"When have I ever done that?"

"When have you ever cared for a woman the way you care about Katie?"

"This isn't just about Katie," he replied, opening the driver's door and climbing in the SUV. This wasn't a conversation he wanted to have with Jordan's brother. Not now, when there was so much riding on his getting to the bridge before Martin made his escape again.

"No. It's not, but you know what I'm saying." Noah put his hand on the door to keep Tony from closing it.

When Tony didn't respond, he sighed.

"Look, this isn't the time or the place, but for the record, whatever might happen between you and Katie, Jordan would be happy for it. If he can't be here to take care of her and their daughter, he would want you to be the one to do it." He closed the door, patted the hood and walked away.

Tony pulled away from the curb, keeping his speed at a reasonable pace, the icy conditions preventing him from flooring it. He refused to dwell on Noah's words. He refused to think about how obvious his affection for Katie must be.

He hadn't had any intention of falling for his best friend's widow, but somehow, it had happened. No matter how many times he tried to tell himself the feelings were nothing but a product of heightened fear and stress, he couldn't ignore the truth. He had had a soft spot for

Katie from the moment he had met her. Now, that soft spot was becoming something more.

He frowned, parking the SUV two blocks from the bridge. The sleet had changed to rain, and he pulled up his hood as he got Rusty out of the back and took off his lighted collar.

There was no sense in announcing their presence before it was necessary.

His phone buzzed as he headed toward the bridge. He checked it quickly, skimming a text Noah had sent. The team was splitting. Half heading for the Queens side of the bridge. Half for the Manhattan side. Patrol officers were joining them, and they'd create barricades to prevent Martin from escaping in a vehicle.

If he showed up.

Tony had a feeling he would.

The guy had one goal and one obsession—Katie. He wouldn't leave New York City without her.

And, Tony?

He had no intention of letting Martin leave at all.

TWELVE

Katie had never used the Queensboro pedestrian walkway. If she had, she certainly wouldn't have done it at night. She preferred bright daylight hours to darkness, and if she did venture out at night, she usually didn't do it alone. Now, though, with Jordyn Rose's life at stake, she was willing to do anything she needed to save her daughter.

She approached the bridge cautiously, the rain drenching her clothes and shoes. She had been outside for too long, and she was cold to the bone, her teeth chattering as she entered the walkway. She'd left her cell phone tucked under the seat of the car, and she could only hope Tony had gotten her message and was on the way.

Otherwise, she was on her own.

About to face the man who had murdered her husband and kidnapped her daughter.

The old steel beams were slick with water, and the wire fencing between the river and the walkway was gray blue in the dim lights. Across the inky water of the East River, Manhattan's skyline beckoned through a hazy fog of frozen air. On any other night, Katie would have thought it was beautiful.

Tonight, it just seemed eerie and sinister.

Several cars passed to her left, and she wondered if a motorist would hear if she called for help. She doubted it. Even if a driver did hear, would he offer help?

She had come because she'd had no choice, but she was terrified, the thought of coming face-to-face with Martin filling her with cold dread. How many times had she seen him at church after Jordan's death? How many times had he told her how sorry he was for her loss? He had even invited her for coffee once or twice, extending the invitation as if he thought company might help ease her broken heart.

She had not realized that he had been the reason for her heartache. She had had no idea that he had created a shrine devoted to her, that from the moment they'd met, he had believed she was God's gift to him.

She shuddered, and the wild baying of a dog sent her pulse racing. It sounded like Reed's bloodhound, Jessie.

Had Tony received her text?

Were members of the K-9 unit hidden nearby, waiting for Martin to show himself.

Please let that be the case, Lord, she prayed silently.

Her foot slipped on slick pavement, and she fell, her hand banging into cold metal, the sound reverberating through the walkway.

"Careful, my love. If you damage your hand, the ring I bought you might not fit," Martin whispered, his voice seeming to come from behind her and in front of her.

She swung around, thought she saw something in the shadows at the end of the walkway.

"Where are you?" she called, her voice shaky with fear and adrenaline.

"Right here, my love." He grabbed her from behind,

his arm snaking around her waist so unexpectedly, she screamed.

He slapped his hand over her mouth, grinding her teeth against her lips. "Shhhhh. None of that," he said gently.

There was nothing gentle about his touch as he dragged her backward, his hand still over her mouth.

When he finally stopped, they were standing in the shadows of a support beam, sheltered from the rain by a metal overhang.

"Are you going to scream?" he asked, his lips tickling her ear.

She wanted to bite, claw, kick, free herself, but he had both of his hands on her, and that meant he didn't have Jordyn Rose.

She nodded, and he nuzzled her neck. "Good girl," he said, his hands dropping away.

She spun around, ready to beg for her daughter.

A car seat sat near the edge of the bridge, the cover pulled up so that she couldn't see if Jordyn Rose was inside it.

"Is she there?" she breathed, darting toward it.

He yanked her back, slamming her against the support beam. Her head hit metal, and she saw stars.

"Ask permission before you touch our daughter," he growled, shaking her hard enough to make her teeth knock together.

"May I see her?" she begged, desperate to lift the cover and see if her daughter was there.

"I don't see why not. Now that we're finally a family, we should all spend as much time as we can together," he said jovially, as if he had not just slammed her into a metal beam and violently shaken her.

"Thank you, Martin," she said, feeling dizzy, weak and agonizingly hopeful. Jordyn Rose might be less than four feet away, hidden behind the cloth cover that was zipped shut over the car seat.

"Call me darling. I always thought that would be a good pet name," he responded, his eyes hot with fanatical glee.

"Darling," she repeated, sidling past him and moving toward the car seat. More slowly this time, because she was afraid that he would yank her back again, that this was simply a game he was playing for his own amusement and at the end of every round, Katie's arms would still be empty.

She reached the car seat, her hand trembling as she touched the zipper.

Please, she prayed. *Please*.

She unzipped it and pulled back the cover. Her head was buzzing as she saw chubby cheeks, a rosebud mouth and a thatch of light brown hair. "Jordyn Rose," she whispered, touching the baby's cheek.

"Alison," Martin snarled, suddenly towering over her.

"I'm sorry. Alison."

"Don't forget again."

"I won't. Can I take her out?" she asked, already reaching for the buckle.

"I guess so. It'll be easier to carry the seat without her deadweight in it."

Katie unhooked the baby quickly, worried he would change his mind.

Jordyn Rose opened her eyes as Katie lifted her from the seat, her rosebud mouth sucking greedily at the air.

"She's hungry," she said.

"I didn't have time to feed her."

"Can I—"

"In the car. If you cooperate."

"Car?"

"I parked on the other side of the bridge. I figured we would be less likely to be found there."

"You're probably right," she said, holding Jordyn Rose close to her chest as he grabbed her arm and started yanking her across the bridge.

Something scuffled on the pavement behind them.

She glanced at Martin, wondering if he had heard.

He seemed focused on the direction they were going. Once they reached the other side of the bridge and got in his car, there would be less of a chance to make an escape. She was certain she had seen something moving at the Queens end of the bridge. She pretended to trip, glancing back as Martin yanked her upright.

"Be careful! We don't have time for your clumsiness."

"Sorry," she said, but she had seen what she needed to—a K-9 officer and his dog creeping through the shadows behind them.

Tony and Rusty. She was certain of it.

"Darling," she said, forcing her voice to be light and flirtatious.

"What?" he snapped.

"I was thinking about our new life. The one you've planned for us."

"Yeah?" He was walking faster, perhaps feeling the net closing in on him.

"Wouldn't it be nicer if it were just the two of us?"

"What do you mean?" He stopped, obviously surprised by her comment.

"The baby." She looked down at her daughter, praying she was doing the right thing.

"What about her? Come on. Speak. We don't have all night for this conversation."

"Let's leave her here. Someone will find her and give her a good home."

His eyes widened, and he dropped her arm.

"What kind of game are you playing?"

"This is no game. I…love you and want to be with you, but Jordan's family will never let us be together if we have his daughter with us."

"You're right," he said, the feverish gleam in his eyes letting her know she had said exactly the right thing.

"Good. Wonderful. Let's put her in the car seat. She'll be fine until morning, when the foot traffic picks up."

"Good idea." He set the seat down, and she strapped Jordyn Rose into it.

She kissed her downy head, zipping the cover back in place as the baby began to whimper.

"Come on, my love," Martin said, taking her hand and pulling her away. "Our chariot awaits."

"Wonderful," she responded, her mouth dry with regret, her pulse racing.

She glanced back one more time.

To say goodbye, and to make certain she had zipped the cover completely.

Tony stepped out of the shadows, easing toward the car seat and lifting it carefully. Seconds later, he was heading back toward Queens, jogging through the rain and fog, disappearing from sight.

The baby was safe.

That was what she had wanted.

It was what had mattered most, but she wanted to be running beside Tony, his arm around her shoulders as they raced to safety.

"What are you looking at?" Martin snapped, spinning her around so she was standing in front of him.

"Nothing," she said, forcing herself to smile at him. "Only you, Martin, my love."

"Liar," he shouted, glancing back and seeing that the car seat was gone.

"Betrayer!" He backhanded her, and she flew backward, landing on hard pavement, the breath driven from her lungs.

"Get up!" he shouted. "Get up and take your punishment."

He had grabbed her by the shoulder and was pulling her upright when lights flashed at both ends of the bridge, the pulsing strobe of emergency vehicles piercing the fog and darkness.

Help had arrived, but she was afraid it was too late.

Martin pulled a gun from beneath his jacket and pressed it against her jaw, dragging her backward against his chest.

"March," he said, moving across the bridge and forcing her to do the same.

She went without fighting.

The baby was safe.

She prayed that she would be, too.

She wanted the life she had been given. All of it. The triumphs and the sorrows. She wanted to live in the joy of knowing that she had been loved by a wonderful man, that she had begun a family with him and that everything she had dreamed of when she had asked God for a family had come true the day she met Jordan.

Maybe the happily-ever-after wasn't what she had expected, but that didn't mean it couldn't be a good one.

If she survived, she wouldn't be afraid of the future. She would walk into it with an open heart, ready for whatever God brought her way.

Maybe even ready for a new love.

The thought settled in her heart, driving away some of her fear as Martin dragged her closer to the end of the bridge.

Tony had his gun trained on Martin, but he didn't dare pull the trigger. Not with Katie there. He had brought Jordyn Rose to an officer waiting near the end of the bridge and returned as quickly as he could.

It hadn't seemed to be quickly enough.

He had wanted to carry both Katie and the baby away from Martin, make sure they were safe and then return to arrest the man who had murdered his best friend.

"Let her go, Martin," he called.

Martin swung around, the gun slipping from Katie's jaw and pointing in Tony's direction.

"I will kill you, Knight. Just like I killed your friend, and I won't have one moment of regret over it. Back off."

"Maybe you will, but by the time you fire the first shot, half a dozen officers will be storming the bridge. They aren't going to kill you. That would make your life too easy. They're going to arrest you and make sure you never see the light of day again."

"That will never happen," Martin snarled, his gaze darting from Tony to the end of the bridge, where half a dozen emergency vehicles had blocked the entrance to the bridge.

"You're trapped. We have officers and dogs on both sides of the bridge. There is no escape, Martin. It's time to face up to what you've done."

"What I've done? What *I've* done!" he shouted, shoving the gun against Katie's temple. "*You* did this! You and your K-9 buddies. You should have accepted Jordan's death as a suicide. If you had, Katie and I would be together, and none of this would have happened."

"Jordan would still be dead," he reminded him, his focus on Katie.

Strands of wet hair fell over her pale skin, and her clothes clung to her. She was shaking with cold and fear, but she was obviously thinking clearly. Getting the baby out of the line of fire had been genius. He planned to tell her that. Just like he planned to tell her how worried he had been, how much he'd thought about her and the baby as he'd driven to the bridge.

He may not have intended to fall for her, but he knew Noah was right—Jordan would have been happy for him. He would have been pleased to know his best friend would always be there for the woman he had loved.

"Jordan deserved to die for what he did to me. You don't take a man's woman. You don't steal another person's property." His voice grew louder with every word, his eyes wilder, the gun swinging away from Katie. Martin seemed too out of control to notice.

Katie met Tony's gaze, and he thought she was trying to send a silent message. Before he could figure out what it was, she slammed her elbow into Martin's stomach, twisted out of his grip and dodged to the left.

Martin fired, and the shot ricocheted off a metal beam, sending sparks flying.

Katie stumbled, fell to the ground and lay still.

"Freeze!" Tony yelled as Martin took aim at her again.

Martin didn't lower the gun, so Tony fired, the bullet striking its target and hitting just below Martin's collarbone.

The gun dropped from Martin's hand, skidded across the bridge and slid beneath the metal fencing.

"Give up, Martin," Tony commanded as Martin stumbled after the gun, "You can't win."

"You don't think so?" he said, blood seeping from his shoulder, his eyes crazed.

"Look around. There are officers coming at you from both sides." He gestured to the men and dogs racing toward them.

"You don't understand, Knight. I'm not like the rest of you."

"That's obvious. The rest of us don't murder people in cold blood," Tony retorted, his pulse beating frantically, his desire to rush to Katie's side nearly overwhelming him. "Put your hands up. It's over."

"It isn't over until I say it is," Martin replied. "Stand back and watch me fly."

He rushed for the fence and clambered over it so quickly that Tony barely had time to react. By the time he realized what was happening, Martin was tumbling into the water below.

"Did he jump?" Katie asked, easing into a sitting position, her face pale.

"I'm afraid so." There was no way Martin would have survived the jump. As much as Tony had wanted Martin caught, he hadn't had any desire for him to die.

"Where's Jordyn Rose?" she asked, her blue eyes desperate.

"With a police officer. Safe," he assured her as he hurried to her side. So relieved that it was over, he did the only thing that made sense. He kissed her. Not the easy light brush of lips that he had offered before. This was a real kiss. One filled with passion and with promise.

"What was that for?" she asked when he pulled back.

"You. Me. Us."

"I like the sound of that," she said, smiling into his eyes, all the tension that she had been carrying since Jordan's death gone.

"Do you?"

"Yes. I was thinking, while Martin was dragging me across the bridge, that if I had a chance to keep living, if God got me through this in one piece, I wasn't going to miss out on whatever He had in store."

"No?"

"No. I've been afraid for a long time. Afraid of losing people I love. Afraid of being alone. Afraid of never having all the things I dreamed of when I was a kid."

"What things were those?"

She smiled, her palm resting on his cheek as she looked into his eyes. "All the things I already have. Family. Friends. A beautiful baby." Her lips grazed his. "Possibilities."

"I like the sound of that," he said, and she laughed.

He captured the sound with his lips, kissing her again, knowing that if he spent a hundred years with her, it wouldn't feel like enough.

"I love you, Katie. I want you to know that."

She pulled back, her smile filled with hope and tinged with sadness. "I love you, too. And, I'm so glad you're part of my life. That you'll be part of Jordyn's."

"I hate to break up the party, but we've got some cleaning up to do and some paperwork to file," Noah said, crouching beside them, Scotty near his feet. "Are you two okay?"

"I'm fine," Tony said, getting to his feet and pulling Katie with him. "Are you?" he asked her.

"Better than I've been in a long time."

"Could have fooled me, sis," Zach said, rushing toward them. "I saw you go down and thought that my heart was about to break. From now on, you stay inside, doors locked, shades drawn. If you do leave the house, I plan to Bubble Wrap you and cover you in Kevlar."

"With Martin…gone," Katie said, some of the tension returning to her face, "I don't think that will be necessary."

"The dive team is ready to go in," Noah said solemnly. "If we can recover his body, that will bring some closure to things."

"It will probably make me feel better," Katie admitted, walking to the railing and looking down. "I wish things could have been different."

"I know," he said as he joined her. "I do, too, but this is how they are. This is where it ended, and maybe, it's where it will begin."

She nodded. No smile this time. No laughter. "I think it will," she said.

"Katie?" Lani called, and they both turned as she hurried toward them, Rusty beside her, the car seat in her hands. "Sorry for barging out here like this, but I've been waiting in the SUV with your sweetie and she's starting to squall. I think she might be hungry."

"I think you're right," Katie said, reaching to lift Jordyn Rose from the carrier.

And, Tony was struck again by the picture they made. Mother and daughter. Looking into each other's faces as they began the process of learning about one another.

"You're beautiful," he said, and Katie looked up, startled, it seemed, by his comment.

"I'm a mess," she murmured, her gaze dropping to her daughter. "And, if I don't feed this little one soon, she will be, too."

"You're beautiful," he repeated, and she finally looked into his eyes again.

"You don't have to say that, Tony."

"I'm saying it because I see it. If I live to be a hundred, I will never forget the way you look right now, standing there with your daughter."

"Thank you," she whispered.

"For the truth?"

"For being you. For being here for me. Every time I've needed you."

Jordyn Rose's face scrunched, and she let out an angry squeal.

"I think that may be our signal to end the conversation," Tony said, touching the baby's face and smiling as she rooted toward his fingers. "For now."

"For now," Katie agreed, and then she lifted Jordyn Rose to her shoulder and headed across the bridge.

"Good job, Tony," Carter said, stepping up beside his brothers.

"I don't think I asked for compliments."

"No, but you would have been getting criticism if you had made one tear fall from Katie's eyes. I figured I would be fair and offer you what you had earned."

"The last thing I would ever want to do is make Katie cry. She has shed enough tears for a while," Tony said.

Noah nodded. "Agreed. I also think we have all had too many long days and nights hunting for answers to Jordan's death." He paused as other members of the NYC K-9 Command Unit moved in. Luke Hathaway and his dog, Bruno. Finn Gallagher and Abernathy. Brianne Hayes and Stella. Reed Branson and Jessie.

They stood together. A team. A family.

"Let's hope the next few months are a little less challenging," Noah continued.

"They will be for me," Carter said, crouching beside his dog and scratching behind his ears.

"What do you mean?" Noah asked.

"I've been waiting for the right time to say this. Now that we're finally able to close Jordan's case." He cleared his throat, and Tony knew he was thinking about the brother he had lost. The friend they had all lost. "I guess now is as good a time as any. The injury I received isn't healing as quickly as I had hoped. My doctor warned me that I may never be able to return to duty full-time."

"Is he sure?" Tony asked, worried for Carter, wondering what he would do if his law-enforcement job were taken away from him.

"No, but I am." Carter stood, his gaze traveling

over the group of men and women who had forged strong bonds through adversity. They had worked together, trained together, fought for justice together. The strength and power of that was in the face of every team member as they returned Carter's gaze. "I can't go back full-time. I don't even know if I would want to. Losing Jordan made me realize that there is more to life than work. But, I can't give you guys up. You're too much a part of me. So, I talked to Lou. He's agreed to allow me to buy Griffin's Diner. He'll show me the ropes over the next few months, and then I'll take over operations. I may not be working with the K-9 Command Unit, but I'll still be sticking my nose in all of your business for many years to come."

For a moment, there was nothing but silence, and then, one by one, the team members began to clap.

"Brother," Tony said, slapping Carter on the back. "It's the very best news I've heard in a long time."

"I agree," Noah said. "Now, how about we save the celebration for after we process the scene. We've got a lot of work to do before we can go back to the office and move on with our lives. Tony, head out. You've worked too many hours the last few days, and I can't afford to pay you any more. We'll meet at the precinct tomorrow, and you can give me your statement and write up your report."

"You sure?" Tony asked, knowing that Noah was giving him an easy out so that he could join Katie and escort her home.

"I am right now, but if you stand there questioning me for much longer, I might change my mind."

"Then, I guess I'd better get moving. See you tomorrow," he called as he took Rusty's leash from Lani and headed back across the bridge.

Cold rain still fell, splattering the pavement and sliding down Tony's cheeks, but Queens was straight ahead, hundreds of lights shining through the icy fog, beckoning him home.

He had never expected to be in this place—where contentment and peace and joy seemed to embody the word *home*. As a kid, he had avoided being in his parents' house. Their violent arguments had tainted the walls and floor and tinged the air with bitterness. To Tony, home had been an elusive dream, a thing that others attained but that he would never have.

Now, though, he finally understood.

Home was peace, it was companionship, it was friendship and community. It was all of the things he had found while working with the K-9 Command Unit. All of the things he had found with the Jameson family. All of the things he had found in his church. And, it was all of the things he had found when he had looked into Katie's eyes, when he had watched her hold her newborn, when he had felt the first stirrings of love in the depth of his heart.

He hadn't expected it.

He hadn't even wanted it.

But, God had led him on a long and winding path to the one thing that had been missing from his life.

"What do you say, Rusty?" he asked as he neared the end of the bridge and the long line of police cruisers waiting there. "Ready to find Katie and Jordyn Rose so we can go home?"

Rusty's ears twitched, his tail swinging wildly. He barked once, tugging at the end of the leash.

"Okay," Tony said, unhooking him. "Find!"

The Lab took off, springing toward the police cruisers, shooting straight as an arrow toward the car where their future waited.

EPILOGUE

Graduation day came just like it always did with the K-9 Command Unit. Only this one was different—a redo of the graduation that should have taken place ten months ago. Katie had been preparing for a couple weeks. Not for the ceremony itself, but for the memories that would come with it.

It seemed like a lifetime ago since her alarm had gone off, and she had gotten out of bed, queasy with morning sickness, wishing she could stay in bed. She had taken the day off work so that she could be there when Jordan congratulated the team for graduating another successful pool of puppy candidates.

He had already been heading out the door when she had dragged herself out of bed, and when he had kissed her goodbye, she had had no idea it would be for the last time.

Even now, that broke her heart a little.

Even with all of the joy having Jordyn Rose and Tony in her life brought, her eyes burned with tears when she remembered waving goodbye to Jordan as he walked down the steps.

"I still miss you, Jordan," she said, lifting the wedding photo that sat on the end table in the living room. She had thought about moving it after she and Tony had begun dating, but when she had mentioned that to him, he had kissed her tenderly and told her that he had loved Jordan, too.

She knew it was true.

"We both miss you," she murmured, setting the photo down next to the one Tony had taken at the hospital. She had come to love the exhaustion in her face and the triumph there. She didn't look anything like the defeated woman who had been afraid she could not raise a child on her own. She looked strong and peaceful and joyous.

It had taken a while, but she finally felt that way, too.

Her path had led her through dark tunnels, but God had proved that there was always light waiting on the other side.

She hoped she would remember that when the next heartache happened.

And, it would.

There were no guarantees in life.

She understood that. Just like she understood that there would always be another celebration, another moment to enjoy, another reason to smile.

She was learning to be present in the moment, to enjoy each day and to embrace the miraculous moments in the midst of the ordinary. The sunrises and sunsets. The snow-laden branches of the towering evergreens. The first sweet call of the songbirds in spring.

The soft cooing of a baby waking to greet the day.

She glanced at the baby monitor and smiled as Jordyn Rose made herself known.

"Here I come, sweet girl," she said, hurrying to the nursery and lifting her from the crib.

Katie had already showered and dressed. She had read her Bible and had her quiet time. All she needed to do was change Jordyn Rose, feed her and grab the already-packed diaper bag, and she would be ready to ride to the graduation ceremony with Ivy and Alexander.

At 9:00 a.m. sharp.

Alexander had called her the previous evening to be sure she remembered. This would be Carter's last official day on the force, and Noah planned to give him an award for exemplary service.

She glanced at the clock.

Quarter past eight.

Forty-five minutes to feed and change the baby.

"Easy as pie," Katie said as she settled into the old rocking chair with her daughter.

Jordyn Rose still had chubby cheeks and a rosebud mouth. Her eyes had turned the same dark blue as Katie's, but her hair color had deepened. It was a rich chocolate brown, the fine thatch of hair she had been born with already growing into a shaggy mop of wild curls.

She was a beautiful baby, but it was her happy-go-lucky personality that always made Katie smile.

"You are a lot like your father, you know that?" she said, as Jordyn Rose sighed contentedly, milk dribbling from her mouth.

Katie should have known better than to get ready before she fed the baby. She was learning quickly that messes happen, and they happen more when you have an infant.

"I am going to be a royal wreck before we even leave the house," she said, glancing at the clock.

"Come on, sweetheart. You need to eat up. We are going to see the puppies today. Grammy and Poppop are coming with us, and your uncles and Tony will be there. Come on. Let's get you burped. We still have plenty of time."

But, of course, when she had said that, she had not been counting on spit-up, or another diaper change.

She also had not counted on a lost baby shoe or a missing pacifier. By the time she finally managed to get them both dressed to semidecent standards, someone was knocking on the door.

"Hold on," she called breathlessly as she balanced Jordyn Rose in one arm and scooped the diaper bag off the floor.

She managed to open the door and nearly stumbled into her father-in-law, who was waiting on the landing.

"Whoa there, kiddo. We don't want to start the day with a wild ride down the stairs." He smiled as he steadied her, his eyes so much like Jordan's, she couldn't help smiling in return.

"It has been a bit of a rocky start to the day."

"Well, it is about to get a whole lot better. Hand me the bag and the kid, and let's get this show on the road."

"I can carry—"

"Are you going to deny me the pleasure of helping my favorite upstairs neighbor?"

"When you put it that way, I guess not," she said, laughing as she handed him the bag and the baby.

"You look lovely, Katie. Make sure you tell my wife I told you so."

"Did she put you up to it?"

"No. She simply commented that every man in her life knows how to give out a compliment. Except me. Apparently, she was the one who taught the skill to our sons and to Tony."

"They are all very good at it."

"Because they are all very good men. It is a nice thing to get to my age, look at your children, and know the values you tried to model and instill made a difference in their lives. I only wish…" He shook his head and headed down the stairs.

"That Jordan were here?" she guessed, knowing this day was as hard on the Jamesons as it was on her.

"What else would I want? I have a wonderful wife, great sons, beautiful young women who love them. I have two darling granddaughters. Life is good, but I will never stop missing Jordan."

"Until we see him again," she said quietly.

He glanced over his shoulder and offered a sad smile. "Until then."

"Are you two going to lollygag all morning?" Ivy called through the open window of the couple's Cadillac. "You know how bad traffic can be. If we don't get moving, we'll be late."

"Then we'd better hurry," Alexander said with a laugh as he opened the back door and put Jordyn in the car seat. Minutes later, they were on the way, weaving through morning traffic as they made their way to the canine-training center. It wasn't far, but traffic made it a long ride. By the time they arrived, the ceremony was almost ready to begin.

"We had better hurry," Ivy said, grabbing the diaper bag from the trunk. "It will be awkward if the chief's family walks in late."

They hurried across the parking lot, entered the auditorium and took their seats near the front. It didn't take long for the ceremony to begin. Noah gave a speech that honored Jordan and the legacy he had left behind—a strong K-9 Command Unit devoted to the community and to justice. In honor of his memory, a German shepherd puppy that had been deemed suitable for training was being named Jordy in keeping with the tradition of naming police dogs after fallen officers.

Surprised and touched, Katie wiped tears from her eyes as Noah put a collar bearing the name Jordy around the rambunctious dog's neck.

"Jordan would approve, don't you think?" Tony said, sliding into the seat beside her.

"I thought you were behind the stage with the graduates?" she whispered, leaning her head against his shoulder, loving the feel of his warmth against her cheek.

"I was relieved of my duty. Apparently, there has been a sudden change in the program. Noah asked all the K-9 officers to sit in the audience during this part."

"A sudden change?"

The last time the program had changed, it had been because Jordan hadn't shown up. Two days later, his body had been found.

She shuddered, pulled her jacket a little closer and hugged Jordyn Rose a little tighter. She had every reason to be thankful for the life she had and for the second chances God had granted her. The day Martin's body had been recovered from the river, she had known she could move forward without fear, but sometimes she still felt haunted by the memories of all that had happened.

"A change doesn't have to be a negative thing," Tony reminded her.

"I know. It's just…"

"A lot of bad memories." He squeezed her hand, winding his fingers through hers and smiling as Jordyn Rose cooed.

"Hey, sweetheart," he whispered. "Want to sit with me?" He lifted Jordyn Rose gently, settling her into the crook of his arm.

Seeing them together filled Katie's heart in a way she never would have imagined could be possible. Even after heartache, love could grow. She knew that now. Understood just how surely God had been guiding her path through the tragedy of losing Jordan and the terror of being stalked by Martin.

Tony must have sensed her gaze.

He met her eyes and smiled, that simple sweet gesture filling her heart to overflowing.

"I love you," he mouthed.

"I love you, too," she responded and felt the joy of that to the depth of her soul.

When Noah finally placed the last K-9 police collar on the last graduating candidate, the crowd erupted with applause. The well-trained dogs stood near their handlers, tails wagging, tongues out. They would be put to good use in the community—searching for the missing, sniffing out explosives, finding drugs and offering closure to families by locating bodies of those long missing. There were German shepherds, Malinois, Labs and retrievers. A basset hound bayed happily as he trotted across the stage.

Jordyn Rose was wide-eyed and alert, her dark blue eyes focused on the dogs.

"I think you have a budding K-9 handler there," Alexander whispered as the last graduate crossed the stage.

"Maybe," she responded.

If that was the path God guided her daughter to, she wouldn't try to stop it.

Go wherever He leads.

That was what Jordan had always said, and that was what Katie planned to tell Jordyn Rose when she was old enough to understand.

Noah approached the podium again, with an unfamiliar young man beside him.

"Ladies and gentlemen and fellow dog lovers, as many of you know, our precinct has had a season of mourning. We lost Chief Jordan Jameson in a senseless act of violence. The day he was murdered, his K-9 partner, Snapper, disappeared. We spent countless hours searching for him. There were several possible sightings, but we were never able to verify them. Not long ago, one of our officers saw Snapper on the adoption website of a local shelter, but by the time we contacted them, and despite the fact that Snapper was microchipped, he had already been adopted out. Since then, we have made several attempts to contact his current owner, but we were unable to reach him. I'm going to be honest, I had just about given up hope of finding my brother's dog."

Noah stopped and took several deep breaths, obviously trying to control his emotion. "Two days ago, I received a call from Mr. Charles Williams. He has been on an in-field study trip with New York University. Charles is working on his PhD in botany. He was studying the flora of the Grand Canyon and just recently returned home. Before he left, he went to the local shelter and adopted a canine friend to bring along. Charles, can you bring him out for us?"

The young man walked backstage and reappeared a moment later with a beautiful German shepherd.

"Snapper!" Katie cried, jumping to her feet.

The dog's ears twitched, and he sniffed the air, and then, as if he finally understood he was home, he broke rank, jumping from the stage and barreling toward her.

She stepped out into the aisle to meet him, kneeling down to accept his doggy kisses. She didn't realize she was crying until Snapper nudged her cheek and pawed her shoulder.

"I am so happy you're back," she said as she looked into his dark, intelligent eyes.

"He looks great," Carter said, kneeling beside her and scratching Snapper's head. Zach joined them, running his hands down the dog's flanks and shaking his head.

"You wouldn't know he had ever been away from training."

"I know everyone is excited," Noah said above the din of the crowd's surprise. "But, if you could all settle down for a few moments, Charles has something he wants to say."

The young man stepped up to the podium, clearing his throat and adjusting the collar of his white dress shirt. He looked around the room, and his gaze found and settled on Katie.

"I had no idea of any of this when I adopted Roosevelt. Sorry, I mean Snapper. I named him Roosevelt after Theodore Roosevelt, but you don't need to know that."

The crowd laughed, and the young man continued, his gaze still focused on Katie. "What I *would* like you to know is that I had no idea Snapper was microchipped or that he was missing from the NYC K-9 Command Unit. I didn't know that his handler had been killed or that he had a family who missed him. I would also like you to know this—Snapper is everything a service dog should be. He's obedient, smart and driven. He is also loyal. He was always a good boy, but from the day I brought him home until the day I learned who he really was, I had the feeling that my buddy had better things to do with his time than lie around in the shade while I collected plant samples. So, as much as it pains me to do this, I've brought Snapper back home to you today. I hope he will have many more years of service to the community. Mrs. Jameson, please accept my deepest condolences for the death of your husband and my heartfelt thanks for sharing Chief Jameson's K-9 partner with me for these past weeks. I'm going to miss you, buddy," he said, not even trying to hide his tears.

Katie was crying again, and she didn't think there were many dry eyes in the audience. This was a beautiful end to a heart-wrenching story, and she was unbelievably grateful for it.

Noah concluded the ceremony by giving Carter an award for outstanding public service. The audience gave him a standing ovation as he walked stiffly from the stage. All these months later, he still had pain from the gunshot wound he had received in the line of duty, but soon he would be taking over the running of Griffin's Diner full-time. With his fiancée, Rachelle, by his side, and his daughter, Ellie, cheering him on, Katie had the feeling he would be just fine.

"You look happy," Tony whispered, his lips brushing her ear.

She shivered, turning so that they were looking into each other's eyes. "I have a lot to be thankful for."

"I think we all do," he said.

"Katie!" Ivy cried, throwing an arm around her shoulders. "What a blessing that Snapper is back." She crouched to pet the German shepherd, and he seemed to sigh contentedly.

"It really is."

"I guess he can retire now," Alexander said, taking Jordyn Rose from Tony's arms and tickling her under her chin.

She giggled and Snapper got to his feet, padding over to sniff her feet.

"See this little one?" Alexander knelt in front of Snapper. "She's Jordan's baby. What do you think of that?"

The baby and dog stared at each other.

Snapper nuzzled Jordyn Rose's cheek, huffed against her belly and then settled down again.

"He really is a great dog," Tony said. "Jordan always said he was the best German shepherd he had ever worked with."

"He did." Noah joined them, his fiancée, Lani, by his side.

"He *is* only five," Katie said, remembering all of the time Jordan and Snapper had spent training together. Hours and hours of work for what should have been eight to ten years of service.

"He'll have a good home with you," Noah said, but there was something in his voice that let her know he had been thinking what she had: Snapper was too young and too good to retire.

"Or, he can be assigned a new partner until he is old enough to retire, and then we can decide where he should live when he is an old man." Katie scratched Snapper's snout, and his tail thumped rhythmically.

"I think that's a great idea," Reed said, joining the small crowd of K-9 handlers, his wife, Abigail, and her emotional-support dog, Jet, beside him.

"Who do you think could handle him?" Luke Hathaway asked, his arm slung around his new wife, Sophie.

"If you want my opinion," Finn Gallagher said, "Lani is the perfect choice."

"Me?" Lani looked shocked, her eyes wide as she studied the faces of the other members of the K-9 team. Her time on the team had been limited, but she would always be part of the family they had become. If not for her relationship with Noah, she would have continued to be part of the team. They all knew and accepted that.

"I think it's a great idea," Finn's wife, Eva, said, her guide dog, Cocoa, beside her. "Not that I know much, but Finn keeps telling me what a great asset you were to the team. And, since you'll be working for another K-9 unit soon, why not be paired with Snapper?"

Soon the entire team was discussing the idea of Lani working with Snapper. Only Noah remained quiet. He probably felt that his relationship with Lani would make his opinion seem biased.

"I think," Tony interrupted, "Katie should make the decision. She has spent more time with Snapper than any of us."

The group went silent, all eyes fixed on Katie.

She looked at each of the men and women who had

known and loved Jordan, and she thought about how much he had loved all of them. This was what he would want—the dog he had worked with so diligently being passed on to a fledgling handler. Both of them working together to serve the community he had loved.

"I think Lani and Snapper will make a good team," she said, her throat suddenly tight, her eyes burning.

Making the decision felt like turning the last page of a wonderful story—beautiful and sad, all at the same time.

"Are you sure?" Lani asked. "It's obvious he is bonded with you, and I don't want you to feel like you have to allow him to keep working."

"It's what Jordan would want. It is what I want. So, yes, I'm sure. And, I do like that he'll stay in the family."

"I can't tell you how much this means to me," Lani said, pulling her in for a long hug.

"You know what would mean a lot to me?" Gavin Sutherland asked. "Going into the reception area and eating something. I don't know about everyone else, but I'm starving."

The group began walking away, but Katie stayed where she was, watching them leave, listening to their laughter. Near the doorway to the reception area, Ivy and Alexander were entertaining Ellie and Jordyn Rose. Noah and Lani were walking hand in hand, with their heads bent together. Carter and Rachelle were standing face-to-face, talking quietly as they looked into each other's eyes. Zach and Violet were just a few feet away, laughing quietly about something.

Katie couldn't help thinking that despite how their

lives had been devastated, they had all found their joy again.

"What are you thinking?" Tony asked, his hands settling on her waist as he turned her so they were facing each other.

"Life. About how one season can bring sorrow and another joy. About family and how happy I am to be part of this one. Maybe even about love and how nice it is to see so many people find it."

"You know what I've been thinking?" He kissed her gently, his lips barely dancing across hers.

"That they probably have chocolate cake at the reception, and that's your favorite?"

He chuckled. "No. I've been thinking about life, too. About how one season brings loss and another abundance. About family and how much it means to be part of one. About love and how easy the word is to say when I'm with you. And, I've been thinking about forever and how wonderful it would be to spend it with you."

"Tony," she began, but she wasn't sure what she wanted to say. She didn't know if she could say anything that would be as beautiful as the words he had just spoken to her.

"I know this is a tough day, Katie. For all of us. And, I know that nothing can change that, but one thing I learned from losing Jordan is that now is never too soon to say what needs to be said."

He reached into his pocket, and her heart stopped. Her breath caught. The world seemed to stand still. He pulled out a small velvet box, and his hand shook just a little as he opened it.

"I never knew what home was until I met you. I never understood what it meant to belong until I looked into your eyes. I don't think I ever felt love until I sat in the hospital room with you and watched you hold your newborn daughter. I can't imagine walking through life without you by my side, and I can't imagine growing old with anyone but you. I love you, Katie. Will you marry me?"

She wanted to say yes. She did. But, the word stuck in her throat as tears flooded her eyes.

She reached for Tony, felt his arms close around her.

"It's okay to cry," he whispered against her ear. "It's okay to mourn what you lost."

"I know," she said, burying her face in the warmth of his chest. "But, I don't want to cry for what I've lost. I want to rejoice in what I have."

She stepped back, wiping tears from her eyes.

"When I lost Jordan, I closed myself off to love. I convinced myself that I would never meet someone who could melt the ice around my heart. I wasn't looking for love, Tony. I didn't even want it with you."

"Is that a yes?" someone asked, and she realized that the team had returned and was surrounding them, a wall of love created by people who knew the weight of Katie's sorrow and the depth of her loss. She didn't see judgment in any of their eyes; she saw joy.

"Yes, it is," she replied, levering up on her toes and kissing Tony with all of the passion and love she had to offer.

This second chance at happiness was a precious gift, and she wouldn't squander it. She wouldn't forget how miraculous each breath was, how beautiful each moment.

His arms slipped around her, and he pulled her close,

his warmth reminding her of every bright sunrise after every long, dark night.

"Congratulations!" More than a dozen voices shouted in unison, the loudness of it scaring Jordyn Rose. She let out a high-pitched cry.

Katie pulled back, still looking into Tony's dark eyes as she took the baby from Alexander's arms. "I love you, Tony. Don't ever forget it."

He smiled, his lips skimming her forehead as he wiped a few tears from Jordyn Rose's face. When he finished, he lifted Katie's left hand and slid the ring on her finger.

She lifted her hand, surprised by the simple beauty of the stunning diamond solitaire, a small pink diamond nestled beside it. "It's beautiful, Tony."

"A diamond for each of my girls," he responded, lifting Jordyn Rose from Katie's arms and then taking her hand.

"Ready?" he asked, and she smiled.

"To eat?"

"To step into the future together."

"You know what?" she responded, pulling him a step closer. "I am."

* * * * *

SPECIAL EXCERPT FROM

LOVE INSPIRED SUSPENSE
INSPIRATIONAL ROMANCE

*With his K-9's help, search and rescue K-9 handler
Patrick Sanders must find his kidnapped secret child.*

Read on for a sneak preview of
Desert Rescue *by Lisa Phillips,*
available January 2021 from Love Inspired Suspense.

"Mom!"

That had been a child's cry. State police officer Patrick Sanders glanced across the open desert at the base of a mountain.

Had he found what he was looking for?

Tucker sniffed, nose turned to the breeze.

Patrick's K-9 partner, an Airedale terrier he'd gotten from a shelter as a puppy and trained, scented the wind. His body stiffened and he leaned forward. As an air-scent dog, Tucker didn't need a trail to follow. He could catch the scent he was looking for on the wind or, in this case, the winter breeze rolling over the mountain.

Patrick's mountains, the place he'd grown up. Until right before his high school graduation when his mom had packed them up and fled town. They'd lost their home and everything they'd had there.

Including the girl Patrick had loved.

He heard another cry. Stifled by something—it was hard to hear as it drifted across so much open terrain.

He and his K-9 had been dispatched to find Jennie and her son, Nathan. A friend had reported them missing yesterday, and the sheriff wasted no time at all calling for a search and rescue team from state police.

The dog had caught a scent and was closing in.

As a terrier, it was about the challenge. Tucker had proved to be both prey-driven, like fetching a ball, and food-driven, like a nice piece of chicken, when he felt like it.

Right now the dog had to find Jennie and the boy so Patrick could transport them to safety. Then he intended to get out of town again. Back to his life in Albuquerque and studying for the sergeant's exam.

Tucker tugged harder on the leash; a signal the scent was stronger. He was closing in. Patrick's night of searching for the missing woman and her child would soon be over.

Tucker rounded a sagebrush and sat.

"Good boy. Yes, you are." Patrick let the leash slacken a little. He circled his dog and found Jennie lying on the ground.

"Jennie."

She stirred. Her eyes flashed open and she cried out. *"We need to find Nate."*

Don't miss
Desert Rescue *by Lisa Phillips,*
*available wherever Love Inspired Suspense books
and ebooks are sold.*

LoveInspired.com

LISEXP1220

LOVE INSPIRED

INSPIRATIONAL ROMANCE

UPLIFTING STORIES OF FAITH, FORGIVENESS AND HOPE.

Join our social communities to connect with other readers who share your love!

Sign up for the Love Inspired newsletter at **LoveInspired.com** to be the first to find out about upcoming titles, special promotions and exclusive content.

CONNECT WITH US AT:

Facebook.com/LoveInspiredBooks

Twitter.com/LoveInspiredBks

Facebook.com/groups/HarlequinConnection

HARLEQUIN

Heartfelt or suspenseful, inspiring or passionate, Harlequin has your happily-ever-after.

With new books published every month, you are sure to find the satisfying escape you know you deserve.

Get 4 FREE REWARDS!

We'll send you 2 FREE Books plus 2 FREE Mystery Gifts.

Love Inspired Suspense books showcase how courage and optimism unite in stories of faith and love in the face of danger.

FREE
Value Over
$20